The Son of Porthos;

OR,

THE DEATH OF ARAMIS.

BY

ALEXANDER DUMAS,

Author of "Twenty Years After," "Viscount de Bragelonne," "Louise de la Valliere," "Man in the Iron Mask."

A New Translation from the Latest French Edition,

BY

HENRY L. WILLIAMS.

NEW YORK:
THE F. M. LUPTON PUBLISHING COMPANY,
NOS. 72–76 WALKER STREET.

COPYRIGHT, 1892, By
THE F. M. LUPTON PUBLISHING COMPANY.

Publishing Statement:

This important reprint was made from an old and scarce book.

Therefore, it may have defects such as missing pages, erroneous pagination, blurred pages, missing text, poor pictures, markings, marginalia and other issues beyond our control.

Because this is such an important and rare work, we believe it is best to reproduce this book regardless of its original condition.

Thank you for your understanding and enjoy this unique book!

THE SON OF PORTHOS;

OR,

THE DEATH OF ARAMIS.

CHAPTER I.

LIKE FATHER, LIKE SON.

THE July sun was flooding with light the calm and radiant landscape offered by the banks of the River Loire, near Saumur, in the middle of the Year of Grace, 1678.

The stage-coach running from Nantes to Paris was on the sandy unpleasant road, drawn by six stout horses, but when the highway rose to cross a ridge, as now, they were none too strong to overcome the difficulty, though lightened of the passengers; these had to walk up in the midst of the heat and dust.

At least, the male passengers trudged on, while the lady inside slumbered. The five men were, a Nantes scrivener, a ship-outfitter, two sardine merchants of Croisic, and a young gallant, half-gentleman-farmer, half-squire of some degree, who hailed from the parish of Locmaria, in Belle-Isle-in-the-sea, of lasting memory from the siege which we have chronicled in our pages entitled - " The Man in the Iron Mask."

Of the country squire he boasted the free carriage, slightly swaggering perhaps, the sunburnt complexion, the long hair coming down upon the shoulders, and the characteristic air of the rustics of that part of Brittany, namely, a medley of the simple and the astute, the timid and the tenacious. He wore the picturesque costume of these peasants, the white wool breeches cut full, the leather leg-boots embroidered with silk, the flower-patterned waistcoat, the braided vest, and the wide-brimmed felt hat encircled by a velvet ribbon, and plumed with a peacock's feather. Of the country nobility, he ofttimes assumed the proud and haughty carriage of the head, the curt and imperious voice, a sort of natural loftiness in the gestures, courtesy in the speech and elegance in the manners. Add likewise, as the nobleman's insignia, a rapier at his side which would have appeared of exaggerated size and length for a stripling, if he had not been gifted with a stature above the common, with limbs which testified to muscular strength and agility.

The view was splendid from the crest, from the bright hamlets under the eye to the red roofs of Saumur and its white citadel; but the travelers had something else to do than admire scenery. The petti-fogger perspired at every pore, as he had wrung debtors into doing; the Paimboeuf ship-outfitter panted and the sardine-merchants grumbled. Still they gasped a few words about the market price of produce, the taxes, the good and the bad weather as they would affect the crops, and the disgrace of the Financial Superintendent Fouquet. Granted that the fall of this treasurer had taken place some time back, you cannot be hard on the rustics for not being versed in the latest court news. The young blade from Belle-Isle slily peeped at the lady-passenger as she napped.

All of a sudden the jolting of the vehicle made her start as to awaken, and in fear of being caught staring at her, the gazer rapidly turned his eyes aloof, and mechanically began to study the road. No sooner had he done so than he stopped short and hailed the guard of the coach who was also the driver, walking beside his horses:

"Ho, ho! what do you call that lot, my Master?"

He pointed to a squad or five or six horsemen, just looming up on a peak of the road, their profiles detached on the clear sky-line with the sharpness of shapes in a shadow-pantomime. Four of these cavaliers carried their musketoons resting for immediate use on the knee. The fifth in advance of the rest, appearing to be the leader, carried no gun; but the sun sparkled on the pistol pummels sticking out of his holsters, and of the long sword slapping against his thigh. Altogether, this was a little troop far from encouraging in a period when the main roads belonged to the boldest highwaymen.

Master Vincent Paquedru, the coach driver, had a flat face, meaningless look and feeble smile ; his cunning was masked under a thick coat of pretended innocence. These rogues out-do any of their race elsewhere in knavery.

"That ? that is a patrol of the Royal Marauders," he answered tranquilly to the question addressed him.

"Royal Marauders ?" repeated the questioner, frowning "a singular title, but no doubt a nickname ; for I do not want to think, Master Paquedru, that you intend to play tricks on me ?"

While thus speaking the stalwart youth laid his hand on the shrewd Norman's shoulder,—only laid it, but its weight was such that the knight of the whip cowered as though he was overburdened.

"Heaven forbid, my gentleman," he replied, in haste, with an obsequious and wary air ; "for it is the real truth— I never tell a lie, on my faith! that is how that regiment is christened in these parts."

"A regiment in the King's service so misnamed ?"

"Forsooth, I am ignorant of that, my good sir," returned the driver, taking his most stupid aspect; "but it is certain, I swear it with my hand on my heart, that it has been out on the campaign, ever so long."

"Out on the campaign ? against whom, pray? as far as I know, for the moment, the province of Anjou is not in arms against the King's authority——However, " added the young gallant, glancing at his traveling companions who had drawn near during this colloquy and listened to it with vague disquiet, " we have nought to fear, for they are just our number—five—and the game is even."

There rose general dissent, and the notary exclaimed : "But we have no firearms!"

"Besides," said the sardine merchants, "it is not our trade to bandy hard knocks!" To which his brother dealer added: "We are respectable merchants who shun stripes and blows like the plague."

"For my part, " continued the ship-outfitter, " I would *not hesitate to* send all my seamen and office-clerks into battle to be slain to the last man—but, unluckily, they are either on my ships at sea or in my offices in Paimboeuf."

"But, say, Master Paquedru," asked the notary, "do you know that martial cohort?"

"I know them without pushing the acquaintance——"

"Do you mean to say you have met them before?"

"Oh, often, very often," was the Norman's reply, with a smile of bad omen, "in fact, as often as I pulled through this spot."

"In that case, how will they act towards us?"

"Never mind," interrupted he young gentleman, "we shall not be long learning, for here they come at a gallop."

Indeed, the little squadron had clapped spurs to their horses, so that they came up rapidly. When arrived within gunshot, they reined in, so stopped by a sign of their commander, who approached at a walking pace. His followers drew up in a line across the way, to block it. Of these four, not one owned a visage that did not have Robber branded on it legibly. All the tanned cheeks wore rakish moustaches, and impudent gaze stared out under unkempt locks; scars ornamented the whole. But what equipments, costumes and steeds! The last as meagre as the lean kine of Scripture; the hats dented, tattered and worn; the bullhide breastplates rotten and cracked, the breeches oddly patched, and the boots showing the riders' toes. But, on the other hand, each carried an arsenal of weapons.

The captain was a trifle less forlorn and threadbare. Some threads had come out in his lace ruffles; only slightly faded were his doublet's purple velvet and his flame-colored shoulderknot of ribbon; and his Spanish boots were not dilapidated all over. Still his plumed beaver was spruced up with a new ribbon and was cocked properly over one ear; his rapier hilt was polished enough to shine brightly; and his show of fashion had a touchy arrogance to impose up to a degree upon the novice and the timid. He would have inspired but scant confidence in the clear-sighted. His bird-of-prey beak bent over a pair of braggadocio's moustaches curled up into hooks at the ends, and turning grey; under them his lips were enlivened by an expression of vulgar cynicism. In his brown-encircled eyes, half-veiled by the bloated, drooping lids, gleamed all the yellow reflections of the **Seven Deadly Sins.**

As he accosted the coach passengers, this character took off his hat with a grand sweep, slow and measured, as he uttered with an exaggerated affectation of politeness, "Gentlemen, I prithee to consider in me the most humble, obedient and devoted of your servants."

"Oh, sir, we are yours," said the scrivener, acting as spokesman for his companions, all trembling like the aspen leaf.

"Since nobody takes it upon him to present me, allow me to do it myself—" here he bowed. "You see the Chevalier Condor de Cordbuff, Colonel in his Majesty's service —when I say, Colonel, it is just a manner of speaking, for the grade is of no consequence at present, and between ourselves, the army is so badly organized that I hardly know whether I am captain or colonel, and my regiment—ahem! company would sound better—is composed for the time being of the four paladins whom you see yonder behind me: namely, Lock-breaker, my lieutenant, Plucker, my cornet, Pillager, my orderly, and Pickpurse, my trumpeter——"

These characteristic names caused the pettifogger to quiver still more, the shipping-merchant to turn frightfully pale, and the sardine-dealers to glance with despair on one another, while the cavalier proceeded:

"But I am going to fill up my muster-list, and I have the recruits. Nothing but the equipments is lacking, which is the reason that I have solicited and obtained from the Provost of Saumur the duty of escorting and guarding honest gentry traveling through the country——"

"What," exclaimed the ship-fitter; "Do you mean that you come only to——"

"To see you safe into the town, and defend you at need from all vexations, criminal exactions or guilty enterprises aimed at your life or your money-bags——"

A sigh of relief issued from every breast.

"And all for a pitiful remuneration," continued the orator.

"Eh, eh? what now?"

"The figure being left to your kind estimate—provided, since I must confine the generosity of my patrons within the bounds of sound sense, that each offers according to his mien, and his means——"

"Alas!"

Astonishment, revulsion and terror had swiftly succeeded

each other in the hearers' minds. One of the sardine-dealers, however, tried to give a proof of heroism.

"Not so fast," said he, roughening his voice, "suppose we do not want any escort and guard——"

"Right," continued his colleague, like his echo, "suppose we do not yearn for the honor of buying your company?"

"In that case," replied Cordbuff, "I no longer am responsible for your precious persons, and that will be a bad lookout, as there are any quantity of scamps in these parts," he said with imperturbable gravity, and with emphasis, "scamps whose arms are longer than their scruples, and who, in so lonesome a spot as this, would shoot me off-hand a pack of traders of your kind as clean as a bevy of partridges——"

He made a sign to his gang, and their musketoons were heard going—clicketty clack! on full cock.

The notary all but fainted; the ship-merchant wiped the abundant perspiration off his nose with his sleeve, and the two sardine-dealers offered blessed tapers to their patron saints if they should be extricated from this hornets' nest.

The Colonel of the Royal Marauders turned to the coach-driver, saying: "Look sharp! Vincent, out with your waybill, and read me out the names and descriptions of your passengers."

The driver had the paper already in his hand and he at once began to read:

"Master Libiniou, notary royal, of Nantes——"

"Good!" said Condor, with an amiable smirk, "men of the gown and men of the sword are both specially king's-men. I wager that you are only too happy for the chance to contribute a hundred pistoles for the harness of my heroes. Besides, as a keepsake of this happy meeting, I will make no bones over accepting that watch which I see rounding out your fob. Mine was stolen lately, in the parlors of the Comptroller-general, in Paris—M. Colbert receives sadly mixed company, as I have had the favor to tell him plumply."

He tossed his hat, crown down, into the road, and concluded:

"There you see the cashier's till! Walk up, gentlemen, and settle. My dear notary, have the honor to lead the revels!"

With many a moan the scrivener did as he was expected.

"Simon Prieur, ship-outfitter, of Paimboeuf," continued the driver.

"One hundred pistoles likewise. I am not going to insult a respectable trader by valueing him under a knight of the quill. To which sum, my honored Prieur will please add the pair of silver buckles shining so bravely on his shoes. My noble father, Hilarion de Cordbuff, always longed to see his dear boy in silver buckles, and the wish of a father is law to a son——"

"Yves Guerinec and Pierre Trogoff, sardine-merchants, of Croisic——"

"Fifty pistoles each, the catch of fish being first-rate this season—not forgetting the gold earrings which you flash, and which I shall offer to my sisters. I hope the gentlemen will not compel me to take them out myself, as I am rather heavy handed and I am really afraid that I should clip a bit of the ear along with the trinkets." As he spoke he toyed with a dagger at his girdle.

The two merchants and the naval outfitter hastened to imitate the notary, but with all kinds of grumblings, complaining and curses, while the Jehu pursued:

"Squire Joel, of Locmaria——"

"A squire? which is he?" inquired the robber, from the height of his saddle.

"I am he," responded the youth who wore the Breton costume.

We have already stated that Joel was a promising scion, having limbs admirably proportioned to his exceptional stature in their supple and muscular robustness. Imagine Hercules or Samson as a boy. Still his countenance did not yet reveal the budding athlete, capable of strangling hydras or carrying away town gates. The abundant curls enframed fine and regular features, a little browned by the sun and the gale; his large blue eyes, inclined to deep grey, had a kindly gaze, where frankness and just dealing were to be read as in an open book, and around his lips, over which darkened a coming moustache as light in hue as his plentiful locks, a boyish smile now was sparkling with mirth, then shaded with thoughtfulness.

During the preceding scene, he had leaned against one of the wheels, motionless but attentive and astonished—the coach having come to a rest, of course, since the highwayman's intervention.

"By the pride of Lucifer," exclaimed the latter, after having examined him, where we have a young chanticleer, haughtily set on his spurs! and if the whim takes him to swell the ranks of my company, deuce seize me but I would make a cornet aide-de-camp of him. What do you say to that, comrade? Do you not understand me, eh?" he added as the hearer remained silent.

"Yes, I do."

"And you accept?"

"I refuse, because I have no wish to die in the hangman's halter."

"The lad has a turn for wit," growled Cordbuff, gnawing his moustaches, "and I doat on merry fellows. So I allow you five minutes to make up your mind——"

"To what, pray?" asked the other tranquilly.

"To take service under my colors, or to count me down 'smart money' as recompense for losing a recruit so stout in make and so jolly in spirit. Well, have you any more on your bill?" he went on to the driver.

"Colonel, we have the Lady Aurore du Tremblay."

"Humph, some old dowager, I suppose. She must be rather old if she belongs to the family that once supplied a governor to the Bastille Prison. And where is the respected Demoiselle du Tremblay?"

"Am I wanted?" returned a sweet and yet ringing voice.

The girl opened the coach door and nimbly leaped out upon the sandy roadside.

She did not appear to be more than twenty. Her strong though willowy figure seemed shaped to do honor to the most sumptuous court costumes, although she was now wearing a dress of mourning and for the journey.

Over her stainless brow, a thick mass of dark chestnut hair formed a kind of crown, in which faint flickers of golden radiance played. Her eyes were of opaque crystal, but from time to time, they were lit by penetrating lustre. The smile of lips so beautiful agitated the heart. She walked with an even step, with no evidence of fear or weakness, to Cordbuff's beaver, nearly filled with the contributions of her fellow-travelers.

"Here, sir, is the ransom you are waiting for," she observed coldly.

"Excuse me, noble damsel," said Condor, perking himself in the saddle, " But I had not seen what you were like.

Otherwise, you should have taken the lead over these gentry. Hang it all, where would we be, if we did not grant the sex, and rank and beauty, some privileges?"

The young lady extended her arm with a queenly gesture and let a purse drop into the hat, saying:

"This is half what I was carrying to town, and this other portion does not belong to me, but to two orphans, for whose cause I am going there to contest with the relatives and entreat the judges' favor. I venture to hope that you will not show yourself more greedy than the former and more hostile than the latter." All this was spoken with tranquil dignity, not devoid of marked haughtiness.

"On my soul, my fair pleader," returned the colonel, twisting up the points of his moustaches between finger and thumb and speaking with mocking gallantry, "the cross kinsfolk are overcome and the judges won beforehand by the might of your attractions——"

"Sir!"

"Whence I draw the conclusion that your orphans have no longer need of the sum of which you expressed the wish not to be deprived, and to boot—you have no farther need yourself of the diamond sparkling on your dainty finger to please and capture——"

"I am at a loss to understand——"

"Yet it is clear: the ring sparkling on your white hand, will marvellously suit that of the dame of my love. You cannot think to keep me from it, any more than from the second half of the sum of which you have dedicated one moiety to my honorable necessity——"

Mdlle. du Tremblay lifted to the bandit captain a look full of apprehension.

"What, do you contemplate despoiling me of this jewel, and the few gold pieces left me——"

"Lord love you! thank me for being so moderate. Some gentlemen-riders of the King's highway would require much beside."

Aurore clasped her hands.

"Sir, sir, I repeat to you: I have yielded up all my own property—and this money which you claim is the lawful share of the heirs, the sole means of the two young persons whom I represent——"

So long as the lady had shown a firm front and some

haughtiness, the brigand had pretended courtesy: but he became bolder and more insolent as she turned suppliant and agitated.

"Come, come," sneered he; "these children will not be at a loss with an advocate having such charms and brightness of wit. Particularly, as you will not fail to find in Paris many rich and generous friends——"

The lady did not feel the drift of this ironical speech, and implored as she saw the eyes of the scoundrel greedily fixed on the precious stone on her finger:

"But this gem has not the value which you fancy—it has no value indeed save to me as a keepsake——"

"Of some gallant cavalier, eh? Of course it is a token of love. But, dash it all! you will have no difficulty in finding another to make a finer present."

The girl drew herself up to her full height and, as her cheek was empurpled with ire and her eyes flashed with indignation, she said:

"Oh, is it because there is no man present to defend me that you presume thus to insult a lady?"

With her tremulous hands she covered her face as though to prevent the additional outrage of the ruffian staring at her. Through this screen she was all the more lovely, so that Cordbuff's gaze became lighted with sudden and brutal lust. He abruptly urged his horse towards Aurore, and from his throat this exclamation hoarsely issued:

"Oho, are we showing anger here? Be it battle, then! I shall not only take the ring but a kiss as well as price of the victory."

"No, you shall only have the chastisement due such insolence, you rascal!" broke in a thunderous voice, as at the same time, an iron grasp caught the adventurer by the waist and tore him out of the saddle as though he had been a feather.

"He-elp!" gasped the wretch, suffocated by the unexpected grip.

His four adherents lowered their muskets to the level; but, already, Squire Joel—for it was none other who had sprung in between the lady and the Colonel of the Royal Marauders,—was holding the latter up and out at arms-length, much as a sportsman exhibits a rabbit to the yelping pack of *harriers*, and using him as a shield against the projectiles with which the muzzles aimed at him were menacing him.

"My good fellows," said he peacefully, "fire away if so inclined; but you will fill only the body of your chief with lead——"

"Oh, no, don't fire, in heaven's name! don't fire, for the devil's sake," moaned Cordbuff, in desperation.

The muskets were raised slowly, but the Breton did not lower his buckler.

"Now, gossips," he proceeded with the same serenity, "suppose we chat about business. I expect your guns carry each a bullet? Well, I have no objection to buying them—all four."

A clamor arose, and Lieutentant Lock-breaker eagerly demanded:

"How much a-piece?"

"Altogether, as much cash as my companions have put in that hat."

The four hangdogs looked at each other with astonishment next to stupefaction, while the young man continued:

"All you have to do is to blow off your powder at the flight of swallows whirling yonder in the open, and I will hand over to you all the spoil. Otherwise, have a care! at the first hostile move, I shall wring your captain's neck,—or, say, colonel's, the rank making no difference to me when I am wringing the neck of vultures—and I shall make use of his carcase to thresh every man-jack of ye, one down, the others take their turn. *Similia Similibus*, all with the same sauce, as wont to say my worthy tutor the priest of Locmaria."

During this address, the unhappy Cordbuff presented the the most piteous aspect; he was no longer cynical and sullenly mocking. The braggart's mask had been knocked off, and laid bare the wicked coward's vertigo of dread. In vain had he wrestled in his adversary's grasp. The wrist was as firm as iron pincers, and still held him like a ball-proof plate between the Breton's bosom and the robbers' bullets. The latter conferred together in an undertone.

"It is a bargain," declared Lock-breaker, finally making a sign to his comrades, who discharged their muskets at the same time as his into the air.

"Take the money!" said Joel, spurning the hat with his foot toe.

The highwayman-lieutenant rode up, alighted, and clutched it. Mounting with the same rapidity, he did not return to his companions, who were awaiting him with eyes blazing with greed, but clapped spurs to his horse, turned to the left side of the road, leaped the ditch separating it from the meadows, and galloped off over the fields as fast as he could go.

Up rose the three-fold shout: "Robber! false brother! oh, stop the thief!" Thus did Plucker, Pillager and Pickpurse protest against such an appropriation of one's neighbors' property, before rushing with a common impulse in pursuit of the renegade.

"Oh, our money! thief, our money!" so roared with one voice the man-hunters in their furious, breathless and disorderly chase.

And "our money! our poor money!" repeated like an echo, on the spot, the notary, ship-outfitter, and sardine-merchants as they beheld the purloiner of the hat and contents disappearing with his speeding followers in the depths of the horizon.

In the meantime, young Joel had replaced on his legs the redoubtable knight of the Road, Cordbuff, still writhing from the grasp.

Drawing that very long and heavy sword of his, he called out:

"Now then, my captain of cut-throats, show us your steel. I do not want to crop your ears without some little defense on your part."

"Monsieur Joel, will you allow me one request———"

The youth turned quickly, for it was the fair traveler who spoke to him. As the interruption was accompanied by a look of fond gratitude, our champion felt his heart dance in his breast. With his cheeks redending with emotion, he respectfully doffed his hat, and replied with fire in his voice, gesture and countenance :

"A request from you to me? say, an order, which I shall be only too happy to obey."

It was the lady's turn to blush and be perturbed, and she cast down her eyes. But, pointing to the royal Marauder, she said :

"Let this fellow go. I ask it as a favor."

"This scurvy knave?" said our hero, shaking his head:

"Really, on my faith, lady, the rascal has offended you—and I must slay him at your feet."

"Holloa!" broke in Cordbuff, trying to brazen it out, "you may have found it very easy to unsaddle me by surprise and to convert me into a corselet, as you had the luck to do, but——" Here he put his hand on his swordhilt, but slowly and without any enthusiasm, for his adversary was already on his guard.

Aurora interposed once more, saying: "Nay, you shall not fight."

"I should like to know why not," remonstrated the young man.

"Did you not just promise me obedience?"

But our hero was as fond of sword-play as a life-guardsman, as wrangling as a theologian and as obstinate as a Breton.

"To be sure," he said, "if I were alone in question, I should make the sacrifice of my wrath and my rancor: but it was to a lady that the rudeness was shown. Now, the old soldier who brought me up often repeated to me: when anybody is deficient in respect due a lady in a gentleman's presence, his sword ought to leap out of its scabbard of its own accord and never be sheathed until the offence is apologized for."

"So, you refuse my request?"

"I entreat you to ask me any other."

"It is still the only one which, at present, I desire to make to you. Come, you are noble?"

The youth hesitated briefly before proudly replying:

"I come of such blood on the sire's side."

"Well, I am Yolande Henriette Aurore of the Tremblays, daughter of Baron Louis Maximilian du Tremblay, in his lifetime, honorary counsellor and register as well as lieutenant for the Marshals of France for the province of Anjou wherein we stand; and I—in the name of my sire and myself, and of the tribunal of Honor which he represented and of all the nobility submissive to its jurisdiction—I forbid you to cross steel with this ragged captain——"

"Whew!" ejaculated Cordbuff.

"Mark this well: it is no longer a matter of doing me a favor for what I am telling you binds you as surely as if the sergeant of constabulary touched you with his crowned staff on the shoulder—I am speaking to you in the name of the King and for honor's sake. To measure yourself with such a creature would be bemeaning your station, forfeiting your own self-respect and that you owe to the traditions of dignity legated to you by your ancestors ; lastly, you inflict on the order to which we both belong, an insult a hundred times more flagrant than that which you stubbornly seek to avenge—an insult," concluded the lady, "which I should never forgive you as long as I live."

When the speaker reminded Joel of his rank, nobility and ancestors, you might see his face suffuse with blushes, and he was as much embarrassed as surprised at the effect of this language upon him. On the other hand, it is a fact that he had but a faint idea of the famous Tribunal on the Point of honor, instituted in the previous reign to prevent duels between wearers by right of the sword, often intervening to stop quarrels after hearing the complaints.

"I yield," he said, confronted with the lady's last words and the resolute tone which emphasized them, and he restored his weapon to its sheath. "Let it pass," he said to Cordbuff. "Begone! you have been begged off."

During the debate between the squire and the young lady, the craven had operated his retreat to his horse. The travelers did not in truth pay any attention to him, or to the dialogue. They were still gazing in the direction in which their "poor money" had flown in the care of the ingenious Lock-breaker, whose trio of hail-fellows vainly gave him chase with all the powers of their mangy steeds.

As for the coachman, Paquedru, he was hunting in the dust to see if any coin had escaped from the stolen hoard.

An outcry of savage joy replied to Joel's boon. It was from Cordbuff who bounded into his saddle, where he took the bridle between his teeth, and drew a pistol from each holster.

"Soho! you grant me mercy, do you, my turtle doves? but I am not going to spare you!"

He took aim and fired both arms at the same moment. But the young man with the swiftness of thought, had flung himself before the other target. A streak of blood was marked on his forehead, and he reeled as he carried his hand to his chest. Aurore uttered a loud shriek.

"Good-bye to you, my Hector!" shouted the robber, in

toxicated with rage and triumph. "As for you, my pretty maid, we shall have a merrier meeting next time!"

Spurring his steed, he was off like a whirlwind. In his way was the group formed by notary, sardine-merchants and ship-outfitter, who were all four rolled in the dust. Before the lightest of them rose to his feet, Condor was at a distance. Let us do them the justice to report that; instead of flying in pursuit of him, they all rushed to assist the wounded youth, whom Paquedru had hastened to support. But here happened an unexpected incident : it was not the shot man who fell, for he stiffened himself on his legs and rejected aid, but the girl. The sight of the blood trickling out of the wound received on her behalf and tearing the defender's brow, had given her a twinge at the heart. She closed her eyes ; her features were covered with deadly pallor : and her body so collapsed that the young squire had barely time to open his arms to sustain her. He bent over the girl with his face bedewed with blood, and forgetful of his own state, from the anxiety which this sudden swoon caused him, he called :

"Lady, return to your senses ! What is the matter? Were you hit? In heaven's name, speak, I beg of you !"

There came no answer, for Aurore's swoon turned to hysterics. Spasmodic movements thrilled her limbs, and dull moaning came from her bosom. Paquedru and the travelers bustled about her to offer their best services.

" Thump her in the back !" suggested the driver.

"Who carries smelling salts ?" inquired the notary, " or has a feather to burn under her nose ?"

" A good glass of cider would fetch her to," counselled Guerinee.

" With spice in it and a pinch of pepper," added his mate.

The ship-outfitter was for the most simple and economical remedies, for he ventured :

"There is nothing like a dash of cold water bang in the face!

At this critical moment the rolling of a carriage, or another coach, was heard on the road.

" If that brings a doctor, it will be a godsend," remarked the scrivener.

And all turned their eyes to see what heaven—or the other place—was sending them.

CHAPTER II.

TWO OF OUR OLD ACQUAINTANCES.

THE traveling-carriage which came towards the coach in distress, was about a quarter of a league distant when the affray was going on. It was drawn by four first-class posthorses which sent the showers in sparks from the pebbles of the road. Around the vehicle galloped, not less as an escort than a guard of honor, half-a-dozen strapping footmen, swart and of martial appearance, who carried a sword by the side and musketoons at the saddle-bow.

On the back-seat cushions, inside, an old gentleman was seated, who still wore the long hair reaching the shoulders, and the fine moustache and *royale*, or goatee, of the reign of Louis XIII.

This venerable man must have been of remarkable beauty half a century back. He had retained of the good looks the eagle-like profile: a broad forehead impressed with Majesty a circumspect mouth, by a miracle preserving enviable teeth, a chin of correct outline, albeit prominent and angular ; as well as black eyes of piercing lustre, and feet and hands of which many a princess would be proud. He was clad entirely in black velvet, with a small skull-cap apparently to conceal where he had been shaven, like a priest.

But hair, chin-tuft and moustaches were blanched into snow. The thin frame seemed near to snapping in two. The yellow complexion would have delighted the lovers of antiques. The features were hooked rather than purely aquiline; the forehead was laden with wrinkles and lips were so thin that the mouth resembled a slit with a knife. Flacced lids drooped to mask the fire of the sight; and the hands had waxen hues and cracked at the knuckles like those of skeletons amid the clouds of rich lace which half smothered them.

On the front seat, facing this man in the sere and yellow of age, dozed another old man, but of corpulent habit.

He affected to maintain the attitude towards the gentleman of an old servant—both familiar and respectful. He seemed to be about the same age as his master, and like him, wore a black suit, of strict cut and clerical appearance. This was worn with as much conceit as dignity on a body which good living had given the rotundity of the conventional abbots of the days of good cheer. His visage was in keeping with his figure. Between puffy cheeks a squat nose withdrew from view, after the former had robbed the other features : his chin retired from a layer of puff pasts, rather than healthy flesh, and this had threatened to blind him. His hair, no less white than his opposite neighbors, was cut squarely and sanctimoniously down at three lines of his brows. Let us hasten to recal to the reader that his forehead in its most open days, had never boasted more than an inch and a half.

At the time when we peer in at them, the master was brooding and the attendant was napping.

At a jolt, the former exclaimed :

"Monsieur Bazin !"

The other opened his eyes, and stammered

"Did your Right Reverence do me the honor to address me ?"

The other replied with a smile

"I am afraid you forget, my dear old Bazin, that I am no Right Reverence; a full score of years have rung out since I was bishop of Vannes and ceased to belong to the Church Militant—having renounced looking after the salvation of others to take care of my own."

"I fear me," sighed the fat fellow, "that it is the sooner to reach it by the way of penitence and mortification, then, that we have quitted Madrid, where life flowed so gently—to race up hill and down dale, instead of dwelling tranquil in prayer and repose over the remnant of days which may be granted us upon this earth——"

"Precisely ; and I would observe in connection with your remark, that we are moving very slowly. I am in haste to arrive as soon as possible. Just bid the postilions make haste !"

"But we are going at a round gait ! The road is a rough one and a horse may stumble. Your Excellency should bear in mind that an upset might be mortal at your age."

His Excellency shrugged his shoulders in unconcern.

"Speak for yourself, Master Bazin. You are five and

seventy, true; but I am but thirty-eight—twice told!"

"But still, my lord duke!"

"Enough!" impatiently interrupted the Duke of Almada. "Do as you are told, and cease to load me with titles which will draw the attention of the inquisitive upon me. Remember that I am to preserve the strictest incognito until we reach Paris."

"Then what title shall I give to my lord the Ambassador?"

"Style me the Chevalier d'Herbaly, as in days of yore."

"The Chevalier d'Herblay," reiterated the servitor, clasping his plump hands. "*Bone Deus!* as in the time of riding at full gallop affrays and running folks through with sword and dagger: verily, why should not my lord assume at once his old habits, the sword and boots and cassock of the Royal Musketeers, with the title?"

Sadly the aged noble shook his head, muttering:

"Nay, ARAMIS is no more. He is dead with his three companions-in-arms, three friends—three brothers! Aramis has gone into the dust with Athos, Porthos, and d'Artagnan. How is it that not one of them has left a son or even a daughter to revive the valorous name? It seemed to me that a spark of such glory should be yet existent! Oh, were that the case, with what joy I should nourish it, and fan it into a flame so that men by that light might perceive what lustre we four shed on the corps of royal lifeguards and on the name of Frenchmen." Resuming a dry voice, he said aloud: "I repeat that I am for the present, and wish solely to be, the Chevalier d'Herblay."

"Very well," grumbled the stout man, who with his grossness had not been blessed with the good humor which had only increased in his fellow-servant, the worthy Mousqueton; "Enough is said. We shall conform to the wishes—that is, the will of the Chevalier. But, if we are going to plunge anew into the life of adventures, I shall hand in my resignation as steward: despite my age, I have not the faintest longing to join so soon in eternity, whither were too hastily hurried by fatigue suffered and hard knocks borne, my poor comrades, Planchet, Grimaud and Mousqueton."

CHAPTER III.

THE EXTRAORDINARY PHYSICIAN.

We have said that the rumble of a vehicle started the consolers of Mdlle. du Tremblay, by the side of the stopped stagecoach. In a few instants up came the Chevalier d'Herblay's carriage, in a cloud of dust, with the swiftness and rolling of thunder. Shortly it had nearly reached the group around the lady and her fellow-travelers who were in the middle of the way. The postilions and the outriders were obliged to curb the horses, whose bits were white with froth.

"Make room there!" shouted the lackeys of the escort, while the postboys yelled: "Look out there, look to yourselves!"

At the same time the old nobleman lowered one of the windows and demanded "What is the matter?"

"Hold, whoever you are," called out Squire Joel, "and come to our aid. This young lady whom you see, is dying!"

"A lady dying? Stop, boys! rein in, lackeys! Wait a little, sir: I am at your orders."

He was obeyed. The carriage door was opened, and the noble alighted with an ease not to be suspected in one of his age. He briskly stepped up to our hero, and with an accent of surprise exclaimed: "But you are yourself wounded!"

"Pooh! less than nothing—only a scratch. I prithee, do not heed me."

The old gentleman had given the fair frank face a look as of one who was reminded of a resemblance, but the girl's had a stronger attraction, and her marvellous beauty, as she reposed in the Breton's arms, drew from him an outcry of involuntary admiration.

"Be of good cheer," said he, after a brief examination. "No danger is to be apprehended. This person is simply under the sway of one of those attacks of the nerves, often felt by females after violent emotions. Without being a great physician, I warrant that I can relieve her." He raised his voice, and called: "Hillo, there, you, Esteban, Pedrillo! bring a mantle! and you, Bazin, let me have my traveling surgical-case."

The two articles being promptly brought, the improvised physician continued: " Spread the cloak on the ground, and lay the poor girl upon it. That is right. Now, I should like somebody to kneel beside her and support her head."

Joel would not resign to any one the care of carrying out the orders of the doctor. From his case the latter took out a bronze bladed knife and a small crystal phial. He bent over Mdlle. du Tremblay and used the knife to force her teeth open, with endless caution. This slight lock-jaw overcome, after a spasm, he introduced past her lips the tiny mouth of the phial and poured out one or two drops of the liquid contents. Instantly, the color began to return to the pale cheeks and the heaving of her bosom subsiding, her moanings and convulsions ceased also as through enchantment.

"What did I tell you?" remarked the friend in need, rising. "This calming extract is sovereign for affections of this nature. Our patient is out of danger at present."

"But she has not yet opened her eyes," objected the Breton.

"Because to the period of excitement succeeds that of prostration which is the obligatory consequence; but the young lady will not be long regaining her senses, and she has nothing to fear from an accident, which, all things considered, is very common in her sex. But," feeling once more a strong and unaccountable interest in the youth, "why do you not think of having your wound attended to?"

"Pshaw!" said Joel, with a careless gesture, "a bandage wet with salt and water, and it will not even leave a mark. 'Tis but a graze—the bullet merely glanced off the temple."

"But you stood two shots," remarked the notary, with professional accuracy.

"Ay, what became of the other?" Simon Prieur wanted to learn.

"It seemed to me that it struck you fair in the chest," continued the coachdriver.

"We saw it stagger you," added both the dealers in sardines.

From the time when the lady was pronounced out of peril, the youth seemed to recover all his good humor.

"Odds bobs!" said he, gaily, "the knave did aim well. I caught the bullet under my breastbone, but, d'ye see, it flattened on a leather belt which carries my little fortune under cover, and my five hundred livres in hard cash are right as the bank. If it had been paper money, it would have been bored through like a sheet of wax, and my breadbasket would have had a leak in it likely to interfere with my hearty meals. As it turnes out, I am merely bruised. Still it was a pretty hard knock."

"Receive my compliments," said the old noble with affectionate kindliness : "you placed your money to good advantage ! I never knew but one who could have stood up against a shock like that. I should like to hear the whole story," he went on, consulting a large and yet tasteful watch set with brilliants ; "but time presses, and, besides, our interesting patient still needs our attentions. Is it your sister, by chance ? Your betrothed, by other luck? and neither relative, nor friend ?"

"My only knowledge is from having travelled in her company these four-and-twenty hours."

"Do you know her destination ?"

"If I heard aright, she is bound for Paris, like all of us."

"Is there no relative of hers among your company ?"

A negative ran the rounds of the bystanders.

"In that case, I offer to see her there in safety," declared the chevalier.

"Take her away ?" exclaimed Joel.

"Oh," returned the master of Bazin, smiling, "only as far as the termination of her journey. Where do you change horses at Saumur ? he went on to inquire of Paquedru.

"At the Golden Heron Inn, in the St. Jean suburb, where the travelers have time allowed for refreshment."

" How long does it take you to reach it ?"

"Say, better than an hour at the least."

"Well, you will find your lady traveler there, carried in my coach in an hour or so before you, and in that gained time she will have rested and received such cares from the servant-girls as her condition can have from women only."

The coachman bowed as one who says : "As it may please your lordship."

D'Herblay waved his hand for his followers to bear the girl into his carriage.

"Put her in my place," he said. 'I will sit with Bazin on the front seat."

"As two of the lackeys stepped towards Mdlle. du Tremblay to carry out the order, Joel took a step himself to interpose his body between them and the lady, still insensible upon the mantle.

"But," he faltered.

The nobleman eyed him with such a lofty manner that he stopped, unable to continue his protest.

"My young master;" said the old gentleman quietly, "I surely am not compelled to ask you by what right you assume to oppose this act of humanity?"

Abashed, the youth hung his head, as the gentleman proceeded, while the footmen carried Aurore into the vehicle, "No matter! Say no more. I accept as expressed the regret to be read upon your countenance, and I forgive you with a true heart for having forgotten that a lady is always safe under mine honor."

Only twenty-five minutes afterwards, his carriage stopped before the golden Heron at Saumur.

Upon the noise of the horses breathing hard, with their froth-flecked flanks heaving and smoking, the bells jangling round their necks, the postboys' whips cracking as hard as they could sound them, and the lackeys shouting " House, ho!" as they got out of the saddle, out ran the landlord, Master Hermelin, with wife, two daughters and all his household, to receive the traveler who arrived with so uproarious and sumptuous a turn-out.

"I want the host?" challenged the latter from the interior.

"It is I, my lord," rejoined the Boniface, bowing like a clown in the circus.

"At once make ready the best bed in your best room."

"Straightway, my lord." With well-founded pride, he added : " The best bed stands in the best room, my lord, and that is my own "

Without listening to this, the speaker had alighted and he turned with gallantry to offer his hand to Mdlle. du Tremblay, saying :

"Come, my dear child."

She stepped down in her turn; she had completely returned to consciousness, but she was in need of support as she was weak and pale from the sudden shock.

"Really, sir, I do not know how to repay——"

"Hush!" interrupted the old noble, laying a finger on his lips, "not another word. Your physician extraordinary forbids you to fatigue yourself by talking." He beckoned the daughters and chambermaid of the host and ordered them to take special care of the lady. "Conduct her to the rooms taken by me, which are at her disposal. My steward accompanies you, to let me know if anything requires my presence. Go, go, my charming patient," he concluded to Aurore, "and take the repose without fear, of which you stand in need, to complete your restoration. I will watch that you may be roused for the resumption of your journey. Then, allow me to be thanked for a service which, however, any gentleman would have shown you in my stead."

Mdlle. du Tremblay gave him a smile of gratitude, and entered the inn, leaning on Dame Hermelin's arm and followed by the latter's daughters, as well as by Bazin, who grumbled in an undertone at the incident and the burden imposed upon him.

The chevalier was about to do likewise when a lounger, seated on the stone bench by the doorway, rose and bowed to him so pointedly that the old noble ejaculated:

"Eh? unless I am in error, we have M. de Boislaurier at Saumur. But any time and place are good where you are met with."

"The pleasure is on my side," replied the other, again saluting, "what joy to meet so unexpectedly——"

"The Chevalier d'Herblay," suggested the traveler, laying significant stress on the title under which he wanted to masquerade.

A wink from Boislaurier showed that he had taken the hint. He was a man of ripe age, and with a face serious and discreet. Booted and spurred like a royal messenger, he was clad in a hunting dress of buff velvet, with feather to the hat and ribbons of the same hue. After shaking hands with the new-comer, he spoke aloud with the intention of being overheard:

"I had an appointment with a friend in this town to go stag-hunting; but some business must have retained him on his estate for I have been vainly waiting a couple of days."

"And you are in desperate tedium?"

"Of course! I commenced to lose patience, and very little would start me back to town."

"If you have no objections, you might do me the honor to share my coach with me this evening."

In chatting thus the two entered the hostelry dining-room.

"Won't you gentlemen do me the honor of taking meals under my roof?" queried the host, bowing as though he had a hinge in the lower part of his spine, for these were customers of importance.

"Confound me, but the appeal is well rounded," observed the chevalier, "and the salutations smack of the court fashions. Little would one think to find the Versailles style at Saumur."

"The reason," said the host proudly, "the reason is that I have not always lived in the country ; I can tell you that I cooked for the Marquis de Villeroy."

"The royal groom-in-waiting ? and one of the daintiest *gourmets* in the realm of France ! Plague on us but the cheer ought to be appetizing here ! Would you like us to test it in company, my dear Lord of the Boislauriers?"

"How can you ask me ! most willingly ! It will be both an honor and a pleasure to sit at your table."

"In that case, it is a settled thing," said M. d'Herblay, turning to the host. "We will take dinner, friend. Serve in half an hour ; and distinguish yourself, without any fear of our looking at the bill too closely. Away to your kitchen! Meanwhile, this gentleman and I will renew an old acquaintanceship"

"I haste away, my lords, and you will be contented, I vow to you." And the delighted landlord-and-cook departed with many a salaam.

CHAPTER IV.

HOW ROYAL FAVORITES DIE.

No sooner had the door closed behind the host than the elder nobleman quickly turned to his guest, and inquired in a low voice, dropping the jovial tone which he had adopted :

"I suppose you came here expressly to meet me, eh, Boislaurier?"

".Just so, my lord the duke," was the respectful reply.

"And you come on behalf of Father Lachaise, the royal confessor?"

"It was he who notified of the route you chose to reach Paris———"

"The sea route, *via* Bayonne and Saint Nazaire———"

"I continue, that it was he who sent me to your grace, and I waited for your coming in this modest inn of this petty town, where I was certain that our meeting would not be noticed by anybody."

"You have acted wisely. For at least some time my return into France should be kept from the King and court. Do you bring me any news?"

"Grave news, my lord."

"Oh! ho! with what a mien you tell me so. Grave rises to the superlative, gravest, in that tone."

"Most grave, indeed. Judge for yourself—the royal favorite is no more."

"Mdlle. de Fontanges dead?"

"Aals! it is so."

"But scarcely over twenty! it is dreadful! no, no, it cannot be!"

"It is only too true; and I am charged by the reverend father to acquaint your grace with all the particulars of the mysterious event."

"Mysterious, say you?"

"So much so, that history itself may remain puzzled to decipher the funeral enigma."

The traveler frowned as he listened, seated. With a wave of the hand, he invited the messenger to take a chair by his side, when, leaning towards him as if he feared that the inn walls had ears to catch the words about to be interchanged, he said.

"Come, come, enough of enigmas! I require facts. Speak without reticence and omit nothing which might enlighten me."

"The new LaValliere," said Boislaurier, slowly, "committed three mistakes: she insulted Madame de Montespan by parading her triumph in winning the King away from her, and the proud Athenais———"

"I knew her as Mdlle. de Tonnay-Charente," interpolated the auditor.

"Does not readily forgive. The second error was to take

into her service, a valet who came from her supplanted rival's household; and the third to accept from this fellow's hand a cup of milk, and drink it off at a draft one evening when she was warm and thirsty."

He who was called Aramis, was not a sensitive man. His heart was dried up, like that of all old men who have been fond of the fair sex or much loved by them. Hence he had listened without wincing to the tragic story of the poor mock-queen of a day, cut off in all the flower of her youth and beauty and royal favor.

"Saha!" he limited himself to saying: "Let me tell you that this is a dreadful accusation that you are setting afloat."

"It is not of my invention, but public opinion circulated under the cloak, in the court and town—it is what circumstances point to—what the inquest has brought out. President Lareynie and his Ardent Chamber being commissioned by his Majesty to investigate the matter of the wholesale Poisoning which terrified the whole capital."

"What has the outcome been of this Inquest?"

"It established undeniably that Madame de Montespan tried to remove her rival of infected garments and gloves offered to her by two villains namely, a servant named Romani and a Lyons silk merchant's clerk named Bertrand; and after applying to a regular professional poisoner, known as La Filastre, the marchioness determined to rely on La Voisin to make away with Mdlle. de Fontanges without the manner being plain. She used, as a go-between, her own maid, the Desœillets girl."

"Is it not in my memory that this Voisin woman was tried, sentenced and executed?"

"Certainly, my lord, and in great haste lest she spoke——"

"I should have thought that she was put to the torture to make her prattle——"

"So they did, my lord, but on an order from the King at St. Germain's, her statement was taken on separate paper from the official records so that his Majesty might destroy them without the tribunal at the Royal Arsenal having any cognisance of them. So were treated the statements of La Filastre. The questioning of Romani and Bertrand was deferred. In the last place, the Minister Louvois brought about a meeting between the king and his discarded mistress in which the latter passed from weeping to recrimination and thence to a very high-handed manner.——

The hearer made a contemptuous gesture.

"I cannot say that it is hard to imagine the interview," he remarked phlegmatically. "Here you have the monarch questioning but not without agitation, and he accuses the woman, there; he calls for admissions which are indignantly refused him and he cannot even wring evidence of repentance. The culprit falls to weeping. Soon, according to woman's inevitable tactics, she inverts the proper order of things—she takes the offensive, and reproaches her judge with his infidelity towards her—the primary cause of her false steps and crime. It was jealousy that forced her to commit it! the excess of her passion—the flame of love which devoured her! Men willingly excused the crime of which they were the origin. Louis, who flatters himself that he is a god, after once smiling on those who told him so when he ought have laughed at them—Louis is as much a man as others. I can see him putting faith in these protests, drinking in this adulation like incense, and growing intoxicated on his adoration as upon so much nectar. After all, it is only a riot in a harem. One of the sultans murders another; and merely to be alone in kneeling to the universal idol. What a piece of flattery for his pride! For your Olympian Jove, whose frown shakes entire Europe, is weaker than a school-boy, simpler than an errand-boy, and more trustful than his shopkeepers of Paris, when pricked by his sense and tickled by his self-conceit. This is so true that he forgave all, pronounced it justified, and sets up the proud Athenais in court firmer and more mighty than ever."

"So mighty," agreed M. Boislaurier, "that the Empire and the United Provinces deem it proper to consult her by ambassadors."

The veteran intriguer stared at the speaker with astonishment.

"How now—what are you telling me there?" he said.

"I say that an envoy of the Prince of Orange and another from the Court of Vienna have been conferring with the royal favorite on the arrangements of the peace to be soon concluded."

"Peace!" echoed M. d'Herblay, with a start; "are we to have a treaty of peace signed? Are you in your right senses, my poor Boislaurier?"

"Peace will be signed, my lord; in token of which it is settled that the town of Nimwegen shall serve as meeting-place for the plenipotentiaries who will discuss the condititions."

"Stay! what about Spain, whom I represent; it went into the coalition against Louis XIV. only on the urgent entreaties of the Emperor and the Stadtholder—is not Spain to be informed of an envent of this importance?"

"It is as unknown at St. Germain's as at La Haye and Vienna. Still, nothing is more certain. It is Holland that is getting ready to be the first to part with the coalition. William of Nassau has despatched a confidential agent to Paris charged to present La Montespan a present of ten thousand ducats, if she will persuade his Majesty not to be hard on the Dutch republic, which has suffered the most from the war and is the most worn out."

"How has the marchioness taken the offer?"

"Her answer was that she will do her utmost to influence his Majesty into evacuating the hostile territory, surrender Maestricht and pay half the campaign expenses."

"How about the emperor, what has he asked and what will he give?"

"He has put an income of ten thousand florins at the favorite's feet, in exchange for which she had promised to restore Philipsburg——"

"And Charles II., my august master, where is he in this carving and distributing?" He spoke with a shade of irony.

"Being isolated, the King of Spain will be obliged to accept these conditions, and will probably have to cede to France, Burgundy and other places which——"

"You need not specify—the more you have to eat the more you want. Decidedly, King Louis should not have taken the emblem of the sun—the crab, which with its legs outspread, does not badly resemble the radiant orb, would suit him better," and the old duke, having extended his fingers to illustrate his simile, cracked the joints. "How did you learn all this?" he finally inquired.

"Entirely devoted to us is this maid of the marchioness's, Descœillets, and she obtained copies of letters exchanged between her mistress and both the envoys, for Father Lachaise."

"Long live letter-writing! the letters fly afar in the mails, but the copies remain."

An instant's silence succeeded, after which the arch-plotter resumed with a wrinkled brow and in a cut tone:

"M. de Boislaurier, what thus is meditated, must not come to pass, for it ought not be so. I grant that France is my country by birth, but Spain is that by adopting me. There was I welcomed when I was, as a proscribed fugitive, hunted out of Belle-Isle with fire and sword under the ban of Louis XIV. Spain made me duke of Almada, conferred the title of Grandee upon me, and entrusted me with the care of its interests at the court of St. Germain's. I must not allow my second mother to be humbled, a little as regards myself and a great deal as regards her. Spain is the Roman Catholic power above all; the lessening of its influence in the European concert will be counter to our justifiable views. Reflect, moreover, that the alliance of France with the Dutch Calvinists and the German Lutherans will deal a terrible stroke to the Company of Jesus, to which both of us belong, while I am the supreme chief. Our enemy is Protestantism. It brings with it that spirit of free scrutiny which is the ruin of the Church's power, based as that is upon the faith of the masses. For a long period France has been at the head of Europe. If Protestantism takes a footing here— and it has long rooted itself in the Cevennes—if it overspreads it and finally gains the upper hand, then it will hold the empire of the world. Persecution will be turned against us; the Sons of Loyola will be dislodged, obliged to disappear under shame, hunted and tracked—glad to take refuge in the exile of Calvin, the dungeon of Luther and even the pyre of Huss and Dolet——"

"Heaven knows that I share your ideas," observed the messenger, "and the same apprehensions; but how are we to prevent it?"

The ex-Musketeer gave one of those smiles which had bewitched while they perplexed "Marie Michon," half a century ago.

"Am I not in the battle's van?" he rejoined. "All is well, since you have apprised me. The old saw asserts that a man forewarned is fore-armed. Unarmed, I should wage a cruel war; armed, I am a thousand strong in my single charge. Is it forgotten how I coped with Cardinal Richelieu, who was a great man, and overcame Mazarin, who was a great politician? I grant that, in those times, I had such aids as are lacking to me now." And a shadow clouded the brow of him who had accomplished such elevated aims when planned and executed in the company of the three Musketeers and the Queen's Guardsman, d'Artagnan. "Still, it was I alone who drew from the dungeon where state reasons consigned him— the twin brother of the reigning sovereign, that second son of Anne of Austria whom I substituted upon the throne of France for the royal lover of La Valliere, Fontanges and Montespan. The enterprise was incredible, unheard-of and senseless, if you like, but it would have completely succeeded had it not been wrecked against the honor of a sublime idiot—Fouquet. Well, he is expiating to-day in the Castle of Pignerol his foolish grandeur of mind and imbecile loyalty, and the true prince, who failed me at the right moment, is also expiating his weakness in an iron Mask, if he has not been done to death in some obscure fortress. Let them rot who broke when they were my valuable tools. Ah, believe me, Boislaurier, when one has undertaken tasks of such magnitude, and measured themselves with such adversaries—he has no dread or care about a court doll."

For want of breath the ex-revolutionist, once Bishop of Vannes, and eternal intriguer, stopped in this recurrence of youthful ardor. It was after a pause that he continued, in a calmer and more leisurely mood:

"Poor Fontanges would have been a precious tool to us, and her lack of intelligence would have served us better than all the wit of all the Mortemarts. But we must replace the instrument out of repair with another. We have to drive out the ally of the Emperor and William of Nassau. We need stoop to have recourse to the criminal hand which distils poisons and the more guilty one which pours it out." He said this without a twinge of conscience, for he may not have clearly remembered how the Franciscan died from the effects of the potion administered at Fontainebleau; and yet Aramis obtained the Generalship of the Jesuits all the speedier through that draft. "We will defeat the marchioness with her own weapons, by opposing to her in the King's heart a woman with charms more intoxicating, subjugating and fascinating. This creature, more of an enchantress, will be no less docile than Fontanges, and devoted to our plans."

"The Reverend Father Lachaise and I have been thinking this over; but it is not so easy a matter as may be fancied. Consider, indeed, that all the court beauties have already tried to captivate the capricious monarch without being able to rule him in any appreciable degree; the reign of such as Soubise and Ludre lasted only for a short while——"

"Hence, I am not going to the court to find this Circe."

"Where else is there a woman to witch a king?"

"I hardly know as yet; but when I must find an object, rest easy about its forthcoming."

"Heaven hear your lordship!"

The King of kings listens also to the lowest of the subjects. It is not for the want of praying heartily that I shall fail to be heard." So spake Aramis, with his smile like the Sphynx's. "In the meantime, let us dine without misgiving," he added in a tone become light, " and happily, here comes our host to announce that it is on the table."

It was Hermelin, indeed, who informed them with many cringes, that he desired to know if they wanted him to set their table in the general dining-room.

" Why not?"

"Only because the travelers by the Nantes coach will expect to occupy the other table under the window."

"Pooh! what matters? good company does not annoy us," replied the old noble kindly.

A few minutes subsequently, the jingling of bells and trampling of hoofs, with the rumble of wheels, betokened that the coach, delayed by the highwaymen, had at last arrived.

CHAPTER V.

WANTED A QUEEN—OF THE LEFT HAND.

THE heavy conveyance lumbered up, presenting an example of the sage's precept : " Make haste slowly." Almost instantly, the passengers made an irruption into the dining-hall. Last of all entered the young squire as he had stopped in the kitchen to apply to his wounds that simple cure of salt and water which, perhaps, after all, was as healing as the famous balm which Madame d'Artagnan had of the gipsy. On the threshold he began to look for some one. Perceiving M. d'Herblay, beginning with the soup, he quickly walked up to him, and questioned him, doffing his hat in his hand:

"Monsieur, will you kindly inform me how I am to act to see Mdlle. du Tremblay?"

"The lady so named, as appears to be the case," returned the chevalier, "reposes at present, in perfect health, I suppose, and I have reason to believe that she will shortly be able to resume her journey."

"I can but thank you, and heartily," with embarrassment the young man pursued. "Allow me to present my most humble and sincere apologies for—for—" he faltered, "a bad thought that I entertained."

The duke's smile became mild and friendly.

"I understand," he made answer with a little slyness; you imagined that I had eloped with your traveling-companion——"

Joel looked down, as the old gentleman continued with a shake of his head:

"Oh, youth, youth! mother of all follies! still you need merely to have glanced at my white hairs to be sure how unreasonable and unseemly was your supposition."

"Say, stupid, ridiculous, odious!" exclaimed our hero, blushing with shame; "you see me in consequence so confused that I cannot express my confusion; but I am fresh from the country, a wild rustic. But, by the sword of my father! I and Falsehood have never walked through the same door."

The old lord made the gesture of patting him on the shoulder affectionately and somewhat as a bishop might do.

"Long ago I forgave you for that. Have your dinner in peace, and sin no more by thinking evil of your neighbor."

" Dinner? Faith, I was not thinking of such a thing— I had such a weight on my heart."

But it would appear that the weight was suddenly removed, for when the youth joined his traveling-companions who had begun on the meal with a quarter of an hour's start, he made out to recover the lost time.

Boislaurier called his friend's attention to the fact.

"Yes; he has a hearty appetite. It reminds me of my poor *Porthos!*" Then, raising his voice, as if to dispel the memory of which he was reminded, he addressed the young Breton at one table from the other, as he was demolishing a rabbit pie :

"My young friend, do you mind telling us in the course of what occurrence you received a wound or two, and what was the cause of the swooning fit of your fellow traveler ?"

"Willingly, since you wish so."

And Joel related the adventure when the coach was stopped by the Colonel of Royal Marauders and his troop, with the result. He told it with a swing and gusto, but with a reserve as regarded his behavior which earned the compliments of the two gentlemen of the audience.

When he ended, M. de Boislaurier leaned towards his companion and remarked :

" Do you not agree with me that this youth expresses himself most fitly and in a manner superior in all points to the peasants whose dress he has assumed ?"

" Yes," responded the elder lord : " he is some younger son out of Brittany, a hobbledehoy or farming gentleman, going to seek his fortune in the capital, with a good prospect of doing it, too, to my mind. A good appearance, a well balanced tongue, coolness, and self-control——"

" And built like Milo of old——"

" Plainly ; built to stop millstones with his finger laid on it, like Bernard del Carpio, or to heave a boulder like a Titan—— "

A cloud shaded the face of Aramis : he leaned his elbow on the board, rested his chin in the hollow of the hand, and mused. The aspect of the stout young squire, the memory he had himself invoked by his comparison—they brought back the image of Porthos, as his name alone had done. Not merely Porthos as he had seen him perish trying to uphold the immense mass of the rocks of the Locmaria cavern after the explosion which the strong man had occasioned by hurling a keg of gunpowder among their pursuers, not the crushed giant—but the Porthos of the happy days of their feast of arms. Porthos colossal Musketeer, active, imposing, magnificent in his lifeguard uniform and the gold-embroidered baldrick which glittered like goldfish scales in the sunshine ; Porthos the lady-killer who had courted "My-Lady" to provoke the proctor's widow into wedding him and bestowing her late lamented husband's wealth upon him;

the Porthos who fought so boldly and whose strength of hand could make a hoop of an iron bar and a corkscrew of a fire shovel handle. And the Porthos, older but still sturdy, who won the admiration of the King at the royal table, as well as of the courtiers, by tucking away lamb chops, pheasants and game patties.

But ever the simple, fearless-hearted Porthos, true, smiling, invincible, disinterested, ready to lay down his purse of life for others as though it was for that heaven had given him strength and riches: faithful to the motto of the Four Friends, he had fallen, crushed by an enormous rock, on the Breton beach where the salty breeze from the ocean waved the heather above his bones.

The repast of the two gentlemen finished in silence, for Aramis was in reverie, and the other respected it. Little more talk went on at the other board, where all ate gluttonously. Was not Paquedru, who was feasting in the kitchen, likely at any moment to make his appearance to call out the traditional words: "All aboard, gentlemen! the delight of innkeepers but the misery of famished, travelers, still used by our railroad conductors at way-stations.

"Have the horses put to," said the old duke to the host. "Do you not think we had better start—for you have accepted a seat in my carriage?"

His friend was fully of his opinion. At this juncture, Bazin, the majordomo, waddled in upon the threshold to announce:

"Mdlle. du Tremblay desires to present her duty to the chevalier."

Behind him entered Aurore, still pale and somewhat agitated. With a noble and graceful step she went towards M. d'Herblay.

"Monsieur," she said, "I have been warned that you are about to depart, and I hope that you have not thought that I should see you go without thanking you from the bottom of my soul for the attentions I owe to you, and the care given without your knowing who I am."

The duke had risen courteously to greet her.

"Lady," he responded, "I am too well repaid for services, of which you certainly enlarge the value, by my satisfaction *in seeing* that they have been of some use. I suppose that *you no longer* suffer from your indisposition?"

"*Thank heaven!* and yourself."

"Oh, do not dwell upon that point: it would vex me and I can crave a truce on account of the service rendered——"

"I keep silent, then, since you require it; but the gratitude which you check upon my lips, will return to my heart to be there preserved, fresh and sincere——"

Turning to the Breton squire, who was looking at her and listening to her as one regards a saint, she continued:

"The same as that I cherish for this gentleman who defended and protected me."

This sentence fell like a strain of celestial music on the youth's charmed ear. He longed to find some eloquent reply, choice and meet, but all that issued from his tremulous lips, from the breast brimful of delight, was this meaningless exclamation:

"It is I who thank you, lady!"

While Aurore was speaking, Aramis had studied her with marked attention. Perceiving it, she felt ill at ease and, courtesying again, she took a step in retreat; but the old lord retained her with a gesture.

"Permit me one question—your name, which I but now heard, is far from being unknown to me. Are you by chance any kin to the Marquis du Tremblay, who was governor of the Bastille, prior to M. de Baisemeaux, and——"

"I am his grand-niece, sir."

"And Grand Huntsman under the previous King?"

"The same."

"An excellent gentleman, with whom I had a pleasant acquaintance—I mean, in the latter capacity—my visits to the Bastille not being in the capacity of his guest," proceeded Aramis with a singular smile which would be only comprehended by those who had been informed, as the readers of our "Man in the Iron Mask," of his inteviews with the governor of that state prison of lugubrious memory. 'Let me see, the marquis married a foreign lady, I believe?"

"A Hungarian, indeed, the widow of a magnate of Pesth province."

"Who brought him a large fortune as her marriage portion?"

"The very fortune," replied Aurore, with a melancholy smile, "which is the cause of my journey to Paris."

"How does this come about?"

"My grand-uncle died some eighteen months ago——"

"My poor, dear friend!"

"He died without children and leaving no will ; his wife had preceded him to the tomb, and his inheritance would have come without contest to my brother and sister and self, as direct heirs, were it not disputed by two sons by the first marriage. They assert that their mother gave her second husband the property only for use during life, when it was to revert to her descendants in Hungary. This leads to a lawsuit, and I am proceeding to town to prosecute the claim, consult lawyers and solicit the judges."

"You are undertaking an arduous task."

"It must be. But do not believe, Monsieur, that it is greed that moves me—it is hard necessity. My parents, whom heaven removed at a brief interval, left me nothing but an honored and honorable name. Were I alone in the world, Heaven knows that I should be content with that; for penniless girls of noble birth, there is always the nunnery open——"

"Do not say that you would enshroud so much charm in the veil in a cloister !"

The speaker had the air of not having heard the complimentary interjection, for she continued gravely and calmly :

"But I have the future of others to look after : my young brother's and sister's. They must be reared as beseems their station in life ; and the young man launched properly upon his career, while the girl is supplied with a dowry. I did not hesitate, but collected our resources of which I made two parts : one, the least, luckily, was to defray my traveling expenses ; that I was robbed of a while since ; the other, preserved to me by this gentleman's help"—she indicated Joel—"is intended to pay the children's board in the school where they will await the result of the case. Heaven grant that it will not be long coming, and will be favorable to us !"

"Mademoiselle," insinuated the chevalier, "I am rich, and it would be according me a signal favor if——"

A flash darted from the full eyes, her brow bent, and all her loveliness assumed a bitter and fierce look.

"Sir," she retorted, in a tone animated by her wounded pride, "I trust that you are not going to offer me your purse ?" But, instantly recovering herself, she softened her air, and said with emotion, "pardon me ! I forgot what I owe to you, and poverty is so sensitive. I am not a beggar," she protested with forced liveliness. "In Paris, I have an old kins woman who will welcome like her own child, and she will not refuse to share her all with me, at need."

In the silence which ensued, Bazin's master assumed a paternal air.

"My dear young lady," he broke it by saying, "It is I who must beg pardon, if I have offended, unawares, by an offer which my three-score and ten years should authorize me to make. I do not dwell on it. But if there be one thing which I have the right to offer and you have the right to accept, from your being the head of a family, it is the support of all honorable men. Come, towards the winning of this lawsuit, do you know anybody in Paris? have you not relatives, protection and influence there?"

Sadly the young litigant shook her head.

"Alas, my lord, this is the first time I have been to town, and I do not know a living soul there, save the old relative whom I have mentioned. The unfortunate have no friends. To triumph over my adversaries, I rely solely upon the righteousness of my cause and the help of Providence——"

"I, too, rely on such aids; nevertheless, had you more life experience, you would know that all the decress of justice are not always dictated by equity and right, but, more often, by means of engaging the powerful intermediaries which pleaders know how to employ."

"The God of the fatherless have mercy on us!"

"Well, I have some credit." M. de Boislaurier, hid a faint smile. "Make use of me without scruples and restrictions. The Chevalier d'Herblay will be happy to serve you with all his zeal and all his power."

" But, really, how do I deserve——"

"It is enough to see you, to be interested in you. By the way, here is M. de Boislaurier, whom I have the favor to present to you——" The gentleman and the young lady exchanged salutations. " I have no doubt that he agrees with me?"

" Certainly," rejoined the other, " I am quite won by the lady."

" M. de Boislaurier is attatched to the household of his Royal Highness the Dauphin, a pious Prince of austere manners," proceeded the chevalier; " when you knock at M. de Boislaurier's door, you knock at mine. Besides." he added good humoredly, " we do not attempt to impose our services; you are perfectly free do decline them. Only, keep the children in mind, as you were just saying——"

"The carriage of my lord stops the way," reported the landlord.

At the same time the coachdriver's voice was heard outside, shouting the stereotyped formula: "Passengers by the stage-coach, take your places!"

The ex-Musketeer bowed to the young lady as he was wont to do to the queens when he was a gallant, and said:

"I hope we shall meet again, my child. My age permits me to give you this title. Remember that you are not without devoted friends. Use them—too often rather than merely wisely, as the only means of proving to them that you are aware of the interest they take in you."

The movement was general to leave the room, and Joel took advantage of it to approach Aurore. She held out both hands to him with an outburst of gratitude, saying: "Wounded—you were wounded! and in throwing yourself before me to save me from the shot aimed at me. Now, you must not be ill friends with me because I did not go and ask how you were at once," she went on with a forced familiarity; "but we are not going yet to part, you know, but go on to Paris together so that I shall have on the journey full leisure to overwhelm you with my thankfulness."

Meanwhile the chevalier was directing his steps to his carriage, on the arm of his friend.

"What do you think of that girl?" inquired the former.

"I say admirably fair," replied the gentleman, turning to have another look at the young lady, who was preparing to climb into the coach, assisted by the radiant Joel.

His companion's smile was a reflection of that which had fascinated the Duchess de Chevreuse.

"Salute her with lowliness," said he, "as the rising star is saluted——as all the court will hail her before a great while; for the country lass, whose existence is not dreampt of by Paris and St. Germain, is the woman whom I have chosen to bring our projects to the desired goal. She will succeed Montespan dethroned: she will be the future Queen of France—by the left hand——the hand on the heartside, remember—and, consequently, the real sovereign of France!"

CHAPTER VI.

THE SWORD FROM THE GIANT'S GRAVE.

Let us go back to the period when Fouquet, the Lord High Treasurer in fact, of France, owned Belle-Isle-in-the-Sea. The estate is six leagues long by six in breadth and it was a fief of the Retz family, to whom we owe the human monster who comes down to us through the nursery as the original of "Bluebeard." After the property had the title of marquis conferred the holder on by Charles IX., it passed into the Financial Seperintendent's hands. It included three hamlets; Bangos, Saugen and Locmaria, the latter having some celebrity in the petty ports of Brittany for the prettiness, gaiety and coquetry of its lasses.

The prettiest, most promising and buxon of all the girls, but the least coquettish, was then Corentine Lebrenn, goddaughter of Master Plouer, a sub-officer of the Marines who had become syndic of the guild of fishermen.

Corentine was eighteen years of age, and her treses of deep yellow shone in the sunbeams like gold. She did not know what to do with them, they were so abundant about her shapely head. Her large, carefree eyes had smiles in them like those on her vermillion lips. Together with natural charms, she was the best "catch" in the island. Her parents were hard-working, saving and intelligent working folk, who had toiled all their life that their only darling should be sheltered from care. They died at the task, but left her a nice farm and land that would sell well.

You may imagine how closely this prize was pursued by the young men, not only on the island, but along the coast. Quite a retinue followed at her heels when she went to sell the farm produce at the markets; she was so enticing in her hooded cloak and short plush petticoat, and with her rounded ankle disappearing in natty little shoes. The young blades, too, formed a double row when she came out of church on Sunday, for then she wore a rich lace headdress, a gold cross, a velvet bodice worked with gold thread, clocked stockings and silver buckles to her shoes. But she little troubled herself about sweethearts

She had enough to do in attending to the farm and house matters, the harvest, the fowls, the stables, her almsgiving and her songs. Her life passed on, sweet and peaceful. Her limpid gaze was never dimmed with tears. Around her shone a halo of glee. All who came near her were the happier for her beaming gladness.

At this time, M. Fouquet determined to fortify his Isle-in-the-Sea. Wherefore? nobody clearly knew. It was his good pleasure, and his serfs asked no farther. The Dukes of Burgundy no longer reigned over the place but the lords of the manor ruled in their stead. Superintendent Fouquet was the most powerful and wealthiest, and consequently the most popular of them all.

He sent to Belle-Isle an engineer and workmen. The former was a cavalier of high stature and robust mien, who wore a doublet laced with gold, and a hat covered with plumes. All the female sex of Locmaria remarked his splendid appearance and his winning air.

Every evening the girl-farmer went to the churchyard where her parents reposed to see to the flowers on their graves and kneel in prayer.

It was in returning from this pious pilgrimage that Corentine was waylaid by a gang of intoxicated soldiers and stone-cutters, at nightfall. In a moment they surrounded her, and dancing drunkenly, insisted on her sharing the bottle and joining in their gambols. In despair she screamed for help, though knowing that the new-comers, both workingmen and soldiers, inspired great terror in the islanders. A man ran up in strides like one on stilts; he knocked the revelers about like ninepins and forced them to flee as much with his prowess as by his post of authority over them. It was the chief military engineer. He escorted her home, although he had so effectually driven molestation afar. The champion was not so much of a Parisian courtier as she took him to be, and with the same rustic frankness which she showed in recounting her name and position, he related that he was not what they took him for. He was, he said, but a Baron at present, but at the close of the honor of dining with the King, it was intimated that he might look forward to be made a duke and peer of the realm. In fact, said the naive Porthos, for our readers will have divined who this engineer was who *felled men* like puppets, his mission in Belle-Isle was not unconnected with the next step to his rising to the rank, for the fortification was on behalf of the monarch, who had no dearer friend than Fouquet.

The Baron du Vallon, we know, was a widower, and ever impressionable: the maid of the farm had never seen such a demigod, and they fell simultaneously in love.

They met again and again, and the love on Corentine's part was so pure, elevated into idolatry, and impressive, that the conqueror, who had perhaps no other defect than a too free tongue, never boasted of the conquest to Aramis; still less to d'Artagnan, who, since the far-reaching and fatal result of his false-play with My Lady, was a model of discretion in gallantry.

As usual, at his last parting, Porthos had promised to come again. He never came. But the siege terminated by the island rebels surrendering to the royalists by command of their leader, the Bishop of Vannes. Corentine did not know that Porthos,(for she did not remember her lover by the titles which he held and which he said were due him,) had not shared the flight of his friend Aramis, but had been stayed by death on the beach of Locmaria.

One person could have informed her how her beloved had perished. It was her god-father, Plouer, whom we have seen valiantly assisting the fugitives to sail from the island. Unfortunately there was nobody whom the poor girl so persistently shunned as the syndic of the fishers, for she had her shame and her sin to conceal from all—she was on the eve of becoming a mother.

She fled to the mainland, where she had an old relative living by Quimper. There she gave birth to a son. It was during her absence from home, and giving an excuse for it, that occurred the arrest of Minister Fouquet, and his transference to Pignerol Castle, and the occupation of the island by the King's troops. Only a confused account of these important events reached Corentine in her retreat. Her distress put her life and her reason in danger. When she returned to the farm, she had lost her virginal smile, her cheek was pale, and her eyes had learnt how to weep. Nevertheless she was happy in a way, in her misfortune and her state of outcast. For her child remained by her—dear little Joel.

Corentine was the Mother, to the point of delirious idolatry. In pagan times, comparing her lover with ordinary—

nay, remarkable men, she would have believed that a demigod had condescended to love her. In the little Porthos, she worshipped the hero whom she had suddenly met and so mysteriously lost. She knew that she had been loved, and she believed that she still was loved by the handsome nobleman whose manly bearing, showy uniform and plumed hat, had struck her with surprise and fascinated her. The conquest was still wonder to her. She knew only enough of him to deplore the loss. She was not ignorant of all that divided them——rank, birth and fortune. Would she ever see him again? Of a certainty she yearned to do so, and with all the ardor of her soul : but not perhaps for her own sake—for the innocent creature who slumbered in its cradle, calm and rosy.

In bringing this child to Locmaria with her, she had braved the local indignation. As soon as the excitement of the war, as they called the affair, had cooled down, the gossips took up the disgrace of the rich girl-farmer. How they did chatter to revenge themselves on her who had been so envied. How they overwhelmed the unmarried mother with brutal humiliation, coarse disdain, and pretended compassion, more cruel and humiliating still ! How the swains whom she had jilted and the maids whom she had eclipsed affected to draw aside from her with disgust, tempered with sneering laughs and cutting remarks ! The unhappy one supported all without complaint. Had she not her treasure to console her, in her solitude, for the scorn of the gross multitude ? Its fresh lips called for the kiss, while the sweet breath of the infantile was wafted through them.

In the midst of this isolation to defend his mother from the public scorn, little Joel grew up. With time he became a youth of stature and strength far above those of the lads of his own years. The parish priest of Locmaria, good Father Keravel, had forgiven the sinning mother on seeing how she had redoubled her charity and with what affection she surrounded the son of shame, and he had consented to teach the youngster. He did teach him to read, write and cipher. And a smattering of spelling and a little Latin; but the highest nobles no longer emulated Fouquet in "living up" to the court of poets and men of letters which he had fostered. But it was undoubted that the young Porthos mounted the wildest of the island ponies barebacked, so that he had won the fame of being a centaur : that he could run down a hare on his own feet and could take the eggs from the highest nest. And lastly, he could fire off a musket with as good a success as old Plouer, who had won the reputation of killing nineteen woodcock out or twenty.

We hastened to say that the old marine corporal had not imitated the virtuous Locmarians by turning his back on his errant god-daughter Old soldiers are usually indulgent in matters of love In his presence nobody dared to speak ill of the pretty farmer-girl.

Plouer was not only the most daring of mariners and the cunningest fisher on the island, but he had been one of the finest and deadliest fencers in his regiment. He could swing a cutlass now so that not one durst stand up to him, steel in hand.

So fond was he of the art without which no gentleman was reckoned accomplished in that era, that he put a little sword in the chubby hand of Joel when he was only five or six years old.

From that time forward, the boy never let a day pass without having fenced with his tutor in sword play for an hour or two. In the course of the lessons, the enlarged knitting-needle had become a cook's skewer, and finally a long rapier, while the unsteady hand was at length firm, the eye sure and piercing, and the stripling was able to stand up all the day, in the position recommended in the fencing schools of the time—which knew a thing or two.

Besides these advantages, our hero possessed at his sixteenth year a height scarcely below six feet in his stockings, without being weedy, and it promised not to stop there · a fist that could smash paving stones, a digestion that could relish them ; and an inexhaustible fount of good spirits.

His mother worshipped her infant Hercules, and he returned her love with interest.

He wanted for nothing. He had the finest broadcloth suits, the choicest hunting dogs, a fowling piece made by the first gunsmith of Nantes. and enough pocket-money to shower alms on the poor. On returning from the chase he always found a copious repast, and the thickest feather bed awaiting him for a good twelve hour's sleep.

Such happiness often covers the worst disasters. A great event was to put an end to it.

One day, one of the beggars whom he regularly relieved and who used sometimes to attend him in his hunting expeditions, was set upon by some fellows who came out of a wine-shop, and not noticing that the son of Porthos was within hearing, pelted him with stones and hurled at him the reproach that he could find no better post than to be the hanger on of a pert knave who could not tell his father's name.

The ringleader of these ruffians was a youth who had pretensions to gentle blood, his father having been a notable official under the rule of Fouquet. Upon the insulted young man showing himself and scattering the brawlers by his presence alone, this one stood firm but refused reparation.

"I cannot fight with a man who does not know who is his sire, he said. "I am a gentleman!—if you are born to carry a sword, go get it with proofs of your right to bear it, and I will meet you with *my father's*, on the beach by the Giant's Tomb."

The gathered crowd supported the challenger in this ingenious evasion, for nobody believed in the hazy story of Corentine's amour, which had oozed out from Plouer in his cups.

In a fit of rage and desperation, Joel had run off at random, and woe to any one whom he encountered in that mad race.

Without intending it, his steps brought him out into the open, in the desert, which the young gentleman had well selected for the duel which he did not expect to have to fight.

The Giant's Tomb was a moss and weed-grown tumulus, about which the superstitious Bretons had woven the usual garland of legends. Here, in plain truth, had been immured Porthos, in defending his friend Aramis and to give him the time to escape in the boat which Plouer and his crew were to launch and direct to avoid the royal fleet blockading Belle-Isle. But the secret had been well-kept by the dead soldiers whom they had destroyed and the fishermen who had conveyed the fugitive Bishop of Vannes to the frigate which carried him to Spain. Plouer was observed to laugh with the low chuckle of the Breton when he heard a villager express his dislike to go along the strand by what had been the cavern of Locmaria.

Corentine, who had discovered the grotto, and had imparted the word to her god-father, had also kept the secret.

THE DEATH OF ARAMIS.

Thus it followed that the rustics went back to the olden times for a cause to account for the convulsion which had buried the pursuers of the Bishop of Vannes and his fellow-rebel in the fallen-in cave. They invented a giant who had been at war with the priests who tenated the spot as custodians of a temple, and who had been defeated by the holy men. Ages after, when the enemies of the good bishop invaded the holy site, the giant's spectre, enraged at the double profanation of the fame of Calonesa and his resting place, had upheaved the rocks and let all tumble in upon the royalists.

When the furious youth reached this mound, the sun was dyeing the gorse and heather with purple and mother-of-pearl tints and the gulls streamed close up to him to scream at him as he took a seat sadly among the melancholy larches which twisted like dead serpents among the stones; some of these showed the blue and black marks of the explosion. In spots a rank grass grew, and in others, only a creeping weed with a blood-red flower like splashes of gore.

Where Joel sat, the upheaval seemed one of the funeral mounds raised by the ancients after a battle where a handful of determined spirits had overcome a host. It is true that Aramis and Porthos between them, with the slight help of Plouer and his crew of two, had slain over a hundred of the foe.

Around was peace: but here the spirit of battle still reigned and whipped up the ire of the youth. He meditated only of killing everyone of the bitter jesters who had insulted his mother and his father's memory. Oh, for such a weapon as the Excalibur of King Arthur,—who lives in Breton traditions. He would attack the slanderers a hundred strong, and strike, and slay, and slay with an unwearied arm. This father whom he had never seen and of whom he thought so constantly but spoke so seldom—who was he? Piously the youth invoked this sire who was but a phantom in his dreams. And it seemed to him on the sombre background of the pines and blackened rocks, that he suddenly beheld one of those human-like figures moulded by the fays out of the ocean mists. This figure had the martial bearing and victoriouss talk of a conqueror of men, and it still seemed to the gazer that the large eyes were bent on him with a glance of blended sorrow and pride. With a noble gesture it drew a long sword from its rich girdle-band, and with a flourish as if to indicate its purpose, placed it on a stone not a score of feet away. Then, with a kind of affectionate nod of farewell, it faded into the other mists which began to wreathe the mound.

Breaking the spell which had held him during this vision, Joel sprang to his feet with a wild cry: "Oh, stay, my father!" but when he reached the stone, all had vanished and, indeed, no weapon of any kind rested on the face of granite —only a dry twig with which imagination had pictured the sword.

But still Joel stared at the place where the simulacrum had withdrawn from his sight: never had a dream been so vivid—he believed that he should never forget the form in its details, plumed hat, with some of the feathers snapped by bullets, glittering baldrick, loose breeches seamed with gold lace and disappearing in the large tops of riding boots. But to his call only the sea-bird's shrill scream had answered. He turned reluctantly, when a sharp pain at his heel wrung from him an exclamation. Something bright but ruddy gleamed in the sunshine; he stooped and carefully examined what proved to be a point of metal. He seized the twig and dug it out—it was a sword, but from its length and weight and the size of the handle it must have belonged to such a giant as was fabled to lay his bones here.

"It is my father's gift," said Joel, kissing it piously, although the rust, which might be blood, reddened his pale lips. "I accept the token and I hop to draw it only in such causes as he would approve and never to sheathe it without the wrong done me is avenged."

He had the weapon for redress, and now, all that he wanted was the proofs of his gentility. He returned home, and entered the house, still pale, but his eyes blazing and his features sternly contracted. Never had his mother seen the usually placid youth so aroused.

"Good heavens, what has happened?"

"I have been insulted," responded Joel, in a deep and tremulous voice. "and I am to meet the principal aggressor in a duel, when I am supplied with the name of my father and the proof that he was entitled to confer on his son the right to bear and use a sword. This sword—his sword— *you see,* I am provided with."

And he related the vision and held up the sword of Porthos which time, the action of the sea breeze and the crumbling of the stones, had fortuitously offered to his hand.

Corentine turned white as a sheet on seeing this **giant's glaive**, heroic in dimensions, which she recognized as having been worn by her colossal lover. She staggered, pressing her hand to her bosom as though she had been pierced to the heart with it. Joel loved his mother and felt a respect for her which would not have been unworthy a saint. On seeing the distress which prostrated the unhappy woman, sudden revulsion drove away his wrath as regarded her. He bent his knee as one does in suing great pardon, and exclaimed with a pang of anguish:

"What is the matter, mother? I have caused you pain! Is it possible that you recognize this sword?"

"It is the offering of the dead," she returned solemnly, and staying her tears; "Well, you shall know at once what must have been enfolded to you one day. I met——"

He held up his hand to silence her, with a kind of authority which he had never felt or shown to her before.

"Nay, be still. I wish to know nothing. I will not fight a duel with this malapert, but cudgel him and his band of jesters within an inch of their lives. Do not speak—unless to utter my forgiveness for having caused you pain."

She disengaged herself from his embrace, and repeated:

"You shall know, my boy, what it is right you should have known; but let it be later—may it be so?"

"Oh, mother, I have no wish but yours. Keep the secret. Like the vision and the gift of my sire, it will be revealed in Gods's own good time."

"I pledge you my faith that all shall be clear," she went on gravely. "If you have seen him—dead—it is because I am to see him soon. You shall know all, all—when—" she muttered the end of the sentence out of his hearing: "when death shall prevent me blushing in your presence."

From that day, there was a change in the life of the mother and the son. She grew gloomy, and her activity waned. She left to him the care of the farm, and shut herself up in her room. She was often heard to repeat with the set frown of one haunted by the same idea: "It is by my son's hand that I am punished."

She had long ceased to go to the churchyard to decorate her parents' graves, for the backbiters would even now have insulted her; in country places, moral feuds rarely die out ; but she took her only walks to the deserted tract of the beach where rounded up the Giant's Tomb. Nobody but Joel, whose curiosity had urged him to follow her one day, divined the object of this strange pilgrimage.

"It was my father whom I saw, as surely as this sword was his." And he smiled with a kind of savage and lofty pride that he was the offspring of so grand and impressive a figure.

Meanwhile the poor woman's countenance grew thin ; around her eyes brown circles formed ; her skin assumed the yellow of old ivory and threads of silver whitened her luxuriant hair. Her son was almost the only one not to remark the alteration, for youth sees everything lively and splendrous as itself.

Yet he was serious at whiles. He had not resented the insult either with the providentially supplied sword or with the cudgel, used for the adjustment of differences between those who were not allowed the gentleman's arm ; but this was because nobody dared repeat the slur on his parentage, in his hearing, from the terribly threatening look which he wore when he suspected it was on the lips of an interlocutor. A jest loses its point when there is danger of no less than death to the joker. No one believed that he had forgotten the insult least of all the young squire who had uttered it. Joel's natural liveliness was often veiled by a cloud of care. His eyes wandered into vacancy and became fixed so that the old crones said that the young master at Corentine's farm had "seen the walkers on the heath," meaning those envoys from the other world who tell us of what it is not possible for mortals to hear without their being made grave for life. He would stroll the beach for hours together, as if an invisible attraction linked his sight with some goal on the other side of the water separating him from the main.

The farm proprietress read what was passing within him; for she would meet him on his coming home, and say in a broken voice as she pressed him to her bosom,

"But you will not go away, my dear Joel, until I am no more?"

The malady under which Corentine suffered was the most undermining of all: it was grief. She was certain that her gallant lover was in the grave, and the sword which pointed to heavan from the subterranean, was a token. She questioned Plouer in a secret conference, while Joel was out of the house, and he described the companion of the Bishop of Vannes, distinguished by his tall form and imposing demeanor so that there was no doubt left that the father of the boy was him they both were fond of, the engineer who had defied the King and his forces. Unfortunately, the soldier had never heard him called by any other title than "Porthos," evidently a *nom-de-guerre*. But he had no more doubt than his god-daughter, of the nobility of the officer. Unfortunately, the Bishop of Vannes had fled as an outlaw. In this remote spot, no one knew how the King had forgiven him, on the instance of his favorite Captain of the Musketeers. That Aramis, escaped by his affiliation to the Company of Jesus, should have attained high rank in Spain, did not enter into the fancy of either of these rustics. They both believed that the secret was entombed in the Giant's Grave. The syndic of the fishermen went there, and tried to unearth the bones of the valiant one ; but the immense boulders defied his single hand to even budge them; and as he did not wish strangers to disinter the remains, he forbore to call in aid.

He returned to tell of his ill success to his god-daughter, whom he had not seen for some days, and met a messenger who was running to the priest's. Corentine was a-bed and in a bad state; her ailment was mental and the physician for the soul alone might do her any good.

As the messenger was an infirm old man, Plouer replaced him in the quest.

In the meantime, Joel had gone into the sick-room at his mother's feeble call. She was sitting up, after an effort which drew from her a piteous wail. He hastened to wipe off the tears which the pain wrung from her failing eyes. He had crossed the room to reach her in a couple of strides, like a lion. But he had not made more noise than the same animal hunting for prey. He threw himself upon his knees by the bedside, and pressed his burning lips on the woman's bloodless and wasted hands. She drew him passionately towards her.

"When you are by me, I suffer no more," she murmured. "You must not afflict yourself," she continued, with gentle gravity, on feeling the boy's tears on her face—for he was ever a boy to her; "we are not to part forever, but shall meet again where my prayers and my repentance will have won me a place, I trust. In that home of peace and bliss, I shall watch over your days. You will see me bending over you, as when you were in the cradle, and the belief of my guard will support you in the task which I entreat our Lord to grant you the power to fulfill.

"Your father assured me—and a nobleman never lies to the woman whom he loves—that he never loved but me—that he had no heir to his fortune, his title and his fame. It is you who must show that his spirit survives in his son. Learn who he was—for I feel that he is not in the land of the living, alas! That is the reason that I reveal to you the secret of my life, my loss of station among the neighbors and this killing grief. It is my duty to avow my fault——"

"Mother," said the young man, "again, let me know nothing. Say not a word, or speak to tell me that this is not the long farewell."

She thanked him with a look which painted the extent of her gratitude.

"You have never so much as questioned me by a look, since the once. Heaven will bless the son who so respected his mother. Nevertheless, you have been seeking here, and you have intended to seek on the mainland, the origin of your birth. Do not deny what I and Plouer have perceived. Besides, you know not how to lie."

Joel raised his head with pride.

"The reverend father is coming," she resumed but with fatigue. "No doubt he will approve of my course, and then you will know all as far as I do."

She interrupted herself to listen to a sound which did not catch his ears, and sank back, exhausted on the pillow. He leant over her, and he received that inimitable caress—the dying mother's final salutation this side of the grave. Without, he now heard the tinkling of a small silver bell: it was the priest coming, guided by Plouer, if the parish priest needed any guide on that often traversed road.

Indeed Father Keravel approved of the woman's wishes, for he remitted to Joel, next day, that of Corentine's death, the written confession which she wished her son to peruse for his search for his paternity, clues to help him, a portrait traced from an unflagging memory, some names and a date.

She had yielded up these when the hour of her liberation from grief and pain came to her. Days after the funeral of one whom he long and sincerely mourned, the young master of the farm announced his intention to sell it and all its appurtenances. But the matter was not arranged without delay, the cunning peasants pretending to be in no hurry to purchase what they were in reality covetting. The formalities and chaffering lasted about a year, in the course of which the young heir gradually fell back into his old habits and moods.

One morning he called upon Father Keravel, and after having begged him to forgive him for the trouble he had caused him as the "Big boy," of the school, and thanked him for what amount of education he had succeeded in imparting, he constrained him to accept a handsome sum for his school and the little chapel, such as a suzerain lord might have offered.

"Father," he said, "I ask to be remembered in your prayers as I am going to Paris."

" Go, my son," answered the priest. "I know the aim to which you tend, and I am not the one to turn you aside, however difficult as it appears the reaching it will be. It is a laudable errand, and you are a worthy young gentleman. The Lord will protect you, and I shall bless you."

Our hero went to take leave of Plouer. At the first words which touched upon the imminent departure, the old soldier grumbled :

" Humph ! it is my opinion that you are seeking a needle in the haystack. But I am not going to wrangle with you, from the time that you have taken it into your head. Why, Paris, though, when to my mind it is here where you should take up one end of the clue ? However, do your best not to leave your skin and bones in town for your pains, and in order to be safe on that score, remember to quickly do unto others what you do not like them to do unto you!"

After enunciating this somewhat perverted Christian motto, the old sub-officer added :

"I see you have girded on the sword you found, and you still believe as I do, that it belonged to the engineer who fought the king's men singlehanded, or nearly so—for though I admit that the bishop saw the blood spilled, like an old warrior—as they tell me once he was—the fighting fell nearly all to M. Porthos's lot. We boatmen only scored dead hounds to our credit." And for the first time, in its entirety, he related the scene in the grotto, where the royalists had been held at bay by the paltry force of the two friends and the three sea-farers. Joel listened with avidity, and his eyes sparkled. This was a father worthy of his owning. But it was the proofs of that parentage that he could alone hope to find—he was sure that he was turning his back in that search, on his sire's grave. At least, he left the admiring Plouer to guard it.

"Let me see it again," said the old corporal, and he reverently handled the long sword. "That is it, I am sure. I see the motto on the blade is ' One for All, All for One'—a very good one for the member of a regiment. There is a Spanish one often seen on good Toledo blades—'Never draw me but from reason—never sheathe me but in honor.' "

Hugging the recipient of his fencing knowledge, as if to crush him, he concluded:

"Hang these fondlings, which are only fit for women! Farewell, and may your journey then turn out well, my boy. Think sometimes of your old fencing-master, and keep in practice for the ward, and the lunge, cultivate the *prime parade* and when you thrust, do it with your whole arm, body and soul. With that correct, you can reach any point."

CHAPTER VII.

ON THE TRESHOLD.

To Mdlle. du Tremblay our hero imparted as much of this romantic story as he knew, and he concluded succinctly:

"The court is at Paris or in its neighborhood, and the place of all nobleman, is at the court. Now, it is clear that my father was a nobleman, and if he be alive, or if he has friends in position, I shall learn there about him. Hence, I am making straight for Paris."

The young lady could not abstain from a start of surprise and compassion before such simple faith.

"But the clues of which you speak—the date—and the *names to aid you* in your searches?"

"The starting-point is the date of the occupation of Belle-Isle by the royal forces. The first of the names is that of my father, 'Porthos,' next those of his three companions-in-arms, for whom he cherished an attachment and devotion above proof—these were Athos, Aramis and d'Artagnan."

Aurore shook her head, and commented:

"Odd names, indeed, and no doubt cloaks to their real titles. What a number of enigmas to unravel!" And she gravely added: "I hope you will succeed."

He looked at her with affright.

"Oh, lady, with what a forbidding look you say that! You will dishearten me. Do you already despair of my succeeding in the quest?"

" No, my friend, for you have a helper—though your only one, but it can do everything for those who trust to it——"

"It?" said Joel sadly: "I understand: you mean chance?"

"Well, I prefer to call it Providence," replied the girl with inspiration.

This dialogue took place on the rich plains of Beauce; for time had progressed, as well as the Nantes Coach, and the acquaintance of the young couple, commenced on the highway of Saumur, was complete on the day after their leaving the Golden Heron.

The night following the departure had been spent by the young squire in watching over the sleep of the lady, she sat over against him, while he shrank back into a corner of the cumbrous vehicle, where all the passengers were huddled higgledy-piggledy.

When a dawning light peeped into the common cell, he had seen the girl's entrancing features gradually become defined, from being vague and smoothed out as in a vision, so as to be still more captivating as they could be more clearly distinguished. The rising sun played with her tresses. As soon as she opened her eyes, their gaze met the youth's, and a rosy tinge suddenly colored her peachy cheeks. In the limpid pupil was a slight reproach as she said to the admirer:

"So you were looking at me sleeping, Squire Joel?"

He, too, had blushed like a boy caught in a fault, and he was confused and could not find a reply. His lifting his hand to his forehead, to collect his wits, disarranged the bandage with which his face-wound had been covered during the night. As he was trying to invent some excuse, to give himself countenance, Aurore asked if she might not help him. And, without waiting for his consent, she proceeded to replace the bandage with a hand which did not tremble.

Our Breton adventurer wanted speech to express his ecstasy, but his ravished gaze was terribly eloquent.

"I am just doing my duty," continued the fair Samaritan. "You ran the danger for me. I thank heaven the hurt is so slight, when it might in such a place have been mortal."

"It would have been a joy to have shed all my life's blood on your behalf," muttered the youth.

"Do I hurt you?" inquired Aurore, smiling.

"Oh, do not think of such a thing!" exclaimed the squire whose intoxication knew no bounds.

The bandage having been adjusted, the impromptu nurse went on to say: "I have spoken of a duty which it is sweet to fulfill; but I have also a right, and it is my desire: I want to know who it is to whom I must be ever grateful for so signal a service."

Thereupon the young man had related the story of his life, until his auditress, lifting a warning finger, indicated that their fellow-travelers were also listening, with ears pricked up and mouths a gape.

"Never mind the rest now. Later—when we are going up a hill."

This was the only means of having seclusion from their coach-companions. So, when a rising of the road obliged the party to alight and relieve the vehicle of their bodies, Mdlle. du Tremblay,—whom her presumed lightness and her sex had excused from this change,—which the shipping merchant facetiously styled "lightening ship—" hastened to step down. The least acclivity tempted her. Encouraged by a smile, Joel offered her his arm, and the two walked on together, leaning towards one another. In these instants of isolation, the orphan had concluded his narration. On her part, she repeated what she had told the Chevalier d' Herblay. After this exchange of confidence, the two had chatted. Of what? it little matters. No doubt of the weather, the scenery, continually varying, the villages they drove through without noticing them, and those trifles, " light as air," which lovers find full of sense when the adored one speaks them. Their glances were caresses, their words incense, and their heart-beats kept time.

On the heights of St. Cloud, Paquedru pointed with his whip to the twin towers of the Cathedral of Nôtre Dame, emerging on the horizon in the floating gold dust of a fine summer's evening.

"Paris!" he shouted.

"Paris!" repeated the others, rubbing their hands with satisfaction at having had no more adventures with highwaymen.

"Paris!" repeated with mutual sadness the Son of Porthos and the daughter of the house of Tremblay.

For the rest, the driver's hail had been the proclamation, impatiently awaited, of the end of their imprisonment in this cage on wheels, rolling at a tortoise's pace. For our pair of turtle doves, it simply meant a parting. Their bosoms shrank, their brows clouded, and their lips became mute.

Meanwhile, the coach entered the city to stop in the coachyard, the name still being applied to the site, though uilt upon in the suburb, without the St. Honoré gate.

The passengers hastened to open the door and climbed out with a sigh of relief when stepping on the pavement.

"Is Mdlle. du Tremblay here?" inquired a quivering voice, as an aged serving-woman showed herself at the coach-door.

"Here I am," responded the girl, leaping out nimbly.

The old domestic courteseyed, and continued : "Your kinswoman, my mistress, Widow de la Bassetiere, sent me to meet you and take you to our house"

"Very well, nurse ; I am with you." But she turned towards the Breton, who had alighted after her from being in the farther corner, and said : " It is the time to part."

His heart was swollen with indefinable anguish, and he could not breathe a word.

"Good fortune," she said, offering her hand, "And I hope we shall meet again."

"Do you hope that?" queried Joel, feeling life return to him at the sentence.

"Certainly I do," in full sincerity : "It is only mountains that never meet," she added, forcing herself to seem mirthful to cheer him up. "I feel sure that we shall meet again,"

"But when, and where?" questioned the Breton, who had learnt from his fencing-master, to reply directly and to the point.

Aurore was "hit." Perhaps she wanted the question to be put, for she answered promptly; "The member of my family offering me hospitality, lives in the Rue des Tournelles. I beleive that St. Paul's Church is close by, and that is in the neighborhood of Royal Place. Every evening, for the vespers, I shall go to that church."

While the young couple were arranging for their next meeting, two men in cloaks, with their hats slouched over their eyes, were hiding under the shed over a shop-front. When the young lady and the old servant went their way towards St. Honoré gate, one of the men leaned to the other and said in the Spanish language, in his ear:

"Esteban, have you noticed those two women?"

"I have, my lord duke."

"Then, dog them whithersoever they may go, taking heed not to let them perceive that they are the object of your pursuit."

"I understand your lordship."

"Bring to me the name of the street and description of the house where their journey leaves them."

"It shall be done, my lord." And the Duke of Almada's trusted myrmidon stated off in the tracks of the unsuspecting pair with a stealthy step and wary carriage which showed that the errand was no new one.

CHAPTER VIII.

THE FASHIONABLE FORTUNE-TELLER.

ABOUT the same time as the Nantes coach rolled into Paris, three women came to a stop before a house in the middle of the Rue du Bouloi. They wore the woolen petticoats, muslin caps with a point, and hooded mantles of the middle-class Parisians. The house had such a mysterious appearance as became one reputed to be the retreat of the heiress, some said the daughter, of La Voisin, the poisoner who cloaked *her deadly trade* under that of soothsaying. Whoever she was she called herself the Manicarde, which meant, if anything, the Manipulator of Cards. The fashion still ran on witches, who sold pommades to ladies of quality to make thin persons stout, and stout ones slender, charms to cause the uimpressionable to love one another; and who showed shades of the greatest; as for instance, to the Duke of Luxembourg, was shown Satan himself to influence a succession to property, and to Cardinal Tour d'Auvergne, Marshal Turenne, whose heir he was, and whose buried riches he was hungering for. The Queen and the King's brother had come to consult the oracles, it was asserted.

If the executed La Voisin's daughter, the prophetess had learnt something by her fate, for she declared that she only told fortunes and did not deal in cosmetics or elixirs of love or, still less, deadly drugs. Thanks to this rule, the Lieutenant of Police, Lareynie, allowed her undisturbedly to pursue her craft in the same street as where he lived, and indeed could count from his house the customers she had.

At the knock struck on the door by one of the women, a hard, sharp, ringing bang as by one accustomed to command, a negro boy, dressed in the Oriental mode, silently opened it and conducted the three visitors into a large parlor on the ground floor where he pointed to chairs.

The room resembled an alchemists laboratory, the hanging lamp showing stuffed crocodiles, owls, alembics, and the traditional paraphernalia of the wizard, covered with dust. On the other hand, the seats which the visitors took were clean as if frequently used. They looked about them with curiosity, and one whispered, with a slight shivering:

"Does it not seem to you that these tapestry hangings harbor a host of muttering spectres? Do you not believe that the witches Sabbath is celebrated here? Really, ladies, I am afraid."

A meeting of witches within a couple of steps of the royal palace and the public gardens—next door to the residence of the head of the police! you must be mad my dear friend!" With boastfulness she added: "I laugh at the whole pack." Turning to the third of the party, she inquired: What are you doing, dear Francoise?"

"I am observing," replied this one tranquilly.

While the first lady shudders in dread, the second laughs and the last observes, let us present all three to the reader, two of them being called upon to play important parts in this work.

The one in terror was small, fresh in complexion, inclined to be full in figure, with chestnut hair, lively eyes and mocking mouth. She is not of much importance to us. The general aspect of her face did not rise above her commonplace attire.

Not so with the laughing beauty: her haughty manners, imperial stature, and lofty carriage of the head formed a striking contrast with the modesty of her dress. She appeared older than thirty, but her loveliness was still "surprising," as her contemporaries termed it. An abundant head of hair, with a ruddy light color, puffed out her cap. Only the slightest space separated brows of jet, seeming to be drawn with a brush, and her imperious lip, of coral red, was curled with a proud smile beneath a nose finely chiselled with nostrils inflated with passion. Still, the masculine and regular countenance wore an expression of unease. The eye was cold and hard; the smile often perfidious and ironical; and the prominent cheekbones betrayed fierce obstinacy.

The third visitor would have been more attractive but for her severe and thoughtful mien. Her face, without being pretty, possessed an invincible charm, for its expression of meditative calm and resolution. Her complexion, of the warm cream tint in colonial beauties, set off the black orb which seemed pursuing some dream flown into vacancy, and when she raised them upon persons, they were scrutinized with deep and comprehensive fixedness. Curls of brown hair clustered on the forehead, brown and smooth, where the work of thought was plain. Lastly, she had the rare and valuable boon of features that collectively could never be forgotten, although no one of them struck attention.

All at once, a doorway hanging opened, and the Manicarde appeared. Her patrons were kept in ignorance of her age, as she gave her audiences *seances* they would be called in the modern jargon of her tribe, in a dark colored, ample dressing gown with hood and cape, pulled down over the eyes for which there were holes cut out; they sparkled with a lustre which might be youth or simply weirdness. For an instant she regarded the three ladies, who had risen on her approach.

"*I greet you, ladies,*" she said in a grave voice.

"Ladies," was a significant term in her mouth, as it was used at the period towards all women of quality, while married women of the lower classes were called "mistress (*mademoiselle*)."

"In you I hail Beauty, Birth and Rank!" she proceeded after a pause. "I hail Fortune which is going to offer its most amazing boon in making one of you a queen."

"Queen? Am I to be a queen?" exclaimed the tall, fair woman, stepping forward as though such a prediction could apply to her alone, but the soothsayer did not take up the direct challenge.

"Is it you who wish to be the first to question Fate through me?" she said.

"Yes, to be sure, wise woman," returned the other, sinking into the common parlance, "provided that there is no obstacle."

The heiress of La Voisin nodded affirmatively.

"You are quite right, inasmuch as your present position gives you the right to take precedence of all womankind. Follow me, therefore, into the study where I am accustomed to receive persons of your quality."

Behind the arras, she had a private room without the hideous and horrifying objects, toads, serpents, magic books, etc., intended to impress the vulgar. On a table was only a pack of fortune-telling cards and a witch-hazel rod. Near the table was a capacious arm-chair.

"My lady the marchioness," said the sybil, standing and speaking with marked deference, "do me the honor to take a seat under my rooftree."

"You know my title?" exclaimed the other with surprise.

As plainly as I know the name of the high and mighty Dame Athenais de——"

"That will do," quickly interrupted the visitor, "do not utter that name in such a place. Walls have ears sometimes, and I did myself quite too much harm, as no doubt you know, by going to consult La Voisin unmasked and without disguise."

"La Voisin was foolish enough to vend the drug that cleared one's way to inheritance—the Power of *Succession*," drily replied the witch, "while I sell nothing but horoscopes. However, I will call you the Marvel, if you please, as you are styled in the circle where you shine with peerless lustre. Now, will you deign to give me your hand ?"

The marchioness seemed satisfied with this arrangement, for she tucked up the sleeve of her robe, and held out to the speaker a hand which might have come from an ancient statue of Cybele; in his happiest inspiration Phidias never sculptured one purer and so perfect.

"Yes," murmured the reader of the future, attentively examining the lines, "it is noble and severe, although graceful in shape and pretty with its dimples. Albiet delicate, it is larger than the average, which denotes a mind virile and decisive, and capable of bold deeds. This hand is fit to wield a sceptre !"

The lady listened with a thrill of pleasure, while the chiromancer pursued : "By these lines I can tell that you were born in 1641, and are consequently thirty-seven years of age——"

"Skip that !"

"You spring from a family in which mental brilliancy is inborn. You were maid of honor to the Queen. In 1663, I believe, you were wed ; but your husband quitted you, and your children have no right to bear his name."

"My good creature," interrupted the Marchioness de Montespan with impatience, "I am not asking to you for what I know better than yourself. What I want to learn is—shall I be Queen of France ?"

The diviner rolled her eyes heavenward as though to consult a higher power, before she answered :

"You are what you wish to become."

Frowning, the other said in a lowered tone : "But there is yet an obstacle betwixt me and the throne."

"It will be removed."

"What ? Queen Maria Theresa——"

"Her days are numbered, and death waits at her door to take her hence." She shuffled the cards and as she spoke threw one down, face up, on the table : it was the seven of clubs. "So many years as there are points here."

"Are you sure ?"

"The cards never speak false," returned the Manicarde, pointing to the pack with a slender finger which might have been an old woman's emaciated with age, or a girl's not *yet developed.*

"Ah!" in this monosyllable, roared out, so to say, the triumph of boundless ambition. The speaker's visage beamed with the intoxication of pride. She drew her hand away, saying:

"Enough! You need read no farther. If your prediction comes to pass, your fortune is made, my pet. Meanwhile, take this purse of gold."

She tossed a heavy one on the board.

"If only the throne be empty, rely on me taking and holding it."

But the sybil shook her head, and said:

"Lady, lady, you have not yet attained your mark. Did you not see that rod move?"

"What rod?"

"My wand which rolled over to touch the cards."

"No, I did not notice it. What would it signify?"

"That there is a stumbling-block on your path."

"Never mind; I shall spurn it aloof, or break it."

"Does the fiery charioteer perceive the rut in which his steeds hurl all to ruin? See—the wand continues to vibrate—Lady, lady, have a care!"

Without any apparent reason, the rod of wood thrilled as if about to turn into a living snake.

"Why should I care?"

"Distrust everybody: those nearest you, in the first place."

"My poor witch, you are in your dotage," said La Montespan, with a smile. "I always take the most precautions against those next me. Ask my son, though he is only eight years old, and my sister, Mdme. de Thianges. Still, if you would be a little more definite?"

"Harm comes from a woman whom you will have reared. Beware of disgrace through a woman-friend."

The hearer reflected for a while, then she rejoined with dark and threatening energy:

"Thanks for the warning I shall not forget it. But whom will dare, in the court of France, dispute with me the inheritance of that wretch Fontanges? Those who would rob me of my royal lover know too well that I am not a La Valliere, and that there it but one Athenias de Mortemart. For all others, the royal couch will be a death-bed!"

The visitress with the pale complexion and fair curls replaced the first client in the diviner's study a few instants after. The prophetess bowed to her with tokens of the deepest respect. She refused the hand which was held out to her.

"I do not need it to raise a corner of the veil over the future. Enough for me to look upon your face where I see the traces of tears but lately brushed away. For you have suffered—sickness, poverty and humiliations."

"The last particularly," said the other with bitterness.

"When but a child, your parents were driven from their native land across the ocean. You fell into a trance on the voyage so like death, that the ship's doctor ordered you to be thrown over the board; but in embracing you for the last time, your mother felt your cheek to be moist, your heart to throb lightly, and you were taken back to the cabin where you opened your eyes."

"This is true—my mother saved me."

"Two years subsequently, when you were drinking milk on the grass, a deadly snake approached you and your mother had barely time to catch you by the hand and snatch you away; but the snake did not pursue you—it stopped to drink the milk."

"That is true: but why revive these memories?"

"Merely to prove that the Almighty hand has never ceased to be extended over you."

"Why should He abandon one who has never ceased to trust in His mercifulness?"

"Fate ruled that you, young and charming, should be wedded to an old invalid who bequeathed you the pension which had helped him to subsist, but which you long sued for until recently———"

"When the munificence of his Majesty restored it to us."

"You have the consolation of another marriage," suggested the fortune-teller.

"Remarry? who would have me?" questioned the young widow, disconsolately. "I am not a girl and I am poor."

"Still," said the soothsayer, "you will marry for the second time, and he who will select you to be linked with him in glorious destiny, will have none above him save the King of Heaven."

"What do you say?"

"I tell you that, the lower your starting point, the higher

you will soar. The goal will not be reached by the proud woman who took the lead of you just now—never will she mount to the rank where her unscrupulous ambition allures her. Your fortune will astound the world and history. A new Esther, you will take your place on the throne beside your Ahashuerus."

"For mercy's sake," whispered the questioner, "speak lower! Were you to be heard and heeded——"

The gleam of brightness in her eyes faded as quickly as it had been kindled, and with apparent calmness, she resumed: "But no, this is a trick of your craft: or you are jesting! in such language how can anything serious exist?"

"Nevertheless, this is not the first time your ears have been thrilled with such a promise. Did not the mason Barbré, one day, in the Albert mansion, on seeing you, burst out with this prophecy: 'Behold one who will arrive at greatness over the thorny path?' The truth of heaven may issue from the lowliest lips. To, and by, the least worthy may be revealed the secret of its impenetrable will. I tell you, that your woes are nigh to ending. You will be guided out of your gloom by a ray from the crown of France, in the same way as your mother's smile called you out of the cloud of death. Adversity will flee from you like the snake that threatened your life. A great monarch will love you, and make you his wife—you will be the Queen."

She paused as if worn out, and raised her eyes to the ceiling as an actress glances towards the prompter, for inspiration.

By a prodigious self-command the hearer calmed her features, and closed her eyes as though the dazzling vision had overcome her: thanks to this temporary abstraction, she did not perceive the passing sight of a face with blue eyes and red hair which appeared at a trap door in the ceiling, and replied to the soothsayer's interrogating look with a smile. At this moment the door tapestry was lifted, and the third visitor showed her head. She also held a purse and she said, in a pleading voice:

"Dear, dear, am I never to have my turn and a share in the good things on fate's table?"

But the fortune-teller was making a low reverence to the future Queen of France, and respectfully said·

"Only when you have the means and the power; be good

to the brave poor, as on the whole the world has been to you who bear your poverty so bravely "

" Eh," said the intruder, advancing a little, " I did the honor to ask if you——"

" Madame," replied the witch to the speaker, " I have nothing to tell you but this. Albeit you are the Lady of Heudicourt, and niece of a marshal of France, you will not the less be expelled from the court on account of your spiteful tongue."

The astonished woman crushed up in her hand the purse, and hastened to withdraw with her two companions.

Hardly had the negro boy closed the outer door on them before the soothsayer, who had sunk on the large chair, was joined by the owner of the fair face with red hair who had peeped through the sliding panel in the ceiling. This familiar, who had no doubt whispered to his *voice* the cues for her foretelling, was an English-looking man of good appearance, except for his eyes being watery and having drooping lids. With such eyes he must be a skillful, hardened, perfidious knave. He was the individual distinguished in the examination of the culprits of the Great Poisoning Case as "the Englishman," or "the wool-merchant," he being neither in reality. He was the leading spirit of the band, and, like most ringleaders, had escaped, where his tools suffered.

"Well, did I do the part well ?" queried the woman, throwing back the cowl and revealing the face of a pleasing and pretty girl, who eyed the man with a sort of terrified, fascinated expression.

"Not bad, Theresa, but for one omission—you ought to have had Mdme. d'Heudicourt's purse before you gave her her prophecy. Luckily," he added, coolly donning a hat hanging beside the arras and a sword and belt in another hiding-place, "they will not have gone far."

"Oh, Walton, what would you do?" cried the girl, trying, but with a timid gesture, to restrain him.

"Carry out the motto of your esteemed mother La Voisin, and your father, now lodged in the Bastille—recover the purse which you allowed to slip your fingers—what the little finger loses, let the thumb regain."

And he darted out of the mysterious house on the track of the three ladies of the court.

CHAPTER IX.

BRITTANY TO THE RESCUE!

LEFT alone on the threshold of the coach-yard inn, Joel felt a deep sinking at his lonesomeness in the great city.

He looked round dismayed at the strange sights and the unknown people. He would willingly have rushed into the arms of the first acquaintance he spied, even had that been the young gentleman who had insulted him at Locmaria. But he was not the man to dwell long in torpor and discouragement. Something drew him forth with a sudden pang: it was his appetite. Our Breton had that of his time of life and of his illustrious ancestor.

He recalled the fact that he had not eaten since the morning.

"I must find a house, and a table well spread within it," he said to himself.

Reflecting on what Mdlle. du Tremblay had said on quitting him, about her going to live in the neighborhood of the Place Royale, he concluded that it was there he ought to find lodgings, but first he had to find that quarter.

Enquiring of a passenger, he learnt the direction, which took him through the St. Honoré gate, and the street of the same name.

The length of the walk did not deter him, for he had stout legs. The long sword of Porthos, however, discommoded him by slapping against his calves, for he had not been in the habit of wearing a sword at Locmaria. This constant beating made him fretful and slackened his gait. Add the multitude of novelties which detained him as he strolled, while the Parisians stopped to stare at him, amazed by his Breton dress and his bewildered air. But the quip and the laugh died on their lips when they saw how he towered above their heads and had broad shoulders to support the rebuke he would certainly have administered to any jester. But still all tended to delay him; so that it was dusk when he reached the Palais Royal, and dark at the Rue Croix des Petits-Champs, where, it being a crossing point of streets, he halted to ask his way once more.

The worst of it was that the passers-by were few. With the twilight, doors and blinds were closed.

In these days, Paris went to rest early.

It was at this hour that the three clients of the witch came into the Rue St. Honoré.

A little beyond them, a man debouched into the same street from a dark and tortuous alley which few would care to tread. It was the man called Walton, who had followed the women in the manner familiar to thieves and police spies—in other words, he divined their route and ran by a short cut to precede them. But he kept under cover of the overhanging eaves and signs, and they did not perceive him at the first. Besides, all their attention was directed towards Joel, who was decidedly endeavoring to accost them. In fact, he had no sooner descried them than, taking them for three good-wives hastening home, he aimed to ask his road of them.

He quickened his pace to catch up with them. They took fright and began to run, which was into the arms of Walton, who had but to turn at any time to entrap them. But the Bretons are headstrong, and in this respect, Joel was doubly a Breton. Fast as the women fled, so he gave chase.

It was a commonplace interruption to the grave thoughts with which the trio had quitted the prophetess. Mdme. d'Heudicourt was still confounded by the saucy retort of the strange witch; the fair marchioness had a crease in the forehead which denoted deep meditation. And the dark-complexioned future queen was dreaming of her coronation robes.

They were hurrying along when they first heard Joel's martial step.

Paris by night had no other illuminators, the moon excepted, than lanterns which the police regulations ordered to be hung out. To the number of sixty, they were supposed to give sufficient light for the half-million inhabitants. The result was that with the last sunbeam, the doleful thoroughfares were transformed into prowling grounds for beggars, mostly sturdy, thieves of all sorts, pickers-up of drunken men to rob them or of any other trifles, and the scum generally.

On finding themselves pursued, the three ladies exchanged

a glance of growing disquiet. Without speaking, they pressed on. But they not only failed to outstrip the hunter, but they did not overtake the ingenious Walton, who kept in advance to execute the manœuvre of separating Mdme. d'Heudicourt, who had not left her purse, from her companions.

"Beyond doubt," said the brunette, "we are followed."

"It is an armed man," said Mdme. d'Heudicourt: "I caught a glimmer of the light through broken shutters on the hilt of his rapier."

The tall blonde said nothing, but she thought: "I daresay I have been recognized, as easily as the fortune-teller told me, I have a host of enemies in the court, and they may have hired a bravo to kill me in the streets."

The three took the turn which led them to the waterside by the Louvre Palace. A prey to growing terror, they huddled together panting, and feeling their hearts thump as though to burst.

"Merciful powers, I can go no further," murmured the marshal's niece.

The dark woman was also nearly swooning, and she breathed: "We can never reach the St. Jacques ward."

"Keep on," said the third to give them courage, "here is the New Bridge (*Pont Neuf*). We may meet some patrol of the night watch."

They did not know that the watchmen were very careful how they marched around for fear that they would meet some band of highwaymen, angry if interrupted in their work of revelers, who would fight with them.

Thinking to reach the only possible protection, they hastened still more but suddenly a fresh terror arose in their path; it was Walton, who thought that his time to intervene had come as he spied Joel, and from his presistency in dogging the fugitives, was naturally taken for a prowler of the like mind. To avoid being caught between the two, the ladies dived into the first opening. It was a dark court, and unfortunately for them, a blind alley, or no thoroughfare.

"Turnagain lane," chuckled Walton, to whom these backways had no secrets: "They are in the trap, pretty pigeons."

At the same instant, he and Joel came to the mouth of the defile. They gave a glance at each other, but all was dark and neither could well distinguish the other's features, or the details of the costume. The sorceress's colleague therefore continued in his delusion that he had met a roamer of his species, and accosted him familiarly:

"They will be obliged to come back into our arms, comrade. I suppose it will be the usual division: share and share alike? The little one, I know, carries a purse."

"Zounds!" exclaimed the Breton, surprised and indignant, "do you take me for a thief and molester of women?"

The mock Englishman imagined that the protest was, ironical, and promptly rejoined:

"Ha, ha! that is a good one. It is agreed, then? the purse to be divided, and the women to fall to us as chance directs. They are not ferocious, to be out after dark, three dolls who seek adventures. Here they come, lad!"

"And there you go, villain!" shouted our exasperated gallant, as, scorning to use even the flat of his sword on such a despicable ruffian, he delivered to Walton so formidable a slap with his hand that the unlucky scamp rolled in the gutter.

Simultaneously the three ladies returned: they had found no way out, and had determined to throw themselves on the mercy of the cutpurses, by giving up their money, and, as a last resort, to threaten them with dire chastisement in announcing their real quality.

What was their astonishment, not merely to see a brief wrangle between the two men terminate by one knocking the other senseless, but the victor, taking off his hat with a flourish, very naturally inquire in a frank, round voice:

"Excuse me, ladies, but may I ask the right road to the Place Royale?"

"The women felt inclined to laugh hysterically; but one, mastering the revulsion of feeling which filled them with relief, said:

"What! was it to ask your way that——"

I was forced to gallop after you this quarter of an hour? Just so, my ladies; and I mean no blame to you when I say that you gave me as much trouble as a rabbit in the open."

"Then you are not a robber?" went on the questioner, ready to laugh.

"That is what that fellow thought whom I knocked into the kennel for the uncomplimentary opinion. Tell me, are there so many robbers in your city that every stranger is taken to be one also? I am but an unfortunate stranger astray in Paris."

"A stranger?"

"I have just alighted from the Nantes coach, and come from where I was born and always have lived—Belle-Isle-in-the-Sea.

The dark woman whispered to the tall fair one:

"It seems right. I recognize his attire. It is that of the better class of Bretons in the country."

Mdme. d'Heudicourt pointed to Walton, wallowing without motion in the gutter, and asked:

"Is he killed?"

"That rogue who befouls the heap of mud? I think not, unless his cheek is as weak as his morals. I struck only with my open, bare hand. But, if you will supply me with the directions I need, I will make my bow and——"

The fact was, hunger was pinching him again.

"One moment, sir!" It was the one of the three who had been greeted by the witch as the Marchioness of Montespan, and her hand was laid on Joel's arm to prevent his retreat.

"What more can I do for your service?" he inquired, rather impatiently and not in the least agitated by the contact—for he could but faintly distinguish the ravishing shape of the unrivalled hand and arm.

"Sir, I take you to be a brave and gallant cavalier——"

"Brave? I do not know so much about that, if the test be to chastise a knave like that. Gallant? I try to be as much so as a poor country bumpkin may be, who knows nothing of fine city manners. As for being a cavalier, I only want a horse for that."

His tone was so clear and sprightly that the marchioness studied him closely, as well as the poor light allowed, and remarked that he was by his carriage, robust but free and even elegant, a man of good race and not deformed by labor in the fields. So she modified the haughtiness in her voice and bearing, and continued :

"My cavalier, I have a request to make. My friends and I have been misled so as to be some distance from our dwellings. Another such misadventure might rise in out path—ugly meetings are so frequent in this quarter. We cannot dispense with the shield of your arm and your ready courage. Do not leave us, weak and lonely, in the dead of night. Pray accompany us, and be by us for defense until we are indoors."

"Oh, indeed, do not leave us to ourselves," entreated Mdme. d'Heudicourt.

The last of the trio said nothing, but her large eyes were most eloquent in their mute appeal.

At this triple call, our hero drew his belt more tightly to quell that wolfish hunger, and likewise overcome a yielding to weariness, he showed he had the mettle of a knight by saying, and meaning it:

"Ladies, use me as your own."

They walked in the direction of the St. Jacques suburb. The convoy was apparently completely encouraged. A very little more would have set them laughing at their recent flight and fright.

"Ladies," said Joel, who found the silence a burden, "there is a saying that all roads lead to Rome. I should be really downright glad to know if you have any such a proverb here, regarding the Royal Place, and does every road lead thither?"

"Are you bound to proceed to that place?" inquired Mdme. d'Heudicourt.

"Rather: for I have acquaintances thereabouts," responded the youth, blushing, "Persons whom I ought to keep near to, in order to lend them assistance at call."

"And would you walk through the town at night to offer them that?"

"Why not?"

"Alone?"

"A man is never alone when his sword is by him."

"Ah! that is rather a neat retort," muttered the brunette to the blonde. What do you think of him?"

The latter made no reply, for she was busy in weighing the capabilities of the youth. To cope with her enemies, besides the poison phial, she might require the sword of the bravo; and one who was attached to her by an affection which she doubted not she could at will enkindle, would be worth the mercenary. Joel did not even guess the scrutiny of which he was the object.

"But good friend as a long sword is," he remarked, "it is, as now, ofttimes in the way, to say nothing of its not suiting my dress—your pert Parisian boys have already made me remark that, a murrain befall them?" Then as they passed under a swinging lamp, he subjoined in the same spirit of apology, "it is a costume that has turned many a head here, all the same; though, for that matter, an honest heart may beat under it as under any other more in the mode."

"What may your name be?" inquired the fair woman.

"I am not sure what it might be, but it is Joel, for want of a better: can I ask yours?"

"Athenais."

"Bravo! it suits you like a glove!"

"Do you mean that?"

"Why, to be sure, for it is noble, majestic and imposing."

"And do you think I am a little that way?"

"Wholly—you look like a great lady of the royal court!"

"Look at that, now! a compliment! it is plain that Brittany has become part of France!"

She kept her eyes on him more closely than before. He had pierced the incognito, though fresh from the daisies.

On the other hand, he was worthy the admiration of the finest court lady. His tall figure, with the long, stalwart limbs, gave his very movement the gracefulness of nature, as in a wild buck. His bashfulness was free from awkwardness, and the fiery energy of his features, when he was aroused out of his placidity, would have been the envy of a prince. The sham citizen's wife, a judge of men, saw clearly in his eyes a whole poem of audacious candor.

"Ah!" here she pretended to slip. "Oh, Squire Joel, the pavement is so slippery—and the night as black as in an oven—let me beg you to offer me your arm."

"Only too proud, Mistress Athenais."

He crooked the elbow, and the arm of "Mistress Athenais" was pendent on his own, but it was hers alone that slightly quivered. After an Aurore du Tremblay, even a Montespan—at past thirty, at least—fell into the second place.

They were now at St. Michel's place.

"Squire," said the monopolizing marchioness, "I wager that you have come to town to seek your fortune."

"Guess again, and you will be wrong. To make my fortune is the pivot of my dreams."

"So Dame Fortune is the only one of the fickle sex that attracted you ?"

"Woman ? On my faith, not a woman, but a man is what I am in quest of."

"Ah, a patron lord, of course ?"

"A lord, I believe ; but more than a patron ; the arbiter of my future, my fate, my all."

But feeling that his frankness was leading him too far among strangers, he interrupted himself by exclaiming :

"A turn to the right—they are demolishing that house, and we run the risk of the night breeze dropping a stone on our heads—to say nothing of that heap of rubbish."

"I was asking you of whom you are in search ?"

"A little to the left—mind that puddle ! you were all but stepping into it."

She caught his eye and, shaking her finger at him, she said playfully :

"Oh, you Breton backed by a Norman ! is it thus that you throw the hounds off the scent ? All your politeness was merely to keep your secret from me."

"It is not mine," observed Joel, gravely, " but that of a woman who is dead."

"Good ! preserve it. That is not the kind they steal in Paris, and I am not in the habit of fawning to obtain my ends. Still, hearken ! If chance brings it about that you do not gain from the person in question, or if you simply do not find him, what will you do ?"

"Become a soldier of the King, and go and seek my fortune where there are blows and strokes to receive and give."

"I am certain that you will make your way in the army—if you boast ever so little of good birth to get you a rank—or if you have a friend to help you on."

"What kind of friend ?"

"One who is devoted, and to be depended upon, and having influence so that you could be presented at court——"

The squire burst into a hearty laugh.

"Ho, ho, ho ! Such a friend must have so long an arm that she could, without stooping, untie the rosettes on her shoes. Even in Paris such friends are not rained down from the skies."

"Spite of that, you shall not die in want of them—I give

you my word on it. With your good looks and your valor——"

The doubting youth began to hum a Christmas canticle, which begins with the well-known words:

"Let's go unto the church
To hear a sermon fine——"

She interrupted the sarcastic lines by abruptly demanding:

"My companion, have you not a sweetheart?"

They were now in the St. Jacques ward. The marchioness' companions trotted on discreetly a few paces behind the pair, pretending not to listen but straining themselves to overhear. Little Mdme. d'Heudicourt—whom St. Simon, the memoir-writer, describes as "merry, but bitter as gall"—she had characterized La Montespan by saying "She would entice all the saints in the calendar, after having entangled the Apostles."

But our wary hero remained dumb to the leading question. It had called up in his mind the image of Aurore, and he saw her walking up the hills of the Saumur highway with her graceful figure imparting sinuous movements to her dress; her straw hat, for the journey, dangling on her arm by its ribbons, and the breeze swung it and tossed her hair.

At length, in a voice that betrayed genuine passion, he answered: "I have not what we call a sweetheart, but one that is my beloved."

"Heavens! and how long have you been in that predicament?"

"To tell the truth, lady—only this evening."

"And how did you find it out?"

"Quite easily: by my feelings. My pulse beat as if I had fever; the blood rushed about me as though it was water when a dam has burst, and the blood seemed an inflamable fluid. My heart grew too large for the breast; and my temples were encircled by a crown of fire!"

"Why, this is the *grand passion,* or I am no judge," she exclaimed with a cooing like a dove. "Such a flame as is not often encountered—the real one, good and ardent."

"Never before did womankind produce such an effect on me! deuce take me if it seemed natural!"

The lady's dilated eyes darted a stream of fire. The guiltless rustic was making her fancy that he was declaring sudden love for her.

"Ah, what could a man give in return for such love?" she inquired.

"All that I have—nothing too speak of—my life!"

He drew himself up to his full height, with the heroism of his ancestors, Antoine, Gaspard, Porthos, glowing in him. She was struck dumb for a space with admiration.

"So you would defend this idol against anybody?"

"Certainly!"

"And if any one plotted her injury——"

Deadly pallor overspread the Breton's lineaments; for an instant he dwelt motionless; then his body seemed to grow; his long locks seemed to turn to rays around his head as in pictures of the Archangel Michael ; one expected a flood of burning words to rush from his lips. But he murmured solely this in a hollow voice :

" I would kill—were it you !"

" What ?" screamed the marchioness, " you would kill, even me ? I do not understand ! then, you did not mean me ?"

" I would stab the King himself, if the King intended mischief to Aurore——"

"Aurore ?" she repeated, eyeing him in stupefaction, "You said Aurore ? who bears that name ?"

" The lady to whom I have given my heart."

" Oh, the lady of your love ?"

" I have never loved elsewhere—I shall never love but her, and she is going to be my wife as soon as I conquer what will make me worthy of her hand and her affection—name, rank and fortune !"

The marchioness tore her arm from the speaker's, and said curtly, as he now looked at her in astonishment :

" We have arrived, and no longer need your kind offices."

Here stood a low, mournful and sprawling house, standing back in a garden with a yard in front, behind high walls. The two stories had a mansard roof, and the two wings were for domestic offices and stables. On account of the color of the stones and the slate roof, the neighbors called it the Grey House.

The coachyard doors were on the street ; at the bang of

the knocker on them, an old servant came to open and show them all into the yard.

"Honorin, have the horses put to the carriage," commanded the lady whom Joel had specially escorted as she crossed the threshold.

"Is your ladyship returning to St. Germain's?" respectfully inquired the man.

"No; I am going to pass the night here. It is to drive this gentleman to the Place Royale."

She nodded coldly to our Breton, who was buffeted from one surprise to another.

"Methinks that is where the lovely object of your flame, so eloquently painted, deigns to dwell on earth?" she sneered.

At this moment, a boy of about eight years appeared on the doorsteps; he wore a royal scarlet velvet suit, trimmed with rich lace of gold and silver thread: he was blessed with an intelligent face, fine but melancholy in the features, but cursed with a club foot and one leg being drawn up shorter than the other. He hobbled along to throw himself into the dark woman's arms, covering her with kisses and crying out in delight:

"So you have come home at last, dear mother! I could not go to bed until I saw you, from fear that some mishap had happened to you."

"My lord," said the recipient of these tokens of affection, "Do you not see the marchioness your mother?"

Thus rebuked, the boy turned towards the Marchioness de Montespan, and wished her "Good evening!" but without going up to her.

"Tut, tut!" said the marchioness, biting her lip, "here's a to-do because your governess has been taken away from you for a little while! Fie! you ought to be asleep at this hour, Louis. Here, d'Heudicourt, take him to his rooms and see that he is put to bed instantly.

D'Heudicourt took a step to carry out the order, but the little cripple-prince burst into tears and clung to his governess's skirts.

"My lady," interposed the latter, "allow me to manage this. The duke will never go off to rest unless I sing him to sleep with a snatch of a song, or tell a chapter from a story."

La Montespan snapped her fingers in indifference.

"Do as you please, thou pensonification of Wisdon! I am ready to drop with fatigue, and intend having rest. D' Heudicourt, come and help my women to undress me."

Joel had stood wonderstricken by all that he saw and heard.

"Young master," she proceeded, "It is always folly to set the burden of real love upon one, but worse when one is trying to reach fortune—then, it is rank stupidity."

She held out her hand to him in a way that indicated he was to kiss it, which he did on the finger tips : and she sailed up the steps with a queenly port. The governess was on the verge of following her, having taking up her pupil in her arms to spare him the pains of mounting the steps : but before departing, she said to the youth, whose tall form gave him the aspect of an exclamation-point :

"Squire Joel, here comes the carriage of the Marchioness de Montespan, which will set you down wherever you like to say. My noble friend has omitted, I think, to thank you for the service done us. I remember it for her. If ever you have need of my services, do not hesitate to come and knock at this door, and call upon Françoise d'Aubigne, the widow of the Poet Scarron."

CHAPTER X.

FRIQUET AT FORTY.

THE inn of the Moorish Trumpeter derives its title from its signboard, which swang and groaned in the wind over its door : this sheet of iron, framed in oak, rusted by the weather, had once been painted by some budding Raffaelle with the portrait of a blackamoor blowing an enormous trumpet. The house stood in the street called Pas de la Mule, which ended in the arcades of the Place Royal. It was a venerable structure having a pepper-box turret on the roof, and the front made of stonework and cross beams. The first floor above ground jutted out over the street, and contained a lattice-windowed room wnere the host lodged for one night or longer, any one not coming on horseback. He himself slept in the garret with his first drawer-of-wine—

the only one. The ground floor was divided between the dining-room and the kitchen, without there being even a partition.

The part bordering on the street was given up to the customers. The other boasted a fireplace in which an ox might have been roasted whole. But on holidays this gigantic feast was replaced with a foul or a joint; now a leg of mutton, turning on a spit before two or three logs on the hearthstone. Nothing could be more primitive, or businesslike, than this eating-house with the kitchen on the premises. Here were the tables and benches shining with the frequent application of elbows and the customer's breeches. There, the kitchen pots and pans, carefully shining like gold and silver ware, though only copper and pewter

In the midst of these objects, was hung a long sword, crossed by the long spit only used on grand feast days.

Master Bonaventure Bonlarron, as was the Trumpet's keeper—had been a soldier before roasting and carving spring chickens. Sergeant in the Laferte Regiment and wounded by a musket bullet in the famous charge of the Duke of Enghien at Rocroy, he had most unwillingly laid down his arms and turned his flag into the innkeeper's apron. Not that he had lost any money by the change of trade, for the inn was well placed to coin for him and was much frequented from its neighborhood to the Place Royale. But only at the first, when it was the fashion to drop in at the Moor's to take the last meal before going to fight a duel, or toast the victor when the party returned from the field of honor. But Louis XIV. had never forgotten the Revolution of the Fronde, when he had suffered much humiliation, and he was severe against single combats.

The golden days of the Moor departed, and rarely did the master see among his peaceful guests one or two of the bellicaose spirits that once rattled his dishes about his ears with oaths and the stamping of foot with which the swashbucklers invited the antagonist to cross steel.

This Sunday evening. Master Bonlarron was alone in his establishment, with his waiter Bistoquet. The former was a tall, bony man wearing a cook's dress of white, but even in this he showed that he was warlike, for he had cocked the cap over one ear, and he walked from kitchen to dining-room with a swagger.

His man was a homely lad of about twenty, with long awkward limbs, and gaunt hands, which broke more dishes than ogling did hearts in that quarter.

"Confound my luck!" ejaculated the innkeeper, coming to a halt in a military position after his uneasy stroll; "the good old days seem gone forever, when handfuls of gold, from the noblest purses of the realm, were scattered over these very tables and the best wines of my vaults flowed like water. If only the citizens would have riots with the soldiery! but, no, they all are content to sling bad words at each other and nobody whips out a knife. It is disgusting! After a good riot, I should dish up my mutton to the survivors, but there it is, roast to a crisp! we shall have to eat it, Bistoquet."

The waiter made a wry face.

"Thank you, master, very much, but I am not fond of dark meat—it is black as the Moor's head over the door, or a lump of soot."

"Well, dish it up and put it on the table, while I put up the shutters and bar the door The day is gone."

And the cook-shopkeeper moved towards the door, where, just as he reached the sill, a joyous voice chirped with the oily accents of the languid Parisian:

"All hail, mine host and the company? Are you quite well? so glad! I feel that way myself Which noble lord is the proprietor of this *casa*, as the Italians say?"

"I, my gentleman,' responded Bonlarron, bowing to the customer, who came so late and addressed him so merrily

He was a man of about forty, but to such age does not count. In vivacity, mirth, quickness and briskness he was ever a boy; but the *gamin* of *Paris*, who would lose his head to have a jest with the Grand Seignior, or to eat the Pope's favorite dish He had a small, round face, scarcely wrinkled although it had seen all kinds of hard weather inextinguishably bright eyes, never at a rest: a turn up-nose: prominent cheekbones, tokens of tenacity and subtility: and a sharp chin. He wore a nondescript dress, which might have been composed on a battlefield by stripping the dead of all arms: the legs were bound with leather thongs like an Italian mountaineer's: the waist had a wide woolen sash like a Spaniard's; his body was encased in a buff leather coat such as used to be worn under armor; he had a dagger and a sword and also the inkhorn and quill which lawyers and clerks carried at the buttonhole in front of the breastbone. And a small cap with a prodigiously long feather, clasped by a monstrous piece of glass which had been cut out of an old church window and in vain would pass for a ruby.

What spoilt him was the small size and fragility of his legs. Sitting down, he would have passed muster as a full-sized man, but on his feet he was but a mannikin.

He skipped nimbly into the centre of the dining-room, which Bistoquet had illuminated by applying a splinter from the fire to a pair of hanging lamps. Thereupon with volubility and without awaiting to be spoken to, he prattled:

"Who am I? gentlemen of the fire and the corkscrew, you see the prodigal son. I am a son of Paris who returns to his native city, the unrivalled, the inimitable, and I grant that I am happy again. I was well known in my youth in the quarter of the Cathedral; the very sparrows that pick up crumbs on the pavement in front, know Renaud Friquet!" He took off his cap to his own name. "I was choir-boy, and at my own hours, wine-drawer in the finest drinking-trap in the Rue de Calandre. Hail to you, also of our noble profession, that of St. Boniface! But do not for a moment think that I am trying to get a free meal on the strength of my being one of the trade. Tut, tut! I am on the high road to a fortune—title, rank, and I know not what. I have not travelled and warred over half the world not to pick up a valuable secret or two. Though I am a Parisian, I can see farther than my own belfries. Yes, I am Little Friquet, albeit the old King-demon may burn me, if I can imagine why!" He flipped his fingers disdainfully. "As if a giant was needed when a hard piece of work is to be done. Why, our King is no taller than I, even on the celebrated high heels on which he stalks." He waved his hand for the innkeeper to close his mouth. "But let us not discuss royalty and policy. Let me rather talk of myself, though that is repugnant to my delicacy, for I loathe to acquaint the whole world and his wife with my own matters. In short, I return to my native city, where I was a boy in the days of the Fronde of lively memory, with a letter of recommendation to the Minister of the Navy, and fifty pistoles which I owe to the munificence of his cousin, Lord Colpert du Terron, Naval Steward, for having saved him from drowning in the port of Rochelle. You see that it needs not being a colossus to put a great man under obligation to you. So I sailed from Rochelle to Havre, and came up to Paris by the boat, which landed me at Celestins Wharf. Now I stand in need of a good meal and a good bed. Are you prepared to supply yours truly with one and the other?"

"My master, I have a room that will suit your lordship to a dot," answered the eating-house proprietor, with the deference due an eloquent speaker who had also a ministerial letter and fifty pistoles in his pockets.

"That is fine! I take the room."

"Besides, if your lordship will deign to be content with a prime leg of mutton that I was reserving for my own table——"

The waiter hid his smiling mouth with his hand.

"Mutton? I have always revelled on mutton. Better and better! I will deign. You shall see, my friend, that though the Parisians are reckoned dainty, I can ply a good knife and fork. Old Nick devour me if I leave you more than the knuckle."

"Hold!" broke in another voice on the threshold, "I hope that you will spare me a slice."

Everybody turned and they had no difficulty in seeing who spoke, for the tall form of Joel of Locmaria filled up the doorway. He came from the part where he had left the noble dames by the carriage which had left him at Royal Place. There he was, wandering in the dark, when he caught sight of the light of the inn, in an anjacent street. He steered towards the beacon, and with unlooked-for luck, recognized the tavern sign swinging in the night wind. The door too, stood ajar for the better welcome to the famished and houseless.

So Joel was striding in quietly and waiting for a favorable instant to make his modest request when he was obliged to hear Little Friquet's harangue, which ended with a prospect of his chance of a meal being blocked.

It is a fact founded on the stupidity of man, that the pigmies have always hated the giants. Friquet was no exception to the tradition, for he eyed the taller guest with impertinence, and in a quarrelsome tone, demanded his business.

"Not business, but a pleasure, I expect," replied the Breton. "I desire, sir, to remind you of a saying which so great a traveler and warrior must have heard in his pilgrimage through the world. It preaches the necessity of charity to your neighbor."

"What do you mean by all this talk?"

Our hero swung his hat in his hand and in the most engaging manner continued:

"It means that I, too, have come from afar, in quest of lodging and something to eat. I shall not be sorry to share with you the delicacies of this no doubt famous establishment."

It was the turn of the landlord to doff his cap and make his bow to this second wearer of a sword. Besides, each pays his scot," said the countryman. " Share alike and pay alike—like comrades. Are you agreeable?"

If the Little Parisian were agreeable, he did not look it. It was with a very sour look that he snappishly responded to the youth who overshadowed him:

"Devil take it! I ordered that mutton and I shall keep it."

"You are not polite," said Joel, tranquilly. "But I am too dry in the gullet to be dainty—dry as an old nail in a vine-stake."

And unceremoniously reaching his arm over Friquet's head and past the landlord's ear, he took up a pewter pot from the counter, and scarcely stopping to test what it was by the smell, he drained nearly a quart of the wine at a draught.

Meanwhile the little Parisian's eyes flared up like a cat's on whose tail one had stepped.

"Not polite?" he repeated in a high voice. "Odsboddikins Have you an idea of teaching me a lesson in etiquette—you who look to come out of the marshes of Brittany, to me, who is a Parisian born? Let me tell you that I deal stripes and lashes to hulking fellows who have threatened to put me in their pocket."

"Stay!" returned the Breton impatiently, "the size of you and me is not in debate: the trouble to satisfy is in our teeth, which seem to be the same length. If they do not set something eatable before us, nothing will be left but our swords and daggers, for we shall have eaten one another alive—and without waiting to strip off the rind. Besides," as he compared the leg of mutton, which Bistoquet had brought into the eating-room, with Friquet's form, "I can never think that you expect to absorb alone a joint of those dimensions."

"Why should I not?"

"Because there is a rule against it——"

"What rule is there against it, pray?"

"The rule of capacity: the container must be lager than the contents."

The landlord rubbed his hands, enchanted at the joke, and the coarser Bistoquet laughed out aloud.

Friquet leaped up in the air as if to crack his heels like a gamecock, and when he came down he had drawn his sword.

"Man, you have insulted me, for I know whether I am small or not. But I do not allow the remark to be made. 'Sblood! you shall pay me for these affronts."

The landlord can put it in the bill. But, think, when we shall have cut a slash or two in our skins——"

"You seem to be tender about yours?"

"Well, yes I did not bring a change out of Brittany."

"The truth is that you are afraid."

"Afraid? I do not know all the words in the Parisian jargon, and I know not what you mean."

While Joel was saying this with a smile, Bonlarron warmed up with evident gratification. His waiter plucked him by the sleeve."

"Good heavens!" he gasped, "are they really going to cut each other's throat?"

"I expect so," replied the tavernkeeper, radiant with enjoyment: "and if only the luck falls that one of them shall be laid out on the floor, we may have the fashion revived to dine here after duels and breakfast before them! proceedings to which I owed the old-time vogue of my clouded establishment."

"But there are edicts against single combats, master."

"Edicts," grumbled the ex-soldier, eyeing his man with profound commiseration. "Edicts are plenty against all recreations of the rich and the people. If there were no edicts how could one have the fun of breaking them? Come, will you bet on the fight?" He examined the pair who were taking on another's measure visually—the Breton, calm, good-humored, taunting, and the Parisian nervous, agitated and lashing himself into fury.

"*Both brave,* but one as flurried as a tiger, while the other is cool as Polar bear. Which will you lay a crown upon?"

"Master, master, you cannot think to let them come to blows. You ought to interfere. You should exercise your authority."

"Exercise my sword, yes." He ran to shut up the house so that the watch should not disturb them and called for his rapier when this care was taken. While it was brought him, he threw off his white apron.

Do you imagine, boy, that I am going to stand with my arms folded while the gentlemen have it out?"

"You don't mean to say that you will fight, too?"

"'Sdeath! but fight I will!"

"With whom? the best man?"

"With the worst, one here—with you, dolt!"

"With me?" repeated the waiter, horrified.

We will be the seconds to these gentlemen, according to the code of honor. You shall take one part, and I the other: so—then, a fight in the good old style!"

"But I do not carry a sword, master!"

"You may use the big silvered skewer!"

"Oh,-Lord!"

"Yes, perhaps it is longer than my toadsticker; but you can have that point in your favor."

In the meantime, Joel had unsheathed his blade; but to make a final appeal for reconciliation, he said:

"Come, let us sup first: plenty of time to cross steel afterwards."

"No, no!" protested Friquet, "straightway—Death of my life! To it?" and with his uplifted sword he menaced the Breton, who had no more than enough time to fall into the position of a *parddein in carte*.

The exasperated Parisian rushed on with such impetuosity that the blades were engaged up to the hilt. Happily the Son of Porthos had as much coolness with the naked steel as with buttoned foils; he disengaged his blade from such close quarters and took a step backward.

"Soho!" sneered the fiery little man, "the Goliath retreats."

"I am not retreating: I am merely breaking free; and in all countries where sword play is a science, to free the blade is part of the game and not a retreat."

While lecturing, the stranger to town parried the thrusts

and lunges of the Parisian, though quick, hot and varied, without making any return.

"Horns of the fiend, I believe you are playing with me!" snarled the latter.

"I am quite sure of it sir," replied Joel, placidly; and launching out a lunge, he said at the same time, "If I had ully let go, you would be spitted like the leg of mutton." In truth the infuriated little hero felt the long sword furrow his side but so lightly that he might have thought it was but the point of a roughened foil.

"This will have to be ended," he exclaimed.

"Just what I say," observed our hero : "I am not asking for anything else, for I am hungry to the very tip of my toes."

Making a feint of a lower *carte*, which the opponent parried with a circular sweep, he entangled the Parisian's blade and with a whip-like movement of violence, sent it to the other end of the room.

"Kill me, kill me outright, instead of disarming me," shrieked the mad little fellow, foaming at the mouth with shame, rage and humiliation.

But the son of Porthos peacefully restored his weapon to the scabbard, with the remark: "You see, were I to kill you, we should not take supper together." He went and picked up the fallen sword and with a bow returned it to him. "I hope now," he went on in his frank, round voice, that you will not draw back from the feast for which you so valiantly fought. Remember, 'none but the brave deserve the *fare*.'"

There was no keeping vexed with such good humor.

"Halloa, landlord, set the board out for two—three—all who like! I invite you all to join me and this hero."

Friquet was for an instant overborne by his defeat; he was red and confused, while he trembled. But won over by the antagonist's loftiness, he took a step up to him, and said in a low voice full of lively feeling:

"My master, I was wrong. I behaved like a curmudgeon in picking this quarrel with you, instead of merely picking that bone. It is my confounded dwarfish stature which upsets my brain, and I wish to the lord that I could grow up or out of the testy mood. It ill becomes the Parisian, that is, the most civilized being on the earth, and before you, too, who are clearly a genuine gentleman. Come, now, will you let this pass, and be my friend?"

"With all my heart," replied Joel, imitating his action. "Our hands on it; we will be friends for life, until death do us part. Now, let us to table," he added, merrily, "this fencing within four walls wondrously sharpens the appetite. We will drink to the prolongation of our acquaintance."

Master Bonlarron was looking around.

"Hang it all," he said, "whatever has become of my man? I believe this king of cowards has fainted away."

"I am here, master," breathed a gentle voice from under the table, where the illustrious Bistoquet had hidden himself by crawling.

The veteran pulverized him by a scornful glance and bade him hasten to serve, "though you are but ill fitted, meseems, to wait at the board where such valorous chevaliers deign to sit."

The guests were soon sitting up to the joint; it was eminently tough and hard, but had it been boot leather, it could not have resisted the teeth of these famished Gargantuas. Besides, the wine at the Blackamoor Trumpeter's was delicious, and by the time the dessert was reached, the four—for the juice of the grape made them lenient even to the waiter—all were jolly together. The ex-sergeant told stories of the camp, march and field, the waiter chirped a song of his own composition, and the new friends chatted about their hopes and dreams.

Friquet, whom we left chorister and drawer in a tavern, odd servitor of the spirit divine and the spirits of wine, had indeed roved far. Finally fostered by M. Colbert du Terron, High Steward of Rochelle, he had learnt a good deal about the navy and war. He had invented a new build for ships to improve their speed; and other "ingenious devices," as they said then, induced the steward to send the Parisian back to his native city to see if he might not falsify the old saying about prophets.

On his side, the rustic squire, no less communicative from the good wine, narrated the events heralding his birth, those of his youth and what had occurred on the road and in the town. What most struck the intelligent hearer was the names of the three brothers-in-arms of Porthos, which were to serve the youth as stepping-stones in his search.

"Hold!" ejaculated he, "at least, I know one of the three who are strangers to you."

"Is it possible?"

"It is Captain d'Artagnan, no less!"

"Captain, eh?"

"Captain commanding for the King, his Majesty's own life-guards, the two companies of the Red and the Black Musketeers. I was only a boy when I was wont to see him, but a boy does not forget those who pull his ears and give him crownpieces. Faith, he promised to cut my ears off once—and he would have done it, for I was riding a stolen horse of a friend of his—and he rewarded me with a kick of which I cherish the memory. What a fighter—you should have seen him the day they arrested Town-counsellor Broussel—that was a riot, such as we see never in these degenerate days," rattled on Friquet, rubbing his hands with a warrior's glee which was shared by the grinning landlord. "Bricks and chimney-pots flying like snowflakes, the citizens flying to arms, and M. d'Artagnan facing two thousand, roaring, rampagious men as if he were a stone statue out of the cathedral. Ah, he was one of them! the paladins that we read about. Then to see the cowardly mob melt away, like the snow I spoke about, when he spied his squadron coming up. 'Present arms—make ready!' but, 'Sblood! which was his pet oath—before he could say, 'Fire!' the crowd had fled on all sides and Broussel was lugged away to the Bastille in double-quick time. Oh, yes, let me alone for knowing M. d'Artagnan, the bravest of the brave, but likewise the most wily of the wily—but then, he was the typical Gascon—the master of the world, if he had wanted it."

"Really!"

"My master the beadle of Notre Dame was also once in the private service of a friend of Captain d'Artagnan's—stop a bit—this, too, may have been one of the three you mention—well, my master Bazin, after he had been tasting the wine which we supplied from our tavern for the sacramental vessels, would let his tongue wag. Oh, the special cohort of M. d'Artagnan and he executed the grandest feats of arms in the reign before my time. They coped with the famous Cardinal Richelieu, and made but a mouthful of Cardinal Mazarin, the Italian sneak! If the gentleman you seek was *a comrade* of Captain d'Artagnan, then he is worth the finding, I warrant."

"What has become of Captain d'Artagnan?" inquired Joel with that relief which one feels when a tangible reality begins to appear where one dreaded a myth was deluding the eye.

Friquet shook his head, already sad at having to disappoint his new friend.

"That is the point where I am at fault; for I have been playing the rolling-stone, when, had I stuck to the ecclesiastical calling—or the taverner's, I should have been a beadle, bar my non-imposing mien, or a host like our worthy Boniface at my elbow. I know no more than you who is head of the church in town or of the royal body guard."

"You need not look to me for aid," remarked the wine-shop-keeper, "since his Majesty offended his good city by living in a palace outside of it, I am no longer informed on the court and garrison news. Captain d'Artagnan may be retired from old age, or dead, although we old soldiers have life rivetted to our bodies."

"It is easy to make inquiries," Friquet suggested.

"In what quarter," demanded the Breton eagerly.

"In the Musketeers' quarters, of course. They are still in existence, and they are only fit to supply the oven of Old Nick if they do not cherish the memory of their old commanders."

"You are right, my friend. The next thing is to find where the Musketeers are stationed."

"That is also easy," said the landlord: "As they are the royal household troops, they will have followed the King into Flanders."

"Right again," said Friquet, "but the campaign is over; I heard that his Majesty had got back to Lille, and so that is where the clue must be sought for."

"Wait a minute," said the master of the Blackamoor, "you need not go so far, for all the Musketeers would not have gone there. A troop will have been kept at St. Germain's to guard the Queen. This I am sure of, as I met the Viscount de Bregy, the other day, one of my customers, who is also a Musketeer—corporal of the squadron left, as I say."

"Do you think he would know anything about Captain d'Artagnan."

"It would be a poor joke if he did not, for he must have served under his orders, as he has been in the corps some thirty years——"

"Thirty years," exclaimed the hasty Parisian, "and not yet shelved? I should think he were more fit to walk on a crutch that carry a musket!"

"M. Friquet," returned the host, smiling paternally. " I have just witnessed that you are a plucky gentleman. You will become a redoubtable master of fence when you wear out your impatience, and fortify your theory. Still, though you have youth on your side, I should not advise you to fall out with M. de Bregy, as I know nobody, unless it be our neighbor here who could match him in strength of wrist and close fighting. Ah, the Musketeers have always maintained the repute of having the best swordsmen in their ranks."

"What, another Colossus of Rhodes," sneered the incorrigible Parisian, "I should like to test this military Methuselah. In any case, his brilliant fencing has not very rapidly advanced him in his company."

"Now, you hit the peg. He ought to have been colonel, or major-general, but he is overfond of the winecup, of whipping out his blade and running after the petticoats; he will drink, and dice and frequent the broad road that leadeth to perdition, as you, monsieur, who have been in the choir, will know better than I. Still, he is a perfect gentleman, borrows money with a lofty air as if he conferred the favor, will drink the hardest heads under the table, and fight while there is a stump of steel in the swordhilt. I know that he has been out in the field of honor ten times, and always laid his antagonist low."

"Bravo! for the Musketeers." said Friquet, grudgingly: "but there is luck in odd numbers—or to them, and the eleventh or thirteenth may lay him out."

"I shall go to St. Germain's to-morrow," observed Joel.

"You could not do better," agreed Friquet; "and meanwhile, let us share that room overhead, which can be made double-bedded. I suppose? as we have shared the mutton." He rapped on the board with his goblet, crying out: "Another cup, host! Then, to rest, all of us. I must be early at the minister's to-morrow, and let me catch any of the clerks make a mock of me." He plumed himself triumphantly and added: "When I wear the royal uniform on my back, it will make me inches taller and no one will refuse me the respect I deserve."

"How long will it take me to go out to St. Germain's?" inquired the stranger to town.

"A couple of hours at the most, on a good post-horse, which you may hire," replied the tavern-keeper.

"That will suit me," said our hero, not forgetting Mdlle. du Tremblay. "I can be back for Vespers."

CHAPTER XI.

ONE CHANNEL OF INFORMATION IS CHOKED.

IT was about two in the afternoon, and the July sun was heating white hot the sharp pavingstones which have always been the terror of foot passengers and the delight of farriers in the good town of St. Germain. Before the front gateway of the old Castle, paced two Musketeers, with the arm on their shoulder which gave their regiment its name, while another pair, off duty, were sitting on the edge of the ditch, with their legs swinging in the hollow, and their swords dangling between them. Other times, other names—we have not now the names in the corps of Du Verger, De Belliere, ect., but Gace and Hericourt, those on duty, and Champagnac and Escrivaux, for those idling.

In the Spanish fashion, the Queen Maria Theresa was taking her siesta and the court followed her example. So the sentinels were yawning fit to dislocate their jaws, and their comrades in the moat were gaping, when one of the latter had just the strength left to nudge the other and say:

"Escrivaux, look over yonder, towards the Tennis-court—what do you call that queer figure?"

"It is a real, live Breton, fresh from his country," returned the other, glancing in the direction indicated. "A strapping fellow, by the mark! But he must be infernally *green* not to be burnt to a crisp in venturing out on the royal highway in a heat equal to roasting an egg, twixt my cassock and my shirt."

It was our friend Joel, entering the town after leaving the nag which had brought him from the city, at the Sully's-Elm tavern, and coming along by the castle rampart.

"He's coming this way," resumed M. de Champagnac.

"Can he have some business with us?" queried M. d'Escrivaux; "as if one wanted to discuss business this weather!"

Coming to a stop, the new-comer bowed to the Musketeers with his usual affability.

"Gentlemen," he began, "may I ask the question if you do not belong to one of the companies of the Royal Musketeers?"

"We do, as the uniform should tell you."

"We are all at your service," added Champagnac politely, while both rose and returned the salute.

"Your obliging greeting emboldens me to address you a question——"

"Do not hesitate, monsieur."

"Only too glad to have it in our power to oblige you."

The bowing went on again, till Joel continued:

"I only am wanting to know if you have any knowledge of Captain d'Artagnan——"

Meanwhile, the sentries had lounged up to the speakers, and were listening, with their muskets held at ease. At the magic name, a chorus of admiration broke from all four.

" Our Captain d'Artagnan! the pride of the regiment whose colors we have the honor to guard! nobody has ever led the Musketeers into more glory, and with more energy and fatherly love! He is a cavalier whose exploits tired the Muse of History to keep the run of. And his memory is preserved as that of one of our bravest and most brilliant officers!"

The Son of Porthos was affected to the heart by this eulogy.

"I thank you, gentlemen," he said. "You make me proud and happy, for the officer you praise was my father's friend."

"In that case, we compliment you," said M. de Gace, "for the captain was not prodigal of his friendship and no man could win it who had not also won his spurs of knighthood on the field of battle."

" One word farther," said the inquirer : " You spoke of the captain's memory, as though he had ceased to exist."

" Why, he has been out of the army list these twenty years," responded Hericourt. " None of us knew him, and it is only by the legends of the messroom that we know what a precious servitor the King lost in him."

THE DEATH OF ARAMIS.

Thereupon, as if all wished to prove that not a chapter in the record of the soldier was unknown to them, they spoke one after another :

"Captain d'Artagnan was killed in the campaign in Friesland—By a cannonball which crushed in his breast—On the very day when he took by storm the last stronghold which his instructions ordered him to capture from the Hollanders—And at the very instant, too, when his Majesty's messenger handed him the patent and truncheon of Marshal of France."

Our seeker hung his head.

"Dead?" he muttered. "I should have expected it, and yet this certainly makes my heart ache. Gentlemen," he said aloud, as he recovered his manlier mood, "since you let me so trespass on your kindness, permit a final inquiry."

"Speak on."

"Has any of the three names I am about to utter, made a previous impression on your ear? *Athos, Porthos, Aramis?*"

The four soldiers seemed to reflect, but finally they replied that this was the first time the singular names had been heard by them. Joel bowed to take his leave.

"Then, there is no more for me to do than offer you the expression of my gratitude as I go."

But Escrivaux, sympathizing with him in his evident disappointment, retained him.

"Stay, stay! Might not those belong to the Three Intrepid Musketeers, called the Inseparables? With M. d'Artagnan, who was a gentleman-private in the Queen's Guards at the period, they held the Bastion of St. Gervais at the Seige of La Rochelle against a large body of the Calvinists? Gentlemen, you remember the story of the dinner napkin which our comrades set up as a standard on the walls they defended and which King Louis XIII. ordered to be embroidered in gold with the royal lily-flowers?"

"Why, of course we do," replied Champagnac. "You have hit the mark. But all that happened so long ago. In the preceding reign——"

"And, mark," said Gace, smiling, "the oldest of us is not over thirty."

"There is only one in the company who could enlighten you on this score," pursued Hericourt, " and he is our corporal M. de Bregy, who is not always in a talkative mood——"

"Not when he has left his money on the cardtable——"
"Or his wits in a pot of wine——"
"Where is your M. de Bregy to be met with?" abruptly inquired the Breton, bent on his own idea.
"In his favorite drinking-place in the Vaches Street——"
"Or the dicing-den of the Poteau-Juré Street——"
"Unless he has lingered by the way to drub some varlet or quarrel with a citizen for having too pretty a daughter——"

"Hold! talk of the wolf and you will see his ears," said Escrivaux; "here he comes from behind the wall of the Royal Kennels."

"You are right, in faith," added Champagne; "be on your guard, comrades. The old bear has cocked his hat awry—a token that he is more cantankerous than usual. Take my advice, and do not accost him just now," he added to the country squire.

"Thanks," was the latter's rejoinder, as he laughed. "This will not be the first time that I have locked horns with a stag and not come off second-best."

In the meantime Corporal Bregy swaggered up, ringing the spurs on his buff leather boots and shaking the red feather of his hat over his ear so that it seemed likely to fall.

This "sore-head," as in military slang was called the veterans galled by the steel cap of service, was of athletic build. Under his scarlet cassock, on which blazed a sun of gold lace with spreading beams, his broad and robust shoulders were prominent, as well as a chest in full proportion to his whole frame. Such a constitution alone could defy prolonged excesses in debauchery and dissipation. Everything in him reflected that brutal and quarrelsome confidence springing from the consciousness of herculean strength and courage above proof. From this, too, arose an impudence which tempted the most pacific person on whom his taunting gaze fell, to take him by the throat and thrash him into decency.

"How now! my pretty pages, is it thus you conduct yourselves on sentry-go? since when, in the devil's name, have the orders been for soldiers to chat with civilians when under arms? By all that is sacred in the army, I do not know any thing but my soft heart that holds me from sending you all into arrest for such behavior." So he thundered.

"Corporal," said Champagnac. "It is only this gentleman who wants to speak with you."

"A gentleman, to speak with me? what gentleman?"

And holding his head back, he scanned the Breton so disdainfully and provocatorily that the latter felt anger flush up into his face. But speedily mastering himself in view of the aim he sought, he began:

"Corporal, I come from master Bonlarrons——"

"The vendor of wine and cooked meats in the Pas-de-Mule Street? a capital host, that, or the infernal fires may roast me! the best *bub* to drink that I ever lapped! I fancy I owe him some ten or twelve pistoles for it. If you have come to dun me, I can tell you that you would have acted wiser to stay in his cellar and drain his biggest tun; for that rascal Vilarceaux, the captain of the keepers of the Royal Spaniels, has raked in my last crown of pay at picquet."

"I do not know anything about your debts——"

"What is the matter, then, by the horns of Belzebub? It did not seem to me that you were tongue-tied as I came up, for you were chattering away like a flock of jays to my soldiers here."

The squire made an effort to overcome the growing irritation which this brutal welcome caused in him, spite of prudence. He laid succinctly before the rough soldier what he wanted of him.

"Athos, Porthos, and Aramis?" grumbled the corporal, plucking at his moustache in ill humor. "Yes, I do remember them all. Athos was a great nobleman, a count of some place which has escaped me—who took the shine out of us with his sovereign style and magnificent manners—which did not save him from dying like an old dog, in his domain down in Blaisois."

"Then, the others—I prithee, the others?"

"Aramis and Porthos? Aramis was a priest who had no business to don the Musketeer's uniform; and Porthos was a beefeater, a gorger and braggadocio——"

"Plague on it!" blurted out the young man, his voice trembling from his biting his lip till the blood ran, "You are not lenient to your old companions-in-arms."

"Ah," growled the veteran with a hateful rancor "They

were the ones who enjoyed all the plums, while I, doomed to rust in a low position, have had to take my belt in two buckle-holes just to save for my daily whet and crust."

"But this Aramis, and Porthos?"

"Oh, Aramis became a bishop, and Porthos, a baron—royal favors that they hastened to requite with rebellion and ingratitude."

"What are you saying?"

"That the Bishop of Vannes and Baron du Vallon were mixed up with Fouquet in the great conspiracy which led to that minister's arrest. They were two leaders who defended Belle-Isle against the King's men, and they slipped away during the hard knocks. I have seen the sentence which condemned the brace of gallowsbirds to death for high treason."

The squire had turned whiter than his shirt-collar; from his eyes darted a flash which alarmed the spectators, and from his quivering lips issued this indignant protest:

"Porthos, a traitor—impossible! You are a liar!"

At this, Bregy fairly roared. His forehead veins swelled like cords; his broad face from red turned to violet, and his hand grasped his swordhandle. The challenger acted in the same manner, but Champagnac and Escrivaux flung themselves between.

"Gentlemen, think what you are about! drawing swords before a royal residence?"

The corporal shoved back his half drawn blade into its sheathe, and stepping up to his living goad, he stared at him and said with ill-contained ire, "Young man, you have spoken a word which makes you equal to me in age."

"I know what it entails," replied Joel, "and I am ready to maintain it."

At this juncture, three o'clock sounded from the bell-tower. Four Swiss guards, with their coporal, came to relieve the Musketeers; when the change was made and the words given, the Musketeer Corporal said to his two sentries: "Messieurs d'Hericourt and Gace, go and leave your muskets in the guardhouse. Then, join us in the Forest. This stranger and I am going to take a stroll for our health. In emphasizing the last word, he showed his tolerably good and strong teeth in a tigerish grin. "Messieurs d'Escrivaux and de Champagnac will also come with us. Each will come alone so as not to attract attention. All are to meet at the Saint Fiacre's Oak cross-roads."

THE DEATH OF ARAMIS.

Side by side the duellists strode through the woods, welcome with their shade on that blazing day. The Musketeer took off his hat and puffed as he hummed an old marching song. His perspiration streamed on his forehead and filled his wrinkles and scars and the brushes which were his brows. Joel was not high-colored, but he was resolved. It is asserted that those about to die see all the events of their past life like a panorama. Joel saw Old Brittany again, the Giant's Grave, the sword which he wore, thrust up out of the mossy ground, and the face of his dying mother. But this time it wore a hard, stern expression, and he believed she was whispering:

"Defend your sire's fame!"

Behind this implacable countenance, appeared another—Aurore du Tremblay's not less imperiously dooming the bully to death.

"Young man, we have arrived," said Bregy, wickedly laying stress on his words of double meaning, "here is the end of your journey."

In this clearing, covered with grass, several roads came to meet and form a star. In the centre rose a hoary oak, shrouded in ivy and lichen, and harboring in one of its decayed knot-holes a plaster statue of Saint Fiacre, who is the gardeners' patron saint.

"We can begin the dance whenever you like," returned the Breton, with impatience.

"Go slow, my boy, go slow, said the other jocularly. We must wait for our seconds, as I do not want it said that I butcher little children, like the ogre in the street-hawkers' ballads."

The four Musketeers came up, each by a different path.

"Gentlemen," said the old swordsman, "two of you will kindly second our young fighting-cock, while the others stand by me. It is understood that you are not to interfere whatever takes place, save as the seconds' duty regulates, and testify at need that the fight was properly managed and that I despatched this gentleman according to the rules."

The soldiers silently obeyed. Escrivaux and Champagnac placed themselves by the Breton, and the other two remained near their superior. All four had a saddened air, and eyed our hero with unequivocal compassion, as he unsheathed his sword. It must be said that the sight of this heroic weapon, deftly wielded, had, however, a lively effect.

His adversary alternatively opened and closed his right hand to test the play of the muscles, and stamp with his foot.

"I am waiting for you, monsieur," said Joel.

The swordsman tossed his beaver on the sod and took out his sword. He bent his knee a couple of times in rehearsing a lunge, and sneeringly remarked :

"Do you not want to make your last speech and dying confession to these gentlemen ?"

"No."

"Then, look to yourself."

"I mean to."

In a deep silence, the two rods of steel clashed and at once an oath was drawn from the corporal's vinous lips for he had perceived that his task was not so easy if he expected to overcome the Breton offhand. The latter had not winced under his attack, but stood like a statue with a mechanical arm playing the sword.

"Come, come, the boy has a spice of the fiend in him," muttered the old soldier. "I did intend only to lay him up for a few weeks. But now I shall be obliged to settle him straight off."

Gnawing his moustache, he successively tried to thrust in carte and tierce, overstepping the fighting-line, and dealing the strokes with decisiveness and expertness which alarmed the beholders, while he was astounded at their being met each time by the inflexible iron, for he believed he alone held the secret of these lunges—a tradition of the regiment. It was a sight of terrible and enchaining interest, with moving incidents which the lookers-on watched with anxious curiosity. The resistance to which the old brawler was not habituated, surprised and irritated him. It caused him gradually to lose his science and coolness ; giddiness affected his brain, obscured his sight and burdened his arm. He felt this defect and redoubled his impetuosity, and became frightful, with his foaming mouth and bloodshot eyes standing out of the sockets. At one time, he shrank back on his guard, and then bounding forward, he delivered one of those high thrusts which would have penetrated the gorget of a foe and transfixed his throat ; but Joel seemed to anticipate this stroke, old and of the Italian school of fence, for he dropped so swiftly that the sword passed straight over his head. As he rose, he and the shotforward and baffled swordsman almost came in contact. He might with a shortened arm have stabbed him who was thus at his mercy, but he contented himself with giving him one of those looks which announce to an antagonist that he must expect no mercy when the time for execution comes.

By a reaction brought about by the phases of the combat, Bregy now doubted himself and the other became confident, and this could be read on his face. Bregy stifled another oath.

To avoid a downward cut upon the sword, he leaped nimbly back but his left foot slipped, and by a natural movement Joel delivered a thrust as straight as a line and the sword disappeared in the Muskeeter's breast. He remained on his feet yet an instant, and tried to speak, but a flow of blood choked him. Reeling, he let go his sword to place both hands on his wound ; then, like a tree uprooted, he dropped on the sword.

The victor leaned up against a tree, with perspiration beading the tip of each hair. He dared not risk a movement. His victory seemed a dream. He stared, affrighted, at his sword, crimsoned to the point, which he had also let drop, and at the corporal, lying on his back near the old oak. The distended eyes seemed to watch him, and a curse or some threat seemed hovering on his lips. Unwittingly he leaned towards him, when something like a sigh exhaled and to the young man alone these words in the faintest of whispers reached the ear:

"The thrust of Porthos !"

Joel had killed the insulter of his father with a secret thrust known to but few in the regiment.

The seconds exchanged a few words like men accustomed to such deeds.

"Nothing can be done."

"Nothing, unless we notify the forest-keepers, who will all carry the corpse into St. Germain's."

Champagnac and Escrivaux approached the conqueror of their unpleasant officer.

" Monsieur," said one, "you will do well in quitting this place as soon as may be, as the royal edicts against duelling are strict and the constabulary cannot be trifled with."

"Of course we may have never seen you." So said the

other. "M. de Bregy must have been killed by some stranger, which is what we shall say when we are questioned. But look! somebody is coming. Haste away! without losing a minute."

Joel stammered a few words in the way of thanks. Picking up the avenging sword of his father, he mechanically wiped it with a handful of leaves, and replaced it in the scabbard. Then, he departed with the step of a drunken man, wildly and without an aim.

Bonlarron and Friquet were awaiting him for supper when he found his way to them—he hardly knew how.

"By the big bell of Nôtre Dame," exclaimed the Parisian, when the recital was ended; "I should have acted in the same way. I should have made that braggart skip into the air so high that the tower of St. Jacques of the Slaughterhouse would have been seen under his flying carcase."

As the fatal duellist flagged in appetite, the soldier-landlord emitted this consolatory maxim:

"The first time you kill a man, it always makes a slight impression; but it is only the first corpse that counts. It is nothing when you get used to it."

HAPTER XII.

ANY PORT IN A STORM.

ON the AnjouQuay, stood the sumptuous mansion built for Lord Nicholas Gruhin, and afterwards the property of Lauzun. But it was taken at the present season for his Parisian residence by his Eminence the Duke of Almada, ambassador of his Catholic Majesty, Charles II., King of Spain and the Indies.

Aramis was seated in his closet, wrapped in a wadded silk gown, before a desk loaded with papers. He had just finished reading the following communication:

"MY LORD; I hasten to inform your lordship that the King will shortly be on the return from Lille to St. Germain's, and that it is urgent to make preparations accordingly. The marchioness seems indeed more that ever assured of the power of her charms and the success of her ambitious designs. I hear that she has secretly vaunted of a prediction lately made to her which, if it come to pass, will ruin our hopes and projects entirely. A fortune-teller of the Palais Royal ward announced to her that the Grand Alcandre (Louis XIV.) would shortly be free to wed again and would, by marrying her, raise her to the supreme rank in the realm. Therefore, it is necessary to produce at the court the counterbane to this noxious influence— the person who will eclipse her. Deign, your Excellency, to take measures consequently and consider me on all occasions the most faithful, devoted and respectful of servants,   BOISLAURIER."

Hot as was the evening, a high fire blazed in the ample fireplace in carved marble before which the desk was placed. Almada crumpled up the letter into a ball, and flung it into the blaze where it was consumed in an instant. Then, settling back in the armchair, he seemed to let meditation absorb him. In a short time, he roused himself and murmured:

"Upon my faith, Boislaurier is right; things must be hurried on. As the mountain will not come to us, we shall go to the mountain."

He struck a spring-bell and a footman appeared.

"See if Esteban has returned and send him hither at once."

In a few minutes the lackey inquired for, was before his master; a fine, sharp Spaniard; he bowed to the old lord.

"Well, what tidings?" demanded the latter.

"I have the honor to bring your Excellency the information which I was charged to gather."

"Very well. Speak—I am listening."

"The young lady whom I followed, dwells with an old relative whose infirmities keep her indoors, in the Tournelles Street."

"Yes, proceed."

"She comes forth in the mornings to call on various lawyers —proctors, judges, counsellors——"

"Go on, go on."

"In the evenings, she goes to worship to the parish church of St. Paul's, which is her habit."

"How have you learnt that?"

"I heard her say to an old beggar-woman, in the porch, as she dropped a coin into her hand: 'You may expect the same daily at this time as I shall come here regularly."

After a pause the ambassador asked:

"Have you not at beck some bold fellow devoid of prejudices, who will do any kind of work if he be paid amply?" He added, smiling as the lackey was about to offer himself; ' I am not mistrusting your delicacy; but private motives prevent me confiding the mission to a member of my household."

"Your Excellency will be suited to a charm," went on the Spaniard eagerly ; " I have met the very fellow for this work."

"Ah, how nicely things fall into place ! What is the quality of this rogue for all work ?"

"He styles himself for the nonce Captain Cordbuff ; he is an old friend, for we served the King together."

"In the navy?"

Esteban shuddered, for he and the highwayman had pulled at the same oar as galleyslaves for the King of Spain.

"How long will he act?"

"As long as the purse of his employer holds out."

"So I may call upon him to do me some slight service?"

"Your Excellency may have him at a reduction from the market price. The poor scamp arrives out of the country where he was badly treated, to judge by his tattered clothing. He will throw into the bargain three more scurvy rascals equally as tattered, whom he drags at the heels—they looking upon him as a hero. All four were the victims of a dishonest comrade."

"Dishonesty among thieves? what is this world of iniquity coming to? but a truce of your confidence. I am not going to profit by the distress of villains to chaffer with their conscience. Bring me this valorous captain in a brief time."

"To-morrow, early, he will await the command of your Excellency."

"You are a precious Esteban. Continue to show the same zeal. My treasurer will often want to see you."

On dismissing his valet, the ambassador wrote some lines in a kind of diary carried with him, in the cipher which he taught to JuanJugan, and anew plunged into musing.

A smile came to his thin lips and gradually became more and more bitter. "Heigho!" he sighed, in fatigue. "How d'Artagnan, Athos and Porthos would look with contempt on the webs I am spinning now. Those valiant champions of the wronged and oppressed queens and lovers, waged manly warfare and measured themselves with such combatans as Richelieu, Cromwell and the crafty Mazarin: they fought for fair ladies and reamless kings, under the flash of swords; they rode desperately; they crossed the seas like Perseus and Jason in the fables."

He had partly risen in his seat, and a spark of fire danced under the curtain of his eye. The memory of dashing deeds of yore galvanized the worn-out frame and awakened the Musketeers in the diplomatist. But this return of youth lasted briefly. The expression of mocking wisdom, his second nature, soon replaced the fugitive gleam of enthusiasm on the aged countenance.

With a dry and broken laugh, Aramis continued :

"But times have changed. The great conspiracies in which a plotter risked his head on the block of Chalais, Cinq-Mars and Montmorency, have given place to bedchamber intrigues, where the disgrace of a favorite or the ruin of a courtier is arranged behind my lady's fan or the minister's fire-screen. And this hand, which has been mighty enough to shake a throne, is reduced to push court puppets to and fro as though they were pawns on the narrow chessboard in the alcove. Ah, 'tis a woman's age—and I must act like a woman, spiteful, relentless, neglecting no paltry action."

Folding his slender, white hands over the silk dressing-gown and gently twiddling the thumbs to counteract his nervousness, a habit of his, he resumed, while his features reflected a satisfied conscience.

"All things considered, is it fault of mine if their is no longer an Olympus to scale? I am more able to climb the molehill. Anyway, the interests I guard are important. 'Sdeath! as my poor d'Artagnan used to swear, the importance of the end justifies the meanness of the methods."

And with this Jesuitical plea, by his position over the Sons of Loyala most appropriate in his mouth, he soon after retired to a sound repose. Not long after he had breakfasted on chocoltate in the Spanish mode, he had an interview with our old acquaintance Cordbuff.

At a result, the valorous Condor, with a couple of his old troop, but no longer mounted, might have been seen in the dust, prowling in the neighborhood of St Paul's Church.

Within, a dozen old women were listening to evening prayers: Mdlle. du Tremblay was kneeling in the Virgin Chapel.

When she approached the holy water font, the worshippers might have noticed, if their sight had been keen enough to pierce her veil, that she blushed. Near the same basin stood a young gentleman, our friend Joel, who dipped his fingers in the blessed water and offered it to the lady. Thus their hands touched. Together, they descended the porch steps.

This discovery of the male escort to the lady whom they were set upon, did not meet the taste of Condor and his comrades; but their orders were strict and their need of gain most urgent. Reviving their courage, they glided after the pair; two of them crossed the street and went to join still another, lurking under a doorway, wrapped in a dull colored cloak and covered with a black felt hat. The third continued to dog the happy couple, who would not have noticed if a regiment were at their heels.

"Well," inquired the watcher, of the others as they met.

"Well, you are quite right, captain," responded one of the spies, "it is the Breton peasant with whom we had the mishap on the Saumur road."

"And the girl is also one of the travelers by the coach—the pretty girl."

"It will be a double prize, then," observed Condor, grinning. "At length I have it in my power to get even with that pert creature's scorn and the rustic's brutality."

"I do not know so much about that," returned one of the twain, "you have acted wisely in having reinforcements; the pretty bird has beak and claws to defend herself."

"Ay," added the second, "and she will not fail to pipe pretty loudly."

"What does that matter?" sneered the Colonel of the Royal Marauders. "Have we not a gag to prevent her making too much noise? As for the clown, we have ten good blades who will put him out of a state to annoy the brave subjects of his Majesty."

With the tone of a general arranging his army in line of battle he went on: "Where is your comrade, Pickpurse?"

"Following the pair of cooers-and-wooers?"

"Where is the hackney coach?"

"Behind the church."

"And the rest of our fellows?"

"Along with the coach."

THE DEATH OF ARAMIS.

"In that case, to work! Mind, no rumpus and rashness: that is the special order of the noble lord who employs us. Take your time and do the trick smoothly."

For three days, Aurore had been coming to St. Paul's to vespers, and twice Joel had had the pleasure of escorting her to her home. But he done it by keeping at a little distance. On this occasion, he made so bold as to walk by her side. As she eyed him with a kindly smile, he muttered, more confused and timid than when first they met:

"Are we going to part so soon?" in a tone of entreaty. "I do so want to speak with you."

"I am of the same mind, my friend," she answered without hesitation, and holding out her hand to him, upon which an expression of delight shone on his face.

They turned into the Petit-Musc Street.

"Give me your arm," said Aurore; "I am frightened."

"Not with me by you, I hope," said Joel.

"Oh" she responded "I know by experience that I may rely on your strength and courage: but this part is so lonely, and night is falling so fast."

Indeed, there were few persons out; the night promised a storm and all the sky was lowering. The girl leaned on her protector's arm. With ecstasy he contemplated her delicious loveliness which the increasing gloom softened and caused to appear more heavenly. They walked but slowly, keeping close to each other. To the Breton's lips the words pressed, but he held them back in order to do nothing but listen to those from the voice which thrilled him to the core with intoxication.

"Well, have you commenced your investigation," she inquired. "I am sure you have, though, as you are a man of immediate action. Do you still count upon a success for which I pray every day?"

The youth felt great embarrassment. Ought he to inform the lady of what had happened when he went out to St. Germain? He durst not.

Still, as falsehood was repugnant to his frank and straightforward nature, he answered the question by putting another.

"And your steps, mademoiselle, do they bid fair to turn out happily?"

"Alack" she sighed, with a shake of the head, "I am

not an adept at begging and praying favors. The art is a sealed letter to me of obtaining general support by reiterated supplications, and I have the great flaw of being proud. Ah, if I were alone at stake, and not the welfare of these children —I—"

" You would give up the task !"

" I certainly should, and leave town on the morrow."

" Leave town ?" repeated the other, with a shudder.

" What else can you expect? its tumult gives me a dizziness."

I am frightened by the traps which I suspect to be set for my feet. Horror and pity are inspired in me by the mingling of passions and lusts which clash in the streets, where the tall houses hide the heavens. Then, again, I feel myself so lonesome, here, deprived of all support, and defense, so weak in a lions' pit where the motto is of Each for Himself ! and where one must fight for a corner in the sunshine and a scrap of bread, with many weakening and shameful compromises. Oh, how much better I should prefer to go home to the country and dwell far, very far from the town? My country is your own, too, where the wild rose and the golden furze mingle on the cliffs and the boundless strand ! and their scent blends with the wholesome breeze from the ocean."

" Could you resign yourself to dwell there by yourself?" questioned the lover, with a tremulous voice.

" I should esteem myself happy above all women if I had beside me one whom my heart has chosen."

"Oh, yes," he muttered, "you mean some opulent and puissant nobleman who would make you a sovereign lady"

" You are wrong," returned Aurore, softly, and shaking her head. " I am poor, and I have confessed that I am proud, but this pride prevents me accepting anything from the man who weds me save the wedding-ring." Her voice became haughtier, and she added: " But as a daughter of the noble, I am bound not to marry beneath my line."

"Ah, me!"

She pressed his arm with hers, and in a grave and penetrative voice demanded :

"Why this sigh? I am patient and we are young. Can we not await in confidence until heaven shall have blessed our efforts, or that, in default of your finding out your sire's name, you make one for yourself?"

"Good heavens," so ejaculated Joel, "is it possible that you have divined my secret?"

They had reached the Celestins Wharf, where there stood a bench by a tree. The girl took a seat upon it, saying:

"Won't you sit beside me?"

He obeyed and she pursued: "I am in the belief that you love me."

He raised his eyes and met hers fixed upon him, and then hers were cast down from his being so ardent.

"Yes, I like—I love you," continued she, "to learn which I had no need to hear the tale from your lips; I had but to listen to my own heart."

Fired up into a fever, our hero said: "I do not well know what my feelings are, but this is sure—I respect no being in the world as I do you, and I should die were you to be the bride of another."

In the brief silence following, a slight stir was heard, which may have been the approaching wind; the storm was nearing them and the darkness augmented. But the lovers saw nothing of either phase; they had no consciousness of the advanced hour or of the thunder growling in the distance. Joel had grasped the small hands which quivered in his tender hold.

"Aurore," he kept on repeating, "Aurore, you are my loved one! My hope and all I long for in the time to come! You are my life entire!"

A heartrending scream interrupted him, for the girl had seen a dark form detach itself from the lesser shadow of the tree. An arm was raised with a heavy holster-pistol held in the hand so that the butt should come down on the young man's head. He fell, stunned, like the pole-axed bull.

As if this fall were a signal, three men swiftly darted out from the same covert, and rushed upon Mdlle. du Tremblay. At the same time, a coach, drawn by two strong horses, came out of one of the alleys ending on the bankside. The three ruffians hurried her away towards it.

She resisted, and shrieked:

"Help, help! this way!"

This appeal of distress worked a miracle. Joel sprang to his feet, like the bull does, sometimes, when the axe has blunted the senses, not fatally paralysed them. The thick felt of his shaggy Breton hat had broken the force of the blow. By the pale gleam of a stray lamp he had a peep at the ravishers, and he bounded upon them, with his sword in his grip. On seeing him swoop, like the charge of a cavalier, one of the three ruffians left his comrades and also bared the sword.

"No passage this way," said he.

"The Colonel of the Royal Marauders!" exclaimed Joel.

"I am your man," replied Cordbuff, darting the steel point at his face : " I am going to mark you this time again where my pistol ball left the trace."

This was only a fencer's trick; for, instead of the blade approaching his eyes, Joel had to parry a lunge which might have cut him in halves.

"Ah, food for the gallows that you are," growled the Breton, "You are not worthy being slain by a noble sword." And, reversing the weapon, he used it as as a club and with the weighty pommel nearly split the bandit's skull, and he rolled in the mud. In one bound the victor had cleared him, and in two more reached his accomplices. With a cut, he left the Plucker howling, and with a thrust, he sent Pillager into a doorway to try to patch up a deep hole : Aurore had no vile hand on her now. She clung to his neck.

"Oh, you have saved me," she said. "Nay, God help us!" she almost immediately cried, "We are lost."

At this time, indeed, a dozen armed bravoes, what were called "the Ferocities," disbanded soldiers who led a vagrant life, seemed to issue from the bowels of the coach, much as troops came from the wooden horse within ancient Troy. They must have their march regulated in advance, for they headed directly for the young spoilsport.

"Curs," said he, "well for you that I am not alone!"

Instead of rushing headlong into their midst, he took up the girl as though she were a feather, and rapidly turning, he began a retreat. The whole band started on the pursuit. Fortunately the first blast of the coming storm lifted the dust into a cloud and shrouded them in its blinding whirls. This for the instant checked their speed, and that space sufficed to give the fugitive a reasonable advance.

Large drops of rain began to fall

Joel ran like a deer. Thinking that to save his dear one, he should not shrink from proceedings which the emergency would win pardon for, he took the girl upon his left shoulder and held her from falling with the arm that side; she did not stir. His right arm was free for his sword. The priceless burden did not slacken his furious stride; if anything, it spurred him on in its giddy swiftness. They who followed hot-foot were inveterate. He heard them breathlessly hastening, with the clash of weapons and formidable oaths. But our champion was fortunately of the build to accomplish feats of this description. He was nimble, spite of his somewhat burly frame. It was not for a poor result that he had trained his muscles in hunting and fowling on the plains at Belle-Isle, and in running over the sand even in the tempestuous nights under the thunderpeals.

The present storm was at its height. The ground rang under the rattling hail. On every hand echoes hurried back the roar of thunder. But the Breton had seen far worse on his native coasts.

In the Equinoctial gales the ocean-rollers come in upon them with the howls of Titans trying to scale the cliffs. He strode onward, undismayed, with a regular pulse and an even respiration.

But not so with the rufflers: broken by drink and carousals, they floundered and stumbled on the miry soil: they choked for breath; at every instant, one stopped short. Joel was bareheaded at he fled, his long hair streaming out on the wind, wet with the rain and his perspiration He crossed one bridge—then, another. He threaded one, two, three streets and with a final effort, reached the end of the outer ward beyond the old City limits. Here he paused to rest on a corner-post, catch his breath and listen.

The sound of the pursuers rose no more. He uttered a shout of triumph:

"Thank heaven, we have thrown the pack off. Mademoiselle, with the help of heaven, I believe we have nothing more to fear."

Aurore made no reply: she remained without any movement.

"Mercy on us, is she dead?" gasped the Breton.

With anguish he touched her pulse, and he found that it still beat.

"It is only a faint," he sighed in relief. "The same sort of thing as she experienced on the Saumur highway. But," as he sustained her on his knee, "she must be attended to. Or, this drenching rain and killing hail will be the death of her. What a place—not a soul about ! All the doors and windows closed, no lights, and the walls so pitiless ! I do not even know where I am," he added, in despair, while his eyes questioned the shadows that thickened around.

Suddenly a flash of lightning glared: out of the dark loomed the house before which he had paused, and the brave youth uttered an outcry of joy.

He recognized the building as the Grey House. Only a few days previously, he had escorted home the three ladies who had asked for his arm, on the Pont Neuf. Filling him with light and cheer, came the remembrance of the sentence which one of the three had pronounced as the most grateful for his service :

"If ever you have need of my aid, do not shrink from knocking at this door, and asking for Françoise d'Aubigny, the Widow of the Poet Scarron."

CHAPTER XIII.

QUEEN-LIKE.

THE great anxiety of the Widow Scarron was for the royal children whose early training was entrusted to her. She feared that the storm would rouse them. At every thunder-peal which shook the casements, she glanced towards their cribs with uneasy affection. But the three children did not stir ; innocence protected them in the battle of the elements. So the lady resumed her reading. At times, interrupting herself, she put down the book and the pencil with which she was making notes, to muse, leaning back in her easy chair, with her gaze on vacancy, and her serious lips fluttering :
" Queen—that woman repeated that I was to be a queen." Still a smile of incredulity curled her mouth, although a ray of hope lighted her eyes. She shook her head as though to dispossess it of the haunting thought. In the midst of one of these tormenting reveries, the royal governess

abruptly started, for a heavy hand hammered with the knocker on her door.

"A call at this hour—what can this mean?"

A few minutes having passed, a servant came in.

"What is the matter, Honorin?" questioned the mistress.

"Madame, it is a young gentleman who craves speech of you."

"A young gentleman?"

"Whom I remember as the one who guarded you and the marchioness hither, and whom her ladyship ordered the carriage out to take him home."

A passing flame glowed on the lady's face.

"Oh, that brave fellow——"

"He is not alone, but has with him a young lady—very pretty, upon my word, and seeming in a swoon, for he carried her in his arms."

"This is most strange," said the governess, rising. "However, conduct them into my oratory, where I will join them presently."

When she entered the pious room, of which the chief secular ornament was a bookcase, containing her husband's works, Joel, who had been awaiting her in faltering and agitation, took a step towards her with a supplicatory gesture and said, as he pointed to Mdlle. du Tremblay, whom he had placed upon a sofa.

"Oh, for pity's sake, lady, help and succor her, and I will repay you."

On beholding the dead-seeming girl, with the treasure of her hair flowing over her shoulders and streaming with wet, the governess could not restrain a low scream of astonishment.

"Quick, call Nicole and Suzette," she said, turning to the footman, who had followed her. "Let the bed in the Blue Room be warmed. And bring me my traveling medicine-chest."

"I must explain to you, lady," began the Breton, again advancing.

"Another time," she interposed. "We have no time now, when we must revive her without delay."

Her two chambermaids having run in, she proceeded:

"Take this lady into the Blue Room, where you will remove those wet garments and put her to bed. I will see among my remedies which will be most fit to bring her to life anew. You, stay here, sir," she went on to the deliverer. "I shall return as soon as the patient will no longer need my presence. Then you can acquaint me with the information of whom I have the happiness to befriend and by what concourse of circumstances."

A half-hour elasped, which seemed half-a-century to the waiting heart. But at last the mistress of the Grey House appeared.

"Be of good cheer," she said to this mute challenge. Mdlle. du Tremblay—for her name came out in the babble of fever —is asleep. I have sent her into it by a calming potion. But she must have been overcome by great terror and a piercing emotion——"

"So they were great, indeed."

Our hero rapidly placed under the governess's eyes the scenes which we have described. When he arrived at the sequel of his mad race through the storm and in the dark streets, she declared:

"Verily, here is an adventure which commenced by a pastoral to end by a tragedy. I now comprehend the poor girl's trouble from which I have sought to spare her by administering the soothing draft. Have no fear: she will be calm on awakening, in a safe place and with her defender by her. If it should not be so, I will not hesitate to have recourse to medical science and call in Fagon."

"Fagon? oh, a doctor?"

"A physician—the new royal physician."

"Oh, then he will save her! For indeed, lady, if he should fail, I should no longer have any heart to live, and would have only one thing farther to crave of you: point me out the nearest road to the river——"

The royal governess shook her finger at him in affectionate remonstrance.

"I repeat to you that the young lady is not in danger of death—at least, such is my belief: what she feels is the consequence of her high-strung character, excessively nervous, it strikes me."

"You are right in that matter," said the Breton, "for I have seen her before similarly indisposed."

"And then, the upset of the mind yielded, I suppose, to

the repose of the body. So will it be to-day. Sleep is the sovereign remedy for these accidents."

"Heaven hear you, who bring to me hope and to her health."

He started to take her hand, but she shrank back from this manifestation of gratitude. As the squire stared at her in surprise, she resumed, to shift the topic of conversation and give herself a countenance:

"At present, M. Joel, meseems it is time to think about yourself."

"You say Joel?" exclaimed the Breton with pleasure. "Then, you know my name?"

"Did you not confide it to one of my companions?"

"And you did not forget it!"

"No more than your generous assistance."

"Pooh, a trifle! It is I who ought to pour out uninterrupted thanks to you this night. Still, as you do me the favor to interest yourself in me——"

"I wish to point out that, as you appear soaked and muddied——"

"It is likely. It is all on account of the deluge—and I did not notice it."

"You cannot remain in such a state——"

"For fear of spoiling your carpets? that is true. I am as much out of place here as though I were a river——"

"No, no," she protested, "I am not talking of carpets, but of yourself who need dry clothes and warmth."

"Tush, a turn before the fire and a glass of wine to warm me through and through, and I ask no more."

"How inhospitable of me," said the royal governess, smiling "Be good enough to accompany me. We can talk as well over the wine you reminded me to offer."

Joel was soon seated in the dining-room, between the fireplace where fresh logs were blazing and the table, which Honorin had abundantly loaded: but the satisfaction of his hunger did not dispel the cloud darkening his brow, usually so carefree and smiling. While he was feasting, the hostess had spoken with her cold, sane, pitiless reason.

"So, you are in love with Mdlle. du Tremblay? you really love her, in full sincerity, in your inner self? it is neither a surprise of the senses nor a freak of youth? You love her so dearly that you would sacrifice your fortune to her if the proposal arose?"

"I would not only sacrifice my earthly possessions but my lot in paradise."

"Breton talk of bartering his salvation," she said mirthfully.

"Good Lord, this is getting serious. Does Mdlle. du Tremblay return the sentiment?"

"She has given me the great joy of authorizing me to believe so."

A slight cloud if vexation shaded the questioner's brow.

"On my honor, this opens like a love-romance," she said.

"But before the *finis* be reached, what disappointments, crosses and proofs! In the first place, you have a rival."

"A rival?"

"To whom do you attribute the attempt at abduction from which the fair Aurore escaped only by your intervention? I vow that there is a thwarted swain in the background—some dangerous personage, no doubt, who does not recoil from the most expeditious practices—" She spoke with more emphasis, and looked hard at him; "For the first time, the method failed: but what shows that they may not succeed on the next essay?"

Our hero dropped upon his plate the breastbone of the cold fowl—the rest of the succulent bird had already gone the way of all (chicken) flesh.

"What, do you reckon that these scoundrels are in hire of someone loftier?"

"Come," she counterqueried, with some bitterness, "do you yourself think that one will easily renounce the desire to secure a girl so accomplished as your idol?"

"Out upon him!" growled the youth, lowering his head like the bull about to charge; "I must kill this man."

"Do you know him?"

"I shall seek until I find him."

"A very problematical result. Has he not as much reason to keep *perdu* as you to discover him? May he not have at call means most plentiful to elude you? Besides, what would you reach? He is doubtless a rich and powerful man, who has an army of cut throats at his back, and you stand alone, except your sword."

This logic choked Joel, who drank a cup of Burgundy to clear his throat.

"In the meanwhile," proceeded the lady, dwelling on her

words as if she wanted to convince her auditor of the desperate nature of the situation "Mddle. du Tremblay is no longer in safety in her lodging in Tournelles Street, do you think? For my part, I do not suppose so. The dwelling must be known to the unknown ravisher, who will multiply his plots around that point, till, sooner or later, the prey falls into them. For you will not always be at hand, like a guard of honor, and the bedridden relative who gives her shelter does not appear to me able greatly to help her."

"But," remonstrated the squire, "above the rich and mighty, there is the law which protects the weak and oppressed."

Widow Scarron smiled sceptically.

"My young master," said she with ironical compassion, "it is plain that you have recently arrived from the rural districts, for the law here is what the Lieutenant of Police Lareyine makes it. He is said to be honest; but is it likely he would take your side, and your Aurore's, two youths from the provinces, without credit or influence—against a rival of your antagonist's rank? From the highhanded manner in which he acts, I may presume that he is a great noble, assured he may brave justice, or a rich one able to bribe it."

Joel rose in sorrow.

"Woe is me!" he sighed. "You see that I must leap with her over the nearest bridge——"

The heartrending outburst was so deep that the hearer was thrilled to her inmost fibre.

"How he loves her!" she thought. "He will kill her sooner than another shall boast of the conquest, and then slay the villain, however high. In all ways, death impends. But he must not be lost—so young a man, who, like myself, belongs to the future Squire Joel," she called out as he staggered towards the door, "return and retake your seat."

As his only reply was a mad shake of the fist, she ran to him at the door, and leading him back, forced him to take his seat.

"You are but a boy to throw away lives like coin. If I were your friend, we might hatch up some means together to extricate you from this quandary. There must be a way when there is a will. So there is!—do you recall the lady whom you served as cavalier—one of my companions?"

"The marchioness?" mechanically queried the Breton.

"Yes, the Marchioness de Montespan," and she studied on the young man's face the impression made by the revelation, or she sought for it, for there was none.

Nothing was there but his personal distress.

"Does the title convey no information to you?"

"By my faith, not a jot—is there anything particular about it?"

"It is not possible that you are ignorant who the marchioness is——"

"I saw that she was a very bewitching and obliging person."

"Is that all?"

"The whole story."

"Really, do you mean to say that you do not know her position in the court?"

"Oh, she holds a position at court, does she? One of the Queen's ladies, I venture to guess?"

The hearer, who laughed very seldom when she became Madame de Maintehon, burst into a peal if hearty laughter.

"You will be my death, the Lord forgive you!" she exclaimed, "I believe you make witticisms as Molière's M. Jourdain composed prose, without trying to do it. Come, come, it is not from Brittany that you arrived, but a journey farther—shall we say Felix Aradia or Nova Zembla?" The youth stared at her, bewildered at this outburst. "How furious the proud Athenais would be to hear that! she who fancies that she fills the whole universe with the beams she reflects from 'the Sun.' But let us look to ourselves. Collect your thoughts. Of what were you two conversing as you came along, she on your arm, from the New Bridge hither?"

The youth repeated very accurately the dialogue.

"It would be so," muttered the auditress. "Heudicourt is right—the woman wants to captivate every mortal son. At all events," she went on aloud, "you did not confide to her the name of your beloved?"

He shook his head, and she approved.

"Good—we have a chance to succeed."

"Succeed in what?"

"In the first place, in shielding your sweetheart from the pursuit of your rival."

"Is it possible?"

"Hearken to me: The Marchioness de Montespan is—how will I explain it? a great friend of the King—his greatest, best friend—up to the present time," she said to herself. "The King can refuse her nothing," she proceeded, for his ear, "a matter of give and take. Now, if my lady agrees to take Mdlle. du Tremblay under her wing——"

"I see," broke in Joel, encouraged. "All you want is this protection, which I will ask of the lady."

"You?"

"Of course! the great lady is not so haughty as you say. We chatted together on the same frank footing. I will declare to her that there is nobody on the earth but my Aurore——"

"Mind you do nothing of the sort, you blundering fellow!"

"Why not? She showed herself right kindly to me."

"That is the very reason."

"I do not understand."

"There is no necessity of your understanding."

"There, you are scoffing at me again," murmured the youth.

"Do not be angry with me for that. I have not had such fun since I lost my poor Scarron. But you are of the most laughable innocence."

"In plain——"

"In plain, then, I charge myself to speak for you to the marchioness. I beg you not to interrupt me; and do not do it, even to thank me. I have been so much somebody's ward that I am happy to play the fairy godmother to somebody else. In the first place, Mdlle. du Tremblay can stay here until recovered from her alarm and ready for me to conduct her to St. Germain, where I will lodge her by Madame de Montespan. Under the roof of the royal residence, her unknown pursuer will not dare to renew his attacks. Hereafter, we shall see what is to be done. I have your happiness in my head, and whenever I make up my mind to anything, it come to pass. In acting thus, I am not purely giving the man of her choice to your adored darling; but a rarity worthy of pairing off with Oger the Danish Knight for wildness and for chastity with Scipio Africanus."

"Oh, madame, how kind you are, and how heartily I bless you."

But though she let him kiss her hands, like the queen she dreamed to become, she receded, and in a calm voice said :

"M. Joel, allow me to part company. I must return to our interesting invalid and the children entrusted to my care. All need my attentions. Besides, it is getting late, and you must be fatigued with your exertions and the long race. Take the needed repose—in this chair—the best accommodation I can offer you; but you must be cut out for a soldier, judging by the way you wield the sword, and you must imagine that you are sleeping on the battlefield, on a night of victory. Good night ! courage and hope !"

Joel slept in the easy chair by the chimney corner, with a leaden sleep till an advanced hour of the morning. A maid-servant came to usher him into the room where Mdlle. du Tremblay was reposing.

Aurore was prey to a violent fever, as was revealed in the lustre of her eyes, the purple tint on her cheekbones and the relaxation of her muscles. When she woke, after a night of nightmare, peopled with frightful panthoms—and opened her mouth to ask where she was, Widow Scarron had bent over her and in a most motherly voice, replied:

"Do not question, my child. At this moment the effort to listen and to speak may be fatal to you. Be it enough to know that you are surrounded by friends." Pointing to her defender, who entered on tiptoe, anxious and excited, she added : "You see that I am not deceiving you. Your champion repeats my entreaty. Friends have undertaken to shield your head from all danger from whatever quarter ; from the malady which keeps you in bed, as from the criminal plots which threatened your honor."

Joel knelt beside the pillow; he took the burning hand and saluted it with a reverent and gentle kiss. She responded by softly and affectionately pressing his hand, and she would have spoken ; but the Widow Scarron again intervened :

"Let me once more, urge no imprudence. I prescribe complete silence. And I represent the Faculty of Medicine here, until the doctor arrives. I have sent an express to St. Germain to bring Dr. Fagon," she continued to the Breton. "I expect him to finish the cure I have commenced. But you must not meet him here."

"Are you sending me away ?"

"Yes; to Tournelles Street to begin with : did you not say that Mdlle. du Tremblay lived there with an aged relative?"

"Yes, old Madame de la Bassetiere."

"Exactly: she must have been mortally frightened during this while; it is urgent to set her at ease on the fate of her young kinswoman, and ask her approval of the measures we intend to take for her welfare."

Aurore, in spite of her state, did not lose a word of this colloquy. Her look seemed to say to the royal governess : "I thank you for thinking and foreseeing everything !" and as clearly on its traveling to Joel, it spoke; "Hasten, my friend, for mercy's sake !"

"But I shall see you again?" supplicated the Breton.

Widow Scarron pushed him gently towards the door, saying :

"Yes, you may come back. Any evening. Is not your presence a remedy, as efficacious as any Dr. Fagon can order: but I must regulate the dose. Now, for heaven's sake, get you gone. Do you not see that as long as you stay, our patient will not close her eyes."

CHAPTER XIV.

DAMON AND PYTHIAS IN THE 17TH CENTURY.

WHEN our adventurer reached St. Antoine Street, he remarked extraordinary animation at about the middle of it, by the Place Royale. Children were running to and fro and screaming; footpassengers stopped and formed groups; The storekeepers came out of their doorsills, and the windows were noisily slammed up to form the frames for curious faces. Our astonished friend inquired what had happened of an honest cobbler whose stall stood in the corner of Val St. Catharine Street.

"Master," responded the disciple of St. Crispin, an arrest has taken place over yonder in the tavern of Pas-de-Mule Street—an important capture—of a heinous malefactor."

"Really?"

"We saw the officer and six provost guards march past a while ago, with their halberds in the fist and in the coats of the City colors. Look, it seems to me that they are coming back."

Nothing so gathers a crowd in a city as a police arrest. Is it because we are all likely to deserve our committal to hard quarters, as a cynic might say? The mob thickened on both sides of an open way hurriedly formed. From all the mouths of the serried spectators a buzz arose, from which these sentences vaguely stood out, so to say:

"It is a murderer—a thief—a counterfeiter—a forger?"
"No, it was sacrilege—arson—a bankruptcy. "Say, rather, a conspirator—a rebel—an accomplice of the traitors!"
"You are all out, stupids! it is a maker of wax dolls which kill the original by inches as they melt away! a poisoner, who went to the witches. Sabbath with Brinvilliers and La Voisin."

In the midst of this uproar, the armed force marched onward with a slowness due to the hindrance caused by the mob swelling on every point. The police officer who preceded it, tried with his long staff to keep back the curious spectators who encumbered the way. His six archers were old soldiers, burly and ponderous, who overshadowed by their bulk the prisoner whom they escorted; among these robust guards he was dwarfed so as to seem a boy. Nevertheless, he did not fail to try by drawing himself to his full height, to remedy the defect in stature. At the same time, he was not a bit discomfited, ashamed or embarrassed. Carrying himself haughtily, with his breast stuck out like a pouter pigeon's, his head held back disdainfully, his hat cocked over the ear and his hand on his hip, he nodded to the male bystanders and winked and smiled killingly to the ladies.

When he strutted by Joel, the latter exclaimed:
"Friquet!"

The mannikin did not hear the word in the disturbance, or perceive the speaker, he was so busy about himself. A girl who was staring, had cried out this expression of compassion: "Oh, the poor little man!" and the little Parisian testily retorted:

"Little, indeed! you impertinent drab! you are pretty watchmen that you let hussies insult a cavalier of my rank and quality under your protection."

Friquet, the protégé of Minister Colbert's kinsman, arrested! The Breton fell out of the clouds, and, seized with irresistible curiosity, he ran to Pas-du-Mule Street. On espying him come up, Master Bonlarron, who was orating with heat in the midst of a crowd of neighbors, hastened to quit them to hurry up to the young man with gestures of alarm.

"You rash fellow," he said, pushing him inside his house. "Why have you come back? away!—or, hide yourself! let nobody suspect you are here."

"Hide? why should I hide?"

"Because they are after you!"

"After me?"

"Decidedly. It is by providence that the police were fooled, for they have been fooled—they never depart from their usual practices. And they have captured the little Parisian instead of you. Yet there is a difference in you two. But those asses can never see clear."

"Arrested in my stead?" said Joel, pinching himself to make sure he was awake. "What do you mean by that? How comes Friquet to be taken for me?"

"Well, he was not sorry to be *taken for* a topping blade of your build."

"What cock-and-bull story are you cramming me with, mine host? I can make neither head nor tail of it. Pray explain."

"Here you have it. This morning, as I was breakfasting, I saw an officer come up with half-a-dosen archers of the City Guard, of whom he posted two at my door. The others stamped in with him. I naturally asked them what the deuce they wanted. Information, said they, and I was not to be chary about it, as they came in the King's name. I was overpowered with the honor, and begged them to be seated, and show how I might be agreeable to his Most Christian Majesty.

"'You must frankly answer our questions.'

"'I will answer to any amount as long as I do not get myself into any snarl.'

"'You have a guest freshly arrived from the country?'

"'Better than that—I rejoice in two.'

"'We mean the one who has just been out to St. Germain?'

"'Do you tell me one has gone out to St. Germain? Good! travel shapes young men—when it does not knock them out of all shape.'

"'The postmaster has sworn to letting him have a horse, and the innkeeper at Pecq that he left him there.'

" 'Left the horse, eh? that proves he is an honest young gentleman, anyway.'

"About this time, the officer perceived that I was toying with him, and he pulled a face as long as a day without a cup of wine; he levelled his glances at me like shots out of a blunderbuss. As if he could daunt *me*, a veteran of Rocroy —— who shouted, 'Devil take you!' to the Spanish guns vomiting grapeshot."

" 'Friend, you are merry,' he sneered. 'Always when I am not bilked by bad customers and have cause to be glum.'

"'We are not talking of your character, but of your lodger's. Where is he now?'

" 'How do I know? he is not here, that is flat, for he forgot to come home last night.'

" 'Are you certain?'

" 'As certain as that this is a glass of ratafic that I am tossing off to your health.'"

" 'Rogue, you are trying to deceive me. The bird is in its nest. The police agent who was charged to watch him, saw light in his room last night, and everything leads us to believe hat he has not come forth.'

" 'If he has not gone out, you had better go and take him.'

" Whereupon they went upstairs with a good deal of caution. After a while, they came down with M. Friquet. The brave lad did not pretend to deny himself, or ratner deny you. He marched along between the halberds like the King among his guards. That Hop-o'-my-thumb ought to be seven foot high, to behave so handsomely as to let hinself be locked up for a friend. The only thing is to see if the police and justices like the fun of the jest."

"But whither are they taking him?"

"I asked one of the archers and he said that the usual process was to bring him before Lieutenant of Police Lareynie at the Châtelet prison."

"Ah!"

"A magistrate with a heart of the same stone as the building around him."

"Well," said Joel, settling his hat on firmly: "I would like to know the straight road to the Châtelet."

"Halloa!" ejaculated the innkeeper, starting; "you never mean to——"

I am going to appear in my place before the bar of justice."

"Why, you headlong fellow," said the veteran, "you cannot think of it. It is about that confounded duel—and the King will be enraged—killing his Musketeer, and in a royal forest!"

"I reproach myself in no way, and I shall await the result of my trial without fear."

"But you forget the edicts which you have broken."

"If the law," tranquilly returned the squire, "if the law punishes gentlemen for obeying the dictates of honor, then it is the law-maker who ought to be punished. Do you refuse to tell me the way to the prison?" he added, proceeding to the door.

"It will be pointing out that to your doom."

"Then I must ask of the first-comer. I do not want M. Friquet to think that I would profit by his devotion longer than I could help."

"Tut! do not bother about him—he will slip out easily. A Parisian always comes out of a scrape with glory—if it be only vain-glory!"

The other frowned.

"Do you, an old hero, suggest such a dastard act to me?"

"What I suggest is, that, without losing a minute, you make for the St. Honoré Gate, quit Paris and hie you home to Brittany, where you will not be sought for."

"You cannot be speaking seriously. If you were, you would be insulting me so that only your age would protect you."

"You stubborn-headed boy," returned the tavern-keeper, stamping his foot, "are you attached to nothing—is there nobody you love on earth?"

"Hush!" interrupted Joel, with a flow of all the feeling in his breast. "It is wicked of you to place a man between his love and his duty. Not another word—make way," he said with an imperious wave of the hand. "Farewell!"

"No," said the old sergeant, throwing himself before him; "You shall not make such a blunder—you shall not go forth, by the pitchfork of Satan! I will not have you go. Come, come, the matter of it is that I like you," went on the veteran, with his rough voice and hardened face softened by tender emotion, "you might be son of mine. It is only three days since we met, but it is just the same as though we had gone through a campaign together. You are an old campaigner, in fact, for you are satisfied with everything—wine, meat, bread, the waiter and the host. You have first class health and a good appetite. And you can fence like the Archangel Gabriel! All this, to moulder in jail! all this, to end on the scaffold—I may say! for running a racketty, riotous sot through the midriff, who owes even his landlord for liquor enjoyed! an old rat—to be paid for as though he were new. I oppose your going. And have a care how you play with my patience. Zounds! I have it in me, to take my rapier down from the hooks and pin you to the wall to prevent you committing a folly which I regard as suicide!"

Joel could but smile at this singular way of preventing self-murder.

"Mine host," he said, "you are an honest man, and you must forgive me for laying a hand on you—but your obstinacy drives me to it."

At the same time, he seized the old man by the collar, but only in fun, as if to drag him away from the doorway where he had planted himself; as the worthy Bonlarron threw out both arms to repel the attack, the Breton thrust his leg between his, and gave him the trip up in so scientific and successful a manner that the result was positive that the noble art of wrestling was well cultivated in Belle-Isle. The veteran of Rocroy sat down on the floor so roughly that every bone in his body had a separate ache.

"Excuse me, papa," said Joel, "but I saw no other way out of it." And, leaping over the dumbfounded landlord, he passed through the doorway.

During this time, M. de Lareynie was passing the time away at the Châtelet by reading and hearing reports of the police. He had a grave and honest mein; his broad forehead wore the legal wig very fittingly, and there was as much integrity as energy in his glance.

He was in the heart of his business, a swarm of details, when an usher came in and whispered a few words.

"Ah," said the magistrate with satisfaction, "so they have caught the Hector at last. That is right. Bring him in."

A few minutes later, preceded by the officer and followed by the six archers, Friquet was introduced into the office

He advanced with his nose in the air and his mouth pursed up in a kind of conceited smile, made a bow according to the rules, and opened his mouth to utter a compliment which he had prepared on the route, to felicitate the magistrate in having the good fortune to set at liberty so shining a star of the future. But the functionary did not allow him any time to do this.

"Hillo, Saint-Jean," he questioned the officer with astonishment, "What under the sun have you brought here?"

"My lord, it is the person you ordered us to apprehend," was the *exempt's* reply.

"Have you gone mad, by chance?" returned the chief of police, shrugging his shoulders. "This, the man in question? you cannot have consulted the description given by all the witnesses whom we examined!" Taking up a paper from the desk, he read, "Here is the paper! Read and compare! Height—over six feet; aspect—herculean; dress—Breton peasant's——"

"But, my lord," protested the officer, "we took the bird in the very room of the very inn where the stranger was said to lodge—I carefully questioned him, and he has asserted that he was the duellist we were after."

"But you do not accept such statements on plain assertion, do you?"

"Why, my lord, when a prisoner owns up that we have the right man——"

"A track to throw you off the scent! Master Saint-Jean, like your name sake, you have lost your head! you are a blockhead who have let yourself be lulled to sleep—you deserve to be broken——"

The infuriated head of police turned upon Friquet who was cooly taking a chair, and challenged him roughly with: "Here, what are you doing there?"

"Waiting, at my ease, until your lordship shall have concluded conversing with this officer on a variety of subjects of which I do not understand the slightest word. At least, it seems to me that you accuse the poor fellow of committing a blunder—while it is nothing of the kind, I assure your lordship, for I am the person whom the King has no doubt talked to you about."

"Indeed, I am acting on the express order of his Majesty—but the description does not apply——"

"A fig for descriptions!" exclaimed the Little Parisian, impatiently. "I am not six feet high, but after all what is an inch under or over? As for the dress of my country, I changed into the present one—just to add to my personal advantages——"

"What, do you claim to be——"

"Claim to be—myself? More than claim, I am proud to declare myself!"

"Is this possible?" muttered Lareynie, fidgetting on his chair. "What a hardened rogue! so you make a boast of what you have done?"

"Certainly I do. I am not beginning my career as a military engineer. But wait, my lord, till I make more progress—you will have the eyes dazzled out of your learned head."

The Lieutenant of the Royal Police turned to his usher: "Are the register and the constabulary sergeants here?"

"They are, my lord."

"Let them enter."

As soon as the new force were in the room, the high official continued: "Clerk, prepare to take down the statements of this man. Sergeants, place yourselves beside him, as he is in your custody now."

Friquet looked with surprise at the new-comers and the speaker:

"How now? what new game are we playing? Statement, clerk, constables—Death of my life! I do not comprehend at all."

"Accused," began the official in a stern voice, "do you acknowledge having maliciously and aforethought contravened the edicts promulgated by our sire, the King——"

It was now the Parisian's turn to fidget.

"Edicts—what edicts? Do I dream? or is it your lordship who has had a sunstroke?"

"The edicts bearing upon duels," continued Lareynie, "consented to, and signed, through the diligence of the late Cardinal Richelieu, by the lamented King Louis XIII., and renewed by the reigning monarch, the Fourteenth Louis, his successor, on the nineteenth of January last in his good city of St. Germain——"

"I, contravened any edicts?" muttered the Little Parisian, with his hands hanging in his stupor.

"By crossing swords, in the royal domain of St. Germain Forest, with Corporal Bregy of the Royal Musketeers, who cannot be pursued by justice for aiding in this deed of rebellion from his having unfortunately succumbed in this combat by your act of bloodshed——"

Friquet cried aloud: light burst in upon his brain. It was to lead him before judges that he was furnished with a squad of soldiers and not to escort him into the minister's presence. He was accused of treason and manslaughter, and was to be shut up in prison—all in the stead of his friend Joel of Locmaria.

Without heeding the terror he inspired as last, the magistrate continued:

"In consequence, you become qualified for trial before the tribunal of the Constabulary and Marshals of France, especially instituted to administer the laws of the realm and the will of the King against those guilty of infringing them."

He paused to give his hearer time to fully realize the redoubtable sense in his speech, before he solemnly resumed: "Misdeeds of this category bearing no less penalty than decaptation by the sword——"

Spite of his bravery, the Parisian sank into the seat, for his legs gave away under him. A red mist veiled his eyes, and on the ruddy background he beheld a vision of the deathsman, with axe and block. "Unless," said Lareynie, the King grant you grace—which I strongly doubt, seeing the heinous nature of your atrocity."

Friquet ran his hand round his neck where a cold chill seemed to strike like a steel edge.

"You must prepare to sign your avowal—provided that you are the true criminal. For you may have agreed with him to dally with justice that he may profit by the time gained to make his escape over the border——"

This suggestion was a ray of light to the Parisian, who was quickwitted. While he was in jail, Joel might indeed be making his flight homeward. His course was taken in a trice: he would support the imprisonment; suffer judgment to go against him, and even let the execution go on—for he would have saved his friend—of new creation but dear. His face grew calm and his limbs ceased to quiver as he arose, and said steadily:

"My lord, I will trouble you for the pen with which to sign."

But at this critical moment, a violent tumult was audible without; above all a vigorous young boy shouted:

"I tell ye again that I must see M. de Lareynie—and see him I will, spite of all the devils! were you five hundred strong, you should not keep me out."

There was a clash of weapons and a scuffle, before the door was dashed open. The Son of Porthos appeared on the sill. The six archers courageously formed a line, and crossed halberds to repulse him. To the rescue ran the two constables, while the exempt and the clerk valiantly formed a reaguard. Joel had not drawn his sword, but, without raising a hand, he cut through the defenders as if he were a cyclone. He planted himself in front of the Chief of Police.

"My lord," he began, "I know what is going on. This splendid fellow is sacrificing himself for me. But I do not accept the sacrifice. It was I who violated the edicts for I drew my sword in the precincts of St. Germain, and slew Corporal Bregy. The King calls for my head—I bring it on my shoulders; but let me solicit a boon of your justice and humanity. Let my poor friend go free, who is at the worst guilty solely of heroism and devotedness."

"Monsieur, what you desire shall be done," replied the Police Lieutenant, moved to the heart by the young man's air, action and language. "You may depart," he said to Friquet.

The latter leaped into the new-comer's arms, faltering:

"Joel, Joel, what made you come here? why did you not let things have their way? I should have been so happy to contribute to your welfare. 'Sblood, why am I thwarted?"

He was choking with mingled grief and joy, as the Breton folded him to his heart in a brotherly embrace in which he almost disappeared.

The magistrate bent towards the police officer, and said with the conceit of one who rarely was at fault:

"Now we have the right man, Saint-Jean! This is the one you should have handled—though it might have cost you some pains. Did I not intimate all along that it would take to lay low a Bregy quite another antagonist than this manikin?"

Manikin? at any other time the derided Tom Thumb would have resented the epithet, but at this moment the Little Parisian was too excited to notice it.

"Constables," proceeded the magistrate. "do your duty!"

The two constables marched up to the youth and one said,

"In the King's name, I charge you to surrender your sword."

The other drew from his pocket a short ebony wand with a white knob and, tapping the youth on the shoulder, said:

"In the King's name, I arrest you."

Within half an hour, the squire was walked out of the Châtelet between the two sergeants to a coach stationed on the waterside. The soldiers made him step into it and placed themselves on the opposite seat to that he occupied: the rule is for one of two constables to sit beside the prisoner, but in this cage there was no room. A mounted archer of the watch rode up to each door, and at once, off went the whole equipage at a gallop.

After a quarter of an hour, it stopped before a fortress, defended by an abundance of moats, ramparts and outworks, and with high towers outlined against the sky.

"Get down," said one of the sergeants.

Joel obeyed. Two soldiers who seemed to await him, took each an arm. A man with a bunch of keys in his hand, took the lead. The little party passed under a vaulted roof, over a draw-bridge, through a guardroom, and a maze of stairs and corridors, after a large yard. Thus they reached the third floor, where one door after another was opened to the number of three. Here the prisoner was thrust into a cell, furnished with bed, table and chair.

"Here you are, at home," said the turnkey.

He withdrew with the two soldiers, and the keys were heard grating in the locks, and the bolts shooting into their sockets. This sound aroused the captive, who had mechanically paced the long way, accepting all that happened him as in a dream the most monstrous conceptions are met without hesitation and without astonishment. He strode to the door and called:

"Hey, you fellows!"

"What is wanting so soon," demanded the jailer through the barred wicket in the thick door.

"One word, I prithee."

"Be sharp!"

"I should be obliged to you for telling me in what place I am."

"Beginning your jokes already, eh?" grumbled the man, as he departed. "As though you did not know, as well as me, that you are in the Bastille."

CHAPTER XV.

THE COUNTERCHECK.

SINCE a month, Louis XIV. had returned to St. Germain, and the little town reassumed the gala aspect imported by the monarch and his appanage. He was then in the apogee of his power, and the "divinity which hedges a king" sanctified even his foibles. He did not dissimulate any of them. Montespan was the titular favorite and mother of his progeny whom the Widow Scarron cared for, and he had just rewarded the latter by conferring upon her the rank of Marchioness de Suggère. Madame de Sevigné, whose friend she was but who spared nobody with her wit, ran off a series of jests on the title, which she misread as "Suggest."

"A happy *suggestion* of his Majesty, she whispered to the courtiers, "indeed, she had from somebody the *suggestion* to wed the cripple Scarron ; it was *suggested* to the mason he that should predict her a great fortune and I should not wonder if envy *suggested* that she should undermine the benefactress who raised her from poverty to confide to her the care of her children by the King."

Apart from the ladies and courtiers discussing this promotion and the bad news of the Queen's health, the officers of the lifeguards were conversing on matters of discipline. They were the Lieutenant of the Musketeers, Maupertuis, and the present captain and his predecessor of the Guards, Gesvres and Brissac.

"What has become of that limb of the fiend?" inquired the last of the Musketeer. I mean that young bravo from the provinces who slew one of your corporals?"

"Yes, with a spledid thrust through the chest. Well, he is still under lock and bar."

"Are they not going to try him?"

"It is in doubt what to do—for he may not be of noble blood as he pretends. He is plain Joel."

"Impossible! where can a commoner have picked up secrets of fencing to kill a royal Musketeer?"

"Ay, and with a thrust known only in our regiment, but which had almost passed out of memory with the heavy swords for which it was invented. It was called the 'Thrust Porthos,' from a famous gentleman-Musketeer of the past reign who used it to fatal advantage."

"For my part," continued Maupertuis, "I should send him home to plant his cabbages and cut them with his huge sword, for, all taken into account, he fought like a brave man. We swordsmen never yet thought a duelist dishonored for having broken the law. The dishonor would have been in his refusing the challenge."

"You are not very kind to your soldiers," observed Gesvres.

"Oh, to tell you the truth, gentlemen, this Bregy was not prepossessing: a toper who drank when not dicing, and wrangled when not dicing. Still, his Majesty is angry at the edicts of his father being laughed at, since he renewed them, and I had hard work to pluck from under the royal paw four of my soldiers who were seconds in the combat."

"And did he pardon them?"

"Well, so far as life goes; but they must step out of the household of troops' uniform and join the active army in Lorraine."

"Why not send the Breton along with them—he seems even more admirably adapted as food for powder."

"Nay, they will waste him in prison or in the galleys—unless they shoot him or hang."

"How old is the poor fellow?" asked Brisac, yawning behind his gauntlet.

"On my honor, I do not know. I have never seen him. Say between twenty and thirty, I suppose."

The guard officer combed his moustache and thoughtfully remarked, "In that case, he had better be done for at once before he pinks more of our fellows."

On the same terrace, in a more remote spot, the Duke of Almada was strolling, leaning on Boislaurier's arm.

"It is very bad," said he, "that all your efforts to trace that young beauty should have been useless."

"Alas, my lord: all our pack of sleuth-hounds have been sent afield, but the best have drawn blank."

"So have those whom I privately employed," continued the ambassador, snappishly. "My man Esteban is the cunningest knave that ever was; the rascal calling himself Captain Cordbuff has a nasty cut to seek revenge for; Desgrais, the sharp police-spy who tracked the Marchioness de Brinvilliers to Liège and arrested her there—he, like the rest, has been flouted, baffled, and foiled to the top of their skill."

"Has your excellency reflected on this point," went on Boislaurier after a pause: "if I am to believe the reports of my spies, that Madame de la Bassetiere, who is her relative, frets not a bit over her young kinswoman's disappearance. From this I infer that she is not ignorant where she is hidden."

"You may infer as much."

"And has not my lord sought to extract information from her?"

"It has been tried without success. Nothing can be drawn. Her old servant-woman is equally as impenetrable. So things come round," he added, with forced gaiety; "in the entire universe, only one incorruptible chamberwoman existed, and luck falls so that she is across our path."

A fresh silence ensued, which the subordinate broke.

"Can Mdlle. du Tremblay have returned home?"

"Into Anjou? I have written thither for news, and the answer came this morning that she has not been seen."

"Then, we must throw down the cards—the winning one is not among them."

"Wherefore?" returned the duke quickly. "It is missing, but we can fabricate another or find one to our hand. At the same time, I do not conceal that this loss puts me in terrible turmoil. Confound that young springald!"

"What springald, my lord?" inquired Boislaurier, looking round on the group of courtiers.

"Oh, that bucolic Amadis who happened upon the scene just in the nick to cut the prey out of the grip of our myrmidons. We must settle accounts one of these days with him." Pressing the companion's arm, he pursued with a dreamy eye, "let me tell you, good Boislaurier, that some indescribable, mysterious sympathy attracts me towards that young man; when first my sight lit upon him, I felt that cold tremor which the superstitious say denotes that one is walking on a grave. He pleased me highly at the Saumur inn. His appearance and his assertive manner remind me of a dear old friend whose loss wrung from me many tears, I should have liked to help him on, but the upstart flounders into the centre of my web and upsets my plans. So much the worse for him! Never has man thwarted me and not repented it. I level obstacles; I overthrow adversaries and I kill enemies."

"But has not this youth likewise disappeared?"

"Yes; a proof that the pair have gone off together. But I shall find them, and——"

A threatening gesture as of one snapping a twig in two, energetically completed the interrupted phrase.

"But what is going on yonder?" he said, in a change of tone. "Why that flocking to one spot? has the King come forth?"

There was a great stir on the terrace and in the grounds.

"My lord, it is the Marchioness de Montespan entering the Bowling-green alley."

"Ah, very well—I understand. Alone in her room sits Queen Maria Theresa; but the gilded throng crowds around the favorite. Is his Majesty accompanying the latter?"

"No, your grace, there are but two ladies by her side—her familiar fiend the Widow Scarron, and—and——"

"One of her sisters, of course?"

"Nay—it cannot be—I am the sport of some illusion!"

"What is the matter?" queried Almada.

The gentleman did not reply immediately; he rivetted his eyes on the marchioness's companion, and finally faltered:

"Still, that step, those features—why, 'tis the same—my lord, it is the girl whom we believed buried in the bowels of the earth—She who escaped all our researches—Mdlle. du Tremblay."

"Mdlle. du Tremblay!" was the outcry of the Spanish duke.

"None other—you have but to look. There, by the edge of the great fountain basin."

Almada shielded his eyes with his hand and after a long scrutiny, replied:

"You made no error. It is she. On my soul, the poet is right who said that 'Truth is stranger than fiction.' Rubbing his hands and cracking the knuckles to overcome their stiffness, he chuckled: "Who spoke of throwing down the cards?

We shall win with ours, because it is in the hands of the opponent. Boislaurier, this time the game is ours."

In fact, they saw Mdlle. du Tremblay.

She walked on one side of the Marchioness de Montespan, who had the Widow Scarron on her left. The favorite wore a silken robe of sky blue ; the governess a dead-leaf colored dress, rather poor in effect; while the new-comer, thanks to the plotter's *suggestion,* and to shine the brighter for her dull array, was clad in a changeable silk. It was trimmed with Venetian point lace and knots of pale green, and amid the pearly and rosy tints of the silk, she was fair to an extent that would have paled the stars. This was not the court type, to which the artifices of the toilet contributed a main part but the loveliness which prolongs the pleasure of the gaze and discloses innumerable fascinations at every turn. Amid these charms must be cited the melancholy and the indifference which were read on the girlish face as on an open page. Aurore considered the brilliant courtiers with neither amaze nor embarrassment, neither curiosity nor interest. Mortal repining was visible behind the immobile and languid mask. Everybody wondered who was this new-comer who soared above the glitter which environed her—the glory of the foremost court in Christendom.

As the three ladies stopped before still another complimenting gathering, a new movement was made in the elegant assemblage. All mouths opened at once and the whisper ran from the forest gates to the terrace balustrade:

"The King, ladies and gentlemen, the King!"

Louis the Great decended the palace sstairs.

He was the Grand Monarque in all the Force of his age, fortune and glory. This day he wore the countenance he put on when, as St. Simon the memoir-writer says, "he meant to transact business." He was clad, too, in black velvet, with worked gold buttons; the Blue Ribbon crossed his scarlet satin vest, embroidered with flowers. A white plume curled around his beaver. The only jewels were in his shoes and garters. He leaned, for effect rather than for support, on a cane with a jeweled handle.

As the courtiers swarmed round him, he looked more careworn, and made a sign that he wished to be alone with the Marchioness de Montespan. On seeing the King draw near, both her companions had started to withdraw, but she had beckoned them back, and said with that bland familiarity which she showed to the greatest personage of the kingdom, and which her lover allowed her to use towards him, though he was a stickler about etiquette.

"Sire, here is the Marchioness de Suggère, who wishes nothing so much as to thank your Majesty for the new favor of which she is the object."

Widow Scarron made a low courtesy, and said:

"Will the King permit the most devoted of his servants to present the expression of boundless gratitude for the boons with which she has been ceaselessly overwhelmed by the most generous and magnificent of sovereigns."

Her voice trembled, which was adding sugar to the sweet, in uttering this studied speech of which the vain Louis delightfully swallowed the laudative epithets. Nothing was more agreeable to a ruler whom seventy years' reign had but partly dulled to the joy of being praised and adored.

"Marchioness," responded he, "I felt bound to reward the care with which you have surrounded my children, for whom I am not unaware that you have been truly a mother."

This was an undisguised fling at La Montespan, but she merely smiled as she plied her fan. The monarch turned to her without having paid the faintest attention to Mdlle. du Tremblay, and said abruptly to the favorite:

"Now for us two, madame."

With the greatest tranquility the marchioness walked on beside him, in silence, for she was waiting for the onset, though she preserved her calmness. On the contrary, the King was agitated.

"Madame," he said, at last finding courage, "to my regret I have to inform you of a decision I have come to, which will certainly afflict you as much as it does myself. It is necessary that we should be most careful in our relations; the Queen is so very ill that I am bound to spare her everything of the nature to distress her and impede her recovery.,

"Ah, indeed!" sighed the marchioness with the utmost indifference. The King was evidently ill at ease, for he did not look at the lady and pretended to flip a white pebble on the path with his cane. She kept her eyes on him, though with the tranquility which was exasperating to him.

"I see," said she trifling with her fan, "that your Majesty

has been listening to the Queen's physicians, who must say something horrifying to earn their salaries."

"No, madame, I have listened solely to my own feelings, which alone I obey."

As if she had not heard him, the favorite went on:

"As you have decided, it only remains to me to bow to your will as to their wisdom. The preachers Bossuet and Bourdaloue are possessed with eloquence to make converts through a wall of stone—I have been converted, and religion and duty justify me in breaking the bonds which are a weight upon my conscience and an outrage on morality."

"What!" exclaimed the monarch, wincing, and at the height of stupefaction, "Do you, marchioness, propose——"

"That we should part? Just so, sire. I take the first step. I am only too happy to spare you the chagrin of telling me to depart."

But she did not cease to smile, and the King could not understand her. It was not without violent apprehension that he had made up his mind to announce the rupture to his left-hand queen. He expected the outbursts of unspeakable furies for which the marchioness was famous. More than once he had felt their lash. But the irritable Athenais spoke without anger and sharpness. This resignation offended him, for was it not an insult to his winning self?

"It is a settled thing" said "the Marvel of Beauty," "I quit the court to-morrow. The sooner the better, methinks, for good intentions should be carried out without delay."

"Do you then quit my court without unwillingness, regret and bitterness?"

"It is thus I go."

Louis bit his lip, unable to admit that *he* could be dispensed with.

"I have no reason to be uneasy about my children, as I so recently heard your Majesty say they would be cared for by their second mother. Besides, I may be allowed to see them in my retreat at Clagny, where I intend awaiting the farther pleasure of the King."

"In that out of the way place, a suburb of Versailles?"

A desert is the fit refuge for one who must look to her salvation: so I supplicate your Majesty not to stand in the way of my holy occupation. Like Mary Magdalen the great sinner, I want to repent of my errors, which are also in some degree your own, so that my prayers must include my Louis, and of the scandal which we both have set before a world too good for me. I shall implore heaven to make those forget me whom I shall strive to forget while praying, trying to be contrite and performing deeds of benevolence."

"Would you try to forget everybody?"

"Without exception."

Louis cropped the head off a magnificent pond lily with a cut of his cane. So he could be forgotten—ignored? His unmeasured pride was stung to the quick: but hiding his wound under a stiff and offended air, he said:

"Enough! go when and whither you will."

"As soon as I shall have discharged a duty—placed under the sceptre of your Majesty's justice a person whom the Queen's friends themselves would deem worthy of your interest."

She beckoned to Aurore, who had stood at a distance, and added:

"Come hither, mademoiselle."

She obeyed, blushing with emotion.

"Sire, this Mdlle. du Tremblay, daughter of one of your old and faithful servants, who has been pursued by villains —perhaps seeking to repay upon the daughter of the former Governor of your royal prison of the Bastille, the grudge which they owed him and your Majesty. She begs to be placed under the safeguard of your justice and authority."

Louis examined Aurore who courteseyed to him, and he was impressed deeply by her angelic appearance and pure looks. La Montespan did not fail to mark the effect and a gleam of satisfaction sparkled in her eyes.

"Sire, the lady has been the victim of an audacious attempt to abduct her in the streets of Paris, almost in the day, and only by a miracle did she escape the ruffians. Speak, my young friend, lest his Majesty believe the event impossible."

The girl related the incident in a few telling words.

"By my soul," exclaimed the hearer, "Such a misdeed is not to go unpunished. The author shall be found out, for which I will give orders to my Police Lieutenant."

"I doubt not," said the marchioness, "that the perpetrator is some considerable personage who is above the laws."

"Madame," retorted Louis, frowning gravely, "know that

nobody in my kingdom may brave with impunity the laws, which are for all."

"Yet," persisted the marchioness, "I should beg measures to be taken for our safety, for I reckon on being accompanied to the Clagny Convent by this poor haunted girl."

The King held out his hand over Aurore's sunny head with a dignified gesture, and answered:

"Rest tranquil. The young lady is now beneath my protection. I shall take heed that everbody knows this, and woe to whomsover is guilty towards her of any enterprise of the kind stated."

"Oh, sire, how kind you are," faltered the girl.

"Thank me not," returned the ruler. "It is a prince's duty to watch over the repose and virtue of his subjects. A sweet duty to fulfill," he gallantly subjoined, without taking his gaze off Aurore, "when the object is the daughter of one of his gentlemen and is herself one of the most accomplished persons whom I have ever had the blessing to admire in my court."

"Your Majesty is too good," stammered the girl, no less confused by the look than by the compliment.

"Ha!" muttered the marchioness; "The fish nibbles—he will gorge this bait."

"If you must go," said the King to the elder lady, slowly and watching her now, "at least I may come at times to disturb your solitude? Besides, you must return when I shall have silenced ridiculous gossips and importunate counsellors —" Athenais shook her head hopelessly, but he continued: "If only to show your charming protégée that your pleading is not forgotten."

"If your Majesty commands, and Mdlle. du Tremblay requires a court presentation, we shall hasten. Otherwise—" She heaved a deep sigh and hid her face behind her fan. He may have thought to hide a tear—if so, it was one of glee and triumph.

The King turned away as well from the two ladies as from all the others and the courtiers, and leaning against a statue pedestal, he was buried in musing when—as if the marble were suddenly imbued with speech, he heard these words whispered in on odd voice:

" Is she not divinely fair?"

The King abruptly turned round and from his lips burst

the name of the Duke of Almada. It was, indeed, Aramis who had noiselessly glided up and saluted the King of France. The latter did not like this interruption; he liked the man as little. He had never forgotten the tragic episode in his youth, which we have related in the works entitled "Louise de La Vallière" and "The Man in the Iron Mask," but which might have borne the name of "The conspiracy of Aramis." Its object, it will be recalled, was to seat on the throne the elder and twin brother of Louis, who was incarcerated from his majority in the Bastille and terminated his wretched life in another prison, where he was seen by Athos and his son Bragelonne, while the prince was wearing the Iron Mask and was guarded by Captain d'Artagnan. The King remembered with horror that Aramis had dared to lay violent hands upon him, when he, assisted by the gigantic Porthos, abducted him by night from the Châteaux of Vaux, and crammed him into a dungeon, where he almost perished of terror, rage and despair. This old man beside him had once dethroned him to place in his stead his other self, and such deeds are never forgiven by kings Hence Louis XIV. would never forgive the Chevalier d'Herblay, the Bishop of Vannes, the comrade of Porthos du Vallon, the friend of Fouquet, and the Aramis who had extorted his terms from Anne of Austria, his mother. But Aramis knew what he was talking about when he assured Athos, during his flight from the royal justice, that he had but to reach Spain to reconcile himself with the King whom he flouted. Indeed, as General of the Jesuits, he had mounted to the Embassy of Spain for the French Court. The necessity of reasons of State Policy constrained Louis to welcome the Duke of Almada, the confident of his brother-in-law Charles II. Still it was almost without precedent that anybody should put a question to a King, and Louis assumed a stiff attitude and chilling haughtiness.

"My lord," he said in a tone in agreement with attitude and look, "methinks that you question me?"

"Heaven forbid that I should so far forget my respect," responded the old duke, bowing. "I only ventured to be the echo of your Majesty's thought, read on your august brow. Overlook, I pray you, my error or my wrongfulness in act."

"Of whom are you speaking?" demanded the King, a little affected by this keenness of sight.

"Of the lady who has just had the honor of conversing with your Majesty."

"Oh, true—Madame de Montespan was announcing her retirement to a nunnery, and——"

"A peaceful journey?" exclaimed Aramis, and then to himself he quickly said: "Into a nunnery. Ah, now she will be dwelling in my states—and I shall know all her moves." Aloud, he observed significantly, "It is of the other, the younger lady that I spoke. The marchioness is indisputably fair, but only the fairest of earthly creatures, while her companion is like an angel come down upon the earth. Mdlle. du Tremblay——"

"Then you know her?"

"Such is my happiness, and I take the liberty to add that never has a loftier and braver spirit inhabited a more perfect frame."

In the silence ensuing, the sovereign's hostility was fought against by a powerful curiosity.

"You began to say that Mdlle. du Tremblay——"

"She is of a good house in Anjou which has proven its value to the realm, and she deserves by her name, character and virtues whatever favors the King may shower upon her."

"For the moment, my lord, she asks for nothing: merely to be defended——"

"Defended? as though such an angel could have enemies."

"An attempt has been made to carry her off."

"Is it possible?"

"Some scoundrel who remains unknown, but I shall have him sought for and dealt with by my officers of justice."

The Duke of Almada did not flinch.

"Hold it as certain," he exclaimed with warmth, "that no one forms more ardent vows than I do for the punishment of the guilty. Ah, if I were half eighty years again, at the happiest period of life, when one is no longer a boy and not yet in the dry leaf—ah! to love, to reward and to punish—with one's own hand?"

His auditor sighed, for the second time.

"That is your Majesty's time of prime," said he, "though of age and death one should not speak to princes, and yet these sighs testify to an alarming state of mind for anyone of the opinion that jollity is the half of health."

"Duke, you are not looking on a happy man or king."

"When the saying is 'Happy as a king!' when from that point my august master is ready to make any sacrifices to preserve the good graces of your Majesty—it must not be as a monarch that you have become the fount of sighs—but, perchance, as a man——"

"The proverb you quote is mendacious like the rest. One of my citizens in Paris is happier than I. He acts as he pleases.'

"Well, why should not your Majesty act as the citizens do? when they are tired of the cold joint at home, they sally forth to dine at the eating-house. It is true that your Majesty may object that he has already tried dining out, and——"

"Duke," sharply, but the smile would come.

"If the triviality of the simile offends your Majesty, I will say plainly that I am afraid that your Majesty has a frightful attack of the blue devils. Take heed, my King!" said Aramis, cunningly seeming to return his old allegiance at this point of serving the sovereign, "The blue devils are the ones who tease one to death if not repelled in time, and the only recourse is to the prescription of Don Juan, who cured the heartache of one donna by turning to have the heartache through another."

The hearer wore a guarded manner.

"Pardy, duke! this counsel does not smack of the churchman, which once you were."

"Ah, sire, the reason is that before I wore the mitre, I shaded my brow with the red-plumed hat of your lamented Father's Musketeers. And then, if your Majesty allows me to babble, it is the habit of men of my age—natheless, there is good sense in the babble of some old men—I am astonished at the backwardness about imitating the citizen, who —disgusted by a servant-maid, sour, or grown beyond tenderness, or what you will, goes and gets another, more soft and accommodating. Albeit the King punishes me for this frankness in excess by revoking his usual kindness so far incessantly shown me, I will believe that the Marchioness de Montespan is the cause of the cares darkening your sovereign brow—it is she who by her impudence—the word is strong but true—has paraded a connection which her very interest and her gratitude impressed her to conceal as much as possible. She, I say, has led the Queen—who has hitherto suffered in silence of an incurable ailment : loving one whom a whole realm adores but who loves her not——"

"Duke!"

"It is the publication of this scandal which has brough\[t\] upon your anointed head the thunders of the preachers——'

"What, do you know—" began the King, fingering his canehead nervously.

"An ambassador is bound by his office to know everything in the court to which he is accredited. I knew also that your Majesty is on the eve of parting with the lady, and that it is done without regret on her side—for heaven has endowed your Majesty with too fine a perspicacity for it not to perceive that she loved you less for your sake than her own——"

"Not thus," sighed Louis, with melancholy, "not thus was I beloved by that poor La Valliere, and Fontanges."

"I know not how Mdlle. de La Valliere died," said the Spanish envoy, as I was not in the pleasant land of France, but as for the guileless Fontanges, whom poison slew, because he had a love for you without bounds or calculation——"

"Duke, this supposition," began the King, looking at the speaker with a kind of fright:

"Sire, the legel axiom, 'who profits by this crime?' is fully applicable here. But I am not going to have the irreverence to insist, since in his high wisdom, the sovereign wishes night to veil an atrocity so abominable. I confine myself to weeping over the inoffensive, unavenged victim."

"Alas!" sighed the monarch, shaking his head, "where shall I find another such as she?"

"Do not slander the sex, sire," quickly interposed the old duke, "thank heaven, all do not resemble the ambitious heiress of the Mortemarts. All do not reign by the ascendancy of a pitiless spirit and by the terror inspired by their transports and violence. To some exceptions, love is an entire, absolute and incessant sacrifice—a complete abnegation of self to the gain of the beloved object. These find all their joy and pride in seeing the first of the kings of earth lay by their side, in shade and silence, the burden of his grandeur and cares of kingship. In their monarch they adore not the glory of the crown or the harvest of honors and favors which crop up beneath his feet, but the handsome gentleman who kneels in passion and ardor to intoxicate them with caresses. They are delighted that the sovereign puts off, on the threshold of the hidden retreat, that supreme majesty which daz\[zles\]

zles the people. They prefer him as he is—asking but his affection and conspiring solely to make him happy. Only too happy to be selected by him from the garden of flowers, they have for him the most shining face, the blandest smile, and the most chaste heart—resembling those vestals of the Hindoo temples who, in the mysterious gloom, administer to the idol whom they are ever fated to worship."

The King's air spoke, as plainly as words : " Continue !' But the wily Aramis answered the mute invitation in this sentence : " Oh, sire, I have finished my sermon, which I greatly fear has taken too long a time. Your Majesty's ministers will accuse me of diverting it to the detriment of the state affairs."

" There is a time for all things, and I have still a question to put to you."

" I am ever at the orders of the King."

" Has this young daughter of the Tremblays no kinsfolk ?"

"Alas! she is an orphan, your Majesty, and it is on this deplorable condition that I wish to call your benevolent attention."

"I am listening to you !"

"This ward of the Marchioness de Montespan—in some degree mine, though she has not charged me to intervene in her favor—has repaired to Paris from her province to prosecute a hazardous lawsuit, on the winning of which depends her fortune, a pretty one, together with the subsistence of her young brother and sister—two children so young that she stands towards them as a little mother. Our Aurore is poor but proud beyond equal, and sues for nothing. Hence it is I who plead for her, thinking if some post could be given her, however humble, near your august person, its income would eke out her meager resources."

"You have reasoned very well," said the monarch gravely, as his countenance visibly cleared. "At the present moment, a post of reader is vacant in the Queen's household, which I accord to Mdlle. du Tremblay."

"Sire," returned the duke, bowing, "one cannot stay by your Majesty any length of time without every instant augmenting one's gratitude."

"Your ward may at once enter upon her duties. I will speak to the Queen presently on the subject, from whom you shall hear her announce the good news to your interesting orphan, should you come this evening, as I trust."

"I shall not think of failing," replied the old noble, bowing again.

"In that case, keep well until we meet this evening again, my dear duke!"

At these parting words, an ironical gleam passed over the arch-plotter's countenance. In the midst of the doffing of hats from the courtiers who had watched this dialogue from a distance, and the smiles of the ladies, Aramis joined Boislaurier whose arm he took once more.

"Well, my lord, have we the point?" asked the latter.

The old peer laughed with the muscles of his mouth without making a sound, and rejoined: "In faith, I am not complaining. The game is as good as won."

CHAPTER XVI.

DEEP WATERS RUN SMOOTH.

The Queen's cardparty was held in the royal apartment occupying the south wing of the palace. This hall, brilliantly illuminated, was literally crammed with the courtiers and ladies. In the midst, before a large fire in the chimney place, for, as a Spaniard, she was always chilled, Queen Maria Theresa was sitting at a card-table, between her ladies, and engaged at her favorite pastime. The Queen was short and stout, and when she walked or danced, her knees gave way, which still farther diminished her in stature: her teeth were spoilt by her excessive eating of sweet chocolate. She idolized her husband, and kept him in view when he was in the same room, and she would be happy all the day if once he smiled on her. If he were more kind than that, she would run around to tell how glad she was, to anybody who would listen to her.

He must have vexed her greatly to have such a spaniel growl at the favorite and hint of a return to Spain unless the marchioness were sent away.

The topic of the chatter was this very retirement of the favorite—in the low whispers some said " disgrace" and "exile" not pretty words, while all eyes were turned upon the proud marchioness. Without flinching she supported the weight of all the stares : gay and yet haughtily, she prattled in a group of her faithful friends, but the Widow Scarron had returned to Paris to look after her royal nurselings. Aurore du Tremblay was isolated in a window recess and looked on without seeing, and heard the conversation without heeding it.

"The King !" called out a page.

The King entered with his Minister Louvois. All the groups made a movement to concentrate where the new arrival should come to a halt: all heads bowed to the sovereign and all the women bent like the tall sunflowers to the magnificent Apollo. Louis wore no fierce aspect on this occasion ; his demeanor was rather contented and kindly.

"Do not let me be a spoil-sport," he said to the Queen who made a pretence of rising. "Let no one be disturbed by me. I wish and desire so. What were you saying, my lord ?" he continued, but addressing the Minister of War Louvois.

"Sire, I have the honor to inform your Majesty that the Duke of Lorraine has thrown his forces into Freiburg, where he menaces our Alsatian strongholds, insufficiently garrisoned, I am sorry to admit, as our troops have not had time to cross the Rhine on their return out of Flanders——"

The King did not heed, for his attention was traveling with his gaze elsewhere; finally, discovering Mdlle. du Tremblay, behind the marchioness, to whom he hastened to make a sign.

"Very well," said he, interrupting the minister, " to-morrow in the Council, we will remedy this evil which you point out."

Meanwhile the Queen had not taken up the cards, and like the rest of the assemblage, who held their breath, she waited—some important event was about to take place.

In the midst of this silence and curiosity, La Montespan detached herself from the group formed by her friends. She crossed the hall with a measured step suiting her figure and bearing of a Juno, her gaze scanning the spectators with the proud serenity of one who despised enemies, of which for three parts the gathering was composed. On arriving by the card-table, and bending to Maria Theresa with a humility too deep not to be ironical, she spoke with calculated slowness and contemptuous tranquility :

"Will your Majesty allow me to inform her of my resolution to leave the court and retire into my domain of Clagny ? in case the Queen deigns to give her assent to this project ?"

Everybody understood the sting in this latter phrase.

"My lady the Marchioness," replied the daughter of King Philip II., with fairly concealed joy on her face and in her tone, "I have no right to prevent your desires being accomplished. It is the King who may retain or grant you leave. No doubt his Majesty, whom you should have consulted before turning to me, will have communicated his will : whatever it decided upon was well decided."

The marchioness courteseyed again with the same emotionless calmness ; she never lost her smile, which crushed feigned compassion and glutted hatred. She took a step to regain her place, when the Queen asked her to stay an instant. The favorite stopped with an inward shudder ; she felt that a stab was about to be dealt to her.

" Mention has been made to me," proceeded Maria Theresa, " of a noble orphan young lady whom you have warmly recommended to his Majesty's bounty. I mean to do something for her. Is this Mdlle. du Tremblay present ?"

"She is here," responded Louis with blundering eagerness, and he pointed out Aurore, who immediately became the cynosure of all eyes.

" Draw nearer, lady," said the Queen, and the girl approached, in a flutter.

The marchioness had lost her color. She seemed to recoil upon herself with a view of leaping in between Aurore and the sovereign.

" Madame," faltered she in a voice wherein anger and astonishment struggled. "Mdlle. du Tremblay needs no help, I thank heaven——"

"From this moment, no need," returned Maria Theresa coldly. "You are right, for, henceforward she belongs to my household. She takes the place left vacant by Mdme. d'Aigueperse, and will be installed by the Mistress in Superintendence into that office to-morrow."

The favorite did not retort, for there is no contesting with the Queen. But her eyelids burned red amid the pallor of her visage, and through them one barely perceived the baleful glance of the bruised viper.

In the meantime, Aurore, however much surprised at this unexpected boon, and tottering under the general scrutiny, bent the knee to Maria Theresa, and murmured:

"Oh, what have I done to merit such a favor?"

"Rise, child," said the Spanishwoman, holding out her hand to help her up, "and recover yourself. I have been told that your father left no property, though he had long and faithfully served the realm. What I am granting, with the assent and from the initiative of the King, is no favor, as you seem to believe—but a beginning of reparation : that is all. Duchess," she went on, to Madame de Montausier, her chief lady in attendance, "place Mdlle. du Tremblay near yourself. It is understood that she is not to quit you until we shall have lodged her in the rooms which you will have made ready for her."

The Marchioness de Montespan walked towards Louis, with her pupils shooting out the blueish flame which may be seen in the wild beasts' eyes after dark. Her voice hissed between her nearly closed teeth, to utter these words:

"Well contrived, sire—my compliments to you. But this is not the last round and I have yet to play!"

On the royal face was a surprise too great not to be assumed for a purpose.

"Really, I do not follow your drift," he said; "did you not beg me to look after the welfare of this poor girl? Am I not giving you satisfaction when I place her for safety under my roof and near the Queen?"

Now, the cardplaying went on. Maria Theresa smiled, though she was losing, for she did not know how to cheat as the ladies of quality did in her day. In all the above, her august master had approved of her by a sly glance. All agreed that the slighted Queen had this time shown good sense, dignity and energy. All likewise hailed the new reader's beauty, modesty, bearing and ease from frequentation of good society. The general sentiment was friendly towards her.

Mdme. de Montespan was shunned, but she was not an antagonist whom one reverse defeated thoroughly. She silenced her rage and hid her spite under the armor of her pride.

Meanwhile the King, circling around like a butterfly, had reached the place where Aurore stood—too unknown for anybody to congratulate her on any pretext.

"Well," he inquired, after saluting her with the respectful courtesy which he lavished upon the sex "are you satisfied, lady?"

She stammered some words of thanks which he interrupted,

"It is not to me you should offer these. But to your friend whose earnest entreaty furnished me with the means of repairing forgetfulness which was growing into a fault."

At the same time, he stood aside and disclosed the ex-Bishop of Vannes.

"The Chevalier d'Herblay!" ejaculated Mdlle. du Tremlay.

"The Spanish Ambassador, the Duke of Almada," the old noble smilingly corrected her. At the Golden Heron, did I not promise you should hear from me?"

Aurore looked at him in astonishment, murmuring:

"It is to you, then, that I owe this benefit?"

He interrupted her by taking her hand with the prelate's unction and kissing it with the Musketeer's gallantry.

"I am your servant—your friend, if you deem me worthy of the title—and your physician, as you may remember my experience on the Saumur highway."

"As though I could forget!"

"Well, it is from that point of view that I forbid any transports of gratitude at present. You may make up for it by-and-by when I shall have done for you all that I intend." He emphasized this pledge with an odd accent. Lowering his voice still more, he concluded: "Meanwhile, allow me to ask a few minutes' hearing—not here, or this evening—a private audience—it cannot be dangerous with one of my age!"

Mdlle. du Tremblay reflected briefly before she resolutely answered:

"My lord duke, I am the more happy to confer with you from my having an entreaty to address to you."

"Is this true?"

"The generous support which you have lent me without my knowledge, and offer to continue, embolden me to entrust to you the secret which torments me and the grief with which I am overburdened."

It was the duke's turn to look at her, stupefied. She hung her head with deep despair.

"Alas!" she sighed, "amid these unexpected boons which Providence sends me, my soul is sad like one's about to die."

"Is this possible?"

"You can relieve me of doubt and ignorance which is killing me."

"Do anything you like with me, my dear child." Laying a finger on his lips, he pursued: "But, hush! this is not the place or the time to exchange confidence, where they are watching and listening. I hear," he added, "that you are to stay with the head-Mistress of the Queen's ladies until you have your own rooms. The Queen does not rise till noon, and I will call on you to-morrow."

As he rose after bowing, a hand touched his shoulder. It was the King's who was returning after going around the room, and distributing those compliments which are known as "court holy-water."

"My lord duke," said he, "I shall have something to say to you on my leaving the State Council to-morrow."

Mdlle. du Tremblay was installed in Montausier House, which had a mean exterior but the apartments were vast, handsome and nicely planned. One of the first floor parlors was given to her to receive the Spanish Ambassador. She sat on the sofa, and her elbow rested on soft cushions as her hand sustained her drooping head. Her eyes were burning. And yet it did not seem that she had cause to fret or weep. In one day, without efforts, she had won the aim of her life—the object of every petticoat-wearer in France—royal favor!

A country girl, blended with the herd, with no money or credit, fighting with bad fortune for her existence and that of others dear to her, she was this day with a footing at court. Her post was beside the Queen; the King had given her a welcome; the men bowed down to the ground to her and the ladies began to be jealous. The whole appeared like a dream.

But the acute suffering which pierced her heart was real enough.

For a month she had no news of Joel. Widow Scarron did not tell her the truth. Made restless by the strange disappearance, the latter sent Honorin to the Blackamoor Tavern, where the servant questioned the landlord, who related how his lodger was arrested, and he had not hidden the cause. The royal governess knew too well with what a dreadful penalty the Tribunal of Honor punished those who infringed the edicts. Louis XIV. had always shown himself severe towards duelists. She recoiled from the idea of driving to despair—perhaps to death, the girl whom she had brought back to life, by telling her for what fate the Breton was reserved.

Subsequently Mdlle. du Tremblay was presented to the Marchioness de Montespan. The latter was admitting to herself that her charms were becoming too mature longer to retain her royal lover. She planned to have a voice in the choice of her successor, whom she hoped to make her own pliant instrument, so that she still would rule. Aurore, without relatives, fortune or will of her own, seemed to her just the obedient doll she looked for to play the part. Hence she had hastened to offer her services.

The innocent girl did not suspect the design. She had accepted with gratitude the favorite's assistance. But the sentiments inspired by the latter did not include confidence : hence she had preserved her heart's secret. She wept for the lost squire, but in concealment.

Her meditation was broken by the footman, coming to announce the Duke of Almada. The latter entered briskly and with a winning mien to take a seat near the young lady, who had risen to receive him. He waved her with his hand to resume her place.

"Come, come, my child," said he paternally : "why is such sorrow on your sweet face ? why are your cheeks so pale and your eyes so red ? Yesterday you were blessed with one of those godsends which most women would covet."

"My lord duke, I am in distress because a witness is lacking to my happiness—" she hesitated.

"Why this emotion?" said the nobleman with an encouraging smile. "I have been in holy orders and was wont to hear confessions much more painful than what you may have to avow. Is there any need to tremble at undergoing the universal fate of being in love ?"

Mdlle. du Tremblay hid her face in her hands, and muttered :

"Have you, indeed, guessed ?"

"With no need to be a great wizard. I had only to watch on your countenance the reflections from your candid mind. Besides, could anything else happen in a court full of dazzling cavaliers, with burning eye and winsome speech?"

Aurore shook her head.

"The man dearest to me is not a noble of the court."

"Oh, then, it is some friend of your childhood, or companion of your youth, some kinsman, perhaps, whom you left in your province of Anjou?"

Aurore repeated her negative gesture, while the ambassador's sharp glance was studying her under the pretence of good humor.

"In any case," he proceeded, "it cannot be any lowborn fellow. A girl of your birth and character does not look below her to make one of those selections which raise a blush. A Tremblay never stoops to conquer a husband."

"My lord duke," quickly protested Aurore, "M. Joel is a nobleman."

"Joel," reiterated the duke, seeming to reflect; 'whose name is this? methinks I have heard it somewhere before. Oh," he exclaimed, "of course! I recall it. The young gentleman of the Nantes coach! Now, I am quite at my ease, after your giving me such a fright. This is not a serious matter."

"I love him," observed Aurore firmly.

"Tut, tut! a girlish fancy! The youth does not lack some nobility in his style and bearing—it is a wayside romance, sketched out, but stopping at the first chapter."

"I love him," repeated Aurore.

"Yes, I am not ignorant that he defended you against some footpad or other and heaven forbid that I should gainsay your feeling some gratitude towards him; but lasting gratitude would degenerate into folly."

"I love him," said the girl for the third time, with the same determined tone and face.

The churchman also assumed a severe mien.

"Then," he said coldly, "you must find the courage to tear this unseemly passion from your heart. Everything at the same time commands you to do so—circumstances, your interest and future, and the prospects of others—even to the providential part which you are called upon to play."

"What do you mean?" exclaimed the girl, revealing all her astonishment.

"I say that the good fortune befalling you yesterday is nothing to that awaiting you to-morrow. In short, reality will surpass all that you may have ventured to conceive most fairylike and magical in your girlish dreams—you will be transported to the threshold of our paradise or the Empyrean of the pagans——"

"Gracious!' faltered she, "I cannot understand——"

"Hearken to me, my child, that all may be clear unto you."

He bent towards her, and speaking with studied slowness and in a low voice, so that she could the better hear and comprehend the sense and range of his words, without any of them crossing the room and being overheard, if by chance there were listeners—he said:

"Buried as you may have been in the country, some rumors must have reached you, so that you cannot be unaware what part was played in the court circle where you are entering, by Louis de La Vallière—the first love of our fickle sovereign. You likewise cannot be ignorant of the position held here at present by the Marchioness de Montespan, whose patronage you accept. You must have your opinion formed upon these two Egerias of a prince who, beginning as a Tarquin the Proud, wishes to end as Numa the Wise."

"It is true that the story has been told me of the former, and how cruelly she expiates not having resisted her heart: as for the second, I accepted her services—not without repugnance and self-resistance, as heaven be my witness! because I had urgent need of a shield of power against a stranger who persecutes me. To appreciate their conduct is a care that I leave to their conscience, which will awaken sooner or later; to the world of fashion, their accomplice; and to history which will judge them. As a Christian, I pity them."

"In any event, you must admit that their fate is worthy of envy. To reign over a king; dispose with both hands of his boons and favors; to assure the peace of Europe, or at pleasure, unchain the dogs of war upon the nations: inspire grand ideas; lead to the fulfillment of great deeds——"

"This, my lord, is the function of the Queen."

"If the Queen were able to accomplish it; in the first

place, she must have her husbands love—but our King never felt more than esteem for his; policy united them and temperament separates them.'

"Then I feel no less compassion for the lady neglected than for her successful rivals. Still, were the choice given me, I believe I should prefer her loneliness to their victory—but I own that I do not see——"

"To what I am tending? to this—the King has had a fresh passion spring up in his heart within a few hours——"

"He has ceased to love Mdme. de Montespan?"

"He is madly smitten with another!"

"Another?"

"An adorable creature, who need never dread the fate of the proud daughter of the Mortemarts, if she will listen to a true friend and second his views, in exchange for a devotion above proof: she will then realize the problem of fixing an erratic star—of making a capricious lover one of the most faithful——"

The temper paused to study on the hearer's countenance the effect of his opening exordium. She seemed to be searching for something in her mind.

"My lord, pray be indulgent," she muttered; "I am but a poor country girl, and really I wonder if——"

"What!" ejaculated the plotter, enjoying in advance the surprise he had ready to finish with, "have you not understood that it is you whom we are talking about?"

He certainly expected an outburst of amazement, real or simulated, and was much mistaken, for the girl remained dumb. It was evident that her intelligence refused to admit what she heard.

"Yes," said the ambassador, dwelling on his words, "it is you whom his Majesty loves; I am offering you a coronet, if not a crown for one word which, falling from your lips, will allow him to hope that you will receive the proofs of this love and its disclosure without anger."

Mdlle. du Treblay sprang up suddenly.

"God help me!" she cried, "the King loves me? loves me?"

In her eyes and her voice was immense apprehension, and she threw up her arms in front of her as though to repulse the words which she had heard. Almada also rose and he laid his hands on her shoulder with familiar authority.

"Calm yourself, child," he said. "You have a superior mind as I have a practical one. Do not let us waste time which we may turn to a better purpose. Therefore, I hasten to play aboveboard. The Company of Jesus, of which I am the General, means to preside in the Royal Council and direct its policy. Help us thoroughly and we will sustain you to the utmost limits. Would you like to govern France with us? I leave you the solid part of the realm and the better task—to do good where others have only done ill. If you were an ordinary woman, I should picture to you the court prostrated at your feet, the dazzling of festivals, the concert of homage, and the incense rising for you to share with the demi-god whom Europe considers as arbiter of its destinies. But you are as good as fair, and I simply say unto you—So far the people have cursed the favorites who preceded you; Let them learn to bless you."

Aramis stopped again, not of his own accord, but from the effect of his words. A burning glare blazed in his auditress's eyes. A purple flush mounted to her cheeks, while she opened her mouth to speak. But the words, though scathing her lips, were not uttered. Her eyelids fell like veils over the lightning glance, and she became calm again. She gently disengaged herself from the old noble's grip, and proceeded towards the door.

"Where are you going?" inquired the other.

"To quit this house," was her curt answer in a broken voice; " I leave the town, too, for return to my native village in Anjou, where the peasants have not yet learnt to cease to respect the daughter of their old master."

"Going away? but this is madness! After what you have heard?"

"It is precisely what I heard that commands me to remain not another instant in a place where I have been insulted. Oh, I do not care to hurt your feelings—I am not one who repays insult in the same coin. Besides, I am firmly persuaded that you did not believe you were insulting me. That is credible enough; for the world in which you dwell and in which I entered yesterday, regards as a glory what I call a shame. I was alone and moneyless, and you offered me the means to become rich and mighty. This is great kindness on your part, and I must beg your pardon for not being on the level of the task which you deemed me worthy to accomplish. How could things be otherwise when I am a Puritan, with odd ideas about honor. I should rather fall dead on the side of the ditch, clad in tatters, with the beggar's wallet slung round my neck, than be satiated with royal favor and endearments, in the glitter of jewels, rank and fortune. I should mar your court with my foolish prejudies: humiliate it it with my silly pride; slight it in my ridiculous innocence. This is why I doom myself to blight, obscurity and poverty; why I do not even await the issue of the lawsuit in which I am engaged and which I feel that I am incapable of winning in the usual way; why I accept for my dear ones the poverty which blemishes my father's name, but which, at the worst, will not stain our family blason. Farewell, my lord duke. We are never to meet again. In the retreat where I shall live between labor and prayer, I promise to remember you only from our first meeting, and I shall force myself to forget how badly a nobleman mistook me and insulted me as the King himself has no right to do. For, granting that he loved me, at least, he did not offend me by proposing I should be his mistress."

While Aurore was speaking in this high and noble strain, Aramis was reflecting. When he had fully meditated, his new batteries were in line. He was now a more dangerous plotter than when he conceived to substitute one royal brother for another at Vaux. When Mdlle. du Tremblay walked with a statue's step up to the door, she found he had glided in between and a complete change had taken place on the duke's countenance. Tears moistened his eyes; his lineaments expressed a joyous emotion without equal; his voice quivered as he said, in turning to the girl with a supplicating gesture:

"Oh, my child, my dear child, how happy you have made me. How greatly I admire you! How great is my love and my esteem!"

Before such a brusque outburst, Aurore receded and uttered not a syllable, but her face was eloquent in its profound amaze.

"To think that I was on the verge of doubting you. Yes I doubted you—I confess—but only for a space. I feared that you would succumb beneath the test."

"Test? was that a test?" almost screamed the girl.

Aramis lowered his head with a chagrined air, and replied *in a reproachful tone:*

"Did yon not suspect it? true, true, I went too for—much too far! But I wished to know the whole." He took her by the hand and led her to the sofa. "I vowed to ascertain what you might secret. And what have I met but the purest honor, and all that embellishes and sanctifies the heart of woman?"

Aurore was still repeating: "A test?" for she distrusted yet. "So," she said slowly, "what you said but now——"

"That was mere fable, of which I beg you no more to think——"

"The King——"

"The King holds no other feelings towards you than any gallant gentleman may declare to any honorable girl—and he is now casting off the Marchioness de Montespan solely to be disentangled as regards the Queen. Alas!" he went on, with a sad shaking of the head, "this furnace, the court, into whose hot breath you have but stepped, must quickly and fatally sear the finest minds, for you to believe that an old man with white hair like me, a nobleman by winning his spurs on the battlefield and by his descent, the representative of a great power and an illustrious sovereign, I, in short, *I* was capable of descending to pander even for a King!"

"My lord?"

"Oh, cruel, unjust and wicked: how you on your side mistook me! But how sharply you have punished me by putting faith in a ruse of which I had not foreseen the effects!" Again his tone and expression altered, while he added with a touch of vanity admirably assumed: "I grant that I played my trick with art. Condemn me if you will, but own that you were my dupe."

She laid a hand on her heart.

"I was caused much pain," she sighed.

"Still again," he said, drawing her to him with a fatherly action, "overlook this. It was that deuced professional pride of ours. We diplomatists fall into such a habit of deceiving and feigning——"

In the pause, the duke secretly observed the girl. At the end of a minute, she raised her lovely, clear and ingenuous eyes and questioned:

"Why was this test made?"

The ex-Musketeer's teeth were impressed on his lip.

"Why did you play this comedy?" persisted Aurore, "Why put yourself to so much trouble? Why cause me so much pain?"

In the time it took her to frame the questions, he had shaped his reply.

"Do you mean to tell me that you do not guess?" She shook her head. "What, you have not reflected that the righteous aim I had, justified my plan? It was necessary for the Queen's future peace that she should not again harbor a viper at her side. How many innocent-seeming intriguantes have sought to mount into the royal favor by first obtaining a hold in the Queen's service? these would have thrown aside the devoted lover who was of lowly birth compared with the ruler of France: but you on the contrary trample on everything between you and the object of the great and holy love filling your heart. I was in my right in asking if in uniting you to that object, I should not expose myself to hearing you reproach me some day for having been the keystone of your happiness, if not of your golden fortune. And he whom you choose will share your scruples. He may be one who shrinks lest you blame him for the humility of his line being an obstacle to your rising with him to where you are lawfully free to aspire—your longings are legitimate for luxury, fame and grandeur. Thus thinking, I tried to tempt you, and the experiment has fully succeeded, at least. You have refused a throne to keep yourself for the man of your heart. What more convincing proof can I desire of an affection and a disinterestedness which nothing in the future can have the power to weaken?"

The girl's charming features had at length brightened. Her youthful beauty seemed to send out rays.

"My lord," she faltered, "you are speaking of Joel."

"Why, of whom else was I to speak save the lucky dog who has the inestimable chance of being distinguished by such a treasure?" rejoined the old duke, with liveliness.

"Do you know, then, what has become of him all this month?"

"Do I know?"

Truth obliges us to admit that Aramis did not have the faintest clue; but a diplomatist of his mark ought never to be caught napping.

"You have seen him?" inquired Mdlle. du Tremblay.

"As you will see him before a great while. But," he added guardedly, "you must ask him for the explanation of his mysterious absence."

"Will he come to St. Germain?"

"Of course," replied the duke, with a goodnatured smile, "he will be forced to come, unless you want to have the wedding celebrated in another place."

"Wedding?"

"That follows since I told you I had made up my mind to make you both happy."

Aurore fixed on him a steady gaze.

"Has M. Joel found what he was seeking, then?" she inquired.

This was not a question for which Almada was prepared and he was disconcerted; he mused: "What on earth was the young rogue seeking for?" But he was obliged to reply, and do so at once, as the girl's eyes were imperiously questioning him. "He has found it?" he said with assurance. "But not without pains, and the task took time."

"But you aided him, I will engage?" proceeded the other with a sincere flow of thankfulness.

"Oh, you inquisitive child!" he retorted, shaking a finger at her. "Nothing can be hidden from her. Well, yes, I aided him with all my power."

She held out her hand.

"How I thank you if, with heaven's help, Joel has found a name?"

"Oho!" thought the ex-prelate, "It is a name he is after? Our loving swain has come to find or make a name in Paris. Well, let us give him one for a present, which will rob no one—A name?" he exclaimed, "A title more like—Chevalier de Locmaria! That sounds rondly and looks right, as he comes from Belle-Isle, where I had reason to remember Locmaria, one of my parishes. And—" here a cloud passed over his brow, " was it not in one of its sea-graven caves that my poor Porthos died?"

He looked so serious that she forbore to speak, but, recovering, he said:

"But I am wishful to leave your betrothed the pleasure of relating all that has happened to him since your parting. The chevalier will be beside you in a few days; for it is a settled thing that you will remain at court?" But Aurore's face wore alarm and repugnance, and he persisted: "You must, my child. The Queen has much need of one like you. The poor lady has not a soul near her to whom she can confide her woes and have them shared. The friendship which she will inevitably accord you and the very high esteem in which the King holds you, will help you to a reconciliation of the couple which all desire and which will be a benefit to the state."

"My lord, I shall remain."

"Ere long, besides you will rest on a husband's arm. I will do my utmost to obtain from both their Majesties the consent to your union. They will feel pleasure in signing the contract as witnesses, and as a kind of wedding present, I warrant the Chevalier of Locmaria will receive some rank which will allow him to be near you. But," he went on, looking at his watch, "the hour is striking for you to go on duty, and I myself have an appointment with the King on his leaving the Council-room. Let us part, my dear Aurôre."

She held up her forehead which he lightly kissed, murmuring "I might easily be your grandfather!" At the threshold, he called: You will shortly see me. With *him!* Meanwhile, be so kind as not to forget me in your prayers."

"Be sure of that, my good lord," returned the girl. "In my heart you have a place like God and Joel."

CHAPTER XVII.

MAKING A KNIGHT OF HIM.

In the renovation of St. Germain's by the famous **Mansard**, a covered way around the building was replaced by a verandah, which was called the Gallery. Here, on coming from the Council of State, Louis XIV. was accustomed to receive applicants for favors and those for whom he had communicaions. Here Almada proceeded after quitting our heroine.

On the way from Montausier House to the palace, the old duke distributed to the passers-by all sorts of nods and smiles and caresses with the hand, which betrayed the former church dignitary. Nobody would have suspected the turmoil in his brain and the mental labor he underwent, to see his smiling mien, the gallant and yet guarded looks at the pretty women, and the exquisite art with which he graduated the marks of politeness according to the rank of those he met.

"This Joel must be found again," he mused as he strolled in the sunshine in order to warm himself. "I have promised her so. It is the sole means to save the situation of affairs bungled by the monstrous innocence of this young girl whom I have arrived in time to place in the contest for the favorite's vacated post. This must be done to retain this virgin at the court, for it is highly necessary that she should not leave St. Germain. It is certain that the King cherishes her under his heart-wing, and I will put my hands in the fire if he has not asked me hither this morning to speak to me about her. Yes, but where am I to unearth this young rustic? He will hamper my projects and, absent, he may upset them. Just think that I believed I knew all about the softer sex from having half-a-century's experience with them, and this one nonplusses me. By Jove! as I used to swear when I wore a sword by my side, to see me beaten by a silly maid's scruples —I, who was the lover of that whirlwind in a fardingale called the Duchess de Chevreuse; the confidential friend of Queen Anne of Austria in her amour with the Duke of Buckingham: the dashing, lady-killing Musketeer; the priest-confessor of a bevy of fashionable penitents; the beholder, if not the actor, of all the merry intrigues which enlivened the end of the last reign and the beginning of this. It is true that I never met any such squeamishness in the Duchess, or the Queen, or Mazarin, or my penitents, or Fouquet's lady-loves, or the early love-conquests of this King. All the same, a philosopher—it might be me—was very right in saying that woman is capable of anything—even of doing good and acting well."

On entering the Gallery, the first persons whom the Spanish Ambassador caught sight of was Lord Nicholas de Lareynie, Lieutenant General of the Royal Police. Under his arm was a large portfolio, stuffed with papers of all kinds. The newcomer walked up to him, and said after the exchange of the usual courtesies:

"Bear my lord, since you are the man who best knows everything going on in the capital, pray try to enlighten me on the fate of a fine young fellow, who much interests me, and who has been missing this month."

"My lord duke, I am devotedly yours."

"This youth has lately arrived from his province of Brittany. From Belle-Isle, if I am rightly informed: honest of face, costume of his country, the figure and bearing of a young athlete. As a special token, the longest sword by his side that any living man wears—I never but once saw its mate."

"Oho!" exclaimed the magistrate, starting with surprise "this succinct portrait puts me in mind of an acquaintance. I declare, it would be odd if you were seeking the very man of whom I came to confer with his Majesty. He had fists to knock down a wall, eh?"

"That agrees."

"He answers to the name of Joel, too?"

It was now the duke's turn to be astonished.

"Joel—it is so. Do you know where he is?"

"He is in the Bastille, of course."

"In the Bastille?"

"In proof of which, I have had the governor's deputy asking me in what style he is to be treated. You may not be unaware, duke, that at the Bastille, each prisoner receives fare and accommodation occording to his position, quality, fortune and the private instruction sent with his committal warrant by the head of the realm."

The old friend of the late Bastille Governor, Montlezun, did know this from afar back; so, interrupting the Police Lieutenant, he asked:

"But why was the poor lad clapped into jail?"

"A very bad case," answered Lareynie, scratching his wig with an ivory back-scratcher carved into the semblance of an open hand, as was the fashion; "violation of the edicts, a duel ending in a man's death—this poor lad, as you call him, in plain, ran a Musketeer officer through the body."

"Heaven forbid?"

"As a matter of course, he was arrested, and the constabulary opened an inquest on the matter; but as he could not supply proofs that he was nobly born, these judges of points of honor would not derogate to try him, and we are all in a quandary. In what court is he to be tried? I have come to have his Majesty's idea on the subject."

As he spoke the functionary drew from his letter-case a sheet of parchment written with a wide margin and inscribed for a heading : " Report for H. M. the King ?" He handed this document to the duke, saying : " Do you mind, while we are waiting, taking a look over it ?"

Aramis had no objections. Thus he knew to a jot all that had befallen our hero. He had finished when the King came out of his closet, with an air of good humor. On his entering the Gallery, Lireynie started to hand him the report on the Joel Case, which the ambassador had returned to him; but the monarch, who had perceived his companion, said : " Presently, my lieutenant," and taking the envoy of Spain by the arm, he observed ; " I am obliged to you for keeping the appointment."

" Oh, sire," rejoined the old courtier, making as supple as it was noble a bow, " the wishes of the sovereign are orders to me. Moreover," he added, after a pause, " if your Majesty had not deigned to evince his intention of meeting me this morning, I should nevertheless have waited to see him come by—having accepted from him the office to offer homage to which I venture to hope the recipient will not show hers altogether insensible."

" Homage ?"

" I mean by that ! to bear to her the expression of feelings with which overflows towards him the most sincere and grateful of hearts."

The ruler's cheeks were covered with bright red, and his eyes sparkled with deep satisfaction.

" Ah, you have seen Mdlle. du Tremblay ?" he greedily inquired.

" I have just left her," replied the diplomatist, smiling to himself at having so swiftly guessed how things stood.

" Then, she does not seem very much displeased with her new position ?"

" Ah, sire, it is more than gratitude which she professes towards your Majesty, but adoration, poorly constrained by the bounds of respect owed by the subject to her sovereign. Yesterday she was stunned and abashed. Think how little she expected the signal favor of which she was the object ! And then her heart's transports were paralysed by the union of gladness, perplexity, amazement, and confusion before the King and the Queen, and the whole court whose bold curiosity, in way of speaking, distracted her. But, this morning, after a night passed in fever from intoxication, almost incredulity, with what eloquence has she spoken of her august benefactor! with what ardor she declared to me her devotion to her royal mistress and her worship for her master! with what emotionful and passionate accents she repeated to me on my leaving : ' Oh, my lord duke, the King is the most generous as he is the most noble of his gentlemen in the kingdom.' "

"Did she really hold this language ?" interrogated Louis, his voice trembling with pleasure.

"And as I merely asked her what had most struck her in the brilliant assemblage which she saw for the first time yesterday, you should have known with what freedom and simplicity she responded: 'Do not question me, for I do not know how to answer. I saw none but the King, and I am dazzled like the rash creature who looks up at the sun.' "

These words were too much like those which poor Louise de la Vallière uttered, in the hearing of the King, twenty years before, under the Royal Oak at Fontainebleau, for the hearer not to recall that scene. All the sweet savor of youth returned with its freshness and sharpness, though saddening, like the scent from a flower found dried in a book. But the memory was sufficiently strong.

"For this girl is chasteness itself" pursued Almada. "Her soul knows no more of falsehood than her lips. It is one detached from all earthly lust, the sanctuary of all lofty aspirations and sublime devotion. Those lips are as strange to coquetry as to kisses."

In hearing the ambassador, the "Grand Alcander," was intoxicated with ambrosia. This affection, mingled with respect and a dread that made the woman prostrate herself before its object, was a dish of spice for one who liked rare delicacies. What flattery could equal, in his eyes, the being taken for a demi-god ? But as he strove above all to seem to be beyond human weakness, he forced himself to dissimulate under a mask of ordinary pleasure the joy and pride which lifted him to the seventh heaven.

"My lord," he resumed after a short silence, "it was precisely of Mdlle. duTrembly that I waited to speak with you. She belongs to a family of faithful servants whom we have **wrongfully** neglected for some time. Were the members still on earth, rewards in proportion to their services should certainly seek the obscurity into which their modesty retained them until their death. In the child we shall repair the involuntary harm caused her parents by our ungrateful forgetfulness. Mdlle. du Tremblay shall be a Lady of the new Palace."

"But, sire, the rule is that the husband shall be the wearer of the honors which carry this title," remonstrated the ex-prelate.

"We will select a husband worthy of our royal ward, and we count upon your excellence to aid us in this act."

"Oh, sire, how your Majesty divines and thoroughly carries out one's wishes! I was proposing to lead the King's solicitude upon the isolated state of this poor girl! it was my design to supplicate my prince to give her a protector and place her in a family."

"This is what we shall do; we charge you to find among our nobility some gentleman who merits obtaining such a treasure, and in the wedding presents shall be a title for the chosen one to some post in our household."

The ambassador smiled as he replied: "There is no need for me to exhaust my power of research to find this privileged person, as I have at hand a young friend who will esteem himself only too happy to unite his fate with the amiable lady's whom your Majesty honors with his bounty. It is a Breton gentleman without ambition as without attachments."

"What is his name?"

"It is the Chevalier de Locmaria, if your Majesty will allow him to wear that title."

"He shall be the Chevalier de Locmaria."

"Only, I am not going to conceal from your Majesty that he has a wild and primitive character, abrupt and rough, badly suited for life in the court, and I daresay he would prefer to make his way in the army."

"Let that be so, too—he shall have an officership."

"And if there were fighting going on, he would gladly be sent to the front."

"Well, we will send him to Marshal Créqui, who is to operate against Prince Charles of Lorraine and Freiburg."

"Good! he will be pleased. I know my Breton, who is a *lover of* battle and hungry for danger and glory. All he longs for is a chance to distinguish himself before the enemy and he will not shrink from the forlorn hopes and other desperate movements entrusted to daring spirits who carry their life in their hands." He laughed like a funeral knell, faintly heard. "But who can help a young daredevil becoming a hero at the cost of his life?" He paused, but he said all that was necessary.

The two had returned to the part of the Gallery whence they started, and Lareynie was patiently waiting, with his portfolio under his arm and the report in his hand.

"Sire," remarkd Almada, "your Police Lieutenant is waiting for the proper moment to have an audience granted, and I should feel ashamed to retain the King any longer."

"Ah," said Louis, glancing at the scroll held out to him, "This relates to that daring duelist who draws his sword under our very windows. A bold rogue, by my faith! How is it he has not yet been tried?"

The Spanish Ambassador interrupted Lareynie, about to reply. "Sire, it is long been said that clemency is the brightest jewel of monarchs as the right to pardon is their finest appanage."

"On my soul, duke," said the King, eyeing him with astonishment, "I like to think that you will not intervene on behalf of this bully——"

"I venture upon this piece of audacity."

"You are going to ask me the pardon of this rebel?"

"I beg more than that—his immediate setting at liberty."

"But a duelist is a murderer!"

"Hence I apply to the royal generosity, not to mercy."

"Do think what you are doing," said the King, stiffening his bearing and tone. "Put the fellow at liberty who has trampled on our signature at the foot of the edicts—killed one of our military servants—and has not even the excuse that he is of noble blood."

"Nay," returned the ambassador, placidly, "it is allowable for a Breton, fresh from his native hamlet, not to know all the edicts——"

"Eh, is the rascal a Breton?" asked the King, softening his voice.

"As for his nobility that is rather dubious—but he can be ennobled at any time by your Majesty. As for the dead Musketeer, there is no lack of them, your Majesty having two companies, each five hundred strong. Besides, judging by the statement, this deceased M. de Bregy was not the finest sample of French chivalry——"

"But still his murderer——"

"Adversary, if you will allow it——"

"Be it so—his adversary seems very dear to you?"

"Not the least in the world; I hardly know him and only once met him, but he is useful to me, which is of much more importance."

"Useful? what could you do with him?"

Aramis looked the speaker in the face and replied, lowering his voice but giving each syllable a value:

"If it please your Majesty, I should make him the Knight of Locmaria, and the husband of Mdlle. du Tremblay."

CHAPTER XVIII.

THE FELLOW PRISONER.

IT is high time to return to our friend Joel.

Fortunately, there is no fear but we shall find him where we left him, as the Bastille guarded its prisoners with only to great abundance of ditches, ramparts, bars, bolts, locks, wardens, soldiers, and spies for anyone to go forth unallowed, unless he wore wings, or had the patience in digging his way out which Latude exhibited.

Joel was incarcerated in that one of the eight towers called the Basinière. His cell was on the third floor of it.

At the first, the unhappy youth was like one stunned by the violence of the shock befalling him: motionless, dulled, he had no sight but the terrible state prison whose name the jailer had shouted to him on leaving him. Shaking himself at last like one casting aside the clinging effects of a nightmare, he had looked around and made the circuit of his room—which did not take long. Instinct being strong, he went to the window for air and light—a small loop-hole, doubly grated with thick iron bars.

Hapless Joel!

This robust countryman, habituated to drink in pure air as he raced over the heaths or on the beach, in the forests or along the cliffs, was now reduced to draw breath through a mere crevice. It was too narrow for him to insert his head. He could barely descry a patch of sky on which nothing was outlined—not even a treetop, a weathercock, or a spiral column of smoke.

The captive examined the worm-eaten table, covered with a worn cloth, which, with a bed and a stool, formed the furniture. He felt the bed, which struck him as hard, and finally returned to a seat on the stool, where he gave himself up to the saddest reflections.

So, he was in jail, under the possibility of being condemned to capital punishment! in that quarter, no illusion was possible: the crime was evident, the law formal; the tribunal would surely doom the culprit, and there were nine chances and a half that the King would sign the death-warrant. Now, our hero did not dread death. But he longed for life. Particularly deplored its being cut short because of how he had meant to employ it: in accomplishing the task imposed by his mother, and afterwards in consecrating himself to making his beloved happy.

But in the midst of his higher, holier thoughts, nature asserted itself—Joel was hungry, thirsty and in need of rest. When his dinner was brought him, a copious one and well served, it must be admitted, which showed that the spirit of the former governor Baisemeaux still haunted the prison—he ate like a starved animal. The furniture was poor but the provender good. After which he flung himself on his bed, and slept as soundly as if he had been in the guest-room of the Blackamoor lulled by the ceaseless babble of little Friquet.

When he awoke at daylight, he had some difficulty in remembering where he was. But a glance on the surrounding walls told him that he was in the Bastille. As this confirmation drew a sigh from him the turnkey walked in and said:

"Exercise-time, master. If you like to come up to the tower top you can get some air that beats anything down in the streets. You can have a chat with the other gentlemen-prisoners, which will stir you up a bit." As he guided the new-comer through the maze of stairs and lobbies, he added: Besides, you will not make any long acquaintances as it appears that your trial will come off pretty soon. The major bade me announce that the constabulary recorder would look you up to communicate the decree, to-morrow."

The exercise took place on the "tower leads," or leaden roof. As there were five storeys, a prisoner to each, Joel met four strollers up aloft. On their countenances and clothes one could almost read the date of their imprisonment. Two of them were men in their fortieth year and were insignificant. The third was a man of medium stature and middle age, square-shouldered, and strongly built : he had a round, good-humored face, with a stupid eye and silly smile ; in short, the aspect of a citizen rather idiotic. The last was an old man of eighty, with long white locks and beard in disorder and vestments in tatters.

On the coming up of our hero into this sky-parlor, the first three eagerly asked :

"What's the news from Paris?"

"In sooth, gentlemen," was Joel's reply, "I am at a loss to satisfy you, from my being arrested when I had scarcely more than arrived from my province."

"So you were arrested?"

"Oddsbobs! I should think so. You did not come here for the pleasure of this promenade, I engage!"

"Well, no, they had certainly not."

"But what were you arrested for?" inquired the dull-eyed citizen.

The Breton related his adventure, at the termination of which the other remarked with a doleful wagging of the head : "By our Lady; your case looks black to me. The King does not joke with duelists. However, you have the advantage of knowing what you are shut up for."

"Do not all prisoners?" quickly asked Joel.

"Well, I do not in the least."

"Nor I."

"Neither do I."

The new-comer did not like to put the question to the old man, but as he looked at him inquisitively, the latter spoke.

"I am sorry for you, my gentleman," said he in a grave voice. "You will certainly suffer the fate of those executed for the same offence. The Cardinal has no pity."

"What cardinal?" inquired the Breton.

The other stared at him with astonishment.

"Can there be any other than his Red Eminence, Cardinal Richelieu?"

"Bless us! he has been dead these thirty years!"

"Are you sure?"

"And his successor, Cardinal Mazarin, is in the same state."

"But there is a King Louis XIII. yet?"

"No, he died before the latter and followed the former into the grave."

"Excuse me, monsieur," said the old man politely. "I was ignorant of these events, having entered here in the year of the birth of that King's first-born."

The Son of Porthos shuddered, for he had not spent as many hours in prison as this wretch had years! Still, out of all the prisoners, this one seemed the most calm and resigned. In the evening when the warden brought supper, he asked who the aged man was.

"That's Number 68," responded the man carelessly.

"And the others?"

"Oh, they are 123, 136 and 141."

The key-bearer condescended to explain that the Bastille's guests lost their names in entering and were distinguished merely by numbers; the servants knew not the motives for their detention, and the governor would not in most cases know unless he himself questioned them. In many cases, however, they knew as little as himself.

"Then, I am a number, too?" queried the squire.

"Not yet," replied the turnkey, "for you are an exception. It has not been seen fit to supply you with one, as it does not look as though you would get blue-mouldy here;—it is given out," he added, with a grin, "you will have your head off next week."

Next day, as had been foretold, the prisoner saw, entering his room, with the gravity of his office, Master Onesime Chamonin, Chief Recorder of the Constabulary. He deigned to inform our captive that he was under watch and ward because of his attire, his appearance and the extreme length of his sword. The St. Germain forest-keepers had been struck by his height and broad chest, his Breton breeches, the peacock's feather in his hat, the unusual length of his rapier, as well as his wild bearing and unsteady step—and having guessed he was the slayer of Corporal Bregy, whose body they were charged to convey to the town, they had hastened to furnish his description to Lareynie's spies. Thus these were enabled to dog him into the Blackamoor Inn at Paris.

The four Musketeers had refused to provide any information on the case, as well as on the survivor of the meeting except to declare that all had passed according to the code of honor.

Chamonin called upon the accused to set forth his proofs of nobility so that he might be tried by his peers, the noblemen composing the Tribunal of honor. As the Son of the Baron du Vallon answered in full sincerity that, while believing himself of blue blood, he had nothing but his word and belief to establish it, the worthy recorder retired with the sentence :

"In that case, you will not be beheaded, but only hanged."

At the issue of this conference, Joel went upon the roof. At first he was alone, as it rained and the guests of the Bastille preferred even their cells to bad weather. Chamonin's declaration had clouded our hero in look and heart. He had seen the execution, by hanging, of a horsethief at Guernab Guerande. What a hideous thing is the gallows-tree! The whole scene had remained in the young man's memory and it made him shudder now after years. And it was this ignoble, infamous, horrible death which was reserved for him, a man so exuberant in strength, courage for grand deeds and such high aspirations!

To drive away such miserable thoughts, he strove through the rain to find among the houses of the city, the Church of St Paul's, where Mdlle. du Tremblay attended evening service, and they had exchanged their hearts and the Grey House in the St. Jacques suburb where Aurore was now sheltered. As he was absorbed in the search, a hand was laid on his shoulder. He turned sharply.

It was one of the four other lodgers in the tower : the one with the dull and guileless air, who had approached, without his hearing him. Joel did not recognize him at once.

"Who are you and what do you want?" he challenged roughly.

"I am Number 141, to serve you, if I may, sir," rejoined *the old fellow* gently. "A prisoner like yourself, a fellow-lodger in this strong box where the King keeps those he wishes held in hand. I occupy the drawer above your own."

"Eh?"

"I mean to say that I am lodged in the fourth floor—not an unpleasant place, but I am going to quit it."

"Changing your room?"

"No, I am going to be out of it altogether," returned the man jestingly.

"Released?"

"Not a bit like it. I am going to make a try to escape to-night," continued the confidential acquaintance in a low whisper.

"Escape?" repeated Joel.

"Not so loud!" said the prisoner, grasping him by the arm. "You will ruin me. Here of all places the walls have ears. Yes," he went on, "I shall be out to-night. Heaven is my witness that I should like to take you with me, but I have misgivings mingled with my hopes."

"How can one leave the Bastille?" questioned the Breton, his curiosity excited to the highest point.

"With patience, skill and tools, in time. With instruments and assistance from without very quickly. I have a daughter who is my life, my joy, all I care for. She has a lover who has come to my aid with all that I need. I have a file and a rope. I have sawn my two window-bars so that they will readily snap, leaving an opening through which I can slip. Towards midnight, I will tie my cord to the remaining bar and lower myself on it as it hangs. In such bad weather as impends, I may have the luck of the sentry, stationed below, keeping in his watch box. If he be outside, worse luck! he will fire on me. If missed, I shall leap from the rampart into the moat, swim across, climb the other side and try to steal into one of the houses by the garrets, unless I can climb down a gutterpipe."

"But you run the risk of breaking your neck a score of times," remonstrated the Breton.

The elder snapped his fingers; he had dropped the mask of stupid content, and his heretofore dim eye darted a flame which would have made the boldest recoil. His companion felt singular uneasiness in parleying with this double-face: it was certainly not fright so much as it was repugnance.

"Why do you behave so confidentially with me?" he inquired.

"Firstly, because you would not betray me; your are an honest youth as I read in your face. We are a family of wizards, fortune-tellers and the like. And again, because I have a favor to sue from you. As you have said, I run many risks of being shot, or my rope may break; I may drown in swimming the ditch, or break my bones scaling the roofs and walls; lastely I might be recaptured, but I will kill myself first. It is for my danghter's sake that I risk all. Afar from her kisses I am eating up my heart; I would pour out all my blood for one of them. I would leap off this tower to die on the skirt of her dress. It is to see her—to embrace her that I will attempt this night the enterprise which to you appears so hazardous, and to me the more as I never put the faith in her sweetheart which she feels. This supply of the means to make my escape may be but a trap in which I shall meet death,—but I shall foil the plotter, if the man is false, by constituting you my executor to convey my inheritance to my child."

"I?" exclaimed the young man, shrinking from the odd desire.

The prisoner drew from within his garments a brass box, about the size and shape of a large coin.

"This is hollow," he proceeded: "it encloses a paper for which my enemies would pay an entire fortune. For my Therese it will be a piece of armor fit to defend her from all blows from whatsoever quarter." Up to the present I have contrived to hide it from all searches. If found on me, it will be destroyed, and so this case must not leave your hands but to be put into my daughter's hands——"

"You are asking an impossible thing," responded the Breton, "How am I to fulfill such a mission?"

"I read in the stars that you will go from this place more easily than I, and not to your death. Even if you were doomed to death, you are not one of those dangerous criminals, who are made to disappear in the dark lest they shout out on the scaffold some destructive secret. You will be regularly tried; the court may apply some dreadful punishment to you, but your exceptional situation will command some *alleviation*. A duelist is not one of those malefactors who *horrify* or are scorned. You have relatives outside or friends with whom you may communicate; your legal defender can confer with you; you may ask a favor of your guards or bribe a keeper. When sentenced, you will be allowed to say farewell to your dear ones. Thus it will be through one of these that you will pass this talisman to my daughter, unless you prefer to give it her directly by summoning her to you."

"Yes, at a pinch, something like this may be done," replied the squire: " but——"

"But?" retorted the prisoner, with warmth," would you refuse to help a wretch who has no hope but in you to preserve an innocent girl from woes without end?"

Once more his face had changed; it now bore witness to so ardent an affection for the girl in whose behalf he prayed, that the hearer was touched in spite of himself.

"Since you insist so strongly," said Joel, without hiding his ill grace, "I will consent to serve you."

"Insist—indeed, I do—in the name of all you love!"

"Enough," said Joel, thinking of Aurore, at this; "give me the box."

"You promise to return it to me or to get it into the girl's hands?"

"I promise at least to try to do so by all the means in my power."

"I do not doubt you. Heaven prompts me. You will hand over the case without reading the enclosure?"

"It is fastened up secretly."

"That may be mastered: the case broken——"

"What do you take me for?" protested the Son of Porthos, repulsing the medallion.

"Nay, I am unfair! pardon me! misfortune makes me distrustful. Take it, but hide it from all eyes."

"Be at ease. I will wear it hung round my neck under my clothes. But what is the name of your daughter? where am I to go to deliver this article or send it to her?"

"My daughter's name is Therese Lesage; she lives in the middle of Bouloi Street, and carries on business, I am informed, as the Manicarde, as fortune-teller—it is our hereditary trade."

This, then, was the soothsayer whom the Marchioness de Montespan and her two companions had visited on the night when Joel had made those ladies' acquaintance; but he did not know the name of the street or on what errand they were out so late. The mention conveyed no hint to him.

"I will make a note of this, and the likelihood is that I shall not be searched from it not being suspected that I harbor state secrets."

"Oh, sir," said the other, with a false note or two in his voice, "if ever I can—or if my Therese can repay you for me——"

"I give you a free receipt, my companion, and the same to your daughter. But one word more: if your project succeeds to-night, as I trust heartily it may——"

"Be easy: if I am free, I will manage to see you and recover the article."

At this moment, the warden's voice was heard: "Time to turn in! come down, all out on exercise!"

Our hero mechanically held out his hand to the other, saying "We must part. Good luck! Before sleeping tonight, I shall pray for your success."

The old man's face twitched and he rejoined with bitterness:

"You are luckier than I in being able to pray and sleep. I thank you for the honor," he added, rejecting the hand, "but not till we meet again."

"In the other world, then," subjoined Joel gravely; "for my opinion is that both of us are in the shadow of death."

Number 141 ironically shrugged his shoulders.

"Where you like," returned he; with a sneering laugh: "But, as you are a good man and I, a great sinner, I do not believe it will be in paradise."

Spite of Joel's assurance about his ability to sleep, midnight came and he had not closed an eye: the talk with the father of Therese Lesage kept him alert.

Not that he was immeasurably interested in Number 141: the shifting and equivocal expressions on his features instinctively shocked our loyal hero, and he divined a dangerous rogue beneath the skillful deceiver. Still, in thinking of the perils the unhappy man was about to confront to reach his daughter and recover liberty, the young man could not stifle compassion or prevent forming vows for the enigmatical person's success in the task, for at least he gave proof of bravery.

THE DEATH OF ARAMIS. 175

Outside, the tempest blew more and more bitterly and violently. The gusts played about the old tower with the howlings of wild beasts. The dashes of water drummed on the walls till they returned a continuous dull beating. Midnight rang from the great clock of the prison, incessantly reminding the prisoners how the hours of punishment went.

Joel kept his eyes rivetted on the loophole over the foot of his bed. It seemed a light spot in the prevailing gloom. Suddenly, it was partly eclipsed by an opaque body: it was the prisoner lowering himself from his cell above.

At this juncture the gale delivered its most furious assault upon the fortalice. It shook it with such rage that it seemed as if it were determined to tear the old fortress from the ground, and bear it away on its wings like a shingle from a roof.

The prayer of Breton seamen in a whirlwind involuntarily rose to the watcher's lips. Some minutes elapsed, long as centuries until a gunshot cracked amid the crash of the unchained elements. A great tumult arose as though everybody in the prison were awakened; there was running about and shouting, orders sounded on all sides, and voices called "To arms!"

When the warder entered his room in the morning, Joel asked what had happened during the night.

"I could not close my eyes. What an uproar there was with the storm, and you fellows rushing about, and shouting, and shooting——"

"It was an attempt to escape," replied Huguenin.

"Anybody I would know?"

"Yes, your neighbor overhead, Number 141, who sawed his window bars and slid down a rope from them. But when the ground was reached, the sentry there challenged him and as the fugitive only set to jumping the moat, he followed his orders by firing on him."

"And then?"

The jailer puffed as if blowing out a candle.

"Number 141 is no more—gone off—killed with a bullet in the head."

Joel, who had begun his breakfast, put down the glass carried to his lips.

"Heaven receive his soul!" he exclaimed.

"It is more certain that they will have it in the other quarter," replied the turnkey, shrugging his shoulders, "for he was a thorough-paced rogue. A hundred times he ought to have laid down his life, broken on the wheel, or lashed to death, or in the halter——"

"That man?"

The jailer was in a talkative mood this morning.

"It happens that he is the very one of my lodgers whose tale I know," he rambled on. "Desgrais, the police-officer who brought him in, told me all about him. His name is Pierre Lesage, said to have been a priest in the house of Montmorency, but that is a flam—he is a half-gipsy, thief, beggar, horse-doctor and horse-thief, vendor of all sorts of abominable drugs. It is a sure thing that he was a wool-dealer at Rouen before he became the principal partner in the wicked deeds of the famous prisoners, La Voisin, Filastre and Vigoureux, three witches whom the Chambre Ardent soon made a finish with. Their victims are said to be reckoned by the hundreds, and high and mighty folks employed them."

"But how came it that he did not suffer the same fate as his accomplices?"

"That is the hitch—they feared that he would raise his voice so loud in an open court that the public would hear queer things, the names of their employers, very great personages, do you see?"

He winked significantly.

"So M. Lareynie suppressed the ugly business, and it was considered enough to *forget* this knave in our tower."

"Which was not strong enough to keep him in," said the Breton.

"Nay, there is nothing the matter with the tower," said Huguenin, assuming a sly and mysterious air, "He had tools to break out, but do not you run away with the idea that they were smuggled in without our knowing all about that. Why, I was charged to mark each day how he was getting on with the work—while he was strolling about with the rest of you aloft. It took a long time, for the bars are good stuff, but he came to an end, whereupon I notified Major du Junca. The bird was about to take a flight! So the sentry was warned, the best marksman we have in the garrison, and he earned his ten pistoles, by breaking that thorn in the foot of many a lofty one at court, beginning with the Marchioness de Montespan."

"Zounds!" exclaimed Joel, thinking to himself that he knew now why he had felt a repulsion to the murdered prisoner, when their hands touched, and now from the locket on his breast. It burned him, as though heated white hot by a flame from below, and twenty times in the day, he felt like tearing it off and smashing it under his heel. But the idea that he had given his promise withheld him, for his mother had always said:

"Do not lightly pass your word: but be a slave to it when it is given, even to a knave."

All day long, the memory and the speech of Pierre Lesage haunted him.

"Comrade, did that monster leave a family?" he asked of the warden that evening at suppertime.

"What monster?" inquired the man, who had already forgotten the morning's conversation.

"Number 141, killed last night."

"I hardly know—wait a bit! Yes, there was something said by the police-officer about a daughter of his, whose mother was La Voisin—who lives with one of the gang who eluded justice."

"Some frightful old hag like her mother?"

"I cannot enlighten you on the head, as I never saw the girl. And very likely, she would decamp when the father and mother were arrested."

"Very likely," thought Joel, "and that relieves me of my promise. If she is not here in Paris I am not required to travel the world over after her. And yet," he said with a change of mind, "I should like to know what has become of her."

CHAPTER XIX.

A MYSTERIOUS TRANSFER.

Days went by without bringing our prisoner any news of his case. In the third week, he began to fret. In his dear Brittany, he used to employ his time from dawn in hunting, shooting, rambling, riding, all those athletic pursuits which had become as much a necessity as the air and the light. Since he came to town, his days had been filled with adventures of all sorts. And out of this free, agitated and extensive circle, he was dropped into the stifling air, stillness and monotony of a prison. The vital fluid, boiling in his veins, had no longer any outlet; it rushed to his head and made his arteries beat as if he had a fever. He remained whole hours, sitting on his stool, his legs crossed, and his chin held in his hand, staring idly.

When evening came, he would throw himself on his couch, closing his eyes but merely dozing as he viewed extraordinary visions: and it was not till morning that he went off into a leaden slumber, in which was engendered some incoherent dream. He had wings sprout out upon him like a bird's or a bat's, and he flew out of his window; but at the time when he was passing over the outer wall, he fell into fathomless abysses or he was shot, and he woke up with a throbbing heart, his chest panting, and his forehead streaming with sweat.

As soon as aroused he would pace his room like a bear perambulating his cage, until, tired out, he would, as before, sit upon the stool, with swinging hands, wondering to God and man what he had done that One should abandon him and the other maltreat him.

One afternoon when he was thus mooning his time away, unusual stir in his lobby was audible. Soldiers were presenting arms; steps approached his door; the key grated in the lock and the bolts were shot back: Major du Junca walked in.

He was the acting-governor, awaiting the King's filling up the post left vacant by death. Making his monthly inspection, he demanded if the prisoner had any complaints of his treatment to make.

"I want for nothing, except the certainty about what is to be done with me," returned the Son of Porthos. "This ignorance in which I am left about my fate is downright cruel. On my soul, since I am to die, it would be humanity to abridge my agony of waiting."

"I am of your opinion," said the deputy-governor, "and I propose writing to M. Lareynie to solicit orders about you. The Police Lieutenant will probably refer to the King, and as soon as the reply comes, I will hasten to transmit it to you, if there is no reason why I should not."

"Oh, may this reply arrive speedily! and may my departure

be soon from this prisonhouse where my stay is daily twenty-four hours torture! I am eager to march forth, though it be between the chaplain and the executioner."

"Oh, sir; I trust you will not be reduced to that extremity," protested the major; "the King will not rear again the scaffold on which perished the noble duelist, Bouteville. He may rather merely *forget* you are here."

"Forget me, like Lesage the poisoner," thought Joel, wincing; "But that is just what I do not want to happen."

"Sir, it is not what you wish, but what the King likes," observed the major.

"Well," resumed our hero, "the King will be misled if he thinks he is doing me any favor in leaving me in this hole instead of having my head chopped off."

"Hole?" repeated the deputy-governor in a sulky tone; "the King never makes an error. I shall have the honor to announce his decision when it comes." He bowed, and withdrew with the four musketeers, who served as guard, and the turnkey.

This time it seemed to the captive that the door banged with a mournful sound, and he felt undoubtedly a prisoner. He fell without strength on the stool, and fastened his lightless eyes on the door which shut out all hope. He shrank mentally and began to muse on his dead mother and his living love. Stories of distinguished captives in this historical prison came to worry him. Nearly all knew their crimes. But this old man met at exercise, who had grown white here without friends to sue for his release, or pester the royal ministers! If so lone, why was he kept here: why, in forty years have made no attempt to escape?

"It strikes me," mused Joel, "that, in forty years, I should have made forty trials to get out. Indeed, why should I not try it at once?"

He had no friends, true or false, to pass him tools like the betrayed Lesage, but he might convert the bars, if broken, into some kind of instrument.

He set to examining his room straightway. The door was of three-foot oak plank; the window was doubly grated; the walls were four foot thick as he had noticed. All this did not leave great hopes. He tried to shake the door; a number of bolts and bars answered for its solidity, to say nothing of the whole series being on the outside; on the inside was not one nailhead or nut; so that the spikes and bolts could not be moved. He shook the window-bars; they were deeply set in the stone sockets. He sounded the walls, but they returned the same sound everywhere to show that they were solid.

A crowbar might have made an impression on the door ; a file on the bars ; and a pickax on the walls ; but Joel had not even the file of the prisoner Lesage.

Stouthearted as was our youth, he felt despair, and fearing he was going mad, he let a wild, hoarse laugh escape him. But after a fit of vertigo, he became gradually calm. In a month, he seemed resigned to the imprisonment. But this was due to his having conceived a plan ; one of simplicity and facility of execution worthy of his father Porthos, who might also have imagined it, though he was wont to confess to his friend d'Artagnan, that his strength did not lie in his head.

"When the major comes round for his monthly scrutiny," ruminated the youth, " I will have ended their plot to murder me by piecemeal by starting to murder them wholesale. I will brain the major with this stool, seize his sword, settle his escort and the turnkey whose bunch of keys I will take in my left hand as a mace. Thus armed, I will run amuck in the jail and, albeit I do not expect to cut my way out, I will die the death of a soldier——stabbed or shot. This is not including the satisfaction of spiting the constabulary which wants to cut off my head and the King who seems to threaten me with eating his prison fare till death ensues."

It was coming to this resolution which restored quiet and appetite to him. He slept and ate as usual. Did he not need all his strength to run full tilt at the garrison of the Bastille ?

One evening when he was feasting himself on this sweet prospect of massacre, he heard the rattle of weapons and fall of footsteps betokening the visit of the acting governor. Indeed, he made no doubt that it was something concerning himself, though at an unaccustomed hour, and he had learned the habits of the place during his six week's stay. Two soldiers marched in and stationed themselves at the door-way; behind came the major, towards whom Joel stepped with his most jovial mien but holding the stool from which he had risen, in a handy though careless manner.

"How now, major," he challenged, " do you come to repeat his Majesty's will—that I am to be beheaded like St. John, hanged like Marigny, or sealed up in this dungeon wall like my upstairs neighbor?"

Misfortune had taught him to dissimulate, for he smiled while speaking and in his merry voice was not to be discerned the least tinge of irony or deadly determination. But he was ready to offer his visitors the stool—on the head!

"Be good enough to accompany me," responded Junca, "I have orders to place you in the hands of one who waits for you below."

Bewildered, the prisoner let the heavy piece of furniture fall to the stone floor.

" I—I will follow you," said he.

The two left the room, and between a double line of soldiers, they traversed the labyrinth of corridors and staircases, the yard, guardrooms, drawbridge and the roofed way which our friend had met in entering. The march took place in silence, for Joel was wondering : "Who can have come for me ? Some officer," he supposed, after a little reflection, " who has to take me before my judges."

At the end of the vaulted passage, a coach was waiting, guarded by four horsemen and having a police officer in a black dress, by the doorway.

"Step in," he said to the prisoner, standing on one side to allow him to do so.

Joel obeyed, and the keeper jumped within beside him ; the door was slammed and locked, and off started the vehicle. At the first, the pair of horses, at good speed, went through three parts of the city without the prisoner understanding whither he was being conveyed. It was one of the dark nights chosen for the transfer of prisoners. It seemed to him that he was taken out of the town through one of its gates known to him. Soon, by the purer and sharper air, he knew that he was in one of the suburbs. By peeping out of the doorway window he could see trees and fields.

"Does the chevalier wish the glass set down so that he may breathe at ease?" inquired the guard. "Only, I beg the chevalier's promise that he will not try to lose his present company. I should at the same time notify the chevalier that four of my comrades, galloping behind the vehicle and armed to the teeth like me, would fire on him, and I should have to do likewise with my pistols at the least offer to escape."

"Why the mischief does he style me chevalier," marvelled the Breton. "Is there an error in the person, as lawyers say? An error of this gruesome looking officer or of Major Junca? After all he reasoned, with a flip of the fingers, "I may as well die under one title as another. Friend," he said to the giver of this advice, "I willingly offer the pledge you seek: not on account of the pistols you and your fellows may carry; if the steers knew that they were being led to the slaughterhouse there would certainly be fewer butchers in the world."

The sashes were let down. Need we paint with what delight our youth from the country, oppressed for over a month with the thick, heavy prison atmosphere, intoxicated himself with the coolness of this summer night, full of starry gleams and floral perfumes! With what inexpressible joy, too did he see, instead of the uniform horizon limited by four walls, the woods, villages, and landscape each side of the highway—that way tracked by the vehicle wheels at great swiftness and the hoofs of the horses going like a whirlwind.

As the rapid journey continued, the prisoner questioned himself with growing wonder if he were not the dupe of a nightmare? Had he not once before travelled this road, gone through those two villages, threaded these windings of this stream, and driven through these woods? Suddenly the moon unmasked itself from behind a screen of tangled clouds, and whitened a new curve of the River Seine.

The coach crossed a bridge. On the left a gigantic elm mirrored its plentiful foliage in the cold, silvered water. On the right a large house stood on stone pillars. Its roof overhang so as to cover a verandah around the second story From this swung a wooden board, on which was painted a picture of the large tree.

"Bless my soul!" ejaculated our hero, "the bridge of Pecq, Sully's Tree Tavern, and that is the new Palace of St. Germain's beyond!" Thinking it over for a couple of minutes, he continued his unspoken thoughts. "I understand whither they are taking me—to the spot where the fault was committed—that it may be expiated there. Where I killed the Musketeer, I am to lose my life."

He threw himself back in the coach, with a slight shiver.

He had a kind of fear of seeing the spectre of the slain duelist stealing along in the moonbeams, in blood-spattered shroud.

The horses breathed hard as they climbed the steep, leading from the riverside into the town.

"Chevalier," said the man in black. "Here my instructions bid me have the windows closed."

Not only did he close them, but he drew serge curtains which intercepted all visual communication with the outside. This man, whose eyes sparkled in a dusky face, spoke with a Spanish accent.

"How is this?" muttered Joel; "where have I heard this midnight bell before? where have I seen that pair of carbuncles light up the night? where have I met this gallows-hawk?"

As he was trying to collect his thoughts, the coach stopped. The "gallows-bird," partly opened the door, and invited the Breton to alight. When he did so, he remarked a singular building facing him. It stood at the end of a vast courtyard, led into under an ornamental gateway and the walls coped with stone and adorned with spikes.

"The town jail, I warrant," mused the new-comer.

"Chevalier, do you mind giving me your hand?" inquired the swarthy man.

"Confound the fellow, with his 'chevalier' on all occasions. But I have no time to quarrel with him," added our friend. "I have no time to dally on this earth."

He was so resigned and prepared for everything which he thought likely to befall him, except a life in prison, that he would have submitted without hesitation if a block, an axe and a headsman had been presented to him and a sign made that he was to kneel down. So he held out his hand with a good grace, and followed his guide without any question or observation. Thus he passed, without heeding, up a staircase into a vestibule, into a gallery and upon one of those flight of steps, broad and high, which would be so much space wasted in the eyes of our modern architects who cover eligible building lots. On one of the steps, leaning on the landing-rail of handsomely wrought iron, an old, fat man held a torch. His white hair was cut short and was shaped on the top as a priest's is shorn; and the fine broadcloth coat, covering a paunch, resembled in cut, case, trimming and color, all austere, the garments of a proctor, a steward, a beadle or a pedagogue.

"The head warden," thought Joel. "He seems to be well fed here. On my soul, if the prisoners are nourished on that scale, they run the risk of being taken out in invalid chairs on wheels."

"Señor Esteban," said the fat man with importance, "your duty terminates here."

The conductor released the Breton and this man went on: "Will the chevalier deign to let me precede him?"

"This tun of a man is very polite," muttered the Son of Porthos. "But why does he also decorate me with the title of chevalier like everybody else? It is a mistake or a hoax?"

They reached the first landing.

"The chevalier has arrived," observed the corpulent man in an unctuous and yet high-pitched voice.

"This hogshead is too polite," mused Joel, shaking his head. "These are the attentions given to a man doomed to death, and I am sure it is a fatal case."

The other opened a door and begged the chevalier to take the trouble to walk in.

"Far too polite," sighed the Breton. "Woe's me! It is certainly in a dungeon that I am to be kept for the dreadful hour."

The old man waved his hand for him to precede him, and the other obeyed. On crossing the threshold, he exclaimed:

"Deuce take it! where am I?"

CHAPTER XX.

BEFORE THE EXECUTION.

CERTAINLY, nothing resembled his cell in the Bastille less than the room into which he walked. The whole aspect was changed. No more barred airholes, cold, bare walls, scanty rickety furniture, and worn beds. All was new, bright and luxurious—mainly pastoral and amorous, for the fashion turned to Cupid and Watteau shepherds and shepherdesses. It might have been believed the boudoir of a fashionable duchess: and the new guest was fain to think that, the prison being overcrowded, they had lodged him for one night only in the rooms of the jail governor's wife. Not even in the house of the royal children, had he seen so much elegance and sumptuosity; hence he repeated his question with growing surprise.

"The chevalier is at home," rejoined the portly usher.

The young man's brow clouded like protent of gathering storm.

"At home? Joker of a varlet, are you trifling with me?"

The fat old man seemed afraid of Joel's irritated eyes. He drew back a little, still facing him, as though his paunch would be a breastwork in defence, and in a voice hoarse with fear, replied:

"I hasten to affirm to the chevalier that no one would mock at him. I am simply carrying out orders received, in pursuence of which I must lock him up when I go forth."

"So I expected," responded the prisoner as naturally as could be.

"Yes, lock you in until to-morrow, when they will come to —to—well, you know better what than I do."

Our hero made the gesture of snapping a branch in two, and said : " So it is fixed for to-morrow ?"

" To-morrow morning, chevalier."

" Early ?"

"In time to have all over by noon—it is the usual thing."

"Whew!" whistled Joel, "they have rapid judges in Paris and its suberb; no lingering delay of the law here. Pooh, when the wine is drawn it must be drunk, and the worse it is, the more quickly! A nod is as good as a blink, to a blind horse, they say down my way. I thank you, friend. I shall be ready."

"Talking of cheering up," said the other, delighted at the smooth way which the peculiar interview was making, "if the chevalier should feel any need of refreshment——"

" I see ; nothing is refused to a wretch in my predicament."

"I will have the honor of serving a cold collation, prepared for the very case, it being contrary to the good old rules of Galen and Esculapius for a man to take his sleep on an empty stomach."

"Take his sleep?" repeated Joel, with a wry face. It seemed to him that in coming up the stairs he had sniffed some appetizing perfumes from the kitchen. "Come to think of it, the condemned is always given a last good impression of the world he quits. Where is this cold collation—previous to the cold *decollation*, ha ! ha ! I do not like to offend the ghosts of Galen and Esculapius whom I may be near to meeting."

The stout man hastened to roll forward a side-table on castors, on which a complete set of table articles for one person was placed in order. He added to it, a golden-tinted thick soup in a Dutch porcelain bowl, an enormous meat-pie in a glazed crust, a roast foul cased in amber jelly, and a ham of such a lovely rosy hue that it seemed "materialized" out of a painting by Jordaens; to say nothing of the dessert, fruit, cheese, cakes and other spurs to the thist.

"Plague take me !" vociferated Joel, on beholding this knowingly devised feast, "his Majesty treats his guests handsomely here. He is a prince jealous about having their last moments go off well. These succulent meats, that feather bed in the recess, these kickshaws——"

" Nay," protested the other, "this is only a light supper; the chevalier will be better able to appreciate our cook when he has breakfast in the morning——"

"Oh, I am to have breakfast ?"

"Certainly, before the ceremony——"

"Of course, how could I forget the ceremony?" queried Joel with a chopfallen face.

"It is the rule——"

"Of course, I know that nothing is refused to those who undergo the infliction of———" And he ran his hand round his neck, as he seated himself, and muttered : "It is settled, then; I shall breakfast on earth though I sup in paradise!"

The old man had placed the eatables on the table with the solemnity of a deacon setting the holy vessels on the altar: he might have been serving a mass rather than a meal. Grave, dignified and beatific, with his broad face congealed in compunction and self-concentration, he stood behind the guest, with a bottle of Chambertin in his hand, in the attitude of the choir-boy holding the chalice, and he complacently listened to the gentleman, who, after finishing the soup to the last drop, proceeded to dismantle the patty.

"It will be a splendid sight—people are fighting for the best places—the chapel is so small."

Oh, they were going to take the culprit into the chapel; probably for the Amende Honorable, or religious ceremony in which the condemned apologised for his misdeed.

"Father Lachaise is going to speak the exhortation——"

"The royal confessor! The King is doing the grand for me."

"Naturally, as he will be present."

"The King is coming to see me turned off?"

"Undoubtedly, as he signed."

"Signed? the sentence? I understand. It is very kind of his Majesty and much honor for me."

"And he brings the Queen, and she, all the ladies. All the court will be there."

"The Queen, too, in at the death! a singular sight for her and the ladies. Verily, your court has lofty tastes! they will be delighted when I lose my head."

He rose and threw down his napkin. After all, the Queen was Spanish, and at her father's court, the court ladies witnessed the burning of heretics. It was necessary that he should show a bold front to this choice audience, and to do that he ought to have a rest. He had made away with the victuals which had loaded the board, like a juggler causing the pea to vanish under the thimbles, and now he meant to see if the bed equalled the cheer in goodness.

"Does the chevalier wish me still to attend him?"

"No, I will go to bed unhelped. You may retire. Good night!"

"The chevalier will please to bear in mind that I am obliged to carry away the room door-key. Please not to think it is through any personal freak, but because my master ordered so."

"Carry it away, my friend: for happiness there is no place like a lock-up."

"There is a bell on the night-table, and if the chevalier requires anything, he has but to ring it, for there will be someone on the watch in the corridor."

"I expected a sentry would be posted there."

"I wish a good-night to the chevalier," said the old man, bowing deeply: "in the morning, my master, the Duke of Almada, will see him."

'Oh, the duke is the governor, is he? I never heard his name before," thought our prisoner, as he was undressing in the solitude. "And I never came across such a novel character as his turnkey. Where did I meet him before—this buckbasket of fat, this full-moon face of purple, and this carriage of a sacred elephant?"

Still puzzled, he laid down, and fell off into a delicious sleep, whether it came from the excellent repast, the generous wine, the softness of the fine bedlinen, or the fatigue from the romance which he was acting lately: the graceful figures in the pastoral landscapes of the tapestry mingled with his dreams and danced in a round of poetical, fabulous and impossible charm.

Having an iron will, our hero could command his body as readily as his mind and heart. Having decided on taking rest, he slumbered without break until the hour when a footman glided noiselessly into the room, and by drawing the curtains, let a flood of merry sunshine cover the bed with a sheet of gold.

We must confess that on waking and recollecting where he was and what impended, Joel heaved half a dozen sighs of which the wind would have knocked down a bull-calf. Persuaded that he was doomed to death, and that the sentence would be carried out without delay, he had resolved to bear himself handsomely. Not to unnerve himself, he gave up the idea of sueing to see Aurore. An interview with her would have robbed him of courage. It was on paper that he would bid farewell to Mdlle. du Tremblay, at the same time that he would entrust her with the deposit for the prisoner's daughter.

By the light, Joel judged that day was well advanced. As they would soon be coming for him, he rose with speed. But as his hand was put forth to find his clothes, left off by the bedside, he was surprised that they were gone.

"At this moment, the stout jailer, as he still took him to be, entered to ask: "Has the chevalier had the repose that meets his desire?"

"Entirely so. But where are my clothes! what has become of them?"

"Consequently he entreats the chevalier to replace his Breton costume by this suit from the first tailor's of Paris."

He waved his hand, and four footmen brought in an elegant court dress in flesh-colored velvet, with Venetian lace trimmings, and complete from the puffed shoes starred with diamonds to the pearlgrey felt hat bending down in the flap with the weight of a magnificent flame-tinted plume.

"This," continued the old man, pointing to an imposing servant following the other four, "this is Master Hardouin, my lord's head valet, who is charged, after the bath, to array the chevalier and assist him in the dressing."

"Gracious!" thought Joel, "What a lot of ribbons for the lamb led to the slaughter! I should have marched as well in my peasant clothes, without fuss and feathers, pompons and lace. Nevertheless, tell your master that I thank him for thinking for me, and that I shall conform to his intentions."

At bottom, our Breton was not sorry to don for once in his life, all the frippery of the fashionables whom he had admired with the like on their shoulders. He felt a secret pleasure in appearing before his judges and proceeding to the execution adorned by all the sheen of a display unknown to him so far. Now he felt sure that he should look well in the deathsman's eyes. His bravery would be doubled by the lustre of his costume. So he delivered himself into Hardouin's hands.

Imprisonment had not injured him. His sunburnt complexion may have been paled a little, and his herculean figure a trifle reduced, but this gave him a delicacy of appearance vainly sought in him before. Strong and handsome he had gone into the Bastille, and he came forth with strength and manly beauty, with the fineness which is the mark of good blood. In short, here stood a perfect cavalier, as he looked at himself in a mirror and acknowledged that he had reason to be proud.

Ah, if Aurore could but see him now!

He took up the hat.

"It is well. I am ready. Lead on."

He went forth with the old stout man.

"How is this?" demanded Joel, in the passage, "nobody to escort me?—no guards?"

"We have only the landing to cross and the stairs," replied the steward.

"Oh, is it here the court assembles?"

He made a wry face, for he was wishful to walk through

the town, and exhibit to the gaping mob the stylish garments, the rich lace and the bold sweep of the plume. The good, vain Porthos perpetually reappeared in his son.

"Deuce take them!" he muttered, "I hope, wherever the trial takes place, they will not execute me *in camera!*"

The steward opened a door, saying:

"The chevalier de Locmaria!"

"Let the dear boy enter," rejoined a paternal voice.

Joel uttered an exclamation of surprise: instead of the stern and impressive show and paraphernalia of justice which he had expected to behold in the room where he was introduced, the Savior on the cross hung against dark drapery, and the long table where the judges would be sitting in a row, cold and solemn in black and scarlet robes, the ushers in inky garb and golden chains, the clerks with longs pens, the guards with ebony wands: here was a large dining-room, where the sun sparkled on Bohemian glass and shone on the magnificent silver plate, arrayed on shelves of an oaken sideboard with a table laid for two, aglow with rare flowers and dazzling with bleached linen, crystal and china.

Near this board an old gentleman was buried in an armchair, upholstered in Cordovan leather, studded with gilt nails and stamped with arabesques. This old gentleman got up as Joel was ushered in, and was at once recognized by the latter.

"The Chevalier d'Herblay:" he broke forth with his astonishment still growing.

"The same," responded the other, running to him with open arms. "And better, besides, if you are agreeable. For, though I kept the mask on during my journey from Nantes to Paris, here at St. Germain there is no need for me to disavow that I am the Duke of Almada, the ambassador of his Majesty the King of Spain."

"Duke of Almada—Spanish Ambassador?" repeated the youth, pressing his forehead between both hands with a stupefied air, " my ideas are buzzing about in my head like fledglings in a nest. However," he went on, putting out his hand to button hole the other as if he feared that he would escape from him, " since I do recover your lordship, will you assure me that I am in my senses, not dreaming while awake, and if not the dupe of a dream, the actor in no fairy tale or destestable trickery?"

THE DEATH OF ARAMIS.

"My young friend," returned the duke, cordially, "I will explain what is to give you pleasure. I think with you that an explanation is necessary between us; but I should like to unfold it while we are taking breakfast, for we have a great deal to get through with this morning, and we must not lose any time."

Waving the guest to a seat, he ordered his steward to serve.

"We can converse freely," he added, as he unfolded his napkin, "as my footmen understand only Spanish."

Joel seated himself mechanically facing his host, who filled his glass and his plate with his own hand.

"If you do not object to speaking while eating, my boon companion, I am at your orders."

"Where am I, my lord?" began the Breton, without waiting to be asked again.

"You are in my house, or I should say, a friend's, as a resident of St. Germain lets me occupy his dwelling when business calls me hither : it is the gentleman whom you saw with me at the inn at Saumur."

"Then I am not in prison?"

"You are in Boislaurier House, near the church, and opposite the palace."

"But I have been in prison, in the Bastille, these six weeks."

"So I heard : from having delivered a swordthrust. Ah, you are a *matador*, a fatal fighter, as the Spanish say, my champion of Belle Isle."

"But I was yesterday in the Bassinière Tower of the Bastille, a vile hole."

"Very true, as it was only yesterday that his Majesty signed the order for your release."

"His Majesty signed the release order?" repeated the Son of Porthos, starting upon his chair.

"He restores you to the world and gives you entire and plenary mercy."

"So that I am free?"

"As air."

"And I am not to be tried?"

"Not at all."

"And hence not sentenced to——"

He made the gesture of cutting his throat with a drawing movement of the edge of his open hand.

"Be at ease," returned the old nobleman, laughing. "Your head may stay tranquil on its shoulders, which it would be a pity to remove as it looks very well there. Now, may I offer you some of this warmed up cold partridge with a glass of Romanée, it will help you to swallow the good news."

"With a good heart—let us drink the health of the King. And yours, too, my lord, since you come to me as the dove to the Ark. But," after he had tossed off a brimming goblet, "to whom do I owe this unlooked for boon ? who has begged it of the King ?"

"You have friends at court, my young master."

"Do you tell me so ? All the friends I know of, are a couple whose acquaintance I formed at a Paris inn, the Blackamoor Trumpeter, of which one is its host Bonlarron, and the other a fellow-guest, one Friquet, neither of whom do I imagine powerful enough to extract a favor from the King."

Almada shook his finger at him with playful threatening.

"My son of Brittany, you are ungrateful, and blink, for you look afar for what is close to you."

"You are right," returned the youth, smiting his brow with his fist. I am an idiot, a blockhead, a heartless scamp, not to have guessed sooner : it is you who have done all this —you are my liberator."

"Say at once that I am your providence," interrupted the other, with his mouth full ; "I find a pleasure in extricating honest folks from straits when they interest me. By the way, will you have another helping of this larded leveret ?"

The Breton held out his plate.

"I am ready for anything," he said. "Shall I be vexed at you if you give me a fit of indigestion, when you have saved me from the courts of justice ? But," he quickly subjoined as a fresh idea struck him and caused him to lay down his fork and lean on the table with both elbows to have a good stare at his host, "how did you learn that I had a duel with that Musketeer, was arrested and clapped into the Bastille ?"

"We will tell you some day," said Aramis, chafing his chin with his hand. "For the present we have other fish to fry. By the way, how did you like those smoked eels last night ? they come all the way from my fishing village by Barcelona, and are appreciated by epicures. You can thank me another time; when we both have time, you to be lavish of gratitude and to receive its expression."

Joel stood up, his breast heaving with emotion.

"At all times, you may have my life, my blood, my arm!"

"Stop a bit, boy," interposed the duke, with good humor, "are you sure that all these belong to you? Did you not give them to the woman you love?"

Joel started, for these words reminded him of Mdlle. du Tremblay. He was free to hasten to the Gray House and learn what had become of the young lady, and explain to her why he had been so long absent from her. All the ideas which had been fermenting in his brain, vanished before this one. All he thought of was hurrying from table. Nothing was capable of paralysing his impulse—not the cardoons in marrow, or the fat young turkey which were now put on the board.

"My lord," he said, "you have treated me kindly, like a father—but I must beg a further favor——"

"You have but to name it, my young friend."

"I want leave to depart on business which will not wait."

"Quit before we finish breakfasting?"

"I am no longer hungry or thirsty."

"What a hare-brain you are, that you forget the ceremony is fixed for noon."

"What ceremony?"

"That for which I sent my man Esteban to bring you out of the Bastille: for which you have been conducted here: for which the royal chapel has been decked, the royal notary called, and letters of invitation issued to the whole court: for which, in short, you have been arrayed in a wedding-suit which gives you the splendrous aspect of a Galaor or a Don Sancho—that which their Majesties deign to honor with their presence."

"Is my dream continuing—am I in a fever?" moaned our hero, at the apex of amazement. "For mercy's sake, my lord answer me what ceremony is on the board?"

Looking fixedly at him, the duke replied: "For what ceremony would you don a wedding-suit, if not for your wedding?"

When the thunderbolt falls on a man's head, he does not

burst out into shrieks and howls: he is deprived of consciousness, motion, and thought. But under the apparent apathy, nature is still acting : the briefly interrupted senses and organs re-establish themselves and when intelligence of the disaster returns, the wretch moves, groans, and strives to be himself again. So was it with Joel, who was for a while thunderstricken, but at last an exclamation rose from his lips :

"But I had no wish to be married."

"You are but a child—the King's will must never be disputed."

"Is it the King wants me to marry ?"

"He desires it, and, as a respectful subject, you——?"

"Why does the King meddle with my private affairs?" cried the son of the Rebel of Belle-Isle. "He does not know me—he has never seen me."

"Chevalier, the King knows all the noblemen in his realm."

"In short, why should there be a marriage ?" said Joel with a shrug of shoulders which rather reflected on his claim to be numbered among the King's acquaintances.

"Because all ladies of the Palace establishment are bound to be married."

Oh, so it is a lady of the royal establishment that I am to be married to—like taking a pig in a poke. I am sorry for her, but may all the wedding-rings in the world be welded into one suit of chains in which to hang me, but if she waits for me to wed her, she will pine in perpetuity! The King is mighty, they say. Let him be the master over his courtiers and his varlets," continued the youth, striding up and down the dining-room become too confined for him; "let him set the law for all Europe ; let him turn the globe into a bubble to obey his breath ; all this is a matter between him and human weakness, servility and foolishness. But he has no right to dispose of my will and feelings, and my free choice—this came from God to me, and not to him by birth or with the crown. I am a Breton, and the men of my land are more or less like their ancestor Duke Conan the Headstrong."

"Young man, young man, take care!" retorted the duke, concealing his merriment, "you confess that the Bastille is a disagreeable dwelling——"

"In other words, I am to be dragged back into it, unless *I yield to* the royal will? The bridal chamber or the prison!

I prefer the latter: for if my body suffers, my conscience will be at ease."

"His Majesty can do more——"

"Yes, I know he can send me to the scaffold or the galleys. It may be imagined that I shall quail; but a great mistake is made. I was ready yesterday, and I shall be the same to-day and hereafter. Does the King want a sample of courage? Let him come and see me die."

While thus speaking the Son of Porthos was a sight to behold. The richness of his attire, its laces and ribbons, went for nothing in the effect, no more than did his athletic beauty: the beauty was in the nobility on his brow, and in his look and his smile.

"He has spoken his mind," mused Aramis. "He is a man, on whose shoulders my old Musketeer's uniform will fit as though he inherited it as a son of the regiment. It is a pity to throw him away to the enemy, but he must not remain here —he would break the King in twain like a dry twig."

There was an instant's silence which the ex-prelate broke with the words:

"Come, come, my lad of mettle, this is all very fine, but we are not in Syracuse and reigned over by the Tryant Dennis. Louis the Grand will not violate your personal rights in any way."

"Excuse me," said Joel, becoming calm. "I was wrong to lose my temper, and forget what I owe you and the goodness of the King. But I am ill-accustomed to disguise what I feel. And, besides, did you know that I——"

"If you yourself did but know," interrupted the Ambassador, "what a blessing was intended for you! a love of a girl—the most winning as the best."

"I do not wish to know her; for I should have to decline her even if with regret were she endowed with all human perfections. You, who are a nobleman, will understand me from all sworn pledges being a holy thing; I am engaged to another. A man does not twice give his heart. I am not my own master, for my heart and my life are in a woman's hands—one who is also an adorable creature, and without offence to the lady you cite, the best and most charming of her sex."

"But if the one of whom I spoke brings you a marriage portion larger than the spotless soul in its ideal envelope?

If to you, a poor and unknown youth, uncertain of the future, and yet open to legitimate and elevated ambition, she brings glory, fortune and credit—the sovereign's friendship, a high post at court and a superior grade in the army——"

"Heaven is my witness," said Joel, with a flash of the eye, "that I often dreamed of the joy of marching among the soldiers of France if not the honor of commanding them as we went into the smoke of battle to seek in the hostile ranks my captain's commission or my knightly spurs, but, though your witch should furnish me with the means of realizing the conception, I would still refuse."

Aramis rested his elbow on the cloth and his chin in his hand, as he spoke with emphasis on each syllable and scanned the young man with piercing eyes:

"Even if this enchantress should be named Henriette Yolande Aurore du Tremblay?"

The hearer was confused, for joy rushed to his brain and occasioned congestion. His temple veins swelled and beat. The floor swam beneath him, and had he not caught at the table he would have fallen.

"What, is the bride to be——"

"It is Mdlle. du Tremblay whom was offered to you for your life-companion—would you reject her?"

"She—oh, heaven help me!"

"Do you love her as she merits being loved?"

"Do I love her?" He pronounced this with fervor in which blazed the most ardent passion that ever fired a soul. "Oh, my lord," he faltered, "if all this be not sporting with me, I shall die of bliss. But it would be too cruel to play with me—better kill me offhand with a bullet in the brain or a swordthrust through my body."

Almada rose and going to one of the windows, he raised the curtain.

"Look, you unbeliever," he said.

Boislaurier House faced the front of the palace. On the open space between there was always a crowd in any season including people who came from town to see the King and court; the populace like the display of the great more than some believe. On this morning, the curious pressed in greater number than commonly over the pointed pavingstones between the church and the palace. Before the latter, guarded by the Musketeers and the Swiss Guards, the handsomest coaches set down gentlemen in brilliant attire and ladies in the latest freaks of fashion. Rumor ran that they came to attend a marriage at midday in the Chapel Royal before the King and Queen.

Suddenly a murmur sped through the crowd :

"The bride, the bride ! make way—this is the bride !"

A coach in the royal colors came out of a street, in which was seated Mdlle. du Tremblay in company with the headmistress of the Queen's ladies and another lady of the bedchamber, with a gentleman, the master of ceremonies, Marquis Montglat. When the gathering beheld her, in her white satin costume, the long white veil floating down her shoulders, and the symbolical orange-blooms in her hair, but one voice arose amid the clapping of hands : " How lovely she looks !"

She was beautiful, indeed, if only for the expression of unlimited felicity to be read on her ravishing features.

Reeling like a drunken man, Joel fell upon a seat.

"Do I continue to dream?" he asked himself. "Will I never awake ? Or am I going mad ?"

The Duke of Almada clapped him on the shoulder, saying :

"Well, descendant of the Headstrong Conan, are you still determined to die in bachelorhood and obstinacy ?"

"Who says that we love one another ?" questioned the Son of Porthos, instead of replying.

"Who would have said so, but the lady herself?"

"And does she consent to marry me?" again interrogated the youth, whose voice slightly trembled.

"Did you think that they were dragging her to the altar?"

"But how has she come to marry me, without a name?" went on the other with distrust.

"You will pardon me," said the old noble; " you have a name and a title; you are henceforth the Chevalier de Locmaria, according to the King's good pleasure."

"But I have done nothing to deserve this favor!"

" Deserve it hereafter. I have answered to the sovereign for your zeal to serve him. The war is not over—a decisive campaign is preparing on the Rhine, and there you may win your spurs."

"I vow to heaven," exclaimed Joel, "that his Majesty will not have a more devoted soldier in his ranks more devoted to the glory of his flag. Furnish me with the occasion to show what I can do, and, as our old Armorican song has it, I will prove that danger and I are two lions born the same day, but I am the elder and the master."

His unusual stature expanded to its full development; a breath of warlike enthusiasm seemed to throw up the mass of his hair; his countenance beamed with flame as from the cannon mouth, and his tones rang as from the bugle sounding the charge.

"I shall remember your words," said the old duke gravely: "though I am sure that I need not remind a gentleman of the sanctity of an oath. His Majesty," he went on in a less solemn tone, "had wrongs to repair towards the family of Mdlle. du Tremblay, so that nothing should astonish in his bestowing on the dear child the husband of whom she dreamed. And there is nothing farther astonishing in that husband being provided by the royal initiative with the means to hold a proper position at court."

As though to efface from his hearer's mind the very shadow of mistrust, he concluded affectionately: "Besides, I do not allow you to imagine scruples where Aurore, the paragon of virtue and honor, has not deemed it proper to raise any obstacles?"

M. de Boislaurier entering at this juncture, the diplomatist presented him to his guest as "One of my excellent friends who is anxious to become yours."

They shook hands warmly.

"My lord Duke," said the new arrival, "allow me to remind you that the King is waiting."

"That is true. And I forget all about him while chatting. Let us be off, chevalier. Quick, Bazin, our hats, gloves and swords. "Make the King wait!" he added with comic fright. "The Lord forbid! Offenders have been put in the Bastille for milder faults than that. And it is not only the King that is kept waiting but the Queen of Beauty. That is a crime to womanhood a thousand times more wicked that treason."

CHAPTER XXI.

ONE KIND OF ROYAL DIVORCE.

AFTER the wedding, performed with utmost pomp, the happy pair were taken in a royal carriage to Boislaurier House, where Aramis's friend had placed the first floor at their orders.

Aurore and Joel arrived there, bewildered by the day so overcrowded with divers adventures through which they were driven blindfold, it might be said. Judge if they were in haste to relate to each other what they had done and experienced since their parting, and try to understand the events of which they suffered the results without knowing the reasons.

Unfortunately, Lady Montausier accompanied the new lady of the royal household in order to edify her on her new duties.

"To-morrow your service will commence," she said; "it is urgent that you should attend early at the palace whence you cannot go away unless by written leave."

"What's this? broke in the newly married man, "forbidden to leave the royal residence?"

"Certainly: the Queen may be seriously attacked and want help at any moment."

"It seems to me that it would be better to keep a doctor and sick-nurse at hand on regular wages," grumbled our hero. "How long does this service last?"

"Three months at a time; still you ought not to go far away from the court, as some attendant may fall ill, and you ought to be ready to replace her, if you keep in favor."

"You seem to be very frightened about illness," said Joel in an audible whisper. "Listen, my good dame, so kind as to give my wife these lessons. If she must begin this task early to-morrow, you will understand that she and I have a lot of private matters to discuss. So you will overlook my apparent rudeness in suggesting that your presence will probably be more in request over the way than in this house."

Mdme. de Montausier went off in high dudgeon, as became an old lady of sixty, and left the pair, at length alone. But, however bold in dismissing the Queen's first lady, our hero was timid and embarrassed when beside Aurore and scarcely dared to speak.

"What delight do I feel under your protection," said she.

"Since I was a child at my mother's knee," returned Joel, "when I was happy without knowing it, I do not recall in all my life one moment comparable to this!"

For awhile, they remained mute, absorbed in reciprocal contemplation.

"You are fair as an angel, Aurore," said the man at last.

"And you appear to me as the archangel, with the flaming sword, from my having seen you twice guarding me with your arm," she rejoined.

The windows were open ; the night was calm, the air pure and the firmament splendid. Only vague murmurs crossed at intervals the silence of the slumberous night. The wind wafted scents either sharp or heavy as they came from the forest or the garden. They were sitting side by side, as they sat on the bench on the Celestins wharf when the ruffians of Colonel Cordbuff assaulted them. The memory of that attack struck her and she shuddered.

"Why do you tremble, darling?" inquired Joel. "Here, we have not to dread the storm or treachery. Let our spirits rest in trust."

"Yes," responded Aurore, "let us forget the wicked. We should enjoy this unique and gladsome hour without fear or trouble."

With a gentle movement she let her head sink upon his shoulder, while her eyelids drooped, but the Breton started up as her lips almost were reached by his own.

"What is the matter?" asked the wife, reopening her astonished eyes.

At this moment, a spurred heel rang again on the pavement of the square, and a vigorous blow was struck on the door panel. A powerful voice was heard to shout: "On the King's service!" before which no one had the right to keep his door bolted, locked or barred.

Aurore recoiled.

"What can that be?" she faltered.

"No doubt, it is some message from the King for M. de

Boislaurier, or the Duke of Almada," replied Joel, though he was not at ease.

They remained apart, staring at each other, while two or three minutes passed. At length they heard the slow step of the steward approaching. A hand gently tapped on the door.

"Who is there?" inquired the Knight of Locmaria.

"A messenger from the King," replied Bazin, to whom the gentleman opened the door for him to enter.

"Lieutenant Maupertius of the Royal Muskeeters," he announced.

In the shadow on the landing appeared the manly form of the guardsman, partly draped in his cloak; behind him were Aramis's emotionless face and the more inquiring one of Boislaurier. On the threshold the soldier saluted the lady profoundly: then advancing towards our hero, he presented a large note with the royal seal and said: "On behalf of the King."

Joel broke the seal, opened the envelope and drew forth a parchment which he ran his eyes over: then he uttered an outcry: "An appointment as ensign in the new artillery company forming at Douai." He turned towards Aurore with his countenance beaming with pride and delight, to say: "Think of that! an officership—I am an officer! Oh, our kind—our excellent King!"

Maupertuis took a second note from his pocket, and handed this also to the speaker, saying: "By order of the King!"

The latter treated this as he had done the former, but the exclamation it drew from him was not pleasure like the first. He read the King's orders over again with astonishment akin to stupor. He examined each line and weighed every word by itself. He had turned whiter than the paper held in his shaking hand.

"What is it?" asked the alarmed woman.

By way of answer the Knight of Locmaria read aloud:

On receiving this present order, the Chevalier de Locmaria will mount horse and ride at speed to report at Paris to the Minister of War, who will hand him despatches for Marshal Créquy, now in his camp before Freiburg, in Brisgau. Under no pretext whatsoever is there to be delay in the execution of this order. Our Lieutenant of the Musketeers, M. de

Maupertuis, is charged to see that the Chevalier de Locmaria is started duly upon his journey.

"(Signed) Louis."

The wedded couple stared at one another in bewilderment.

"But the Lord forbid that this should be possible," muttered Joel.

"What should not be possible?" haughtily demanded the Musketeer, who probably knew that he stood before the duelist who had made a vacancy in his corp

"What his Majesty requests."

"His Majesty does not request—he commands," replied the successor of d'Artagnan with the same stiffness.

"But his Majesty cannot think—he must have forgotten—The devil take me! I cannot quit in the evening the woman whom I married only this morning!"

The piteous accent and the despairing mien of the poor fellow touched even the officer, who said:

"I appreciate all there is painful in what is commanded you; but you are a soldier, sir, and you should know that a soldier's first duty is obedience."

"Still, take me to the King!" implored the young gentleman; "I must speak to him, explain to him—he will hearken to my prayers and grant a delay."

"The King has retired for the night, and nobody is allowed to see him until his hour of rising. At that hour, you ought to be on the road to Freiburg."

"But would you have me take up the march in this dress?" remonstrated Joel, glancing on his wedding garments.

Almada came forward to say: "My dear chevalier, in your dressing room is a complete outfit for a chevalier, such as a cornet would wear in the cavalry; besides there is the sword which you handed to the constables and which was restored by them, an attention which is unusual in those gentry and a surprise which I reserved to you."

"And the pick of my horses in the stable is yours," added Boislaurier.

"Alas!" said the ambassador, taking the husband's hand, "You see me afflicted. Pardon an old man who is the cause of all this. Not suspecting that it would be so soon brought to the test, it was I who had the unlucky idea of boasting to the King of the ardent zeal with which you burnt to serve him. I must have been too eloquent in picturing how impatient you are to prove your gallantry. I was wrong to repeat these words you uttered on your wedding morn."

"Oh, then, the chevalier has made an engagement," inquired the young wife.

"To sacrifice everything to his King and country," replied the diplomatist. The chevalier hung his head while the old plotter continued: "Consequently the King, wanting a messenger on whom he could rely, fixed on our friend, from my language, to favor him with this token of his esteem."

The Breton looked up at him supplicatorily. But he went on, after a slight pause, "His Majesty cannot have calculated what such a separation would cost you at such a moment, although it is but temporary; and if it were allowed me to make my voice heard, I am certain that he would revoke his decision. Unfortunately, we have no time to act thus."

"Give me some advice," muttered Joel.

"My child," said the old noble, shaking his white head, "a man of heart and wits like yourself should at such times take counsel of himself."

"To make a long matter short," interpolated the lieutenant, "what am I to report to his Majesty?"

"You will announce to him," Aurore took it upon herself to reply, "that his orders will be executed. Do you believe, Joel," she continued while her husband looked at her in astonishment, "that I love you so little and take so little pride in you that I would try to hold you back? Honor orders and we must obey. This new parting will cost me many tears, and heaven alone will know how sad and lonesome I shall feel in your absence in this court where I shall be left. But you offered your service to the King, and it is not right that you should draw back when he requires them. Go and make ready, therefore, without weakness or hesitation. The thought that we are both doing our duty, you, on the journey, I, in my solitude, will console us."

Half and hour subsequently, the actors in this domestic tragedy, came down into the yard of the Boislaurier House where a groom was holding a pair of horses by the bridle. The wedded couple were arm-in-arm: the woman's eyes were dry and her visage calm, for she wept inwardly in order that she should not shake her husband's courage. He appeared no less resigned. He looked handsome in his military harness: a breastplate and buff gauntlets, a steel gorget, a blue coat laced with silver at every seam, scarlet breeches, high boots and a hat with a red plume. The sword of Porthos again was in a fit place at his side.

"Chevalier, I have selected my best war-horse," observed M. de Boislaurier.

"And as you will want a lackey," added Almada, "I give you Esteban, one of my faithful Spaniards, who, however, speaks French as well as any Parisian citizen. He is a brave, skillful fellow who can help you in any work."

Joel bowed his thanks.

"If you please," said Maupertuis, " I will accompany you to the town's end, to give you instructions."

Joel leaped into the saddle: the two married ones regarded each other with deep melancholy but with supreme serenity of heart.

"You are not traveling alone," breathed the young woman, "for you take my soul with you."

"Aurore, you are great and noble," whispered he, as she held out her hand as if to point out his road.

"God will bring you home to your dear one again ! We shall meet again ! Remember that you will find me what you left me—your wife, proud to wear your name, and happy that we love one another."

The Son of Porthos leaned over and, catching her round the waist, he lifted her upon his saddlebow without an effort.

"Yes, we shall meet again," he repeated : " God shield you, my adored wife, till then ;" and the last syllable of the wish died away on their lips uniting in a kiss.

Already true to instructions, Joel rode straight to the offices of the War Minister, but Louvois, who had been kept late at St. Germain's overnight, would not receive any one until noon. Thinking of the Widow of Scarron, the Knight of Locmaria, heedless of a kind of remonstrance from Esteban, remounted and proceeded direct to the Gray House.

The lady welcomed him, though her surprise was great to see him in the soldierly attire.

" I am the King's soldier," he said, explaining what had occurred to him. " I come to say good-bye to you, our good angel, our providence, and thank you for all you have done for us both. You must have had a hand in the good fortune showered on us, for I presume that it was due to you that my wife obtained a footing in the court."

"Let me see: you are the Chevalier de Locmaria and you have married Mdlle. du Tremblay?"

"You know all this—but with what an odd look you stare at me! any one would think that you ware not glad for my happiness. It is true there are crosses with it," he went on, shaking his head. " We had barely time to exchange half-a-dozen words before an order from the King dropped on us, and here I am, obliged to ride off in the first peep of the honeymoon."

" Sit down there, M. Joel," said the Widow Scarron, indicating a seat in front of hers, " and tell me the whole affair with all the particulars. The sympathy you inspire in me makes me curious to know to the least detail this event which I so little anticipated."

When he had again but more fully related the story, the lady, who had listened with religious silence, muttered to herself : "He is speaking in good faith. Does your wife love you?" she inquired with abruptness.

The Breton burst into a peal of hearty laughter.

"That is a good joke," he replied, "certainly not more than I love her. To doubt her love would be to offend the most virtuous heart in the world. But I am at a loss to understand—" he said, with surprise in which anxiety began to show.

" Have you any reason to distrust this Duke of Almada, the principal engineer in this match-making?" she interrupted him.

"Why should I distrust a good old man like him? He is the best and most generous of men."

"You cannot suspect him of any wish to deceive you?"

"To what end—by what means—under the sway of what interest?"

"Has Mdlle. du Tremblay ever spoken to you about the King?" proceeded Widow Scarron, after a silence. "I mean in any peculiar way?"

"Never! what a funny question! why do you put me to the *question* thus?" His voice was choked as by some sudden pain : not that he suffered any, but he feared he should through the promonition of misfortune. The **lady scrutin**ized him attentively, muttering to herself.

"Such a clear eye, honest features, frank speech, and this real and sincere grief are not the traits of husbands who traffic in their wives' honor. He may be a victim, but not a guilty accomplice. My friend," she said to the chevalier, "you do wrong to feel alarmed. I do not really know what could have been in my head to pester you thus with my silly questions. Forget them and pardon me. There are times when the blue devils dance in one's brain and speak by one's mouth."

The Breton was yet boyish, as prompt to cool as to heat. He sighed heavily in relief at these final words.

" Good again !" he exclaimed in serenity. " You frightened me, though, for I was going crazy, I believe. To think that I was on the point of suspecting the most perfect of human creatures !"

" Well, to punish yourself for that wicked doubt," returned the royal governess, affectionately, " you must still more dearly love her who is so worthy of your passion, consecrate the whole of your life to her and watch over her happiness as a miser does his treasure. Go away in confidence," she added, holding out her hand. " Go quickly, too, that you may the sooner return."

" Thus did I determine," said our hero, rising. " I am in haste to get through with a disagreeable piece of business before I quit Paris with all speed. But promise me one thing before I leave you : in my absence, watch over my darling."

"I will do better than hover around her—I will keep by her and confer with her about you."

"You must yourself see that you are an angel !"

If any peril threatens her whom I call your treasure, I will warn you of the plot so that you, whose duty it is, shall defend her."

CHAPTER XXII.

THE BLACK VELVET MASK.

On leaving the widow's, Joel proceeded to Bouloi Street, to use up the hour before him until Louvois should receive him, and to acquit himself of the mission Pierre Lesage had entrusted to him.

The first person he met had pointed out the right road, and he soon found the house in the street, where the ladies of the court had gone to consult the oracle. By day the whole scene was so different that Joel did not clearly recognize that here he had defended Mdme. de Montespan and hurled the confederate of the Manicarde into the gutter.

Even in the broad light, the dwelling had not a less mysterious appearance. But the fittings of the pythoness had been removed, and in the room where she had performed her conjurations nothing was left but an old table, not worth burning, at which was seated an old hag and a man was standing. He had brought in a pot of wine and two pewter goblets were there to receive its contents; they had been playing cards and the winner had brought the liquor now at hand.

The man was the Walton mentioned in the case of the Poisoners and he was ruddy, red in hair as a fox, with large teeth under a bristling moustache: his pale blue eyes seemed of glass—so cold and unfeeling. The world had acted like Joel of late—that is, kicked him into the gutter and kept him there, for he was unkempt, dirty and tattered.

They were beginning to drink when they heard the steps of Joel, who had found the door ajar after the man's entrance and boldly intruded.

"Who can come in here like that?" demanded the man, feeling for the sword which no doubt had been sold for old iron.

"It is some horseman," replied the woman, "for I hear the jingle of spurs and the scratching of the sword-scabbard along the wall."

"This looks bad," muttered the other, "though I hoped the matter had blown over, especially since Therese ran away. She may have been taken and told of us, eh? However, they can get no proof against us. I have destroyed what existed when I was caged, and then they could not hold me."

The sound of steps approached, and a lusty voice began to shout in the deserted corridor: "House, ho! is there nobody at home? let me see some Christian soul who will supply a brother in a fog with enlightenment?"

"Singular address," muttered Walton. "Yet it may be a spy of the police come to extract some clue to Therese The Lord only knows what she may have dealt in without my knowledge since I was knocked on the head by that cowardly giant." He leaned towards the hag, saying: "Mind what you say; I am the public-writer Latour, from the corner: you are the sick-nurse Bosse, and we have just moved in and know no more than Adam and Eve who were the previous tenants."

With a few rapid turns of the hands he executed some changes in the arrangement of his hair and moustache, and awaited the new-comer.

The old woman rose and as she went to the door, she screamed:

"Do not be so noisy there, you! here I am."

She opened the door without hastening so as to give her companion time to finish his alteration in appearance.

Joel strode in without a pause.

"Good people, excuse this riot, but I have not a minute to lose. And your dark corridor is as difficult to navigate as a sea of ink."

Walton stared at him with hate and rage, for he recognized the tall man who had not only refused him assistance to nab the three ladies, but had felled him to the mire. On the other hand, the new soldier of the King did not give more than a glance to the scamp who presented nothing to interest him.

"Captain," said the two together, "we are at your orders."

"I only want a little information: two words about a girl or woman named Lesage—Therese Lesage."

The man's face expressed surprise not to be concealed though he was an adept at self-control: but he turned to the woman, and said "Therese Lesage? do you know any one of that name, Mother Bosse?"

"We have only just moved in," was the hag's reply, "and I do not know any of the neighbors or who was living here before we came."

"You do not know who lived here?"

"We do not want to know them: they were a bad lot, who told fortunes and who sold drugs, and the police routed them out. I never heard that name before, eh, Latour?"

" Is there no other tenant, who has been here all along? it seems a large house," persisted the inquirer.

" I am going to take lodgers—I occupy the whole house," returned the woman with a kind of pride.

Joel looked his defeat.

"I already knew that this person whom I have never seen," he said, "may have strong reasons to keep concealed; but I do not wish her any evil. I do not come from any enemy of hers, but from her father, who died a short time ago, in the Bastille, almost under my eyes."

At the news of the death of Lesage, the pretended Englishman's glassy eyes flashed with a serpent's glitter, but Joel did not notice it as he pursued:

" The unfortunate prisoner charged me to hand to her an article which is of some value, I was given to understand— a locket in brass or gilt——"

At these words, the fire of greed blazed up in the old woman's eyes and she was about to speak, but with a terrifying glance the man froze the words on her lips.

"This medallion," said Joel, "contains a paper said to be of capital importance to this Lesage girl—something like a weapon of defence, if I clearly understood it. It is therefore urgent that I should find her, so as to acquit myself of my undertaking."

"Captain," replied the man in a cracked voice, "I should be happy to help you in the matter, but it is no use my cudgeling my brains, I cannot furnish you with the slightest clue. But if she were one of the infernal crew who held witches' sabbaths in this house, I suggest that you should apply to the police. The house of their Chief M. de Lareynie is only a few doors off."

"This honest fellow is quite right," mused the inquirer. "And Huguenin the jailer hit the nail on the head. She will have left Paris, and perhaps the kingdom. This couple seem truthful, although they are not prepossessing and the man's visage is a patent of rascality. Ought I question the neighbors? no, for I have no time, since it is going on for midday, and Minister Louvois will expect me. After calling on him, I must take the road. When I return from Freiburg I will resume this errand, which weighs upon me, with more activity. And if I cannot reach the intended depository of this locket, Faith! I shall destroy it, paper and all."

To the joy of the couple, he proceeded towards the street. As he was crossing the threshold he almost ran against a woman who was on the point of entering. She was masked in black velvet, and was wrapped in a voluminous black silk mantle. The gentleman stood aside to allow her to pass. It seemed to him that she uttered a faint scream on seeing him, but that might be only from the fear that there would have been a collision. However, she plunged into the dark passage with a light step, leaving behind her a cloud of perfume, which had previously struck the provincial youth.

"Where did I smell that before? where have I seen that tall and elegant figure ? where did I catch the glance of that bold and fascinating eye?"

He turned round instinctively, but the lady had disappeared in the very path which he had trodden. The way was not wholly unfamiliar to her, but she missed the black boy who had ushered her into the fortune-teller's presence, and she stopped at the door of the room.

"He, in this den—what business had he here ?" she said to herself in astonishment.

While she was hesitating, the man and woman who had received the squire so churlishly, were disputing.

"What a blunder you have made," reproached the hag: "we might have 'nailed' that locket, and sold that secret paper to whoever is most concerned to suppress it, and that would have provided funds for our flight. If that game would not work, we might have handed it to Therese, who is as generous as the theif's daughter usually is, and one way or the other we should have made a good thing of the affair."

"That is all right," returned the other, with a shrug of the shoulders, "unless the whole thing is a fable to trap us. I know this fellow to be a prowler whom I mistook for one of our kidney the night when I was following home the three great ladies who would have been our reliance in a rainy day. Instead of joining hands with me and despoiling the court hussies, he upset me into the channel—curses on him ! that is more like a bully of the police than the gentleman of leisure that he affects to be. Besides, who would be in the Bastille to see old Lesage kick the bucket, but a prison guard or such? The sleuth-hounds of Larevnie have so many faces that we must be aways on our guard." He filled his cup from the pot, and continued: "We are the last of the old gang in town. La Voisin was burnt alive: Pierre Lesage came to grief as you heard that person tell us ;" he made a malignant face ; " their daughter has crossed the frontier, waiting for us to join her, especially me, her sweetheart; the rest are scattered—in fact, we are completely broken up. We expected to be let alone, as we are thought small fry, not worth hauling in by the net ; but we may be under the ban, and this is as likely as not a spy ——"

"Spy or no spy, we have missed a chance. If only he came again—" grumbled the hag.

Three light taps were heard on the door, and caused the couple to look at each other in the same anxiety as before. The knocking was repeated, more loudly than at first and a woman's voice articulated with a remarkable tone of authority :

"Whoever is within, open this door : you are wanted."

The expression was that traditional with the police, but the feminine voice had encouraged Walton, who smilingly said :

"This is one of your customers to have the future told. She falls in timely, by all that is good in wine, for I am kiln-dry again and my *red rag* (the tongue) feels like an old kernel in a last year's nut."

The woman ran to open the door, and let in the masked lady.

Her eyes, glittering in the holes of her vizard, rapidly made the circuit of the room, which she failed to recognize from its having being stripped of its adornments and furniture. She scanned the countenances of the pair, as they bowed obsequiously.

"Are we three without hearers here ?" she demanded.

"Yes, noble lady," said the man, respectfully.

"Oh, is this you, Walton ?" she said as she approached the table. "Hand me a chair."

"Do you know me ?" said the man starting.

"Since some time back, gossip. I need not know you by name to guess what sort of a finished villain you are, to inhabit the old haunt of the daughter of La Voisin."

She sat on the stool which was presented to her. Her nonchalant attitude contrasted with the rogues' trepidation as much as her satin with the sordid aspect of the room.

"You are the sham Englishman whom the great lady saved from the gallows. You are called 'the Author' by the gang because you can write a good hand in various styles, and have pretended to publish philosophical works. You were latterly the factotum of La Voisin and Pierre Lesage, whose daughter you have inveigled. It will not conduce to the warmer intimacy between you if she should be informed of the part you played in his sham escape, which has resulted in his decease."

Both her hearers started at this accusation.

"As for you, Bosse, you were in the service of Lesage before the band was dispersed. Am I sufficiently well informed?

"You know more than I know myself," returned Walton brazingly, though there was as much dread as curiosity in his tone.

"After the scandal died away, you thought to resume the old craft, but anew the police became vigilant and the Lesage girl has thought fit to flee, it seems, for the paraphernalia of the so-called La Manicarde has disappeared. You are under the ban: you are closely watched and you fear that you may not even attempt to go lest you be arrested. In short, you run the risk of dying of starvation in this house where your confederates and masters made a fortune."

"Alack! moaned the woman, "this is true. Our powders and salves no longer sell, and our pills and drafts go begging. If our medicines were only harmless we would be forced to live upon them."

"Bah!" growled her companion: "one can get used to doing without meat, but not without drink. It is the days without a draft that are so hatefully hard and long." Walton uttered the phrase with solemnity and his face was convulsed with genuine horror.

"The great ladies are just as frightened as the common folk," went on the hag: "the flames that consumed La Voisin have daunted them, and the lesser dames act like them in the spirit of imitation."

"I do not share this terror or those scruples," coldly observed the visitress; "and if you consent to serve me, I shall pay your help—never mind your conscience—what is it worth?"

"Speak, lady," said the man, more accustomed to such negotiations than the woman, "we are ready to obey you."

'On more than one occasion," began the visitress, lowering her voice, "I had recourse to the talent of Lesage and La Voisin ; are you as skillful as they in the art of fabricating that elixir which given in a carefully calculated dose, invigorates ; in a larger one, plunges into sleep ; and in a still larger one, or in a prolonged series of small portions, causes the sleep without awaking ?"

"Madame, I was initiated into all these secrets and have studied with all the masters of my time : from them, and perfected by myself, I hold the incomparable receipt, by which I make the elixir to wihch you allude : it leaves in the subject experimented upon all the semblance of life ; while it is carrying into every article a stream of inevitable death."

"Enough ?" exclaimed the dame, " I see that you are the man I want."

She dropped a heavy purse upon the table. "Bring out to a follower of mine what you speak of, and if I be content with you, you will be fully recompensed. You are watched, so do not attract the attention of the Police."

"So I said," remarked Walton, turning to his confederate : "that was one of Lareynie's spies."

"That officer that I met at the door ?"

"Oh, he was an officer, then ? At all events he did not glean much here."

"What did he do ?" demanded the masked lady imperatively. "I want to know. Speak !"

Walton did not hesitate, but related briefly the interview with the Knight of Locmaria. From the commencement the hearer violently trembled. Her brow frowned behind the black velvet ; her eyes were surrounded by a brown ring, and her feline glances explored vacancy.

"A locket ? what is a locket ? a token of affection to his daughter on the eve of the death which he divined. There is more in this wizard's craft than all acknowledge. Yet, nothing was found upon him that incriminated me. He would have never destroyed that letter of mine—oh, that letter," she muttered, pressing her head between her hands, "what can have become of it ?"

Walton had been straining his ear. On catching these last words, he made bold to speak.

"My lady, the old fox passed the paper into the medallion, and that over to some hand which he believed he could trust. But permit me to finish my story."

He did so swiftly with the masked lady silent on her seat. Her features had become as still as though they were sculptured in marble ; but her eyes blazed and her brain was working furiously.

"So, so," she mused, "it is this intruder from Brittany who stands in the way ; he repulsed my advances ; he is the associate, unconscious or otherwise, of this woman who is trying to displace me beside the King ; he is now the master of my secret and of my fate ! By my faith, he has gone too far in braving me and being a fetter upon me. You are a spoil sport, Chevalier Joel, and I begin to believe that you will not arrive at Freiburg without some thorn catching you in the hedges. Friend," said she to Walton, "can you procure for me two stout swordsmen who will do any work set to them, if they are roundly paid."

"When do you want them?"

"Immediately."

The sham Englishman reflected a moment, then slapping the hag on the shoulder, as she was dozing or pretending so to do, he said:

"Get you to the tavern of the Dry Well at the Croix Rouge. Your brother, the Lock-breaker, should be carousing there; bring him with another of his stamp, for there is gold to win with their steel."

The woman shuffled out with a more nimble stem than might have been expected of her, but there was the prospect of many a revel

The acquaintance of Lock-breaker, the treacherous lieutenant of Colonel Cordbuff, we have had the sad necessity of making ; the comrade cut-throat whom he brought was an ex-soldier of the royal guards, with a bully's face, bony brazen and hardened, with his moustaches waxed and hooked upwards on strong jaws. The pair saluted the masked lady, with one hand on the sword hilt, the other to their moustache curls.

" You understand me clearly then." said she; "at present this man is on the road to Lorraine. You should recognize him from the description which I gave. You are to get horses and run him down. He carries a locket of which I have need. Rid me of that gallant and bring me the token, and I will give you a fortune."

"*Fortune* is a relative term," observed Lock-breaker, "How much do we get in advance?"

"Fifty pistoles, and you shall have three times as much after."

"Lady, it is a bargain."

CHAPTER XXIII.

EVIL TO THEM WHO EVIL PLAN.

AFTER receiving from Minister Louvois's own hands the despatches for Marshal Créquy, the Knight of Locmaria left Paris by the St. Martin's suburb. He was in warlike array; spurred with pistols in the holsters, and sharpened sword by his side, and the horseman's cloak on his shoulders. Esteban rode by him as his lackey.

The journey opened sadly, as, under his apparent resignation, the newly married man quitted with regret the part of earth where he had been about to be so happy. In the ride from St. Germain to Paris, the beat of his horse's hoofs carrying him away from that lot in paradise, had sounded like a funeral knell. As the horizon enlarged, and the future, full of mysteries, unfolded itself before him, he felt the need to reason with himself, and be completely his master to parry the eventualities and dangers of such a journey.

He rode now with a free spirit if not in gaiety, for the unconfined breeze had refreshed his forehead. His broad chest drank it to the fill of his lungs. The world seemed vast, and he knew he lived and might hope.

In his recollection, Aurore was smiling, and all the more charming a memory for that phase.

Two things annoyed him. First, the companionship of Esteban, whose swarthy complexion, piercing eyes and honeyed voice inspired in him scanty confidence. Again, he had not had time to continue his leavetaking at the Blackamoor. What had become of Host Bonlarron, with his sword as long as Friquet was tall, and that brave lad himself, the jolly companion so tender about his statue? Never mind! he would hunt them up on his return.

For he had but one thought: to distinguish himself before Freiburg, and return as quickly as possible. Hence he had decided to go twice the usual distance in one day. He planned to pass Chelles and sleep at Lagny. Unfortunately, a little before reaching the skirt of Bondy Forest, as they were passing a little wayside blacksmith's, the man, who was hammering on his anvil, shouted:

"Cry you pardon, my gentleman, but your man's mare will cast a shoe before she goes twenty lengths, for the off-hind shoe hangs by only a couple of nails."

The remark was true, and they were obliged to stop. While confounding the delay, Joel addressed the farrier who had warned him: "Friend, it is not enough to point out this unlucky mishap; but you must help us remedy it."

"Right willingly, master; only I am run out of nails, and must send to my brother-smith at Noisy for a supply; but it is only a skip, and I will fasten the shoe on in four blows of the hammer."

"At Noisy?" and the young traveler's brow became more dark. "It is a good distance and the job will take a lot of time."

"Why, no, for I have my bellows-boy here who has legs like a deer, and will get there in a short half-an-hour and another to return, while it will only take me ten minutes to do the job. In better than an hour you will be off and away again."

"Yes, but this prevents my supping at Lagny."

"But you can have the supper at Chelles, at the Shield of France inn, where they do not flay alive honest folk, and it has not its like in all the county for roast duck in a paste."

"Send your prentice off at once," said the gentleman, dismounting and walking into the smithy. "But how am I to kill the time of waiting?" he muttered, while Esteban led the horses into a yard behind the forge. "Stay, I know. I will send news to Aurore—the darling will be uneasy, no doubt. Let us prove that we do not let a moment pass without thinking of the adored wife. Master Vulcan," he called out, "can you furnish me with writing materials? and find me some corner in your house where I can sit at a table, and not be disturbed? I pay for any inconvenience I cause."

The peasant pointed to a ladder-like flight of steps leading up from the smoked corner.

" Go up into my room, there. The paper, ink and quill are there with which I make out my bills. And do not *hurry yourself*, for we will let you know when the job is done."

THE DEATH OF ARAMIS.

When the Breton had disappeared in the loft, Esteban went up to the smith and made a sign to him.

"Your man is there?" replied the blacksmith, pointing to the partitioned-off place where he stored his small coal.

A door creaked slightly on its hinges, and they saw the hangdog visage, long body and hooked moustache of Colonel Condor de Cordbuff; on coming forth from the hole, he stretched his limbs like a wild cat leaving its lair.

"In good faith," grumbled he, "I was afraid that the fresh orders would not arrive in time to you."

"It is plain," observed the lacky, "that if we had not been made to dance attendance on the War Minister, up to noon, his excellency's emissary would not have met me in Paris." In a confidential tone he resumed: "So my lord the duke is bent upon finishing the affair straightway, eh? Are we not to go on to Freiburg? is it here the journey comes to an end?"

The ex-colonel of the Royal Marauders pointed towards the sombre forest line as he replied: "Twenty muskets lie behind the outmost bushes? ten a side. From each hand of the road the lightning will flash."

A ferocious smile lit up the Spaniard's face, as he approved.

"*Caramba!* I like to hear the guns speak, provided it is not to me they have sharp things to say."

"But we must await nightfall," went on Cordbuff, "otherwise this confounded Breton may perceive the glint of the barrels under the leaves."

The Spaniard took a look at the sky.

"Waiting for nightfall when there is a gale in the air. I have a seaman's eye for storms. Before an hour it will be as black out there as in this forge chimney."

Condor rubbed his hands.

"That is wonderfully good! Though our lads blaze away at random, they will not do the worse work. After we do it, each must shift for himself, leaving the bodies in the middle of the road, so that whoever finds them will lay the blame on the robber Vide-gousset, who infests this part round Paris."

"Pardon me," interrupted the lackey, pricking up his ears; "You spoke of 'bodies' in the plural—from *some slip of the tongue, I suppose.* You meant the body."

"That's it," Cordbuff rectified the error, but biting his lip. "The body of the master and the carcase of his horse—that is what I meant, for the beast will hardly go scot-free from such a volley? But I must hurry to join the ambuscade. This cursed fellow knows me from a brush I had with him on the Saumur highway and the attack in Paris, and it would never do for him to come down, for he would recognize me."

"Stay, for one word. Take care that no bullet goes akew in my direction, please, as I am quick to reply in kind. Remember that I shall be close behind him, and I do not want any *fatal blunder* in a jest or by premeditated forgetfulness."

"How can you think of such a thing, my dear comrade?"

Indeed the sky was clouding over. At the gallop sped masses of storm-lined vapor, producing a changeable chaos of light and shade. One of these eclipses of light prevented Esteban remarking the perfidious intention which glistened like the serpent's scales on the adventure's lips and in his eyes while he said:

"It was the duke who gave the orders to my men. So no mistake can be possible, and we shall carry them out."

In the meantime, Joel continued to write, on the upper floor. His pen ran rapidly and he was hardly conscious how time was coursing, too. He was speaking to his dear Aurore whom he saw before him and expected to hear her speak. On the sheets of blackened paper, the phrase "I love you," was often repeated. But it was time to come to an end; he folded up the epistle, and wrote the superscription.

"What a slowness they show in notifying me of the time to start again," he muttered. "How dark it has become," he added, with some astonishment. "Can it be dusk already, or is it the weather turning bad?"

He rose and went to the little window to verify his prognostic, but he had barely cast a glance without before he recoiled like a man who does not want to be seen.

"Halloa!" he exclaimed to himself, "this is singular!"

The road took a curve before passing the smithy. One of the branches, that travelled by our pair, led from the city; the other went into the Bondy Woods, at a few hundred paces, yet to be threaded by them. The room window commanded the forest skirts, and the squire mechanically examined the brush. A sunbeam slanted through the slaty gray clouds, and left the house in the shadow; but, on the other hand, it lighted up the thickets and penetrated the foliage to some depth. Thus it came that the looker-out thought he saw men in the coverts, and luminous points like the glint of light upon polished metal. Keeping up his scrutiny, but remaining hidden, Joel could count a score, ten on each side of the road.

"The deuce, this looks like an ambush," he thought.

At this juncture, one man appeared among the glittering dots and waved his hand, so that they faded out of sight : evidently he had perceived the oversight and wanted to prepare it, before he, too, vanished in the copse.

"Zounds !" muttered the Breton, "if I had not smashed that scoundrel Cordbuff on the Celestins wharf, I should swear that he is yonder, organizing this little waylaying enterprise.

But who would this party be arrayed against ? As the young knight was putting this question to himself, he heard the clatter of horses' hoofs on the road from Paris. On account of the bend, the new-comers could not perceive the thicket until they passed the forge. Besides, the sun did not shine at this period, and the whole sky was a mass of sable clouds. The wind raised whirls of dust, and heavy raindrops began to sprinkle the ground.

The sound rapidly drew near, and presently two men on horseback rushed by the smithy at full gallop; their steeds were fleckered with foam, as if from a precipitous race. One of them was no doubt better mounted than the other, for he preceded him by three or four lengths. Both were pressing on without heeding the rain, or the dust which strove to blind them between them.

Scarcely had they turned the elbow before the men in hiding moved in the foliage and Joel saw them coming forward to bring their guns to bear.

"How now?" muttered he; "can it be for me, or those fellows that these warlike preparations are made ? In either case, I cannot let the unsuspecting fall into the deadly trap." He lifted his voice to call out to them, but it was lost in the uproar, and in a trice, the cavaliers were out of earshot.

The brave knight rushed down the stairs, shouting:

"Our horses—let us have our horses—quick!"

They stood ready before the forge. Near them was Esteban, his saturnine countenance contracted by anger which in the haste his master did not notice.

"Plague take those outsiders!" muttered the Spaniard, "whom our bullies will mistake for us, and shoot them instead of this new-fledged knight."

Joel had bounded into the saddle, crying: "At full speed and have your sword drawn—we must save those travelers or at least lend them aid"

But, as he dug his spurs into his steed's flanks, several gunshots resounded. In spite of this, the chevalier dashed off with the bridle between his teeth, and in his hands the rapier and a pistol. The lackey followed at the same pace.

"It looks as though I shall be obliged to put a bullet into the back of his head," though he, streching out his hand to his holsters.

But a few scattering shots whizzed about them like angry hornets, and the servant of Aramis uttered a scream of pain: a slug had broken his pistol-arm near the wrist and a bullet had entered his throat. Uncontrolled, his frightened horse carried him in the wake of his master's, which burst into the wood like a hurricane.

Twenty paces within the skirt of the wood, between natural hedges of undergrowth, two bleeding corpses were stretched, at the side of which Joel with difficulty reined in. Into the pool of blood which they had lost,—Esteban was pitched, by the sudden stoppage of his steed—horrified by the blood and the smell of powder.

The two dead men were those who had caught the volley intended for the Son of Porthos. One of them was held down under his horse, which had a broken thigh. The other's horse was racing through the forest, which was becoming hushed as though its glades were unpeopled once more. But at a distance was audible the tramp of a troop of irregular cavalry, fading away. It was the company of Cordbuff, obeying the order to make off at will.

Joel hitched his charger to a tree, and examined the dead before he attended to the dying, less interested in his own man than he could account for. The strangers were beyond hope: the first was slain outright as though struck by lightning, and the other was riddled like a sieve. When the young knight terminated this task, he saw that Esteban had come to his senses, and, propped on the elbow of his uninjured arm, was curiously contemplating the two corpses.

"I see," muttered he, careless whether he were overheard or not: "if I had been riding behind the master, as I should have been, I would have received all that shower of lead in my body, instead of two pellets—which, by all that is unlucky, will do the trick, I fear me. Orders were out to slay the valet along with the master: or Cordbuff sought to get rid of a rival who hampered him in trying to enjoy my lord's good graces. Be it as it may, the lesson comes too late for me to profit by it. But I can be revenged," he continued, with a scowl of evil augury.

Joel lifted him up into a sitting position, and propped him against a tree. His wound had ceased to bleed outwardly, but he held his unhurt hand to it as if choking. A deathly perspiration bathed his livid brow; his eyelids closed despite his will, and a red froth bubbled about his mouth.

"Drink," moaned he.

Joel took a flask of wine from his saddlebow and held it to the swaying head, of which the teeth chattered against the cap, used as a cup; but he managed to gulp a mouthful.

"The saints reward you," he gasped.

"Take courage," said his master. "I will ride to the smith's or carry you thither."

An ironical smile flitted over the lackey's lips.

"Do nothing—it is over—I have my account settled."

His eyelids slowly opened, disclosing the vitreous orbs, and his unsteady gaze wandered over the scene of slaughter; suddenly, kindled by the forerunning of his doom, it shone with a fugitive lustre. "I trust you will revenge me. Oh, that I had a priest ere I die—but it is impossible here. Since there is nothing else, you shall receive my confession, by which you can profit to save yourself perhaps——"

"You are wandering! how save myself?"

"This ambuscade was directed against you and me—that wretch of a Cordbuff would not have spared his accomplice.

"Cordbuff, do you say? then, it was he whom I spied. Has that cut-purse turned cut-throat?"

"He is your mortal enemy—and not the only one—and the others are more powerful and skillful. They send to Freiburg to be rid of you—they wanted to kill you, lest you might return."

"But why? who are these enemies? who longs for my death?"

"All is spinning round me," muttered the weakening sufferer. "My very heart is melting within me. For pity's sake, give me something to clear my swollen throat."

Joel offered him the wine again, and on his swallowing a few drops, a slight flame mounted to his cheeks.

"Yes," said he, hastening as if he feared a crisis would stop his revelation, "listen now, and grave these words on your mind with the indications I give you. Those men fell instead of us, but, you see, I was marked down. My master, the Duke of Almada, has bought, on the margin of Marly Woods, a summerhouse not far from the royal residence. In the principle room of the house, on the left of the fire place, is a secret panel, moving, if you press the spring, in a brass knob concealed in the dado. This opens a way to a subterranean gallery communicating with the palace, ending in one of the rooms of the king's apartments."

"But what is the good of these particulars?" quered Joel. "In what way do they concern me? what use are they?"

"I see that you do not understand me," breathed the wounded man with difficulty. "You think I am in delirium, raving and out of my senses—but you are wrong—I see clearly, and you will understand me later. That secret way is to be used to arrive in time to outstrip the King and prevent——"

"Go on, go on! prevent?"

"Prevent the plot which I overheard arranged, being brought to pass."

His breathing had grown hard, his vision dim, and he held out his hand as his head fell backward.

"More drink!" he panted, "I am dying."

The knight held out the flask this time, but he had hardly more than carried it to his lips than he repulsed it so roughly that it fell on the mossy ground, and he hoarsely uttered:

"No, would you send me drunk into the presence of my Judge?"

His features became broken up with frightful rapidity; his upturned eyeballs half disappeared under the distended

THE DEATH OF ARAMIS.

lids : the flaps of his nose sank, and the scum on his lips changed to a yellow hue.

"What does all this signify?" demanded the Breton, leaning over him; "answer me! what did you hear plotted?"

"I know not—I remember no more. The mist clouds my eyes, and a bell seems booming in my brain. But that passage will be guarded. Cordbuff and his murderers will be posted to dispute the entrance. *Caramba!* crush them as they did that pair there : and the old chief, too. Ah," he shrank back as if to enter into the substance of the tree against which he rested, "it is he who is coming, the sinister white-beard ! he comes to strangle me lest I make the confession !" he rose along the trunk as if to resist or flee from a spectre; his eyes widened with intense terror, and his unhurt hand again clawed at his throat.

"He has seized—he is strangling me !" His skin turned an ashen color; from his swollen throat a hoarse gurgle issued, and the froth on his mouth was a blackish red.

Joel grasped him, for he would have fallen full-length.

"Once more, Speak, I urge you ! I beg you—I want to know——"

No reply came from the lackey, whose head dropped forward on his chest, for he was dead : the wound had flowed inward and his last words were stifled.

Meanwhile the storm had suddenly been appeased; a last gust had cleared the sky and the sunset was clear and serene. Joel gave a last look to the ghastly battlefield ; on the two *bravi* he saw the vile expression which death had not lessened, but he could not guess that they were the hirelings of the Marchionesss de Montespan, engaged to pursue him and bring to her the locket in which Pierre Lesage had secreted the incriminatory paper in her hand which he hoped to be the weapon for his daughter's protection. To earn their pay, the ancient lieutenant of Cordbuff and his partner had started forthwith on the man-hunt. They had not spared the spur to overtake the young knight, and had so strained themselves that they had shot in advance of him and received the musketry discharge intended for their betters.

"*Errare humanenness!*—" which may be translated as "Evil befals those who meditate evil."

Joel went to the blacksmith's for aid, but that worthy, fearing that his complicity in the outrage might be suspected, had abandoned his house. The young man was therefore compelled to leave the corpse, and take the two spare horses in leash, to the bailiwick of Vitry, where he related the matter to the *lieutenant-criminel.* After signing his statement, the King's messenger resumed the journey, less troubled by the sanguinary scene than by Esteban's strange and incomplete revelations.

Ought he take them seriously? or consider them the fancies of cerebral derangement inherent to the passage from life to death—the ramblings of a mind filled with incoherences and chimeras by the death throes? was there anything behind the last words, with an enigmatic sense which the dying one had no time to make clear?

What could signify this mysterious stuff about sliding panels, assassins lying in wait, a summerhouse, the royal residence? who were the powerful and skillful enemies who threatened the days of the young knight and had already delivered one bow at those who had by chance been substituted for their victims. What was the aim, and what the reasons?

The Duke of Almada could not be the "old man" of whom the Spaniard had passed away in such terror. He might have let him moulder in the Bastille : but he had made him the happiest of lovers, by uniting him to Mdlle. du Tremblay.

The King could not be an enemy. He had but to frown to be disembarrassed of a dangerous subject or of one simply importunate. In the case of the knight of Locmaria, he need not have interfered with the march of justice : but he had been great and good, and granted mercy. Besides, in what way could a humble country squire have offended the most Christian King or annoyed the ambassador of the Catholic Majesty of Spain ? It is needless to say that no idea struck the honest youth that Aurore had any part in the schemes woven against him. The dying lackey and not spoken of the young lady. So the newly married man was very deeply perplexed. It was in bewilderment that he reached Nancy, where two letters overtook him in kindness to his poor head : he was obliged to stop a couple of days to rest his charger. One missive was from *her*.

Aurore was already beginning to feel impatience over the return of the husband of her heart. She was in attendance on the Queen at St. Germain's, her royal mistress manifesting *more* and more affectionate kindness every day. Her companions seemed to like her. Those called "the wise ones," in that frivolous court, surrounded her with attentions and deference. The King was absorbed in the important negociations at Nimwegen. He came seldom into his consort's apartments. The writer added that she had seen nothing of the Marchioness de Montespan, while she often met the Widow Scarron, who was located at Pecq with her royal nursery.

"She is a friend whose great mind and heart I value more and more. Need I tell you that you are the topic of all our conversations? and how she endeavors to comfort me, strengthen me, and restore my faith in the goodness of heaven and hope in the future, when my thoughts, running before you on the remote highways, look for you amid the horrors of a siege, the fury of storming parties, and among the dead and the wounded! Oh, my dear and valiant Joel, take care of yourself for the sake of her who lets no moment go by without thinking that she is your wife. Be prudent as you are brave. Preserve your life as I should your honor."

"How she loves me!" muttered the knight, "and how deserving she is of love!"

He kissed the paper in a transport of delight.

The second message was from Widow Scarron. She stated to her correspondent that Aurore won admiration by her candor, loftiness of character, and frank revulsion against vice and wickedness.

"The King, whose confidence I sometimes have the honor to enjoy, since I am nearer St. Germain, has declared to me on several occasions, that none among the ladies of the royal household better merits the tokens of esteem and sympathy with which the Queen kindly favors her. Aurore is yours, my friend, as the priest is wedded to heaven. You must be the same towards her. Besides I keep my promise, and I watch over this angel of perfection with the solicitude which I have for the royal offspring confided to my care."

The words in both letters were a cordial to him. In neither was there mention of the Duke of Almada. It was clear that the agony and the fever of death had embroiled the wits of Esteban when his heavy conscience was in turmoil.

Hence our traveler resumed the journey with both head and heart relieved of depression which had almost stifled him.

The roads were cut up by the wheels of the artillery, among which he was glad to hear was the battery of the new engines of war, the bombards, of which Friquet held himself the inventor, and which it was understood would give the signal for the grand attack on Freiburg. Besides, the roads were also dangerous from the numbers of banditti, disbanded soldiers and deserters from both sides who foraged for their own gain, and put all the inhabitants of the Vosges to ransom. For that matter, the chevalier would have preferred to face a company of these highwaymen than ride with the black thoughts which had harassed him before he received the letters.

The night was clear when he reached the Black Forest, which had not stolen its name, for it was black as an oven in the glades. Before him, after passing through a vale, dark masses of pines covered the gloomy ridge of a hill. A light sparkled there, of so much greater volume than a cottage candle, that Joel believed it would be a rendezvous of soldiers or an inn.

He was right in the latter conjecture, for he recognized by the sign of a Cooked Crayfish and the general aspect that he was before one of those humble houses of entertainment which have earned this quarter in more recent ages the title of a land of hotels.

CHAPTER XXIV.

THE MAID OF THE INN.

ALTHOUGH there was no welcome when Joel rode up, he dismounted on being assured by hearing voices within that it was not deserted, and tying his horse to a ring in the wall, strode boldly into the place.

It was composed of a common room, with a staircase at the back, a table in the midst, and a fireplace where several pieces of meat and some split crayfish were broiling and baking.

A tall, brawny man sat by the window, cleaning one of those long-barrelled fowling-pieces which are good for any kind of game. Before being an innkeeper, Kaspar Braun was a soldier in the Thirty Years' War, devoted as now to his Emperor and his country. When the French invaded the country, his loyalty set him against him, but on the otherhand his good fare and the sacred laws of hospitality through which he had often saved a guest, earned him a kind of truce. The excuse of his age sufficed, but his sunburned visage, breathing indomitable energy, and the melancholic gravity special to men living in the solitudes of nature, did not express the weakness of many years. Over his green cloth vest and breeches, the uniform of a forester, he wore a goatskin jacket with the hairy side inward; his high leggings of buckskin were tightly laced over iron spiked shoes; and his hunting-knife hung at his belt. When he rose to receive the guest, he showed the subdued ferocity of a bulldog under restriction not to bite till further orders.

"What can one do for your service, my gentleman?" he challenged, with a slight bow, and using the French mixed with German common on the border where the armies of both powers so often warred.

"In faith, many things, my good man of the woods," gaily rejoined the cavalier: "accommodation and food for myself, and shelter and provender for my steed at the door. I suppose a supper is possible?"

The old forester smiled grimly.

"Everything is possible even now on the frontier, if the money is forthcoming, and you give enough time."

"You shall take your own time, and as I have escaped the knights of the road, I need not look to the expense."

"Arouse you, you sluggard wench from Paris," shouted Braun. "Go and put the gentleman's horse in the stable and hurry back to do the cooking."

This was spoken in German, but the guest had already acquired a smattering of the dialect and the result of the speech enlightened him as to the meaning. To his surprise, a recumbent figure which he had not suspected, rose in the fireplace: but he did not utter the exclamation risen to his lips as, while the German put his gun in a rack on the wall, this woman laid her finger signifying caution on her mouth. The word Paris had been cue enough, for her person, small and brisk, her manner, petulant, quick and restless, and her saucy and brightly vulgar features spoke of the daughter of Lutetia. In her peasant's dress she no more resembled the buxom girls of the Rhenish inns that an actress the countrywoman whom she personates in silks and costly jewelry. But she nimbly crossed the room and disappeared without.

"There is a basin of fresh water yonder," said the innkeeper, sullenly pointing to the farther end: "you may want to get the dust of the road off you. And if your trappings are in your way, I will hang them up."

Braun alluded to the guest's rapier and horse-pistols which he had brought in with him, stuck in his belt.

"Thank you, my good friend," said Joel, without losing his smile: "I am used to the articles and they do not inconvenience me."

The other seemed vexed in a sulky way, but he spoke calmly enough: "Just as you like, my master. Then, since I can do nothing for you, let me go draw some wine."

He stole to the rear of the room and lifting a trapdoor, descended by a short ladder into a place hallowed out in the rock among the roots of the pinetrees which had contributed their substance to make this house. Hardly had he gone than the young woman returned; but she seemed afraid to venture many words to the new-comer, to whom, as she passed to blow up the fire, she gave a look meaning: "Be careful. We are listened to."

To kill the time and give himself a countenance, the Frenchman pretended to study the coarse prints stuck against the wall to relieve the monotony of the plastering. They were mostly pictures of saints, or battles.

"What can all this strange reception mean?" he wondered. "A German host and a French servant, who is certainly not his wife or his daughter, but in as much awe of him as though she were either."

In the meantime, the man had returned and placed two bottles of Rhine wine on the table, where the woman arranged a cloth, two china vases with woodland flowers, a slice of cold roebuck with berry sauce, a hare pie, some sliced smoked sausage, and a polished pewter goblet. While busying herself at the board, she made the Son of Porthos a sign which meant that he might drink without apprehension. Then she returned to the revived fire, where she deftly and rapidly cooked an omelet, and dished a rabbit stewing since some hours.

On sniffing the aroma of these warm edibles and feasting his sight on the cold side-pieces already ranged on the board, our hero flung his hat on a chair, and cried: "To table!"

Braun darted an angry look upon the woman and said: "Well, do you not see that the gentleman's weapons are in his way?"

This return to the previous charge irritated the guest, who retorted testily: "Never mind! I am learning to be a soldier, and I am trying to get used to eating and drinking in my equipment."

"Oh, the gentleman is a soldier?" broke forth the innkeeper, in a voice which he tried to make more innocent than it would have appeared to more experienced ears.

"Yes: though I am more of a despatch-bearer than anything at present time, being on my way from Paris to Marshal Créquy."

The fact was, the good dinner was doing its softening work and, besides, Joel was on the very verge of accomplishing his mission, and he did not even feel a twinge at this too frank admission of his errand in a debatable land where both parties roved.

The innkeeper's face darkened as much as the strange waitress's brightened at his refusal to lay aside his weapons. Braun had reckoned on the influence of the meal and the sex without success. The Breton showed the thickness of his skull by drinking a bottle to the omelet, a second to the venison and he called for a third to wash down the preserves, the cheese and the fruit.

Night had fallen and lights were lit.

"How do you like the wine? it is a little vintage of my own," said Braun, rather more amiably.

"It is exquisite. I shall like this country!"

The host proposed fetching some more, but at this time, as the young soldier caught the eye of the servant, he saw her simulate nodding off to sleep. That he had in this fellow-countrywoman a friend in the possibly hostile camp, he did not doubt, and he took the hint.

"But it flies to the head," went on he, gaping frightfully; "either that or my long ride has made me desire rest. The Sandman has got into my eyes."

The landlord rose from his bench at a respectful distance and took up a candle to light it with splinter at the fire.

At this chance of gesticulating behind his back, the waitress took a step or two, reeling as if it were she who had imbibed too much wine.

"Right," thought the knight. "I shall conform to these suggestions, which have a purpose."

And rising to take the candle, he tottered as if the floor were oscillating.

"Dash it all," he said, clutching at the table, "one would say that the wind is high in the hills and rocks your old chalet like a ship at sea. Oh, it must be the little vintage of which you brag. Satanic beverage—I shall have a headache for this if I do not sleep it off."

Braun laughed heartily.

"It is mild as milk," sneered he, putting the candlestick in his hand, as if to prevent the servant seeing the guest to his room. "Dr. Slumber will cure you. After a good night you will not feel a bit of it. You will wake up to-morrow morning as gay as a woodpecker in a hollow tree. But let the maid hang up your iron appendages. You see that even I hang my gun up; we live in the peace of heaven, since the French drove away the duke of Lorraine; and they shall be cleaned like my old ducking-gun, when you don them in the day."

The woman surreptitiously shook her head, and as, with a calmed face she extended her hand, Joel gallantly chucked her under the chin and said: "Hold there! the old priest who taught me latin, told me a pretty tale of Venus in the armor of Mars—but pooh! all has become mixed in my head— to bed, to bed!"

He had the heavy gesture, thick tongue and falsely sparkling eye of the cavalrist who has drunk too deeply.

"As you please, my honorable guest. It is only to oblige you. Go right up—there is but one room at the head of the stairs. The bed is under the window. Do you want anything more?"

"No, I have lost my man along the road, and must get used to tucking myself in. Good-night, master, and my pretty maid! Peace on all under your rooftree!"

Braun echoed the wish but in the tone of a funeral oration. He fastened his eyes on the woman, who looked demure and guileless, as both listened to the irregular tread of the stumbling youth, who reached the door in front of him on the landing, kicked the door open and staggered to the bed, on which he seemed to fall. The couch was heard to groan and creak under the unusual weight, and soon a loud snore thundered in the loft. A sinister delight showed on the forester's browned face and he muttered:

"Drunk, tired and asleep. The cat is in the bag. A bearer of despatches, eh? I must have a word with Walton on that point before we settle him."

He took his gun down and put on his tall felt hat, adorned with an eagle's wing.

"Madame Therese," he went on in a low stern voice, "I am going to meet Walton. If the man upstairs moves, blow the cow's horn, and we will hasten to your aid."

Joel was listening overhead and as soon as he heard the innkeeper depart, he quickly rose; there was nothing painful or uncertain in his steps and no vestige of the drunkenness or fatigue existed in his whole frame. He had no need to be a soothsayer to divine that his money, his despatches or his life were at stake. So he freshened his pistol priming and loosened his sword in its sheath.

At the end of a time that seemed long, he heard a light but incautious step on the stair, and he opened the door so that he might have free swing to his sword and a broad opening for his shot. It was the petite figure of the woman which appeared, and he lowered the weapons' point and muzzle.

All was in darkness as he had prudently extinguished his candle but his sight was accustomed to the gloom, and her eyes sparkled like gems.

"I hope you have come to explain?" he began.

"To explain enough to satisfy you. We have an hour before us as the man has gone to keep an appointment and gather help, perchance. This estimable forester makes it a practice to get soldiers and travelers drunk and do them to death in their sleep. Thus he serves his cause and gleans secrets of military movements by which his employers profit.'

"Why did you not tell me at once, when I should have cut him down on the eve of his abominable project?"

The two were out on the landing now.

"Because I had my doubts of the outcome of the fright—Braun is a hardy old soldier. When he heard that you carried despatches, he knew that you had a greater value than a chance passer-by, and he goes to consult with one who is a past master in rich secrets. They have suggested to me before, as I am French, that I should decoy young officers and thus deliver the generals' plans to our enemy."

" Well ?"

"The opportunity has not happened before this, and I ——"

" Patriotism would make you repulse the suggestion?"

" I do not know—this man whom Kaspar Braun has gone to meet is my tyrant—a demon. Have you never heard in Paris of the criminal associate of La Voisin and Lesage, the chief who contrived to escape after a temporary arrest—the 'Englishman,' the 'Author?'—and author he is of many an atrocity."

" I know little of Paris, but I learnt something of the affair of the Poisoners."

" Hereafter, I will acquaint you with what he is: enough that he is a thorough villain who will not need the whet of your carrying despatches to ally himself with Kaspar to kill you in your bed. He had told me, on rejoining me from Paris, whence I was a fugitive, that he must obtain information of importance in order to sell it to Prince Charles for his protection, a shelter and money, so that he may gratify his horrid ambition."

"This wretch is your gallant, then ?"

"My torturer—the living reminder of a past of which the recollection sears me like a burning iron. Fate has chained us together like two convicts in the galleys. Perhaps I adored him once. To-day, I submit to him—I am forced to serve him, but I hate him. Never mind me, though," she went on, drawing nearer Joel, who towered above her on the stairs: I repeat that the innkeeper will soon return with Walton or another. In these frontier villages are plenty of deserters whom a piece of gold converts into murderers. At need, Walton would persuade Braun, who has some human weakness in him, to join hands with the camp-followers and villagers who throng the woods."

"Let them come," muttered the youth, clapping his hand on his swordhandle with a joyous, fearless gesture.

"Yes, I understand that you will defend yourself against a score or more, but at the sound of the affray a scouting party of the Germans may run up and then you would be overpowered. Besides, though Braun would attack fairly enough, it is not the same with Walton who employs the devil's weapon, fire, with all the devil's cunning. He is capable of setting fire to the house."

"Who cares——"

The young woman grasped his sword-arm, saying in a sweet voice: "But how about her?"

"What 'her!'"

"The woman whom you love and who loves you—whom you left behind?"

"Aurore!"

"Ah, her name is Aurore, is it? I do not know anything about her, but this is true—a man who loves and is beloved has no right to rush rashly into death."

"Aurore!" repeated the chevalier, with pendant head.

"If you were to get slain, what would become of her? who can tell but she may need your sword and arm one of these days! Again and yet again, think, oh, think of her! Think of me, too, for heaven's sake! when that scoundrel learns that I betrayed him and his accomplice to save you, my life will no longer be my own. I do not want to be murdered before I have time to plead to the Judge on high by my repentance—"

The Breton felt overcome.

"In short, what do you ask?" said he.

"I have not only kept the harness on your horse, which will be rested, but I have equipped Walton's, on which pair we may flee. All I beseech you is to place me in some asylum where he may not penetrate—a convent or the like—But follow me without sound——"

"Run away before such scum?" said Joel, with a rebellious movement.

"I will show you how to meet him another time," said the woman savagely.

He followed her down the stairs with as light a step as possible. They reached the inn door but Therese only stopped there to listen to the sounds without.

"The better way is to leave by the rear door," murmured she. "It seems to me that the road is not lonley. Come on."

But on passing through a low, narrow door which gave the Frenchman's robust body a squeeze, and finding themselves in a kitchen garden, where the vine flourished on trellises, the guide suddenly seized her companion by the arm and dragged him under a kind of bower: here, in the hot weather, boon-companions discussed the vintages of which Braun boasted beneath the leaves of the vine which bore them.

Three dark figures entered the stableyard by the simple process of striding the hedge at a gap. Joel recognized the tallest as the innkeeper's; he was accompanied by wearers of cloaks and swords, but only one of them had a soldierly bearing in keeping with the weapon. This one seemed treated with respect by both the others.

"What meant that light going out as we came up?" questioned this man in a voice trained to give orders.

"My lord," answered Kaspar, "I should say that it was the wife of this gentleman, who thought all was ended for the night and she has gone to bed. But I can make sure——"

Then, leaning towards the mute and cloaked third party, he whispered: "Get through with your business with the prince, that we may attend to this French officer. Confound it all, I fear that your wife may give an alarm."

"Fear nothing,' replied Walton in the same undertone; "she is as suppliant to my will as the cane which I wield."

He carried a cane with a horn head, like the gentleman of fashion in town who wish always to be accustomed to holding a weapon.

The person addressed as a lord had impatiently waited for this brief colloquy to come to a close. Thereupon he said: "Disturb nobody. We can confer just as well in one of these arbors. As for you, Kaspar, go and stand guard at the gap on the road. There are too many prowlers about after dark for precautions to be neglected, and as an old woodsman, I know your eye can be relied upon."

At this, Joel shrank farther back behind the leafy screen.

Whether by instinct or that he had not the profound faith in Therese which Walton manifested, Braun was reluctant to take the designated post and he muttered:

"Will not your highness do his faithful servant the honor of sitting within his doors—after a few minutes to rid the house of vermin—and accept what I have in the cupboard and the cellar?"

"Be easy, my dear Kaspar," said the prince affectionately clapping him on the sturdy shoulder, "I will go into your house and sit at your board, but not until we shall have cleared the land of these accursed foreigners, who have impudently come upon the imperial soil. Then, I promise you, we will drink the best vintages of your Rhenish wine to the disgrace of the vanquished foe and the joy of Freiburg with the siege raised."

CHAPTER XXV.

THE INVOLUNTARY SPY.

"CAN this be the Duke Charles?" said Joel in a low tone: but he received no explanation from his companion: frightened into stupor, she had sunk upon a seat in the arbor and wrung her hands in muteness.

Braun, with a glance up at his house, quiet as if only the dead were inmates, strode to his post to act the sentinel: the other two, occupying the bower adjacent to that which concealed the knight and his guide, began their dialogue. The prince sat on the bench, leaning both hands on his knees, and projecting his chest so as to study the face of his interlocutor and not miss any words. The socalled Englishman remained standing, with his hat off, in a respectful attitude, and as the starlight out lined his features, the watche was amazed; it was the man who had met him in the house of the Manicarde in Boul-i Street and stopped his searches for therese Lesage. The coincidence of the woman's name, a common one, furnished no clue, but he could not help thinking that this meeting was strange: he had no time to indulge in trying to solve puzzles for the interesting dialogue had commenced. They used the same border language as Braun to the Chevalier de Locmaria, that is French peasant talk with German words, but Walton spoke with choice phrases here and there like one who had communed with the great.

"Yes, my lord," said Walton, "I have ridden all the way from Paris to furnish your highness with news."

"Good or bad?"

"Both, your highness."

"Let me hear the bad news at once, sir!"

"For the success of the campaign, no further reliance

should be placed upon the Duke of Saxe-eisenach, who, after having shamefully retreated before Montclar's French forces, stupidly let himself be cornered on an island in the Rhine, by Strasburg, where he has surrendered."

"Yes," said the prince, turning pale, "you are right; this is bad news—worse—disastrous!" He wiped his perspiring forehead with the back of his hand. "What next, sir? quick!" he said in a tone becoming steady by his will.

"Well, my lord, you must not count on the sixty thousand men with whom you promised to relieve Freiburg and re-enter Lorraine——"

"How is this?"

"His Imperial Majesty, from whom you expected this succor, requires all his troops to put down the insurrection in Hungary."

"Ah!"

"Besides, his ministers judge the position of France so strong that they have resolved to accept without discussion the conditions, which that power imposes at the treaty-congress held at Nimwegen."

His hearer was whiter than the handkerchief with which he wiped his face as the cloaked spy continued:

"The fact is that the army which collected under Basle, and which you were to take the command of and relieve Freiburg before a forward movement, has started this very morning for Vienna, with orders to march quickly so as to deal with the rebels."

"Ugh!" growled the prince, gnawing his fists, "so fade my hopes and expectations! Fie on this Prince of Saxe-Eisenach and this Leopold, suggested to be my brother-in-law! two Varuses—one, a coward and the other, a perjurier! who will restore me their legions?" he rose and stood in a shaking fit of rage. He breathed hard, and opened his coat as if to bare his breast to his dagger. Is there nothing good left on the earth? nothing that men hold in respect? gone are plighted faith, the ties of family and the soldier's honor!"

He seemed choking; but mastering his emotion after falling upon the seat, he said with a wearied gesture:

"Have you some more gall from that cask to pour out to me?"

"My lord, I have finished with the bad news."

"It is true—you said some was good. Well, speak, my

man. Please heaven, what is to come is not so disagreeable!"

"Your highness is the judge. In the first place, Your highness is aware that the French are short of artillery before Freiburg."

"But it is being sent them: I hear of a battery being planted."

"Of guns on a new system and of recent invention?"

"Precisely; of terrible execution."

"Possibly; but it will be a long time before this battery comes into play."

"Do you think so?"

"I know so, my lord, because the pieces are useless without the proper powder and projectiles, which are loaded in wagons, mired down on this side of the Vosges Mountains; it will have taken days to dig and haul them out; and though they are due to-morrow night they will not arrive if they are cut off."

"Eh?"

"The wagons will be escorted by dragoons; say, some thirty men at most—enough in a safe country, and your regular soldiers are withdrawn; but I have had a chat with an old freelance captain, and he has a band of fifty desperadoes waiting at Colmar to intercept them."

"Did you order this?"

"They await my word, my lord. And I have done better than that as I came along. On hearing that peace will be signed at Nimewegen, a number of brave lads who dote on warfare, for what profit it brings them, have deserted from all armies so as to co-operate with fellows of the same stripe, and there they are at Oppenau, upwards of eight thousand strong."

"Eight thousand rough soldiers at Oppenau,—only a few leagues away?"

"I, who knew most of their leaders when we campaigned in Flanders, had the idea of enrolling them under your highness's colors. Your highness has this extra legion, then, to lead to victory and booty—or death."

The prince frowned.

"Is it partisan war that you propose to me, sirrah?"

"All kinds of war are feasible when it serves one's gain"

"I am a general of armies, not a captain of plunderers."

"But a general is none, when he has no army!" returned Walton with rare boldness, at which Joel conceived a higher opinion of him.

"Fellow!"

"Pshaw! I imagine your highness to have a mind too superior to cavil at mere words. Come to this pass, what were the companions of Romulus? a handful of blackguards scooped up along the highway for the organised robbery called conquest! what the grand companies of freelances which Duguesclin gathered to fight the King of Navarre? what the knights who helped William the Conqueror to take England? Adverturers all! Allow these desperate soldiers to place you once more in possession of your states. You can discipline them into regiments and their captains will make as good a figure in history, I warrant you, as those who burnt towns under Marshal Turenne, pillaged Lorraine under Créquy, ravaged Germany under Gustavus Adolphus, and nearly upset your Emperor under Wallenstein. Besides, your highness has no time to be dainty. The hour is decisive for you. The capture of Freiburg by the French will mean your impotence to fly to the help of those whom you led to ruin—all Europe will see this clearly and pitying you to-day, it will scorn you to-morrow and repudiate you thereafter. Do you wish to act over again the part your uncle Charles IV. palyed vagabond, dispossessed, and starved—and which you have had some experience in? do you want Louis XIV. to cast you a slice of teritory as a crust is tossed to a dog? Would you like to rule over the three Bishoprics, with Toul for a capital—that hencoop! If you be this kind of sovereign and commander, I am your servant who takes his leave. Consider that I never came so far to seek you out; and that I sounded the secrets of the intriguers in Paris for another confidant than you. Think you that I have pretended to sell drugs with the risk of being burnt alive, for the purse of gold they earned, now and then? No? I will go straight to link my fortune to some one's more ambitious, more audacious and more enteprising than your highness."

"The Author" had found a hearer if not his opportunity at last: be sure that Joel listened to the whole with avidity. Therese had heard some such sentences before, and the eloquence was wasted on her : sitting on the bench, she hid her eyes in her hands and went silently.

The Prince of Lorraine meditated: he was a well-read man, and he muttered:

"Qui jacet in terra non habet unde cadat."

Which meant on his lips that he was on the ground and had no farther falls to dread. If he moved, he might risk all to win all. While he reflected, the tempter regarded him covertly, dusting his fine boots, which he owed to the bounty of Mdme. de Montespan, as well as his suit of riding clothes.

"But," said Duke Charles, finally raising his head, "Supposing that I consent to use the soldiers whom you offer me, do you fancy that they will have any chance to vanquish an army full of bravery, discipline and cohesion like Créquy's?"

"Yes, if the Freiburg garrison, also good regular troops, makes a general sortie at the same time as these irregulars, not so irregular in movements as in morals, attacks them in the rear."

"It may be."

"That is not all. I should want this day of attack to be that when the French made an assault in force on the stronghold. I am told that a secret mine is ready loaded for such a storming party. I would lure the enemy upon the wall so undermined and apply the torch when a simulated retreat brought them over the volcano. Then, when the most daring spirits of the foe were hurled into atoms, I would have the free companies charge with your regulars and the garrison issue by the other gates to rout the demoralized foe."

"This implies that you are to be inside the fort?"

"I must, in order to notify your lordship when to make the attack with the combined forces."

"You would enter the place?"

"I shall be inside in a day or two."

"But you must pass through the French camp?"

"I am French, though born in London: I see no difficulty in this—it is my business: I shall find some pretext, some disguise, some means. Trust to one who has an inventive wit when I decide on anything, the devil, somewhat related to me, I believe, never fails to assist me to carry out the scheme."

"If success crowns your efforts, sir, I shall lie under great obligations to you."

"In working for your highness," said Walton, "I am working for myself. I built up a fortune in Paris, but as I was putting on the roof, a gale arose, and all has tumbled in. I have fled with my mistress, my lord, and I come to your highness, because we are birds of a feather—I mean in the like straits.

Lorraine frowned, as this resemblance did not more than half please him.

"But," went on the other, understanding this repugnance; "let the more pressing case be attended to. Is your highness willing to take measures in connection with the plan I have the favor to propose? May I know on what day he would give battle to the French marshal?"

The duke reflected, before replying in a determined tone: "This is Monday. To-morrow I shall go over to Oppenau to put myself at the head of your partisans; on Friday night we will rush upon the besiegers. May this day repay us for that at Consarbruck when we were defeated! But," he resumed, turning to the other, "I repeat to you, this ultimate effort has only the hope of success in the concurrence of the garrison, the explosion of the mine beneath the storming party, and of the population of the town."

"I say again; the storming party shall be lured to the site of destruction, for I shall be within Freiburg to-morrow. On the fixed night, signal to me that you are ready to fall on."

"A rocket from this house should forewarn you that we are about to attack."

"A rocket: that will do; hold it as certain then, that all the men able to carry arms will sally out to crush the French between them and your army like two branches of pincers. Rely on me, my lord, for our aims are alike."

The duke rose to the relief of Joel, to point out that the interview was over, but Walton did not budge.

"Still a few minutes, my lord! all is not settled between us. Your highness has apparently omitted one essential point."

"Hem!" said Lorraine, "I have forgotten that all services must be paid for and that we have not yet fixed the price which you have the right to claim for yours."

"Your highness is wrong," returned Walton, shaking his head. When success has come, then your highness may value it in proportion to the gains."

"Deuce take him!" muttered the general. "He asks for *nothing*, and so his terms will be terribly dear."

"A last point, my lord: it is settled that I am to enter the town. Ought I not have some credentials to present to the governor on which he will obey the instructions which I carry from your highness, and show me the mine, which I want to fire with my own hand," said he with a fiendish grin which caused the warrior to shudder. "Otherwise the worthy officer will see in me only a spy, a secret agent of the French Marshal, and he will apply to me the expeditious methods of the laws of war—which will not sensibly advance your highness's affairs."

The duke pondered.

"You are right," he said, taking out a note-book, of which every page was stamped with his cipher so as to be recognized by his military officers. "Braun answers for you to me, and I can answer for you to others—to a certain degree. I will furnish you with the pass you desire." He wrote on the page with pencil and read these lines aloud.

"To Colonel Schutz, our Military Governor of Freiburg Castle and town. Colonel: We desire you to receive the bearer of the present note with the attentions due an envoy of ours and to favor him with all he may wish for the good of our service and the defence of the place."

"Wonderfully good!" observed Walton.

"Wait!" said the Lorraine prince, who resumed

"If however this said envoy proffers the advice to surrender the said place, or he appears to commit any act hurtful to the defence, or seems to be in collusion with the enemy, do not hesitate to punish him straightway with the penalties prescribed by the law for spies and traitors. Watch him carefully and at the first suspicious move, hang him for me or wash his head with some ounces of lead. This is our express will."

He looked at the traitor fixedly and asked:

"Have you understood this writing?"

"Yes, my lord," rejoined Walton, who indeed followed the text with a clearer head than Joel, brought to the task of comprehending German.

The duke signed and detached the leaf.

"The colonel knows my hand," said he, "and consequently the authenticity will not be disputed. I warn you that he is the sort of man to execute the orders though he had to do so with his own hand."

Walton snapped his fingers, so naturally that the prince was deceived. He held out the paper, saying:

"Take it, and take heed that it is not found upon you, if you run up against the soldiers of Marshal Créquy."

"I must come near to him, my lord, since I reckon on him to help me into Freiburg."

"Ah?"

"I shall call on him, as the bearer of despatches from the War Minister Louvois. I left Paris with the hope of securing them; I have distanced the messenger on the road, and I know where to lay my hand on them."

Joel shuddered in the ambush, to think that he might have been sleeping at this hour, unconscious of his impending doom.

"I shall transmit to your highness a copy of the documents, and as for this pass, I have a secret receptacle here in which I defy the cunning ones to perceive the real hollow."

He unscrewed the head of his cane and showed that it was innocent enough of preparation; he detached the ferule, and the stick sounded solid to the rap of the nail; but about half way down, one of the ornamental knots, whence the twigs were trimmed, proved to be fictitious and disclosed a pocket. He rolled up the paper and inserted it therein. Fastening the pieces together, he cut the air with it and said jauntily: "It is done, my lord. It is not the French who will ferret out the tablet of your highness."

The chevalier had missed no detail of the manœuvre. Duke Charles V. and his ally proceeded towards the door of the stableyard and exchanged some words with Braun, who had stood like a statue, surveying the road.

The prince's features were depressed with lassitude, disgust and repugnance as he went out to join his escort in a hollow.

"What a great shame and pity that a prince of my race, related to the most illustrious houses of Europe, should be reduced, to fight destiny, to ally himself with the accomplice of the Poisoners of Paris!"

"What a pity!" sighed Joel in his ambush, "that I cannot make this capture—the Lorraine prince, the implacable adversary of Marshal Créquy, his Majesty and France! I must let him fly away when I had but to put my finger on him. The marshal would have congratulated me before the whole army; the King would have called me home to overwhelm me with honors, riches, and decorations—but all is lost! it is not so sure that I shall capture this renegade."

Indeed, the sham Englishman and Braun were speaking by the hole in the hedge. The silence in the house gave them a twinge of suspicion.

"Bah!" said Walton, at last, as he preceded the German on the way to the house, "I am sure of the woman. We will send her up to see if the man is asleep, as you assert, and as he answers or is silent, we will charge to make an end of it. Did you hear? those papers he carries must be my passport into the presence of Marshal Créquy. He will be too glad to get them to look closely at my story of how I met the bearer, wounded to the death by bandits, and confiding them to me. He will welcome the Frenchman who did his duty and would not try to sell them to the Prince of Lorraine."

He drew his sword, and with the innkeeper armed with his knife, he entered the house.

"Now is our time," whispered the woman, who had been electrified by the nearness of her persecutor.

They ran to the stable: the large door was on the jar, and the two had the horses out in a twinkling. Joel swung himself into the saddle and helped the woman into hers; the saddle was not suited to the feminine mode, but there was no time to rectify it, and she mounted as best she might. To add spurs to their flight, they heard in the inn angry words, oaths, and shouts, and divined that their absence was discovered.

Side by side the two horses leaped the hedge at the gap and Joel, half-turning, asked:

"What direction do we take?"

"To the French camp at Freiburg, of course."

"No, the very one they will pursue us upon: did you not hear that the roads which lead thither are infested by camp-followers. Loss of time is nothing compared with the loss of my despatches. Let us take some bridle path and let them give chase as they may at random."

You are right. They will also try to throw themselves between us and the only bridge, while we can cross at another spot, by a ferryman's boat. We are sure to reach it by keeping to the riverside as soon as we strike it."

"Forward then, into the woods; but I am sorry not to have given the traitors a taste of my steel and to have exchanged shots with the villainous innkeeper, he, with his long gun, I, with my pistols, which I am glad to retain in my girdle."

CHAPTER XXVI.

A TRICK OF WAR.

Joel and his new companion were riding through the wood as the false dawn peeped: but it was gloomy under the trees; their horses were fatigued by the soft soil of rotted leaves and the vines which caught at their fetlocks.

"Alas," the young woman continued her revelation, "one may not choose one's parents, and my mother—God forgive her! one whose name will ever arouse a shiver of terror and horror. She was a midwife when she fell in with my father, who under the pretence of teaching her black magic—for she practiced white magic and told fortunes to ladies—instructed her to manufacture poisons, among them the superfine powder which floats about so that the maker must wear a glass mask, and the elixir which is distilled from the jewel in the toad's head. My parents kept a store where all vices and passions could find help and satisfaction, and they had numerous customers—wives whose husbands were a clog upon them, husbands whose wives were their incubi, high-born dames who were hampered by a rival, heirs to estate who had run through their patrimony, ambitious statesmen impatient to be promoted, place-hunters, enemies who flocked hither to buy the means of rapidly contenting their interests and wicked propensities."

"Hearken:" interrupted Joel, as he heard in the distance the passing of a troop of horse.

In the silence of the morning, the hoofs on the clayey soil of the highway could be heard distinct as blows of a hammer.

"They are our pursuers," continued he: "they are at about the spot where we turned out of the main road: they are going on—they have gone on."

The sound indeed lessened and soon died entirely away.

"It was there that I first saw that man Walton," proceeded Therese. "He went by the name of the Englishman, because he was born in London of gipsy parents. He is cowardly, perfidious, cruel, rapacious, and abominably perverted: but he is active, intelligent, educated, and of good-manners and artful language. It was he whom the band employed to negotiate with the Marchioness de Montespan, through her maids, when she purposed compassing the King's removal."

"The King's removal?" repeated Joel, starting in the saddle.

"At the period," went on the woman, emphatically, "when the Beautiful Fontanges was preferred to her by Louis, for the moment——"

"Such a crime is impossible," protested the knight, "and by the favorite of the King?"

"She would not have hesitated to sacrifice her royal lover to the pain, and wrath, and shame of seeing him ensnared by another. Besides, the proof of what I assert exists, couched at full length in a letter written by the marchioness to my father to ask for the poison."

Joel did not hear this last sentence, as he was listening to a sound in another quarter. A rumble was heard and a damp chilly wind came to fan their cheeks, hot with the riding.

"It is the river," said Joel.

Ten minutes after, they came out on the bank of an arm of the Rhine, swollen by rain and spread widely; the moon slanted as it paled before the aurora and made the willows seem an army of spectres. As they followed the water at a slow pace, the woman pursued:

"How was I entangled by such a miscreant? Can I explain the infatuation otherwise than by the circle in which I was brought up? Panderers and witches, sham priests and homicidal chemists, who professed nothing but the cult of evil, feared nothing but the police officers, and were ignorant of a conscience. In short, he became my master, to the applause of my mother, for I was a reproach to her as long as I remained honest; my father, however, who loved me as the tiger loves his young master, alone tried to wrest me from the claws of this devil.

"He will kill you some day," he warned me.

"At least, he beat me, robbed and deceived me, but I adored him all the same——"

"Is not that the house you meant!" inquired Joel.

While listening to the tale, he continued to scan the ground, and as he spoke he stretched out his hand to a cabin of logs and rudely shaped timber by the riverside, on a knoll. A boat was bobbing up and down on the tumultuous tide among the reeds, at the end of a chain attached to a stake. Leaping down from his horse, the chevalier knocked on the door, until a man's voice hallow'd from within:

"Who are you, and what do you want?"

"Friend, we are in want of your help," replied the Breton.

"We will pay anything you ask for your services," added the woman also alighting.

They heard the clicking of flint and steel as the fisherman struck a light. The door opened warily, and the ferryman made his appearance on the sill: an old thickset man, with a tanned complexion, who held up a lantern to examine the visitors, and in the other hand held a boathook to defend his home.

"Goodman," said Joel, "we want to be put on the other side."

"It is not easy in the morning fog; the current is swift and my flat boat is leaky."

"Service of the King," returned Joel, "and if we are drowned the price will not be exacted of you. And on my own service, you must obey or I shall be forced to deal with you summarily. Steel or silver—take your choice." And he slapped his sword-pommel.

"If it comes to that," replied the other, frightened, "I will do my best with a nail, a scrap of tarred canvas and a plug——"

"How much time is this work to take?"

"Not more than twenty minutes, I suppose."

"Be it so," said the young officer, with a stern tone that was terrifying: "if in half-an-hour at the farthest, we are not *in the* middle of the stream, you will be going down to the *bottom* of it, with a stone round your neck."

While the old man hurriedly made the repairs to fit the boat for the three to cross, by the lantern light, the pair entered the cabin and sat on a pile of rushes.

"How did you come from Paris to this part of Lorraine and Alsace?"

"Alas," said the daughter of La Voisin, "what was fated came to pass. Divine clemency was worn out, and human justice was goaded on. One morning, M. Lareynie had all of us arrested, and the Chambre Ardent took up our case. My unhappy mother was condemned to capital punishment and was executed on the Execution-place with over thirty of her accomplices. My father was kept in prison, by the royal order: a form equivalent to perpetual imprisonment. I was benefitted by my youth, and my lover by his turning evidence. We were banished, but, after a tour in England, we slipped back into Paris where I carried on the harmless par of my mother's trade in the Bouloi Street, under the name of the Manicarde. I was soon fashionable, as I had my mother's craft at my finger's ends and Walton knew all the stories of court and city ladies. But I was in fear of a descent of the police, and, unnerved, sick of the business, I made a bold step and took to flight. I came in this direction because I thought that war would be a bar to justice. I hoped, too, that my lover would never meet me. In this I was wrong, for he overtook me at Brisach and the bond was fastened on me again. He talked of entering into the pay of Duke Charles, sure to welcome any enemy of France. If we had nothing to sell him, he proposed pushing on to Vienna, where he expected me to dupe some court lady and obtain state secrets which we might dispose of to the highest bidder. In short, we might thus return to Paris, to resume the old trade. But this time the scales fell from my eyes. I understood that this man was an enemy of our race, and shame drove out of me the mad passion for him. But I am a woman, feeble, and seeking an aid—you came across my path and——"

"Unfortunately, I cannot take you into the camp," objected the chevalier.

"It matters not, I have already spoken of the convent. Well, I have jewels to pay for my entrance into some holy house; I am eager for oblivion and repose. I wish to sink into the protective shadow of the cross, where I will kneel to implore pardon for my faults. I wish to repent and pray —pray for my mother, who has expiated her crimes upon the pyre, and for my father, who will expiate his in some dungeon——"

"You have spoken some names, but I do not formally know what are those of your father and mother."

"It costs me something to utter them, before which the Parisians cross themselves as at sight of an infernal apparition. Nevertheless, if you insist——"

"Do not believe that it is mere curiosity which impels me. My persistancy has another cause and another aim. I am charged with a deposit, and you may be the very person for whom it is intended."

"What deposit—what person—speak!"

If he had spoken, she would not have heard, for louder than his voice sounded one on the bank:

"There the are! I recognize my horse, tied to that tree. Ten crowns to whoever will dash down and prevent them mounting."

"The boat," shouted Joel, springing out of the cabin.

"It is fit. Step in! I am in haste to put off."

The chevalier took the woman up in his arms and placed her in the boat. But the old man lost his wits as the enemy came down the bank, forced to dismount and lead their horses, and threatening to reach them in a mass. His trembling hand made a blunder in detaching the rope on the stake and he gasped: "Holy Mother!" without any progress.

"Never mind that—get to your pole to push her off," said Joel, and seizing the stake, driven deeply into the bank, he plucked it up as easily as a gardener draws a radish from the soil.

"Take care chevalier, take care!" screamed the woman.

Three of the ruffians whom the prisoner had already picked up on the road, ventured to ride down the steep bank. Two had their swords flourished, the other held a pistol in hand. On the water's edge, they reined in, pulling up their horses on their haunches, and encircled the young officer. He had in his grasp the stake, a pile fit to be driven under a bridge. He swung it round like a mace, and for a minute the medley was dreadful of the crushing blows, the crash of falls, the shrieks, the oaths, and the neighs of horses. All three *reiters* were hurled from the saddles:

the two swords flung fifteen paces off, and the pistol imbedded in the fist of the man who had discharged it, he lay on his back in the ooze, senseless. His comrades had a broken arm and a broken jaw. The victor's cheek was black with powder and his luxuriant locks were singed, but unharmed, he stepped into the boat and with a vigorous push of the stake, he sent it off into the flood.

When the rest of the ruffians reached the verge, the scow was out of reach. Walton and Braun foamed at the mouth with ire. He urged his horse into the water as if to swim it after the fugitives; and shook his cane at the Son of Porthos, as he road in the stirrups, yelling:

"Ah, you dog!"

At this insult, Joel's temper was ruffled, and snatching a pistol from his belt, he fired at the speaker. But at that moment, the horse floundered in a mudhole and Walton's head was at a lower level. It was Braun who received the large bullet in the chest and he staggered back and slowly slipped down out of the saddle.

"Go no farther," said one of the party to Walton: "The river is treacherous—if your horse loses footing in the deeper places, you——"

The scoundrel did not hear: green with bile and anger, with a bloodshot eye and a quivering lip, he hissed:

"They are escaping—no, they shall not escape me!"

The second shot from Joel cut off one of his lovelocks as clean as though scissors had clipped it, and left a red seam along side his temple. The pain only maddened him and he roared:

"You have your muskets. Fire on them, comrades, fire on all in the boat!"

The scow was but slowly leaving the bank as the rapid current was full of eddies, and it went badly in spite of Joel, laying down his empty pistol and taking the pole to assist the old man in punting.

The reiters hastened to unhook their guns from the saddlehorns.

"Lie down," commanded Joel to the woman while he placed himself like a bulwark to the boatman. Thus they awaited the discharge of about half the battery already in position.

Six or seven shots sounded, and the bullets whizzed

around the flatboat : the fisher peeped back, but at this, a whirl swung the boat so that he was left uncovered by Joel, and a straggling bullet pierced his brain by the ear, after grazing the Breton · the unfortunate man lost his balance and fell over the low side, still convulsively clutching the pole. This loss was hailed by a shout of coarse exultation by the rude soldiers on the shore, and those who had not fired, levelled to obey Walton's order. He on his horse were swimming in the wake of the boat, of which Joel took both oars to try to navigate it across the channel.

"Down, down!" cried he to Therese, who had lifted her head, but the caution came too late.

"Aim low," Walton had shouted, hoping that the boat would be injured if no one in it were hit : and most of the missiles flew along the surface of the stream

Again the volley was followed by a straggling shot or two, and the woman, who had thought that the general discharge was all to be feared and who rose a little to make sure that her defender were uninjured, was struck : she rolled in the hollow of the scow, murmuring :

"Lord, have pity on me—have pity on the daughter of Therese Lesage—and La Voisin !"

What deepened her pain was to see the stalwart form of the chevalier reel like a tree to the trunk of which an ax had been vigorously laid : he let the oars drop, but inside the gunnel, and was soon extended across the thwarts without a tremor.

"Hussa!" laughed Walton, who had fallen into the current and was being sped towards the scow, itself turning round and round on its centre in a whirlpool. "Cease firing, or you will hit me—I can deal with them now."

But again the conflicting flows played a trick: one current caught the boat and spun it towards the opposite bank at good speed which made the next shots unlikely to fall true : besides, the same flux carried Walton and his horse into the line of fire.

The dawn had fully come, and objects began to be defined as the mists rolled away.

The sham Englishman laughed as he beat his horse to swim more fleetly. Then, shifting the cane into his left hand, he extended the other to seize the gunnel of the flat: he gloated on the splashes of blood, on the pale and still figure of the woman and on the huge body of the Breton, who had baffled his schemes. All his triumph was in hand's reach, indeed.

"I have them," he called out.

At the same moment his exhausted horse failed him, and as he felt it sinking from between his legs he grasped the edge of the boat with both hands; the cane fell within the side. To his horror, Joel rose with a turn upon his knees and made his hands encircle his throat with a grip impossible for a man thrice his strength to disengage.

"Pray your last," said the Breton, "the French dog gives a deadly bite!"

Then rising, he held up the strangled adventurer in clear view of his friends on the opposite bank and contemptuously hurled him into the stream in their direction. A shower of bullets played ducks and drakes on the surface about him, but he was out of range. In another instant the boat came to a stop, in shoals by the edge. Joel lifted the motionless body of the woman in his arms and bounded upon the shore.

He was climbing the ridge when a body of armed men appeared on horses and with musketoons ready for use held by the thigh.

"Who goes there?" was their challenge in French.

It was a French patrol.

"France!" replied our hero, who felt in safety.

"Drop weapons and advance!"

As the bearer of Therese obeyed, the sun rose behind the forest, the whole scene was suddenly illumined, and a flood of exclamations broke out on both sides:

"What a meeting!—The Breton of St. Fiacre's Oak!—the adversary of our Corporal Bregy!"

"What a providential chance," said Joel, no less astonished. "My Musketeers of St. Germain Forest—Messieurs de Gace, Escrivaux, Hericourt and Champagnac."

The cavaliers poured question upon question on him:

"Where do you spring from, in this dress, and loaded with this blood-sprinkled corpse?"

"Gentlemen, I will explain all later," rejoined the young knight, "but let us think of this hapless woman now. In heaven's name help to what he needs—shelter, a bed and succor!"

"Hump," coughed the old officer commanding the patrol "it is my opinion that the sufferer has more call for a confessor than a doctor, but, never mind, let us do the usual thing. Those gentlemen may help you to carry her to the first house on the road to camp, while I attend to this knot of rough-looking gentry on the other bank."

With the oars a litter was improvised, and wrapped in a horseman's cloak, the woman was transported to a farmhouse. In the meantime the rioters had decamped on seeing the armed force able to exchange shot for shot. They had no wish to stop under fire to fish for the body of Walton, doomed to feed the fish of the Rhine.

The farmer's wife undressed the woman and put her to bed. Temporary dressing was applied with lint and bandages, but the wound left little hope: the projectile had gone clear through the body. On her sniffing vinegar and rubbing her temples with it, she appeared at last to recover life. A fleeting color tinted her cheeks, while her lips fluttered and her eyes opened. She cast a dim look around her, vacillating and without brightness.

Joel, who had not quitted her, bent over her.

"Do you know me?" he inquired.

The gaze brightened in token of recognition.

"Can you hear and understand me?" he further questioned.

The eyes made the same response: and he turned to the bystanders, saying: "Leave me alone for a space with her, as I must speak to her."

Everybody went out, leaving the man beside the pillow: he held one of her icy hands in his.

"So you are the daughter of Pierre Lesage and La Voisin?"

"Yes," she nodded, ashamed, and using a voice scarcely above a breath. "I horrify you, do I not?" she said with pain and with an effort.

"I have been looking for you, my poor Therese, in order to hand you this object," and he drew the locket from his bosom and presented it to her. Her eyes dilated with astonishment as she recognized the memento from prisoner 141.

"Yes, I know this trinket—it belonged to my father. How did it come into your possession?"

"I had it from the rightful owner—Pierre Lesage——"

"You have seen him?" she faintly screamed.

"I have seen him and spoken to him, in the Bastille——"

"Was he detained there? I thought it was in Vincennes Castle. Good heavens! how long may he not be imprisoned there?"

"He has already left it—more than six weeks ago, he died."

He related his meeting with his fellow-prisoner and how he had a doubt about the sincerity of the provision of means to escape which he owed to Walton.

"The villain—how right I was to quit him. He alone escaped the quick doom of the transgressor."

"Not so: he was—drowned in the river," said Joel.

"All have gone to the other world," muttered the woman, "after their strange destinies here. How will the heavenly Judge receive my father and my mother? How will their daughter be received?".

She repulsed the locket.

"Keep it," said she. "It is a talisman, which will bring to the bearer who knows how to use it, all that human ambition can dream of: riches, credit, honors, and power! it is a letter which proves what I affirmed to you in the boatman's hut, but which you refused to believe. In this the Marchioness de Montespan, furious at the King casting her off in favor of La Fontanges, asks Pierre Lesage and La Voisin for poison with which to rid herself of her rival and revenge herself upon her lover. This avowal is complete and signed. She must have been love-sick to have made such a confession, monstrous imprudence! but is it not written that they whom heaven would destroy is first made mad? However that may be, that scrawl placed under King Louis' eyes, may send the proud marchioness into Lesage's prison or to La Voisin's pyre! Either he or she will buy it at any price, for though the sovereign escaped, poor Fontanges lies in the grave. From one or the other, you see, the holder is sure to obtain whatever he likes to demand. I give you this paper and the locket."

"To me?"

"To him who witnesses my last moments, as you almost witnessed those of my poor father."

"What would you have me do with this poisoned weapon?

I am not of the school of the Montespans. Besides, she has retired from the court in disgrace."

Something like a smile flitted over the dying one's lips.

"Oh, chevalier, it is plain that you are a novice in court matters! A favorite never falls so low that she may not on the wings of evil soar to the point whence she fell. Time and again she seemed to have lost her power, but each time she retook her place and marked her return with cruel blow of revenge."

"But deuce take me if I hardly more than know your marchioness!" returned Joel, animatedly. "I am neither her liege nor her enemy. Why should I be armed against her?"

The woman raised upon him eyes in which were the dark depths of the eternal night. With a tone that seemed that of a spirit of another world, she said:

"The veil over the future is rent for those about to die; and moreover, I have the gift of second sight. I see that you must struggle with that woman for your dear ones——"

Joel started, for a vision of Aurore rushed across a scene and his heart felt a pang.

"Keep the locket—preserve it for her guard—to save her!" persisted Therese in a weakening voice. "And as a keepsake from me, who would have loved you with all her soul—had you been free and I not unworthy of you!"

As though ashamed of the avowal escaping her, she seized the sheet with both hands and tried to cover her face; but her arms relaxed and then stiffened. The linen fell, and her eyes closed as the door opened to admit the doctor who had been sent for. He looked for a moment on the white face, idealized by death to the extreme of human beauty, and taking off his hat with a grave movement, he said:

"This woman is beyond our cares."

CHAPTER XXVII.

TO WIN HIS WIFE!

THE town of Freiburg was a difficult place from its strength of position and sorely teased the rough and fierce captain who beleaguered it, when Ensign Joel de Locmaria arrived at last before it.

His new friends had accompanied him as mourners when Therese Lesage was borne to her grave in Alt-Brisach cemetery, leave having been accorded by their captain of light horse, M. de la Berange, although every man was wanted in the trenches. On their reaching Waldau, they found that Marshal Créquy had left his head quarters for a reconnaissance in force, and they persuaded Joel to await his return.

As they approached the trenches freshly dug before the Herdern suburb, they saw a tumult among the soldiers: light cavalry men had alighted, tied up their horses and surrounded a group of officers whom they were threatening with voice and fist. The friends of Joel rode up with him, also dismounted and hitched their horses, and ran up.

"What is the matter?" they inquired.

"It is the marshal," said a horseman. "He is making fools of us. Not content with using us as footsoldiers, he wants us to go into the trenches and use the pick and spade like sappers and miners."

In the thick of the riot, Captain Beranges's voice arose, addressed to someone whom the Breton could not perceive.

"You see, sir," he said, "that my soldiers refuse to lend a hand in such dirty work. I will try to dissuade the marshal from requiring it—in the meantime, pray seek the diggers and delvers somewhere else."

"But I tell you again, captain," replied another voice, "that Major-general Basset of the Artillery has given me orders to take fifty of your men to help finish this trench and mount my mortars—and by all the gods! take them I will? though I have to grasp them by the collar and drag them to the work."

"I beg to advise you to try nothing of the sort, as my men are very excited and they may forget the rules of the service."

"How now?" muttered the Breton, "do my ears deceive me? I seem to have heard that captious voice before—and that style of carrying all before him!"

Meanwhile the disputatious officer, picking out one of the light horsemen, said:

"I say, you with your elongated body, begin by taking that mattock and set an example to your comrades."

The person addressed did not move.

"Did you not hear me?"

"I heard you plain enough."

"Obey then, or——"

"I obey only my own officers, gentlemen who wear my uniform and who measure more than a span from the crown to the sole!"

There was general laughter and the officer grew more angry.

"You rascal!" he said.

"Softly, softly, Master Bombardier," returned the cavalryman jokingly, "Do not rush at me like that—you might stumble into the funnel-tops of your boots and it would be the devil's own work to find you in them!"

The hilarity increased, and the exasperated bombardier called out:

"Sergeant Bonlarron!"

"Present" and a tall old fellow in a steel cap, scrambled out of the trench.

"Sergeant, take hold of this saucebox of exaggerated dimensions for a light horseman—the one who is laughing so loudly—and take him to the provost-marshal to be corrected with the strappado."

"Very well, sir!" and the tall soldier strode towards the horseman designated: but when he stretched out his hand to seize him, he drew back and laid his hand on his sword, growling:

"You mud-splasher (footsoldier)! don't dare to finger me!"

"Beware, sir," said Berange, "I warn you that my men will not allow their comrade to be pulled about."

"Not by a mannikin!"

"Mannikin! these insults must not be borne. Here, my bombardiers."

The gunners darted out of the trench, brandishing their digging implements.

"Sir, I shall hold you responsible for any bloodshed," said the cavalry officer.

"And I shall hold you responsible for the disobedience and insolence of your soldiers—mutineers whom I shall chastise—hang, draw and quarter for their abuse. At them, my lads, and well flog the foul-mouths!" He whipped out his sword, in which act he was imitated by his sergeant and men.

"Come, come," muttered Joel, "it is high time that a cool head intervened."

THE DEATH OF ARAMIS. 257

He plunged into the riot and appeared among the flashing blades, picks and spades raised in attack and defence.

"My friend Joel!"—"My lodger of the Blakamoor."

So exclaimed the bombardier captain and his sergeant, whom the Breton cordially saluted.

"But put up your swords! I must say that you are both wrong. You in the first place, my comrade," he went on to Friquet, "with such bullying, imperious and aggressive manners in asking even for a proper thing that one is always tempted to send you to the deuce with your touchy, quarrelsome temper. Hang it all! it is not the fault of his Majesty's lighthorse-men that they should stand a head and shoulders above you. Overlook this accidental superiority and comfort yourself with the old saying that the best things are done up in the smallest packets."

"That is certain," grumbled the pigmy, sheathing his rapier, "and the ladies always give the preference to the neat, little, dapper gallants who never attain the bulk of your Olympian Jupiters."

Joel had turned to Berange and said: "Captain, in all deference allow me to observe that it would have been handsomer of you to carry out the King's orders, for you are no less his man because you have a horse between your legs. What are we all sent here for but to take Freiburg: and to do so, a blow with the pick is as good as a cut of the sword. There is as much honor in being shot at while digging a ditch as in galloping across the field."

At that instant, as though to give point to the speech, a puff of white smoke rose on one of the bastions of the stronghold. A cannon shot resounded, and the ball buried itself in one of the sandbags covering the trench's epaulement. The bag was burst and Joel disappeared in a shower of dirt: emerging and dusting himself, he continued calmly: "Now you will see the utility of this work."

A second explosion was heard, and this time it was followed by a deathcry, for a splash of blood half covered the speaker: the besieged had improved on their aim at the crowd, and the ball had struck Captain Berange in the chest. A terrible clamor uprose from the men in dread as the captain expired. Champagnac threw a cloak over him, while the rest looked on in silence, pale and awed.

"Had the front of that trench been opened," said our

hero coldly, "that brave gentleman would still be alive."

Without a further word, he picked up a spade and set to filling a gabion. Everybody followed his example, as if fever moved all. Light-horsemen and artillerists, officers and privates, they ran for tools and to fall into working-order. A furious cannonade from the enemy did not throw a damper on this ardor, so that by nightfall the cutting was a fit lodgment and strongly occupied.

"'Sblood!" exclaimed Friquet, as he and Bonlarron felicitated Joel, "this is fabulous, stupefying and pyramidical! to renew old acquaintance under the enemy's cannon fire! Oh, my valiant, faithful Joel!"

"But only look at this," went on the sergeant, "he sports the uniform of our regiment—with the officer's insignia—he must be the ensign we were expecting to see!"

There was an exchange of stories. Bonlarron had sold out by reason of the police having plagued the Blackamoor since the substitution of Friquet for the duellist, and he had enlisted under the flag of the new corps of bombardiers which Friquet had the appointment to command.

"As for you—we can see that you have found your sire, and the happy Porthos has procured his son a grade suitable to his birth and rank——"

Joel felt his heart smart as if burning. Violent color, a hot flush mounted to his cheek and he stammered in embarrassment:

"No, it is not as you think—I have not had that great good fortune——"

His confusion was interrupted by Captain Friquet being called away by the major-general of the artillery. Silence and rest presided over the camp and town at night. In the outposts nobody was awake save the sentinels and Joel. He could not sleep from the remorse which Friquet's words had aroused in his bosom. Was he acting right in what he was doing? conscience answered no! He had not quitted his native place to be a happy man; to win the love of Aurore du Tremblay and marry her for a life of peace, no more than to lead one of war: but to seek out the unknown. On her deathbed his mother had imposed this task upon him, and he had promised to devote his entire life unto it. He said to *himself* that he should not have acquired the right to enjoy *his bliss* until he found it impossible to ascertain the fate of the companion of Athos, Aramis and d'Artagnan. His resolution was taken in a minute. He would lay the case before Marshal Créquy, who would no doubt excuse him from lingering out his time at a siege which was a work of duration in those days. He would return to Paris and apply to that old man of such experience and wisdom, the Dude of Almada. Surely he would point out the means for the young man to recommence and carry his investigation to the end.

This course debated and settled within himself, he was tranquillized and could slumber, awaiting the morrow. He was right at first in his conjectures for, on reading the despatches, the general gave the bearer a kindly glance. Unfortunately there was a postscript to the paper recommending the young cornet, and the signature of " Louis the King," made the veteran start. He read it over again with deliberation, like one who has a cipher despatch under his eye and fears he is missing some hidden meaning. At intervals he observed the officer as the latter was preparing to utter his petition to be sent back to the capital.

"Chevalier," said the marshal, "the King asks me to keep you by me to the end of the campaign to spare you not any occasions to distinguish yourself. You have commenced very well by bringing your messages through, over a very dangerous route. Still I shall conform to his Majesty's desires, as he wants you to return to the ladies of the court like a Cyrus, Achilles or Hector."

Alackaday! all the young officer's hopes were blown to shreds. He could not think of quitting the army, as the King had written to the contrary and he must obey.

"Meanwhile," said Créquy, "if I can do anything special for you——"

"Forsooth, general, I have a great favor to solicit of your bounty; but I comprehend that it would be taxing too far, and I shall content myself by doing my duty in the company to which his Majesty appointed me ensign."

"The new cannoneers, I believe! I will recommend you to the captain——"

"Captain Friquet and I are old friends —we once met in a duel. But all I wanted was a piece of information, a clue to the length of the campaign and if I dared to ask on what it depends——"

Créquy stretched out his hand towards the town, saying:

"There is the end of the campaign. That is the eyrie from which Duke Charles reckons to swoop to tear Lorraine from us; that imperial fortress is the sword of Damocles, impending over our Alsace—his foothold when he springs forward in attack, his rest when he wants to recruit, his line of retreat in case of defeat. Freiburg taken, young man, is the key to Vienna in our grasp : the ruin of the Lorraine Prince's hopes : the proof to the Emperor Leopold of the rashness and invanity of his plighted brother-in-law's enterprises against France and a preliminary to his repudiation of him. That is why I am bound to take Freiburg," he concluded, after a pause."

"Why not at once," cried Joel, with eye ablaze.

"Young man, you are too hasty," said the old war-dog, "it is meet to be brave but one must take heed not to be presumptious. Do you not see that citadel encrusted in the mountain—the Castle. Do you talk of taking that, without my having hippogriffs on which to mount you young gentlemen? I might reach that point with the loss of half my men —but, then, there would be that fortalice to take ! a garison to subdue and the population who would fight behind walls and use against us fire, stone, water and iron! No, no, dash it all! let us be patient, and play the mole, with sap and mine ! When the beach is open, your old general will show you the way."

"I see," thought the young ensign, "since it is to be a duel at long shots, I will jog Friquet to hurry up matters, otherwise——"

"What would happen otherwise?" questioned the marshal who had overheard the monologue.

"Well, I shall have to take the citadel myself," rejoined the Son of Porthos without hesitation.

"Whew !" and the old marshal joined in the laugh of the aid-de-camps and the officers : "go ahead then, my boy. and do not wait for me : If you have an idea, you may have the means to put it into execution. I authorize you at need to make a sublime madman of yourself."

"You are looking quite radiant," said Friquet when his new officer returned from the visit to the commander-in-chief.

"Yes, I shall soon be going to win my wife !" replied the Son of Porthos with gladness and fervent belief.

CHAPTER XXVIII.

JOEL'S IDEA.

HERR SCHUTZ, the governor of Freiburg, ate and drank heartily but he slept with one eye open. He was sheltered behind thick walls; he had food in abundance; more guns than were set against him and munitions to spare. The townspeople were devoted to the Emperor; Duke Charles had promised to come to his relief, and the prince had never been known to break his word. From all these reasons the corpulent colonel had been but slightly uneasy about the investment of the place. But he kept up a good guard, and he ceased not to pound away at the entrenchments advancing towards him. He was going to begin a meal when an orderly announced the arrival of an extraordinary messenger from the Duke of Lorraine. This news made him swallow some of a glass of Moselle the wrong way.

"A messenger from Prince Charles?" he repeated; "how the devil could he get to us? I cannot imagine that the enemy would let him penetrate their lines at his ease. Unless he fell out of the skies or came riding astraddle of a comet——"

"Colonel," said an officer, "we spied him running towards us, pursued by the shots of the French and our pickets treated him to pepper out of similar castors—but he stood the double fire finely, and jumped into our moat, shouting: '*Freund!*' so that I cast him a rope and he hauled himself up on the rampart. He is now in the guardhouse drying himself as you may expect after a bath of that kind."

"What is he?"

"Not a Frenchman—more like a Saxon—a giant of a fellow who would cut up into half-a-dozen frog-eaters. It is my opinion that they could have caught him if they had tried, but none of them had the bravery to get near enough to him."

"Let him be brought before me at once. I will interrogate him while taking a bite; and if anything double-faced appears in his tale—" He snapped off the end of a sausage between his stumpy teeth with ferocity of ill omen.

Ten minutes afterwards, the personage announced was e»-

corted into his presence between four imperial fusileers, tall fellows whom, however, he towered above by half a head. He had black moustaches streaked with grey, strongly outlined creases on the face as from age and a hard life in military harness, but an eye of inextinguishable youth. In this feature alone would Aurore herself have recognized her lover, whose disguise was the work of art of the hairdresser of the young Duke de Villars, who had associated himself with our hero in this enterprise. Needless to say that the cane of Walton, picked up by the patrol and brought to Joel, had reminded him of his idea and furnished a means to commence it auspiciously.

"Are you German?" brusquely demanded Colonel Schutz.

"No, colonel, I am a Lorrainer, from Oppenau."

"You say you are charged with an errand by Prince Charles?"

And with the assistance of a soldier who used his bayonet as a knife, he extracted from a seam of his cothes a paper which was nothing else than the note confided to Walton by Duke Charles in the garden of Kaspar's inn. The governor read it over twice and carefully examined it.

"Well, it is right enough; it is my lord's memorandum-paper, branded with his cipher."

There was no doubting the note, but he had still a remnant of distrust as he inquired: "How did you manage to cut through the enemy's lines?"

"I went into the marshal's camp under pretence of selling cherry brandy of my own make, out of a cask I had in a cart. At a chance that was given me I slipped into the trench. Unfortunately," with a rough laugh, "my bulk betrayed me among those midgets of French in the ditches and the hue-and-cry was raised. I jumped out and ran for your works. The rest happened under the eyes of your men and they can tell you all about it. I am glad that they do not shoot as straight at your friends as they should at the enemy to repulse them."

Schutz drew a wry face.

"What are you bringing me—news?"

"Instructions from my lord, private, precise and confidential."

"Verbal, do you mean?"

"I should say so! what I carried in my vest was enough

to have me hanged—but the duke would not let his liege carry, save in his head, the plan by the means of which Freiburg is to be delivered in three days."

He pointed to the soldiers, whom Schutz dismissed with a jerk of the thumb.

"Now, unfold yourself, man," he said when they were alone. "I will listen while I eat—my breakfast is my heartiest repast."

Word for word the mock Lorrainer repeated what he had heard Walton and the general arrange in the inn garden. The colonel approved as he laid it open.

"That was good!" he said, clacking his tongue. "A rocket as the signal—that was better! the double attack at one time—the prince and his troops on the one hand, and I, with the garrison and the people on the other. Ah, Créquy and his men will not be able to stand that, ha, ha!" He crushed the wing of a fowl between his ponderous jaws, coming together like a portcullis. "By the way, comrade," he added, eyeing the jolly old Lorrainer who was still echoing his laugh, "do you chance to guess what was in that note about you?"

"Ay," said Joel tranquilly, with the grim merriment of a peasant, "my lord advised you to make a bullet-pouch of my head or halter me with a new rope if any thing in my behavior struck your excellency as suspicious." And he laughed again, as though this doubt of him were the cream of good-jests.

"Oh, you knew it, did you?" and he snapped his piggish eyes on each side of his high-colored and fleshly nose.

"His highness kindly read the lines out to me with stress on those concerning yours faithfully."

"Then remember, *landsman*," said the colonel, thumping the board with his glass, "that Colonel Schutz has never broken his word. And may the thunder-weather crush me if I do not carry out the duke's orders, though I have to blow your brains out with my own hand or wind the noose round your neck."

"Pshaw!" returned Joel with the same serenity, "there is a plain way of making sure that I walk straight in doing my duty to my prince and my country—keep me by you so that you can read my very thoughts——"

The colonel caught the ball on the bound, so to say.

"*Der Teufel!* the very thing I had decided upon. From this moment forward, my watch over you will not be taken off you, and you are to be rivetted to me as the shadow to the body."

The pretended envoy of Prince Charles gravely said: " I am glad to become, if only for a while, the shadow of the eminent warrior, Colonel Schutz, whose prudence, valor and military science are a house-hold word among the soldiers of Europe."

This blunt flattery operated a fresh change in the colonel. His face showed amiability in the highest power.

"I like you," he said with gruff good humor. "In fact, we are old war-dogs together—about the same age, I judge. What grade did you hold in the army?"

"I have long retired to cultivate the patch of pine woods I wrested from the forest—but I was a sergeant in the Vaudemont regiment when we fought at Rocroy for the right cause. Only," with another broad guffaw, "the right cause was well thumped that day. Herr Gott! how our allies the Spaniards were threshed—by that mere greenhorn the Duke of Enghien!"

Colonel Schutz joined in the laugh.

"What did you say your name was?"

"Niklas Hummer, at your orders."

"Then, *Major* Hummer," said Schutz, holding out his hand, "Not only shall you accompany me when I go forth on the requirements of duty, but you shall share my board, and sleep in the inner room of my own bedchamber. I will see that you fare well. Can you eat well—can you drink?"

"Try me!" responded Joel, who never felt anywhere more at home than when this proposition was put, and opening his mouth to show a set of teeth, which, spite of his assumed age, seemed fit to devour a wild boar at three sittings.

The governor soon seemed enchanted with his guest, who not only was his shadow, as has been well said, in his round on the rampart, and in the inspection of the barracks and the works, to say nothing of the mines, including the famous one which was to overwhelem the French if they made a grand assault, but at his copious banquets.

All Freiburg feasted likewise. The people had wind of the approaching deliverance, though there was no suspicious *babbling* of the plan from the pretended envoy. They made preparations to receive the prince when the French should have been driven away.

The governor's suit of rooms was on the ground floor, an old guardroom converted for his pleasure: in spite of the low, vaulted ceiling, short columns supporting it, and the dark walls covered with armor and trophies, it was gay when the two carousing companions, as Joel and the colonel had become, entered on the second dozen bottles of the pure juice of the grape.

Nine o'clook was ringing from the cathedral tower when an officer intruded on them to get the word and countersign. Herr Schutz raised his enflamed, puffed and mottled face and made a beckoning sign for the officer to stoop to have the word whispered to him. But he forgot to alter his voice to the proper key and almost roared in his subordinates's ear: "*Vater* and *Land*—*Vater-land*,—did you catch them?"

"Very well, governor," said the officer, departing.

Another officer succeeded him who brought a bunch of keys to his superior, as was the usage, every evening after the tattoo was beat. Not the keys of the town gates, which were locked, bolted and barred, with the portcullis lowered and the drawbridge hauled up since the beginning of the siege ; but of the citadel, communicating with the town, as well as a grated door, preventing access to the stairs leading up to the castle roof. On receiving them and stuffing them into his pocket, Schutz asked if he had any news.

"Nothing to see, colonel : the night is as black as the muzzle of an uncleaned gun and the rain is beginning to fall."

"So much the easier for the watchers," said the head officer with a guttural laugh: "those jackshapes of Créquy's will not venture forth for fear of taking the curl out of their feathers and the starch out of their lace. Go and get to bed," he added to the two soldiers who had brought in the meal, as soon as the officers had retired. "We do not want you to pull the caps off these ladies—" alluding to the sealed bottles. "When I drink, I do not like folks looking over my shoulder to count how many glasses I took."

The soldiers obeyed.

"Now it goes between ourselves, dear Major Hummer! Much as I hate the men of France, so much I love their wines. There they stand—off with their heads, jolly fellow !

down with the wines of France!" Seizing a bottle he wrenched out the cork and began to fill the two glasses.

"Let us drink," said Joel, knocking off two necks of bottles, one held in each hand, against another with the dexterity of a juggler.

So commenced the bout; to the mild wines succeeded the heavy ones: and the liquors followed. They sang while they drank, and to Schutz's muffled ears, the Breton ballad was good enough Lorraine dialect to excite no comment. Soon, though, the musical notes were merged into snores. Both guests seemed to sleep, but at the end of twenty minutes as the church bell sounded eleven o'clock, one of the drowsy ones made a move. It was "Major Niklas Hummer," who lifted his head warily and let his eyes wander to find Colonel Schutz. The host was leaning back in his armchair, letting sound rumble through his immeasurably opened mouth which defied the trombone to imitate. He was deeply wrapped in a heavy sleep. The Frenchman scanned him, without any tokens of drunkenness on his part.

"To think of his expecting to drink me under the table! and with wines of my own country, too! Intoxicate one whose head has mocked at home cider and the wine of Bonlarron!" listening to the churchbells striking after that of the cathedral which had given the cue, he said: "I have just an hour before me. More than I want."

Schutz snored more loudly than ever and with his bared throat, a sanguinary enemy might have been tempted to spoil his gullet for wine bibbing: but Joel shook his head.

"All I want is his bunch of keys," he said: "and they are there." The keys puffed out the governor's pocket and were not easily extracted, but Joel accomplished it, as he was not pressed for time. He also borrowed the governor's hat with a black and a yellow feather and his gold-laced mantle, from the chair where they had been flung, and arrayed himself in them. He took down a sword from the wall pegs, and left the room.

The vestiblule led him into a gallery, where he was stopped by a grating across the way to a spiral staircase.

One of the abstracted keys opened the lock of this grating, and our hero entered on the stairs. The chief defence of the *Schloss* was the principal tower roof, over two hundred feet above the moat; it communicated with the town by a very narrow way. While all the troops were placed at points along the circumvallation, one battalion of the imperial regiment guarded the tower. It was not supposable that the enemy would attack a part reputed impregnable, and to reach which the whole of the fire from elsewhere would have to be endured. Still there stood on the tower top, six heavy pivot guns which could be turned against the town, once the castle were captured. In a stone watchbox on the roof was a sentinel who could survey the country roundabout. Here also Schutz had posted a squad of twenty men, under an ensign who was charged to watch the French.

Where the stairs came out on the platform a sentry was walking up and down.

"*Wer da?* who is there?" he challenged, as he heard steps coming up, stopping and lowering his bayonet.

Joel had not neglected his recent opportunity, in accompanying Herr Schutz on service, to acquire at least many phrases of military German.

"Officer going his round," replied he, in a deep voice worthy of his stature.

The slouch hat concealed his face in the mist, and the cloak mantled his shape. He stooped a little as he went up to the man and said:

"Vater!" to which the soldier replied "Land:" as he raised his musket to the present.

"Soldier," said Joel abruptly, "who posted you here?"

"The *anspessade* officer."

"Anspessade—idiot! *lumpen hund!* sentinel—mid staircase! go, finish rest of service there!" The broken sentences might pass for those of a man who had sat too long over the wine and beer. Without rejoinder, the soldier let the pretended officer go by while he descended the stairs.

The rain began to fall in torrents and it was cold at this height: the wind roared as a gale. In the wooden shelter serving as guardhouse, the officer and his score of men were sleeping on the plank bed. In his watchbox the special lookout was dozing, but on hearing the new-comer, he peered out. Thinking he knew the person by the hat and cloak, he let the false Schutz come up.

"Vater——"

As the German was about to return the password, Joel's resistless hands fell upon his throat and his waistbelt: he lugged the wretch bodily out of the box and hurled him over the battlements. His strangled shriek was indistinguishable among the many curious noises made by the wind around the stone parapets.

"One less to deal with," muttered he, "I hope, though, that he has not fell on any of our boys!"

He alluded to his friends whom he had arranged to meet him on the main tower at midnight.

"I had no choice in the matter. Besides, it is one way of notifying them that I am at work."

The bells began to ring for twelve o'clock.

He hid behind the watchbox, and through the loophole in the wall lowered a rope, which he had worn coiled around him under his clothes and which had given him the roundness of corporation which had excited Schutz's fellow feeling for a lover of good cheer.

Weighted with a loose stone tied to the end, this rope slowly descended: but in time Joel felt the weight removed; then a shake was given and as he drew upwards, he found that another and increasing load had been attached.

"A rope-ladder," he thought tugging at the burden which few men could have pulled so far, but he "walked" it along, hand over hand, like a sailor. At length he had the end in hand, to which a bar of iron was bound crosswise. This bar he placed within the battlements so that it would not slip and shook the rope. Bending over the profundity, he soon descried a string of shadows ascending, and with the reckless levity of the old soldiers, whose manners he was prompt to adopt with the imitativeness of youth, he muttered:

"Passengers for heaven, this is the way!"

In twelve to fifteen minutes he had the majority of the thirty men, under Friquet and Bonlarron, around him.

"In the first place," he said, pointing to the guardhouse, "Make sure of the fellows in that shed. They sleep, so you need not flash a weapon, but blind them with their belts and gag them with their pompons. Do not fire a shot, whatever you do."

The little party, shod with strips of blankets over their boots, proceeded to the spot. The ensign was aroused, but Joel caught him in the left hand as he recoiled from this column of silent phantom's and pointing the sword at his eyes, said:

Not a breath or you die!"

THE DEATH OF ARAMIS. 269

The officer saw by the frown on the face that the wisest course was to obey and he remained, flattened against the wall like an owl nailed to a barndoor.

"Only a sentry on the stairs is left. I will attend to him. Reverse the guns." And Joel descended the tower steps. A few minutes after, they saw him reappear, carrying under his arm the soldier who had been given no time to snap the trigger at him.

Meanwhile, the six privet guns were turned round to bear on the town, and threaten it with a torrent of flame and iron.

Joel looked round with a proud and gladdened eye.

Up with our flag—said he.

There was nothing more for them to do but conduct the water from the tank where it was stored against fire, to the receptacle for the great mine, which was inundated during the hours before dawn.

Immense was the joyous surprise in the French camp, and equal that of another kind, of the town, in the morning, when the white standard with the gold lily-flowers, was seen waving in the sun over the main tower of the citadel.

As the signal to their friends, the French fired one of the guns trained upon the town and the ball decapitated one of the statues in front of the cathedral : the town was at the mercy of the party who held the tower top :

"The French—the French advance ! " was the cry, as they saw the army of the marshal leaving his lines in three columns. But before they came under fire, a sphere of iron, with side pieces which gave it a peculiar rotary movement and an awful sound, rose from the French battery of Captain Friquet, and described a trajectory which landed it on the City Hall square, where it crushed several in the vast crowd assembled in agitation. It was the precursor of the Little Parisian's infernal work, for three more bombs spread destruction and carnage.

Under these shooting stars, the enemy continued to advance. There was no hope of entrapping them at the undermined wall as it was discovered that the powder was swamped. On the other hand, a fourth shell exploded in the magazine and the only thought of everybody was to escape this fire raining from heaven.

At the height of a panic, Créquy sent the order to cease the bombardment, which Friquet had witnessed from the height At nine o'clock, the French general made his entrance good into the place.

He threw his arms about the neck of the Son of Porthos as the latter presented him with the keys.

"It is to you, my lad, that we owe the opening of the place to the King's arms."

He called Friquet to him and complimented him and Bonlarron.

Here they brought him the flags taken from the enemy: that of the imperial regiment, the Kornach and the town guards.

"Chevalier de Locmaria," resumed he, "I charge you to convey these trophies to St. Germain, to be placed at the King's feet. I shall acquaint his Majesty with the large share you had in the capture, in my report. Captain Friquet and Sergeant Bonaventure will accompany you; having shared the peril, it is right they should share the glory. Take the keys and the flags, gentlemen. I have no need to say that I am proud to command lads of mettle like yourselves and I am your friend whenever you want one."

That same evening, the three friends set out. All three had active bodies, free minds and contented hearts. They passed joyfully over the returning way. Everywhere the news ran before them so that they were proclaimed as the heroes of Freiburg. Thus they were hailed at St. Dizier, where they put up at the Cross of Lorraine Inn, when a man ran out of the mob towards Joel.

"The chevalier!"

"Honorin!" exclaimed the knight at seeing the old serving-man of the Widow Scarron.

"I was coming after you, with this message from my mistress."

Our hero took the paper and read these two lines:

"Come home without losing a minute. Aurore's life and honor are in danger.   YOUR FRIEND."

"Halloa, my horse!" he shouted. "Join me later—I must make straight for Paris, though I had to walk there—nay, *drag* myself on my knees. You may join me there—if I be *still* alive."

"But the flags?" suggested Bonlarron.

"And the King?" added the Parisian.

"'Sblood!" ejaculated the Son of Porthos, with a snap of the fingers in mighty disdain, "it matters little about kings and flags. My wife is in question. My wife, do you hear, whom they want to rob me of or kill!"

He leaped into the saddle, and, getting ready to drive in the spurs, he shouted:

"Farewell! if you love me, say a prayer for me—for I know not what kind of devil I have to fight!"

CHAPTER XXIX.

THE SALARY OF SILENCE.

THE hunting horns sounded the start in the courtyards of St. Germain Palace, and on the place in front and the streets where the royal hunting party were to pass, there was a noisy affluence of people, insatiable to gaze at so many carriages, horses, plumes and golden decorations.

The brilliant cavalcade paraded the town and left it by the slope which leads to the deeper parts of the Forest. There were non-equivocal tokens of storm, but all the orders were given out, and the King would not pospone an engagement which concerted with a secret arrangement with the Duke of Almada. But the order was given to make haste and the whole cavalcade dashed off at the gallop.

When all had disappeared in whirls of dust, the multitude dispersed, and the good town subsided into its usual state when its mighty lords and ladies were absent—as silent, dull and deserted as at the present day.

Towards dusk, as the clouds immensely enlarged and their line of battle, outlined on the slatey sky, borrowed some purple tints from the setting sun, which made the hue more lugubrious—the shoes of a horse ridden at the top of speed, smote fire out of the courtyard paving-stones It was the Son of Porthos, with dusty clothes, flaming countenance, hair dropping perspiration, and bloody spurs, who was stopped by the sentry at the gates, lowering his partisan to bar his way.

"Courier from Marshal Créquy," said the Breton from the height of his saddle and his own superior stature, as he waved the Swiss guardsman aside with an imperious gesture.

The officer at the gates ran up.

"Do you come from Freiburg, sir?" he queried eagerly.

"Yes, sir, and all haste, as you may perceive."

"But his Majesty has gone hunting at Marly, and will probably spend the night there as usual."

"How is Mdme. de Locmaria?" demanded Joel after a frown in disappointment. "My wife, that is—one of the Queen's ladies. There has been no mishap to her, I trust?"

"I have not the honor to know Mdme. de Locmaria personally; but I have not heard of any accident to any lady of the household. The Queen has gone with the hunt, and takes all her attendants with her."

"The road to Marly?" said Joel curtly, and on its being pointed out, he darted off in the direction followed by the King and the court in the morning. Our enfavored rider recked little of the dust, the wind and the storm overhead : all he thought of was Aurore, who might at that very instant be in need of his arm and his sword. He hurried his course : his saddle burned him, his steed, with sides furrowed by the rowels, neighed with pain as it whitened its bit with foam. He thus went two leagues in fifteen minutes.

Distant flourishes of the hunting-horns guided him.

Suddenly a black curtain, drawn across his path, was ripped by a blade of steel-like color—it was the lightning—signalling the downpour of a torrent. He was in the woods, but the old trees seemed a frail defence to the shower. The horse was almost broken down by this new disaster, but the rider was invulnerable. He had taken one of the bridlepaths which seemed to lead to the centre where the horns now sounding the rally. The storm had spoilt the sport. This alley led to a clearing where ancient oaks surrounded a natural circus. At the instant when Joel's foundered horse stopped, dead beat, at this space, a singular party crossed it. Two of three men carried a burden which seemed to be a dead body; the third guided them : he bore a resemblance to M. de Boislaurier. By a flash of lightning, this confused mass became defined and the cavalier recognized that the apparent *corpse* was a woman's. Fainted or dead—what was more to the purpose, and drew from him an outcry which was an appeal, a sob and a roar of wrath—it was his wife!

But all sank back into gloom. Standing up in the stirrups, Joel stretched his arms towards the vanished vision. Unfortunately, in this movement of despair and entreaty, his hand let go the reins. At that, another flash of lightning zigzagged the foliage and the thunderbolt fell on a tree which it split, with such a detonation that the echoes seemed afraid for a space to repeat the roar. The frightened horse reared violently, and the unsaddled rider was thrown so that his head struck the foot of a birch tree where he remained stunned.

For nearly an hour he was left unconscious until the cold and the wet restored him. The storm was as short as it had been tremendous. He rose painfully to his feet. His intelligence triumphed, not without an effort, over his bewilderment, and one memory surged up above the whirl in his brain—that of the strangers carrying off his wife. He wished to spring off in chase of the wretches, catch them, tear their prey from them, if yet she lived, and kill them to a man, exacting blood for blood!

Yes: but to what side had they turned—where was he to begin the hunt? Time had gone on and they had a start. The Breton was utterly unacquainted with the woods. His horse had disappeared. He went on at random, staggering as if intoxicated: his limbs were benumbed and he did not feel his heart beat.

Suddenly, at the end of a windfall row, he spied a light.

He instantly directed his steps to this beacon; it was burning in old ruins, thatched, dilapidated, with a door hanging by one hinge, and with a small window like a loophole. He approached the latter, and looked in, before knocking at the door, from some unaccountable reason. It was easy to see the inside, as there was no blind or curtain, and the wind freely circulated from the absence of a pane of glass. A kind of murmur came through it, such as is made by a priest reciting prayers.

Despite the anxiety mastering him, Joel was deeply attracted by this singularity. He stood on the grass to deaden the sound of his spurred heels, glided up to the wall, and stretching his neck, peered into the gap with uneasy curiosity.

In the room with naked walls, was a table covered with a

black cloth which after a fashion resembled an altar. At each corner burnt a wax candle. On the cloth, holy books were placed exactly the reverse and contrary to their proper positions. To complete this burlesque sacrifice, a cross was placed foot upwards, with a long knife and a brass basin.

Before this mock altar stood a woman, dressed as a priest, whom Joel recognized as the hag he had met in Paris, associated with Walton in barring his way to reach Therese Lesage. Her chasuble was worn inside out, and she was reciting prayers *backwards*. Two kneeling women were making the responses in a whining way. Still another, wearing a Spanish mantilla, stood in an expectant attitude.

The veiled woman was the Marchioness de Montespan: the two kneeling ones, her maids.

At the period of the Consecration, La Bosse took the brazen bowl to raise it above her head as the priest does the chalice, but in turning it upside down, she shook out an enormous toad.

The marchioness stepped forward, threw aside her veil, and appeared like Medea, with a deep and feverish eye, the tresses of her purple hair winding among a crown of vervain, ivy sprays from graves and the violets of death. The toad was hopping upon the altar as she caught up the knife and with one sharp stroke beheaded the unclean animal. The viscid blood daubed her patrician hands:

"By this sacrifice," said she in a strong, grave voice, "I ask for the love of the King to return to me and to remain ever mine; for my obtaining from him all I want for myself and my kin; for my friends and servants to be cherished by him; myself respected by the lords, whom I may call into the councils of his Majesty, and who are to let me know what happens there: in short, that his love shall grow above what it was in the past. Let Louis cast off this execrable Aurore as he did Louise de la Vallière, and let me marry Louis when he repudiates his Queen or she dies!"

"Madame," said La Bosse, "it is time to proceed to the evocation."

The lady turned her back to the altar. Her hair twisted as though serpents were writhing in it and gave her forehead the aspect of the Omenides. With quivering lips, and panting bosom, she called out three times:

"Satan! Satan! Sa——"

But the last syllable of the Cursed Angel's name was lost in a terrible shriek from herself and her trio of accomplices.

The door was dashed in with violence, as a tall figure whose proportions were exaggerated by the dubious moonbeams, stood, silent but threatening on the threshold. The officiatress and the maid servants flung themselves down with their faces to the ground while their mistress shrank up to the wall.

Had the prince of Darkness responded to the impious vocation?

The colossus entered; with a wave of the hand he dismissed the minor sacriligists, and the wretches did not ask for him to repeat the stern: "Begone!" They scrambled to their feet and darted out into the forest like three owls hurrying to their nests.

The intruder walked up to the marchioness, and stopping before her and folding his arms on his breast, he said:

"Woman, what have you done with my wife, Aurore de Locmaria?"

The lady stared at him in stupor and drawing back her head to shun the double jet of flame from his eyes, she murmured:

"Oh, is this his spirit? do the dead come out of the grave? or has Satan taken his shape to manifest himself?"

He grasped her wrist roughly.

"Madame," said he, "no falsehood or trickery. I am alive, indeed. I must be answered promptly. Minutes are worth hours in such an emergency. What have you done with my wife?"

By the grip the royal favorite felt that she was not dealing with a phantom and her courage came back, so that she tried to combat.

"I do not know what you are talking about," she replied.

"You lie!" retorted Joel. "You uttered my name just now in your abominable practice of sorcery. I saw two men in your hire, no doubt, not long ago, carrying her in a swoon through the forest. By all that is holy, you will tell me without delay, or——"

"Would you lay your hand on a woman?" sneered Athenais in bravado.

"Well, no, I will leave the executioner's to do that!"

"The executioner?"

"Is it not he who will deal out justice to the poisoner?"

"I say to you now that *you* lie!"

"Mademoiselle de Fontanges stood in the way of your ambitious projects, and you slew Mademoiselle de Fontanges: I hold the proof in this locket, enclosing your own death warrant, your confession—your order for the poison of Pierre Lesage."

At sight of the trinket, she recoiled as if for a leap.

"Madame," he said coldly, reading the intention in her dark eyes, "Let me tell you that, in my country, I once strangled with these hands a wolf that sprang upon me. Now, let us finish this. Tell me where my wife is and I will give you impunity by restoring to you this paper. If you hold your tongue, I swear to God that I will with my own hand place this before the King to-morrow, after having shouted out the story so loudly and widely over Paris that all the world, nobles and people, will demand that the special tribunal shall send you into Lesage's dungeon until they light the fire again which consumed La Voisin to ashes!"

"But, I have not had Mdme. de Locmaria abducted. Go and ask the Spanish ambassador for her, who in this matter is rather the agent of our King—he projects to make her the mistress of the King."

"My patron—the King—where is the King—where is Almada—where is Aurore?"

"All three are probably in the Château of Marly. The lady fell ill during the hunt, and the duke ordered her to be carried to a summerhouse he owns next the château."

"Enough!" interrupted Joel. "I know all that you could tell me."

He remembered the dying words of Esteban, and as he recalled the details he recovered self-command.

"The road to this summerhouse?"

"The path by those rocks—in twenty minutes——"

"I thank you!"

He tore from his neck and flung down the medallion, saying: "There is your salary, madame."

He drew his sword and he marched forth without heeding the marchioness. He went at a good pace, firm yet quick, and as he shook his locks as the lion does his mane, he might *be heard* to say:

"We three will fight this out—I, the King and the duke!"

CHAPTER XXX.

THE DEATH OF ARAMIS.

THE King was supping at Marly, sitting at a small table higher than the others for his guests. But let us leave him and the courtiers discussing the delicate storm which broke up the hunting-party, while we enter those private apartments which were prohibited to the frequenters of the palace. In this sanctuary the King ceased to be anything more than a mortal man.

Here we shall find Aurore again. At the cold collation on the turf, which had preceded the letting slip of the buckhounds, the Duke of Almada had stepped up to Mdme. de Locmaria.

"What ails you, dear child?" he asked with affectionate interest:—"You appear to be in pain. Are you not well?"

"Not very. But do not busy yourself about me, as it is but a passing indisposition."

"Then you must take some stimulant not to mar the sport. A dash of malvoisie——"

He beckoned to a butler.

"Will you not drink to the good health and speedy return of our friend Joel?"

"With all my heart, my lord."

Thus she had accepted the drugged wine he offered her. A few hours afterwards, the storm burst and the frightened Queen ordered her ladies to return in all haste to St. Germain.

Aurore tried to keep up with the riders, but a sudden weakness overcame her. She had not strength to guide her horse or to stop him. Her cry for help died in her throat. She wrestled with serious depression. She was slipping out of the saddle when Boislaurier ran up from the distance where he was watching her, and, with the help of two valets, caught her in his arms.

Now she reposed in a huge bed, with a plumed dome, heavy blue velvet curtains, with clasps and tassels of bullion, while a gilded rail separated it from the rest of the room. It was lighted by a silver lamp on a table, by which the Duke of Almada sat. At length he rose and taking the lamp, went up to view her.

"A lovely statue in rose marble," he muttered. He returned to his seat. "In an hour the operation of my narcotic will be exhausted. On my faith, the King is slow to come. Will he never have done with that supper? It appears that Joel is still alive and has written to his wife. It is certain that he worships her and it is no less certain that my future favorite would give him the last drop in her veins. This does not displease me, for by threatening to reveal her shame to her husband——"

He interrupted himself as though to reply to the objection of an invisible objector:

"Granted that this is vile and odious! Against the indignity of the act and the scoundrelism in its execution, would revolt the lofty gentlemanliness of Athos, the simple honesty of Porthos and d'Artagnan's valiant uprightness. D'Artagnan would swear with all the oaths in his Gascon vocabulary that what I do is of the meanest rascality. With the curl of his disdainful lip, Athos would let the one word fall: 'Fie!' The good Porthos would say nothing, but his frank visage would broaden with amaze to see his comrade of the Bastion St. Gervais and the Locmaria sea-cave—Aramis the Musketeer, the prelate and the conspirator; the man who has juggled with the crown and sceptre of France and with royal persons and destinies—acting the spider—the panderer——"

Disgust contracted his features, which had remained handsome and noble in spite of age and intrigue ravaging them. He took a crystal phial from his breast, hidden at the end of a gold chain amid the lace, and sipped a drop. His eye was brighter and his voice refreshed as he proceeded:

"Everything is interwoven. This woman must become the royal love so that, as her master, I may put into Louis's hand the pen that will strike out Heresy on the book of the Rights of Man. Then with the order of which I am the head remain erect over its prostrated foes, my numerous, invincible, disciplined army, and when I command from the chair of St. Peter——"

Again he was hoarse, and he had recourse to the elixir.

"Why not? are not my shoulders strong enough to support the pontifical purple? would not the tiara become my silver hairs, and is there not in me the making of a Gregory, a Leo, or a Julius? The end justifies the means. What does the mud in the road or the twig snapped under the foot matter to him who has scaled the mount? What value is the virtue of one woman, the happiness of one man, when their loss ensures the triumph of religion? Well, no! these are sophisms with which I vainly try to lull my conscience. Religion is not in this game—I am playing it for my ambition solely." He laughed more like one of the drolls of Italian comedy than the great pontiffs whom he had mentioned. "*Basta!* who cares? Has not the Holy Father power to absolve all crimes? when I am Pope, I shall clear myself."

He had barely expressed this ironical jest when a violent surprise was manifested upon his features.

"What is that?" he muttered, half rising in his chair, and extending his neck as he listened.

"I can't be mistaken," he said with growing astonishment. "Some one is in the underground passage." He rose fully. "Tush! no doubt it is Boislaurier—it can be nobody else: but what can he want? What can have happened so important that he comes after me?"

He went to a door so artfully secreted in the woodwork that the most expert eye could not have espied it. He touched a brass knob concealed among the ornaments with the same care. A spring worked, the panel opened, and, master of himself as was Aramis, he could not help exclaiming in affright:

In the square opening, pale, solemn and threatening, appeared with a drawn sword, smeared with fresh blood, the Son of Porthos!

Almada receded to the table. This apparition was the one he least expected: it scattered his plans like the bombs Friquet's gunners had flung into Freiburg. But the former Musketeer was not to be discomfited so easily. Had a bombshell really fallen at his feet, he would have plucked out the lighted fuse. His first feeling was of surprise, but it lasted only a moment, and this redoubtable wrestler quickly recalled his wits and collected his powers.

"Chevalier, how came you here? you have a post in the army—desertion is a grave offence."

"Sir," replied the Breton with terrible calm, "I have nothing to do with the army—Freiburg is taken—by me! I bring Marshal Créquy's report attesting that, in my pocket,

But that is not our business. You want to know how it is that I come upon you by the secret stairs? I have no time to go into particulars. Suffice it that Boislaurier is dead—so is your chief of cut-throats, Condor Cordbuff—executions which I will account for to those who have the right to question me on the point. Now it is for us to settle accounts."

The ambassador remained cool, like the wild beast in his lair, who watches with apparently indifferent eye the movements of the hunter:

"Ha!" he haughtily said, "Have we an account to settle? I leave such matters to my servants. This is neither the time nor the place for such trifles. This is the King's home? Do you not know that?"

"To be sure I do, since I come here to regain my wife."

"Your wife?"

Joel stretched out his unweaponed hand.

"My wife who lies there, on the couch of which you have not even drawn the curtains, so surely did my visit deprive you of prudence and precaution. You put her to sleep with a potion—so that she should not know of what crime you would be guilty—a potion such as you finger there——."

Aramis so felt the necessity of strengthening his nerves that he had indeed drawn his elixir from its nesting-place.

"Mdme. de Locmaria is dead," said the old man drily.

The other laughed menacingly in his face.

"If I believed that, you would already be in the lower region with your myrmidons. But your greed is my insurance—the King will not pay you for a dead body."

"What, do you know?" and Aramis blushed slightly.

"I know that you found me that wife in order that I should be the mate of the King's favorite! that you sent me to Freiburg in the hope that I should never return—that the German bullets were hoped to do the work in which your secretaries failed——"

"Young man," returned the ambassador, shaking his bold head, "if you knew so much, you should have had the wit to be silent. Do you think that I am going lightly to renounce the prospective gains of what you term my infamy? let us share, or I take all! Come, my boy," went on the prelate, assuming the most unctuously paternal tone, "reflect that the highest state reasons constrain me to play this part: the sacrifice I require is necessary to political combinations

THE DEATH OF ARAMIS.

which concern the peace of the world. You are a lad of wit, who must understand and without plain speech: sheath your rapier, cease to roll your furious eyes, and get you gone——"

"I go with my wife."

"Oho!" snarled the duke, his eye blazing with choler and the effects of the cordial which he had sipped: "You are wearying my patience. Yet I do not wish you harm, Away— or I shall kill you."

"Who have you to help, old man?" You forget that I have swept the earth clear of your scoundrels. You are nearer the grave than I."

Aurore made a movement, and Joel took a step towards her. But Aramis, who had drawn his courtsword, sprang in between with the factitious activity of the elixir:

"With that toothpick do you talk of killing me?"

"Defend her, and yourself!"

Joel thought that he might soon dispose of an adversary of this age, and he did not lose time in "trying" him, but almost at once delivered a straight thrust, rapid and flashing as a lightning stroke. The lunge was parried with a strength, ease and agility the Breton had not expected to meet in that frail body. So were met the others he gave, and however fleetly this long blade described circles, the thin feil followed it closely as the magnet the iron, twisting and hissing like a viper. The young man comprehended that he was pitted against a fencer of the first class, and that caused him to moderate his mode. Aramis plied the steel with a vivacity akin to that he must have displayed in his youth. It was in vain that the soldier multiplied his attacks: he found no weariness in this antagonist. His wrist seemed of steel while the other, fatigued by his long rides, his fall, the events of the day and his conflict in the subterranean with the duke's bravoes, became daunted by his inferiority. The blood flew to his head, and his arm lost its usual vigor and liveliness.

At this moment, Aurore gave a sigh. The Breton heard it and it was the signal for a truce. Joel looked at his wife, while the old duke again sipped at the phial, doubling the dose. When he resumed the action, it was he who attacked, and with a fire which astounded the adversary.

"You are caught, my fighting-cock," said he, with a sinister smile, "and I shall serve you out with the favorite thrust of my friend Porthos——"

By a strange coincidence, the same way of ending the conflict had occurred to both swordsmen. As a consequence, the swords glided along one another to the hilts, where the slighter blade snapped off short. But the defenceless state of Aramis did not matter at this juncture, for the name had caused Joel to utter an exclamation:

"Porthos—he was my father!"

"Your father? Then I was his friend—I am Aramis!"

The old man recoiled and flung down the stump of his sword. Before him he thought he saw, as the false life and warmth of the elixir faded away, the phantom of the friend of his youth—the Porthos with simple grandeur of soul, and real superiority of heart—more mighty than splendor of mind. Sublime in vigor, courage and disinterestedness—smiling, open, unconquerable—the strongest of the Four Companions, and yet the first to die; to die, because he, the Chevalier d' Herblay, had drawn him innocently and unwittingly, into the tragical adventure of the Château of Vaux.

At last, his gigantic shade had come out of the tomb, and with it was ranged the spirits of Athos and d'Artagnan. They seemed to adopt their old friend's son, and stood ready to defend him. But there was no cause for them to stand between. After the flame which had coursed through the old man's veins and made him lose the weight of eighty years, a chilliness had crept over him. But in an instant, wherever the dangerous liquid had mingled with the blood, all the channels ached and seemed to be consumed.

"I am deceived," he muttered, staggering to the nearest chair and leaving the way clear to Joel who bounded over the rail to his wife's side. "The liquor of long life is ephemeral and I have but hastened my death. Oh, I so wished to live—to reign—to have all the world for one, and that one—I——"

When Joel, carrying his wife in his arms with her heart again beating in unison with his own, passed the old man, he saw but a bent, gathered-up form in the chair. Aramis had died, without consciousness that *he* was, an accomplished courtier, committing the unpardonable sin, of thrusting death before the eyes of a king.

CONCLUSION.

A *fortnight* later, on the deck of a sailing vessel crossing from Croisic to Bell-Islle, some of our characters would have been seen again.

With an emotion which thrilled every fibre, our hero saw once more the sombre girdle of rocks rise on the sea-line where his infancy had past. His young wife, lovelier than ever, leaned against him and watched him smile again as he heard the grumblings of Friquet to Sergeant Bonaventure.

"Our prince is a curmudgeon: not a bit of ribbon, medal or gold lace—not a coin with which to drink his health. Death of my life! what a joke it is to call him Louis the Great who is anything but tall."

The rising sun gilded the boat as it ran into the port of Locmaria under full sail. A cannonshot from the fort saluted the arrival. Instantly the drums beat in the castle, and the bells in the parish were set ringing. When they disembarked, they found the garrison ranged in battle array on the strand; the soldiers had bunches of flowers in their muskets, and streamers of ribbons to their halberds. Behind them were all the inhabitants in their best clothes, the women and children carrying flowers by the armsful. The men waved hats and caps, and all vociferated:

"Long live the count! long live my lady! long live our new lord!"

"A deucedly civilized country," said Friquet, " just look, sergeant, how the pretty girls perk up as we come along."

An officer came up, hat in hand.

"May I ask for M. Joel of Locmaria?"

"It is I, " responded our hero, with the same civility.

Drawing his sword, the officer made a sign with it, on which the drums beat, the soldiers presented arms and the principal inhabitants advanced with bows.

"Welcome to the Count of Locmaria, Governor and Lord of the Manor of Locmaria!" was the universal shout.

There was news for Friquet at the Townhall to which the new-comers were escorted. He was appointed commander of the fleet of bomb-ketches to be sent to ruin Algiers; Bonlarron was named lieutenant in the same expedition.

Among the other documents, confirming the boons of the generous King—not to call his act of reparation—was a letter from Widow Scarron. It announced that she had been the bearer of the order to the Marchioness of Montespan that she must confine herself to a nunnery. Her place was taken by the governess, to whom Louis gave a large sum to buy the marquisate of Maintenon, and support her in that title.

"I shall start soon to take command of my fleet," said the Little Parisian, an inch taller as the Admiral of the Bombardiers Navy.

"And I am with you," said Bonaventure, who had renewed his liking for the soldier's life.

"I shall stay here," said Joel, turning towards his wife, "beside my father's grave——"

"And the home of our children," added Aurore, blushing.

THE END.

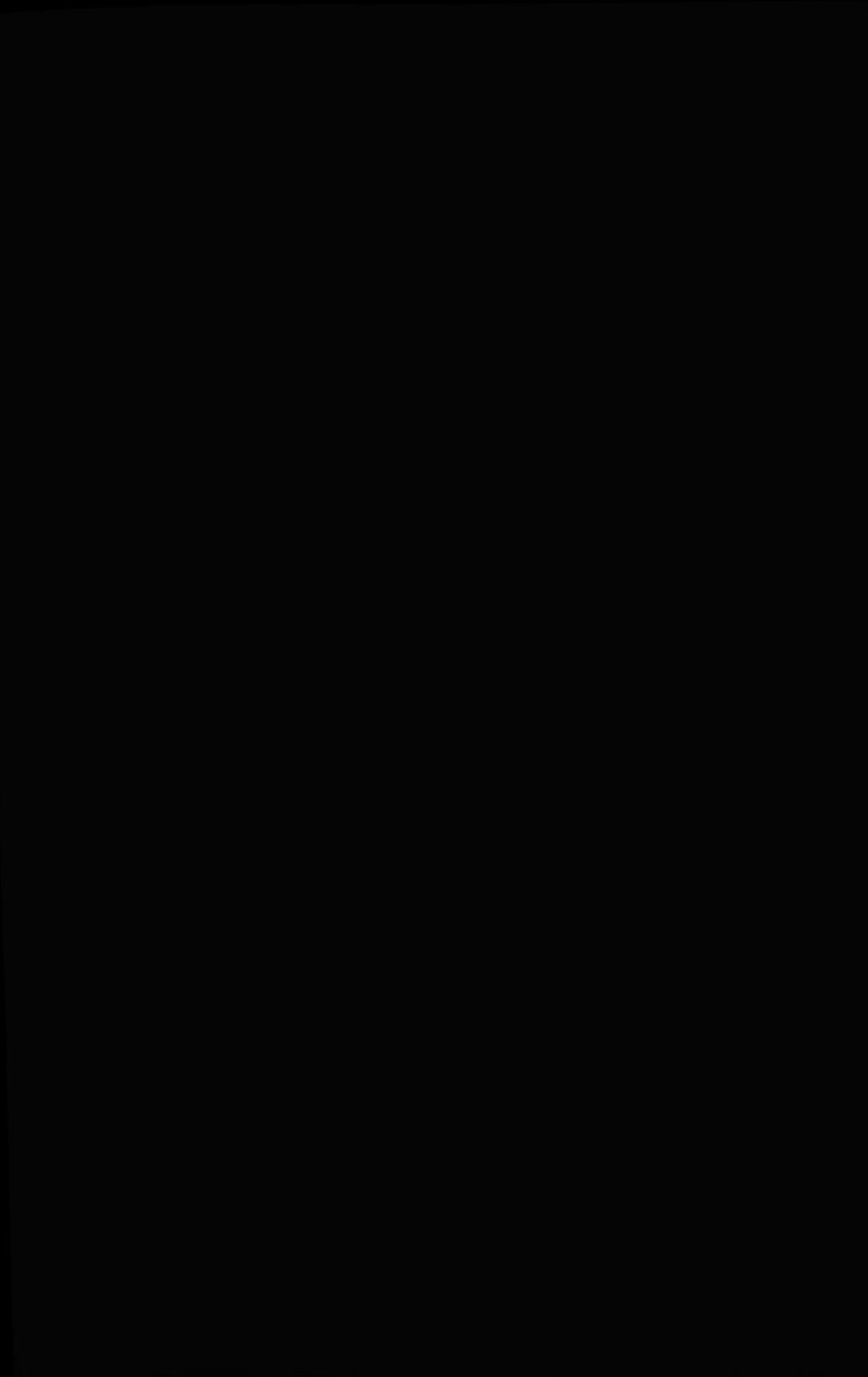

Printed in the United States
91653LV00005B/149/A